THE VERY THOUGHT OF YOU

ERIKA KELLY

ISBN-13: 9781677305605

This book is a work of fiction. Names, characters, places, and incidents are used fictitiously or are a product of the author's imagination and any resemblance to actual persons, living or dead, business establishments, events, or locales is entirely coincidental.

Cover design and formatting by Serendipity Formatting

Praise for The Calamity Falls series

KEEP ON LOVING YOU

"I adored this book! It is exactly what I love in a second-chance romance. The characters are so vibrant and real, I was rooting for them with every page." —*USA Today* Bestseller Devney Perry

"*KEEP ON LOVING YOU* is such a fun and sexy second-chance romance that I didn't want it to end. Their connection is a swoony blend of tender first love and sizzling heat, and Erika Kelly delivers a highly entertaining and sigh-worthy romance that shouldn't be missed."
—Mary Dube, USA Today

WE BELONG TOGETHER

"I loved every sweet, heart-wrenching, crazy, mixed-up minute of this book. It was an emotional journey from the first chapter to the last. This is Erika Kelly at her best, and this is a not-to-be-missed book!" —Sharon Slick Reads, Guilty Pleasures Book Reviews

"Erika Kelly damn near pulled my heart from my chest with Delilah and Will's story. It's so well-written that you feel everything. My heart got tugged so hard! I honestly cried at a few moments in the book. I fell all the way in love with "Wooby." It's hard not to, really." —Ree Cee's Books

THE VERY THOUGHT OF YOU

"Wow, THE VERY THOUGHT OF YOU was simply OUTSTANDING! This second chance, friends to lovers romance is enchanting and entertaining." —Spellbound Stories

"I just finished this story, and I want to start all over again. Or maybe at the start of series. To once again feel the events, the emotions, that brought these amazing characters together. To hear the banter and the arguments, the sorrow, the loss and the happiness that brought a family together and closer." —Nerdy, Dirty, and Flirty

JUST THE WAY YOU ARE

"An alpha cowboy and a smart, sassy princess collide in JUST THE WAY YOU ARE in Erika Kelly's latest, and it was fabulous! I was cheering for Brodie and Rosalina with every page. If you love stories with heart, steam, and plenty of swoon, don't miss this one!" —USA Today Bestselling Author J.H. Croix

"With the Calamity Falls series, Kelly doesn't shy away from charming. She captivates with delectable characters that wrap themselves around a heart. From the first hello to the final goodbye, Rosalina and Brodie are a match made out of the unpredictable, but the sweetest kind of heaven. JUST THE WAY YOU ARE is the perfect example of why I am hooked on this series. SWOONWORTHY READ!" —Hopeless Romantic Book Reviews

IT WAS ALWAYS YOU

"This book was full of every emotion you could ever feel. Gigi and Cassian proved you can conquer anything with true love." —Cat's Guilty Pleasure

"I could not put this book down! Erika Kelly always delivers a great love story and never disappoints! I recommend this book for romance lovers looking to get lost in a great love story." —Reading in Pajamas

CAN'T HELP FALLING IN LOVE

"I love everything about this emotional and sexy, second chance story. Erika Kelly writes a story that makes me feel like I'm right there with the two main characters, Beckett and Coco. It is a slow burn, passionate story with lots of underlying tension. I not only enjoyed this story, but I found it impossible to put down." —Cocktails and Books

"I loved everything about this book. I loved all the characters, from Beckett, 'I don't believe in love,' to single mom, small business-owning, closed-off Coco, to a fairy-believing five-year-old who will steal your heart! I cannot gush enough about how spectacular I thought this book was." – Bookcase and Coffee

WHOLE LOTTA LOVE

"BRILLIANT! This book was incredible, I could not put this book down, that is how good Lu and Xander's story was. I fell in love with these two characters instantly." – Harlequin Junkie

"Whole Lotta Love was absolutely perfect! You will instantly love this couple and their journey to find happiness!" – Just Love Books

YOU'RE STILL THE ONE

"Griffin and Stella really are soulmates. They bring out the best of each other, and when they're together, everything is better. Their world is better with the love they feel for each other. And I think they made my world better a bit, too." – Jersey Girl's Bookshelf

"WOW! WOW! WOW! Welcome to all the feels! I ADORED Stella and Griffin's story. I was completely lost in this book and didn't want to put it down. I FELT everything, and I can't tell you how much I loved it." – Books According to Abby

Titles by Erika Kelly

Sign up for my newsletter to read the EXCLUSIVE novella for my readers only! You'll get two chapters a month of this super sexy, fun romance! #rockstarromance #teenidolturnedboyfriend Also, get PLANES, TRAINS, AND HEAD OVER HEELS for FREE! I hope you'll come hang out with me on Facebook, Twitter, Instagram, Goodreads, and Pinterest or in my private reader group.

This book is dedicated to Superman….my heart.

Acknowledgments

- To Superman: you're the love of my life. Thank you for always listening, always being there, and always loving me. Also, thank you for being the best plotstorming partner EVER.
- To Olivia: thank you for always braving that first pass through my books! Also, sorry.
- To Sharon: thank you for your unconditional love and for making me a better writer.
- To KP: thank you for your friendship and for sharing this journey with me.
- To Kristy DeBoer: you always make my book so much better! Thank you for your friendship and support.
- To Amy: you are such a great friend. Thank you for stepping in when I needed you most.
- To Melissa: your help is invaluable to me, and your graphics are the best!
- To Erica: I can't thank you enough for being there for me with covers and formatting…and friendship.
- To the romance writing community: I couldn't do this without the bloggers and reviewers like Obsessed with Romance, Guilty Pleasures Book Reviews, About That Story, Reading in Pajamas, Zoe Forward, Shirin's Book Blog and

Reviews, Reads and Reviews, and Isha Coleman—to name just a few; and my friends in writer groups like the Dreamweavers, the DND Authors, and my local plotstormer girls.

Chapter One

HURRY UP, HURRY UP, HURRY UP.

As the ocean roared through the open bathroom window, Knox Holliday snatched the towel off the rack and quickly rubbed her body dry. Wrapping it around her head turban-style, she eyed the line of surfers waiting for the next set.

She could feel it—the grip of her toes on her waxed board, the churning of the sea under her feet, and the slap of salty water on her skin. Her body yearned to be out there.

A storm somewhere in the Pacific had delivered massive waves to the island—rare for September—and she hated having to miss it. Her cell phone trilled from her nightstand. *Crap.*

Hurry.

Padding into the bedroom on bare, damp feet, she picked it up and accepted the FaceTime call. Setting the screen so it faced the ceiling, she said, "Hey, Luc. Just give me one second." She bent over, unwinding the towel and shaking out her hair.

"Are you all right?" he asked in his thick, French accent. "What is going on?"

She reached for the red satin underwear in the top drawer of her dresser and stepped into them. "Just running a little late."

"Why? Is there a problem?"

She could hear the panic in his voice. *Such a diva.* "Everything's perfect." Hitching up her panties, she eyed the line of dresses and blouses in her closet and yanked off a crepe mini dress with spaghetti straps. She stepped into it at the same time she shoved her feet into high heeled sandals.

"Why am I looking at your ceiling and not you?"

Her boss checked in every day at the same time. Normally, she'd be ready to show him the progress she'd made, but she'd had to make an alteration to one of the gowns, which had her running late.

"What is that...why is your ceiling bumpy?" He gasped. "Is it warped?"

She'd rented the cheapest house she could find on this stretch of beach in Maui. Of course, Luc had offered her his homes in the Maldives and Portofino and his flat in London, but she still hadn't gotten over what he'd done to her, so she needed boundaries.

Mostly, though, she wanted to keep him from feeling any sort of ownership in her collection. "It's called a popcorn ceiling, and what do I care what it looks like when I'm getting the place for a steal?" As if she hadn't lived in much worse conditions. She'd learned as a child to create beauty in her mind and with her own hands.

She slicked her hair back into a high ponytail and grabbed the phone. His handsome face came into view from his bright and airy Paris office, seventy-five hundred miles away. "Well, hello, there. Nice to see you."

"Bonjour, ma chère." His features pinched. "Why is your hair wet? You showered, when you knew I'd be calling?"

Maybe she couldn't get over what he'd done to her, but she still hated to let him down. "Yeah, sorry about that. I'm a little late this morning." She had a show in six weeks, so she'd barely been getting five hours of sleep a night as it was. Last night, she'd gotten even less.

"Hmph. Every day for one year I have called you at ten o'clock in the morning."

That was because he didn't finish his day until nine or ten at night. His assistant brought him a baguette, some smelly cheese, and a bottle of wine, and he caught up on all his phone calls.

"And for three hundred and sixty-four of them, I've made it right on time," she said. "Ready to get started?"

She turned the phone around and headed into the living room, panning the sea of taffeta, silk, organza, chiffon, and tulle. Even after all this time, she still got a rush of happiness from seeing all that frothy gorgeousness.

"Stop, stop. Oh, dear God, what is that?"

Of course, of all the beauty in the room, he'd notice the one problem. A low beat of anxiety pulsed through her. *Please don't freak out.* "What's what?"

But he ignored her teasing tone. "On the floor. What is that?"

"It's nothing to worry about." She lifted the puddle of charmeuse and lace. "I made a slight alteration."

"To La Danseur? There was nothing wrong with La Danseur."

3

"Luc, I promise, it's all right. I tried it on my neighbor, and I didn't like the drape, so I'm redoing it."

"No, no, no. Does your neighbor have a portfolio with Elite? Is she a Ford model?"

Her sixty-two-year-old neighbor was fit and tall but not what Luc would consider a model. "Trust me, it wasn't working. It's going to be much better."

"It's in pieces on the floor. And Martine is coming on Monday to pack up the gowns. Ach, I'm growing a migraine. Stop this nonsense right now. We'll do all the tweaks when you arrive in the city."

A thrill shot through her. Thanks to Luc's support, she'd debut her haute couture wedding gown collection at October's Bridal Fashion Week in New York City. A big deal for a twenty-five-year-old, just four years out of college. In return, she'd had to create a year's worth of collections for him.

"I'll have everything ready by the time Martine gets here, I promise. When have I ever let you down?"

"When you left me." For a fifty-eight-year-old man, he had the pout of a two-year-old.

"I guess you shouldn't have *stolen* from me."

His eyebrows shot up into his thick, gray hair. "Take that back. I did not steal from you. Everyone who works for me signs the same contract. I own everything you create while under my employment."

Technically that might be true, but he'd devastated her. He'd swiped her sketchbook out of her apartment, designs she'd done on her own time. "Luc, you broke my heart." Since she didn't give her heart to many people, that was an even rarer occurrence than a storm in September. It had been scary to quit her job, but she'd believed if she was good enough for Luc Bellerose to steal from her, then she was good enough to go out on her own.

"And now I have healed it. Trust me, ma chère, you will take the world by storm with this show." He gave her a smile heavy with pride. "In my four decades in this business, I have never fallen so in love with someone's style. You are magic, Knox Holliday, and I'm going to make you a star. Ah. That's it." He reached for his laptop and his fingers went to town all over the keyboard.

"What's it? What're you doing?"

"Emailing Victoire."

"Why?" What did his publicist have to do with this conversation?

"I've been looking for just the right tagline." He tapped the final letter with a flourish, then shoved the laptop back. "You are the white-hot wedding gown designer." He grinned, obviously pleased with himself. "The hottest star in the bridal galaxy." His smile faded. "I mean that sincerely, you know. They're not just empty words."

Often, he drove her crazy—like when he stole from her—but sometimes she loved him. "Thank you, Luc. Your opinion means the world to me."

Tires squealed on asphalt. A shout pierced the air. Knox spun around to look out the bay window of her living room but couldn't make sense of what she was seeing. Her house, situated on a sharp bend in the road, saw a lot of traffic. It sat close enough that she could catch a glimpse of the drivers' faces as they whizzed by. But this car...this dark green Jeep...it was driving *across her front yard*.

Holy shit, it was careening toward the house.

Toward *her*. "Oh, my God." She dropped the phone and bolted into the kitchen, seconds before the car crashed

5

into her living room. Glass shattered. Wood splintered. The Jeep sheared off wallboard.

The engine idled, and an Eddie Van Halen guitar riff screeched in the air.

"Knox? *Knox?*" Her boss's tinny voice got her moving toward the phone. She had to call nine-one-one. Brushing debris off her phone, she picked it up. "Luc? I have to call you back." She didn't give him a chance to respond, just hit End. Seeing no movement through the tinted windows, she called, "Hello? Are you all right?"

Swirls of dust filled the room. In her sandals, she made her way across glittering glass and chips of wood to the driver's side, focusing on her keypad as she dialed.

Someone answered right away. "Nine-one-one, what's your emergency?"

She had to shout over the music. "A car just crashed into my living room." As she gave her address and answered questions, her heart squeezed at the sight of crystals and beads and strips of delicate—filthy—lace under the big black tires. That lace…it was handmade. Literally irreplaceable. She tried the passenger side door, but it was locked. "Are you okay?" Peering into the tinted window, she made out several bodies.

The radio snapped off. The driver's door opened, and a woman got out. Wearing a bikini top and jean shorts, she looked dazed.

"Hey, are you all right?" Knox lifted the phone. "I just called nine-one-one. They'll be here in ten minutes."

"I'm fine. I just…" The young woman covered her mouth with a hand and took in the scene. "Oh, my God." She turned back to the car, pumping on the back door handle. "Guys? Open up." When it popped open, she stepped aside to let several large men out.

Knox moved toward them, her ankle twisting in her stupid heels. "Is anyone hurt?" Three of the men were shirtless, one wore a thin white tank top, all wore board shorts. Five surfboards were strapped to the roof of the car, the front edges snapped off by the wallboard that covered the windshield.

"What the hell?" one of them said.

"Whoa, man," another one said.

Her phone chimed, and she glanced quickly at the screen. Luc. *Not now.* She silenced the ringer. "What do you guys need?" She could grab some kitchen towels if anyone was bleeding.

"Knox?"

She'd know that deep, gravelly voice anywhere, even after all these years. A shock of recognition had her looking over to see—"*Gray?*"

What the hell was Gray Bowie doing in her living room?

"This is *your* house?" He scraped his fingers through his hair. "Jesus. Of all the people…" Fear twisted his features. "Did we *hurt* you?"

"No." *At least not in the way you're thinking.* "I'm fine." She deliberately didn't look at her gowns. It was the only way to keep her panic at bay. That…and she'd need her full attention to assess the damage. "What about you guys?" She gestured to his friends.

His gaze lingered for a moment, as if he couldn't believe he was seeing her. *Believe me, I feel the same way.* It had been seven years since she'd last seen or talked to him.

His choice.

With a slight shake of his head, he turned to the driver. "You okay, Amelia?"

7

"Yeah." The woman wrapped a hand around the back of her neck. "Shaken up, but I'm okay."

She looked disoriented, so Knox wasn't sure about that. Grabbing a kitchen chair, she said, "Maybe you should sit down."

For a moment the woman looked confused. Then she pulled her hand off her neck. "No, it doesn't hurt. I guess I'm just expecting it to." She tipped a chin to the others. "You guys?"

The passengers all spoke at once, clearly stunned.

"I'm good."

"Fine."

"Jesus, man."

Hands cupping the sides of her head, Amelia turned to survey the damage. "Oh, my God. How did this even happen?" She blew out a breath, glancing at Knox. "We were just so stoked, you know? He"—she pointed to Gray —"literally got the call ten minutes ago. And we've got to head to the airport right now." She scanned the room, her attention zeroing in on the white tulle. "What *is* all this?"

With everything in her, Knox did *not* want to look at her beautiful, perfect gowns, wasn't ready to see their condition, dreaded that feeling of total devastation…but she had no choice, did she? Slowly, she turned to take it all in.

The three dress forms she'd placed in front of the living room window lay trampled under the wheels. Terror sliced a vein, and she bled pure adrenaline. She went light-headed, her vision narrowing.

Her showstopper gowns were destroyed. They couldn't be salvaged. Not a chance.

She drew in short, shallow breaths.

You don't have time for a panic attack. She forced

herself to rally. *It's only three dresses.* The others might be okay. She could still show twenty-two dresses. She dropped to a crouch, and the world spun and teetered. She blinked away the wall of tears, fingering the sheer organza with handmade petals that overlaid her favorite gown.

A hand came down on her shoulder with a firm grip. "Knox?" Gray knelt beside her, wearing nothing but bright blue board shorts. He smelled of coconut oil and ocean breeze. She could even see a trace of dried salt on his skin.

It was enough—the destruction of one year of her work—she didn't need *him*, of all people, compounding it. "Just...give me a second." Some of these could be salvaged. *Right?* She could fix anything. But no matter how hard she blinked the room was still a blur. It made her frantic, so she swiped at her eyes. She needed to see, to assess, but the damn tears wouldn't go away.

There's still some fabric left. Plenty of embellishments.

I can fix anything.

The fist gripping her throat eased. She drew in a deep, calming breath. First, she had to get these people out of here. She couldn't think with them in her living room. She'd assess the damage the minute they left.

It'll be fine. Promise.

Everything felt surreal. The Jeep in the middle of her living room, the glorious dresses she'd hand-sewn lying beneath it, and...Gray Bowie right here talking to her. Especially since he looked so much bigger, broader, more masculine than the eighteen-year-old boy she remembered. The only thing that remained the same were his startlingly blue eyes.

But, holy cow, with his thick, powerful muscles, bronze skin covered in ink, shoulder-length dark hair that curled at his neck, and a strong jaw covered in scruff, he'd turned into every woman's bad boy fantasy come to life.

"What is all this?" Gray jerked his chin toward the mass of white, blush, lavender and a blue so pale it looked gossamer.

She tried to hide the panic from her voice. "Wedding gowns." Assaulted by a tumult of unwelcome emotions, she stood up in a rush. She needed him—all of them— gone. "You—"

"Wait, we ran over your wedding dress?" Amelia sounded horrified.

"Not mine. I'm a designer. I've got a show in six weeks." *Six weeks.*

But Martine is coming on Monday.

Oh, God. She couldn't fix this much destruction in three days.

Wrong. She would, because the alternative was unthinkable.

"Fuck," one of the guys drew out the word like a balloon leaking air.

"Well," Gray said. "Let's get this Jeep out of here and see what we've got."

A rush of energy had her practically tackling him. "Absolutely not. Don't move anything. I have to see what I can salvage before we back over the dresses."

"Good point." He turned to his friends. "Guys, let's pick up whatever—"

"No." They all froze at her sharp tone. "I need you to go outside and wait for the paramedics." At their perplexed expression, she explained, "There are beads and crystals and panels of lace…fine details that I need to handle on my own." Material created from Luc's heritage atelier and fabric mill. Nothing she could ever recreate.

Okay, that's enough. She had to stop catastrophizing. *You can't fix anything if you're freaking out.*

"We can at least pick up the dresses," Gray said. "Get them out of the dust."

The careless son of a billionaire, who spent his life chasing waves and snowstorms, Gray couldn't begin to understand that he'd destroyed not only a year's worth of work but the launch of her career.

"No. Please...just leave." No matter how in control she needed to be, nothing could stop the trembling from deep within. "I have until Monday to make it look like your Jeep didn't mow down my gowns." At their stunned expressions, she eased back. "I'm sorry, but this is my first show, and I've got the backing of the biggest bridal designer in the world. I swear to God, I don't want to lose it in front of you guys, but this is my life's work, so please, please, just go. I have to figure things out."

"Yeah, sure," one of the guys said. "Come on." Two of them headed out across the wreckage.

Amelia stood there, slack-jawed, looking destroyed. "I'm so sorry. I…" Her jaw snapped shut. She reached into the Jeep and dragged out a slate gray leather messenger bag.

A five-hundred-dollar Longchamp. It looked totally out of place with these laid-back surfers.

The woman pulled out a crumpled receipt and wrote something on it. "I'm Amelia Webber. This is my contact information. I'll pay for all the repairs. That includes your house, supplies, and whatever your dresses need." With a plea in her eyes, she said. "Anything I can do to help, I'll do it. I'm so sorry." She stood there a moment, looking helpless, and then turned and moved carefully out into the bright sunshine.

Only Gray remained. Stroking his scruff, he examined the tires. "I'm sure the car's got a jack. Instead of backing out over them, we can jack it up and let you get the dresses out." He turned those bright blue eyes on her, and a shudder of recognition traveled through her. "That sound good?"

God, she couldn't stop shaking. This time, when her phone vibrated, she glanced at the screen. How many times had Luc called? She knew he was going out of his mind with worry, but she couldn't talk to him until she had a handle on the situation.

With the others in the front yard, huddled together and talking quietly, and Gray opening the back of the Jeep and leaning inside, she had a moment to really take in the damage.

Destruction.

Dust swirled in the slanted morning sunlight, and sparkling glass, beads, and crystals lay scattered across the wood floor. A fine layer of debris covered the dresses heaped on the kitchen table--dresses far too fragile to clean. The dresses under the Jeep were a total loss. The tires had shredded the delicate fabric. Luckily, the fender stopped right before the couch, saving the dresses draped over it. They were covered in particles from sheet rock, though. Picking it out would tear the delicate material. Still, she'd try. She had to try.

Gray slammed the trunk, wielding the tire iron like a trident. "Called for a tow. Better to have a professional lift it. He'll be here in twenty minutes."

She gave him a skeptical look. Nothing on the island moved that quickly.

He shrugged. "I know a guy."

Of course he did. Everyone loved the Bowie family. All

four brothers were elite athletes blessed with good looks, ridiculously cut bodies, and the kind of confidence that silenced conversations when they entered a room.

He looked at her a little too long—his expression revealing nothing—until a smile softened his features. "I can't believe you've been here a year, and I never ran into you."

Choosing a house to rent on this beach for her year-long seclusion hadn't been random. Both her ex-boyfriend and Gray's families had houses here, and she'd come with them on vacations for many years. She might have godawful memories of her hometown of Calamity, Wyoming, but she had the best ones in this place. "I've been working."

"Right." A hand on his hip, like a marauding invader, Gray surveyed the living room. "I'm going to send the others back to the house. While we wait for the tow truck, we can take all these dresses"—he gestured to the kitchen table—"to the bedroom."

"Gray, I'm going to be dead honest with you. I'm about two seconds away from losing my shit. Literally, the only thing between me and a total meltdown is the absolute false hope that I can still somehow make my Monday deadline. So, I'd be really grateful if you'd leave right now and let me get a handle on this disaster. Can you do that for me, please?"

He stood there, this mountain of a man, with his potently masculine features and that same aura of confidence that had always allowed her to lean on him at the lowest points of her childhood. She knew what he wanted. To be her hero. To fix her problems. *That's our pattern.* He'd been the one—not the school, not her mom, not her ex—to knock her bullies into next week.

That pattern had ended the night of the prom, when he'd walked away from her. She'd vowed to never be anyone's pity project again.

Her phone's screen lit up again, and then, just to make him leave, she held it up. "This is my backer. I was talking to him when your friend drove into my living room, so he's going to want to know what happened. He's a total drama queen, and when I tell him, it's a very big possibility he'll cancel my show."

"Don't tell him."

"He hired me out of fashion school, included me with his family over the holidays, and backed my show even after I quit on him. I have to tell him." The adrenaline rush was subsiding, allowing the slow tide of fear to roll in. "He's sending someone on Monday to pack up the dresses and ship them. And, unless you have a superpower beyond being unnaturally good at everything you do, there's not a chance in hell I'm going to have…" She glanced around the room, making a quick count of the unaffected dresses. "More than ten dresses ready to go. And that's not a show."

He stalked right up to her. "Trust me?"

She'd never known her father. Her mom was a good person whose lust for life meant a lot of lonely days and nights for Knox. Other than her ex and Gray, she'd had no friends growing up. And she still had few…okay, fine, no friends. So, it was safe to say, trust didn't come easily to her.

But she *had* trusted this man. "Not since the day you walked out and never looked back. Goodbye, Gray."

Chapter Two

Cool morning air whipped through the open windows of Gray's rental car, bringing the scent of the sea and a hint of plumeria. The road followed the coastline, nothing but white sand and swaying palm trees.

He got a flash of Knox's ruined dresses, and cold dread prickled his skin, making him sick to his stomach. *What the hell did we do to her?*

As she'd surveyed the damage, she'd looked utterly stricken. He would fix it, though. Whatever it took, he would get her back on track.

He couldn't stop thinking about her comment. *Not since the day you walked out and never looked back.* She'd meant to deliver it cold and flat, but he'd heard that edge of hurt. Seen it simmering in the depths of her hazel eyes.

It shocked the hell out of him to find out he'd hurt her. What had Gray ever been, but her informant, her therapist, her window into her messed up boyfriend?

Of course, he'd thought about her over the years. *You don't break a habit that easily.* He'd checked out her social media sites enough to know she'd left town not long after him, moving to New York City months earlier than she'd planned. He'd figured, if she could put Robert behind her, then she wouldn't have spared him a single thought.

To have hurt her, though, meant he'd mattered.

He steered the car into her driveway, pleased to see the contractor he'd called had boarded up the living room window and cleared the yard of debris. Shifting into Park, he got out. It didn't sit well that he'd hurt her by walking away all those years ago, but this time...Jesus, this time he'd fucked up her *career*.

The Jeep had taken out the front door, so he knocked on one of the remaining support beams. When she didn't answer, he walked around the side of the house, across a row of uneven stones lodged into dirt, and landed in a tidy plot of green grass. A rickety, waist-high wooden fence separated the lawn from the beach.

He climbed the cement porch steps and rapped on the back door, turning to face the thrashing ocean.

He could see why she'd chosen this house. Surfers lined up, waiting to hit those juicy waves. Man, they'd had some good times on this beach. Back in middle and high school, they'd spent their vacations surfing and hanging out. He smiled at the memory of Robert thinking he could teach Knox how to ride. As if he didn't know she was the kind of person to learn by experience. It had taken her awhile, but she'd figured it out on her own. She'd been fearless, graceful, and athletic.

Damn, he'd loved her. Watching the waves—he estimated about twenty footers—ten feet taller than yesterday's—he reached behind him and knocked again. In a few days, he'd be riding fifty-foot monsters. Excitement slammed him. He couldn't wait to get to California.

If they'd stayed friends, would Knox be going with

him? Hell, would *she* have gotten the invitation for Titans with him?

Nah, she'd always wanted to be a fashion designer. She wouldn't have time to enter competitions on a whim like he did. She'd never have become part of his—as his brothers liked to say—posse. She had a big life, just as she'd always wanted.

Or she'd been about to have one—until they'd destroyed it.

Shit. He'd fix it. He'd bet his Burton custom snowboard that she'd spent the entire day and well into the night assessing the damage, writing up a list of supplies. She'd know by now exactly what she needed to repair the dresses.

"Come on, Knox. Answer the door." He needed to tell her about the conversation he'd had.

Right then, one of the surfers leapt to her feet on her board. The bright red bikini stood out against tan skin. *Knox.* He knew the way she surfed. He knew everything about her.

At least he once had. Seven years was a long time.

Folding his arms across his chest he watched her board flip back and forth. She rode with the same fearless energy she'd always had. She was so fucking hot.

Old feelings stirred, and he shut them down. *Don't go there, man.*

She rode the wave to shore and then jumped off. Gathering her long hair, she squeezed it, wiped the ocean water out of her eyes, and then reached down to pick up her surfboard. Carrying it under one arm, she sashayed up the beach, features tight in concentration.

Watching her from afar…it was all so familiar. The terrible ache of wanting someone he couldn't have, the tightening of his skin as she approached, the compulsion to do something—anything—to make life better for her.

He couldn't think of a time she wasn't alone and fighting.

He caught the moment she noticed him. Her easy gait stiffened, but she ignored him and went straight for the outdoor shower just steps from the house. Leaning her board against the wooden frame, she turned on the faucet and stepped under the spray. When she tipped her head back, all that dark hair fell in a glossy sheet down her back. He'd always loved her body, lean, toned, with that sexy round ass and perfect, lush breasts.

Desire struck up a low hum at the base of his spine. *Jesus, not now.*

Weirdly, she'd never known it, that she was smoking hot. Because of the way she'd been bullied, she'd believed she was lowbrow. But he'd seen the way their classmates looked at her. She'd been cool and aloof, mature well beyond her years. They'd made fun of her because they'd envied her.

After a quick rinse, she patted the wall for her towel.

She wouldn't find it. Her eyelids flew open to find him holding it out to her. She snatched it. "Come on, Gray, I'm not in the mood." She slid her feet into the sparkly black flip flops she kept inside the shower stall.

He noted the slight tremble in her hands. She was panicking. "Is it worse than you thought?"

She nodded, turning away from him to let her hair fall forward over one shoulder. She patted it with the towel, then sent the terry cloth sailing over the wall to dry in the sun. Grabbing her board, she climbed the porch steps.

He followed, too aware of all that bare skin, the tiny

freckle on the inside of her thigh that he'd always wanted to kiss. "How bad?"

"There isn't a single chance in hell I can have twenty-five dresses ready by Monday. It's over." She crouched, peeling back the ratty welcome mat to retrieve a key. Unlocking the door, she stepped inside, blocking him from following. "Thank you for calling that contractor and getting the tarp on the front of the house, but I swear to you, Gray, there's nothing more you can do. Please, just go."

"Not until we talk."

"I can't talk. If I talk, I'll fall apart. Look, bad timing, bad situation, whatever, I just don't have it in me to catch up with you or hang out with you or anything but try and fix my life."

"Fashion Institute of Technology, critic award winner for the Future of Fashion, job at the House of Bellerose Atelier in Paris, and now preparing for your first show in fashion week." He gave her a look that said, *See?* "Thanks to social media, we're all caught up. Now, we can get to the reason I'm here." He stepped forward and, where he expected her to back away—being six-four had its advantages—she blocked him. "Look, I did this. I'm going to help fix it. Please let me in so I can tell you about an interesting conversation I had last night."

Whatever he'd said hit like a slap to her face, because it reddened. "*You* didn't drive over my dresses, Amelia did, and as much as you want to help me, this time you just can't."

"Why don't you give me a chance?"

Casting her gaze to the ceiling, she drew in a deep breath. "Look, I know you feel responsible for what happened but, unfortunately, in this situation you don't know my business, so you're just going to have to believe me when I say there's nothing you can do to help. If you really want to make it up to me, please give me a chance to regroup. If I think of anything I need, I'll get in touch with you, okay?"

Nope, not okay. "I can't fix your dresses, and I can't get you in the fashion show, I get it." He stepped into her kitchen, with its faded yellow Linoleum floor and bullet-shaped refrigerator. "But how about a swerve?"

Something shifted behind her eyes. He caught a whiff of hope. "Swerve how?"

"I happen to know two brides with unlimited budgets who'd like you to make their wedding gowns."

Hope crashed and burned on the landscape of her expression. "That's not what I do. Look, thank you for trying. Really. But I'm making a name for myself in couture, and my only hope at this point is to get another job with a designer. Start all over again."

"When you say start over…?"

"I was about to debut my own designs. If I go back to work for someone, I'll be creating collections for them. It'll take years to build back up to having my own show."

"Is there any chance making couture dresses for my future sisters-in-law would fast-track it?"

She eyed him warily. "A wedding gown is special, Gray. They shouldn't have to wear something of mine because you feel sorry for me."

"Feel…what? No. This has nothing to do with me. I told them about the accident, and they looked you up online. They *want* your dresses."

"Okay, okay." With a palm to her forehead, she turned away from him. "It's hard for me to think right now. I still haven't processed all that I've lost." She shot him an apologetic look. "I'm grateful for the offer. I really am, but...I'm just having a hard time wrapping my head around everything." She paced across the small kitchen and stared out the window, though he doubted she saw the beach. "My only thought is how I can resurrect the show, my career. I keep racking my brain, trying to think—what if I talk to some of my design school friends? We could all put some dresses together for a show. I've got at least ten that are okay. We could create a group collection. Or...what if Luc could get me into someone *else's* show—like a little side thing?" She drew in a breath, lowering her gaze to her feet. "I mean, even as I say it out loud, I know how ridiculous I'm being."

"Your backer, is that Luc?"

She nodded, and he didn't think he'd ever seen her look so defeated.

"Is he going to help you?"

"No. There's nothing he can do." She turned away from the window and gave him a brief but sweet smile. "I'm on my own."

Jesus. As a kid that smile made his knees wobble, turned his bones to jelly. *Why is it happening now?* "Okay, so let me ask you this. What was your end-goal with this fashion show? You get great reviews, buyers go nuts over your dresses, and then what?"

"Brass ring? Jack Abrams Couture offers me a contract, and I get to design my own line of wedding gowns."

"Can you get his attention by making dresses for high profile bides?"

After she gave it some thought, the pain and confusion cleared. "I mean, yes, I definitely can." A moment longer, and she seemed a little surprised. "All I really need is the right kind of visibility."

Now we're talking. "Don't know if you've been paying attention, but there's this meme going around."

"Fin's thing?"

"Yeah, that one. It's brought a lot of attention on us. Making dresses for the bride of The World's Worst Boyfriend would kick up all the noise again, only this time it'll shine it on you. Maybe you could launch your business that way."

With a thoughtful look, she nodded. "I can't believe I'm saying this, but it does make sense."

"So, maybe there's an opportunity here."

"Maybe." And there it was, that smile that lit a fuse from the back of his neck all the way down to the soles of his feet.

"I'm thinking, with the attention we're still getting from the meme, it might drive some more custom orders your way." He saw the alarm in her expression. "You'd only make them for high profile brides, and only until you got that contract you want."

She turned away from him, gathering her wet hair and twisting it into a bun, before letting it drop down her back. "My renter's insurance doesn't cover the loss of my dresses. They said I would've needed to take out a commercial policy for that. And there's no way Luc's going to pay for new materials." She let out a defeated breath. "Which means there's no way to fix my dresses in time for April's show. And I really don't want to go back to designing for someone else, so...I think you're right. This might be the only direction to take right now that makes sense with my long-term plans." She smoothed her hands down her stomach. "Look at me. Standing in my kitchen with Gray Bowie."

With that invitation, he took in the gentle slope of her

shoulders, the sexy curve of her waist and flare of her hips. He'd seen countless women over his lifetime, but no one stirred his blood like this one.

After a moment, she rubbed her forehead with her fingertips and turned to him. "Yeah. Okay. Let's do this."

He was happy beyond reason that he could help her. And—not a small part of it—get to know her again.

I'm a sucker for this woman.

"Great," he said. "Then pack up. We'll head out in the morning. Don't worry about the dresses. Amelia will get them shipped home."

"Home?"

"Calamity. Isn't that where you'd make the dresses?"

"Okay, that's not happening. The only way I'm going back is if you cart my dead, bleached bones there in a wheel barrow."

"Thanks for the ride." Knox hauled her tote off the floorboard and opened the truck's door. Her fight or flight instinct had been raging since he'd picked her up at her house in Maui that morning. It had lasted across the Pacific Ocean and reduced her to a bundle of throbbing nerves on the drive from the local airport.

It had less to do with coming back here than with sitting in such close quarters with Gray Bowie. She supposed everybody had a unique scent, but Gray's did something to her on a cellular level. It triggered that same sense of exhilaration she'd get from reaching the summit on a hike, when she'd gulp in all the fresh, cold air and take in the panorama of jagged gray peaks capped with glistening snow and endless Wyoming blue sky.

He was every good memory she had of home.

Brushing up against his tanned forearm, thick with muscles and covered in black ink, and listening to his deep rumble of a voice drove her back to the days when she was the girl in the trailer, and he was the boy whose presence chased the shadows and scary noises away.

Just as she got out of the truck, the engine cut off. She shot him a look of warning. "What're you doing?"

Gray got out and shoved his keys in the pocket of his jeans. "Going in with you."

A car whizzed by, and every muscle in Knox's body tightened. Her soul turned into a pill bug, curling into its protective shell, even while her middle finger shot up. But, of course, it was just someone traveling on the highway, heading into Grand Teton National Park.

No one had his head out the window, hands cupping his mouth as he barked like a dog at her.

So this is how it's going to be, huh? The minute she hits Calamity, she reverts to the same pissed-off girl who'd flipped the bird to her tormentors. Seven years might've gone by, but her body obviously didn't understand the passage of time.

She soothed herself with the certain belief that everyone had grown up. Most had probably even moved away. "No need. I'll just settle in and catch up with you later."

The late afternoon sun glinted off the trailer. As a little girl, she'd loved the safety and comfort of her cozy home. Loved the wide-open meadow surrounding it, the scent of sun-warmed sage drifting in through open windows. The tall grasses shushing in the breeze had soothed her, and the sight of a bear or moose wandering across the land had thrilled her.

"Place's been empty a while. I'll just check it out." The soles of his boots crunched on the dry grass.

"Even squatters don't want to live there." She'd meant it as a joke, but she heard the bitterness in her tone. Her perspective had changed in fifth grade, when Sean Devane had pierced her bubble with his comment. *You don't even have skirting around it. How poor are you?*

The jab had stayed with her forever. Which was strange since, at the time, she hadn't even known what skirting was. It was more his genuine shock—like, she was *that* poor?

Was *anyone* that poor?

Of course, now, looking back, she totally sided with her mom. Who the hell cared about *skirting*?

Gray watched her carefully. "You don't need to stay here, you know."

The concern in his tone did two things to her. One, it made her sink down into it, as comforting as lolling around on a hammock on a warm summer day. Gray had always been her soft place to fall. But, at the same time, it made her bristle. Because the days of being his pity project were over. "My only income this past year came from bartending at The Rusty Scupper, so I don't have a lot saved, and I don't want to spend my insurance money on a hotel when I can just stay here."

"Don't forget about the deposits from Callie and Delilah."

"That money will go for very expensive fabric and crystals and seed pearls. Not for living expenses." And, honestly, she didn't have the energy to keep explaining things to him. She just felt so…depleted. "Thank you for setting this up for me, but…don't you have a surfing competition to get to?"

"I do." He said it with that lazy grin that made all the girls swoon. "But I'm good on time."

Right. The Bowie private jet meant he could head for California whenever he wanted.

"And I'm not leaving until I introduce you to the brides, and we get things set up."

"Okay." His time management wasn't her concern. "How about I settle in, then come meet you at the ranch?"

He glanced around the property. "How're you going to get there?"

The weight of disappointment squeezed out a big exhalation. "Excellent point." Her mom was on the road for the next couple months. So, no wheels. "If you give me two minutes, I'll drop off my bag and get this place aired out. I want to do a quick inventory, see what supplies I'll need." She started for the trailer. "I'll just be a few minutes."

With a curt nod, he pulled out his phone and leaned against the truck. He swiped the screen, reading intently.

Another truck roared past. This time she ignored it. *See that? Progress.* Until Sean's comment when she was nine, she'd never noticed that she lived in a trailer on Highway 191. Growing up on the other side of the national park boundary, just twenty minutes outside the town center of Calamity, she'd thought she'd lived in heaven.

She and her mom had spent most of their time outdoors, so someone pointing out that she didn't live in a mansion like the billionaires or a ranch-style house in a neighborhood like the business owners or even a huge apartment complex like the seasonal workers, flipped on a light she could never shut off.

She dragged her suitcase across the knee-high prairie

grass, dread building like soot on her lungs, making it harder to breathe with each step. She did *not* want to go in there. Her mom, a seasonal worker herself, spent April through August working on a dude ranch and November through March on ski patrol at the Jackson Hole Resort. In what her mom called the freedom months—September and October—she hit the art festival trail around the country selling her giant found art sculptures. Which meant she was rarely home.

It would've been more pleasant to go inside if her mom had been around, but...*buckle up, babe. We're going in.*

With both hands, she dragged the suitcase up the metal stairs. A cool mountain breeze brought in the scents of pine and sage, rustling up memories from her childhood. Good ones. Running through the woods, jumping into the lake. Her, Robert and Gray, wild and free.

She glanced back at the man who'd been there for her —when her boyfriend had not— expecting to see him buried in his text messages. Instead he watched her, one foot braced against the tire, knee bent, face turned toward her. Everything in her just sort of crashed because, even when she didn't want him to, he was still there for her. Still caring. With a grateful smile, she held up a finger. *One minute.*

Inserting the key into the rusty lock, she turned it and pushed the door open. *Gah.* The closed windows had trapped the summer heat, but it still smelled like cinnamon from the scented pine cones her mom kept in a basket by the electric fireplace. Before hitting the road in her camper, her mom had obviously cleaned, so Knox didn't see a single crumb or mug on the kitchen counters. *So, that's nice.*

Leaving the door open, she stepped into the living area and set her suitcase down. With her mom's lifestyle, Knox had spent a lot of time alone in here. After school in the winter, she'd boil water in a saucer and make a packet of hot chocolate, and then sit with her legs crossed under the coffee table while she did her homework with the television on. Mostly, her mind would wander, and she'd wind up spending more hours on her sketchbook than her school work.

Through the open door of her bedroom, she caught sight of the white quilt she'd made from scraps of fabric. Lace, tulle, organza, everything bridal she could get her hands on from the fabric shops in Jackson County.

She'd taken such care with the delicate material and had been distraught when Robert's belt buckle had torn it. The sharpness of that memory delivered a stab of anxiety.

Was he in town? Did he live here?

Doubtful. He'd hoped to make films with his dad, but even if that hadn't panned out, she couldn't see a reason for him to be in Calamity.

The edge of a clear plastic storage container peeked out from under her bed. *My sketchbooks.* A punch of energy got her moving toward her room. Getting on her knees, she pulled out the box and pried off the top. Excitement buzzed under her skin at the familiar black covers.

Throughout her childhood, before she'd had to design for her senior year fashion show, before she'd had to impress Luc's couture world, she'd sketched for the brides in her dream sets.

Growing up, she couldn't wait to go to bed, eager to return to her imaginary worlds. The stories unspooled like movies, always involving a group of friends and inevitably leading to weddings. They helped her fall asleep at night and got her though many lonely hours.

Opening the top book, she flipped through the pages. *Serena. Oh, my God.* She totally remembered Serena, a free spirit she imagined had moved to Calamity from a small beach community in southern California. *Look at these bohemian gowns.*

She'd have to buy a new sketchbook for Gray's sisters-in-law. It would be fun not to worry about couture, to get to know the women, and come up with dresses that fit their personalities.

Snapping the book shut, she dropped it back on the pile. Just as she reached for the lid to seal the box, she noticed a sheet of heavy drawing paper. A memory tickled just under her skin, until she pulled it out to find the wedding gown she'd designed for herself.

It was a fairytale dress with a plunging beaded lace bodice and an ethereal ballgown with wispy layers of tulle. Hand-sewn flowers on top of the illusion foundation gave it an outrageously feminine look. She'd spent a lot of time on this one.

Do you know something? I'd choose this same dress today.

Well, marriage was so not on her radar. Maybe one of Gray's brides would like it. But even as she thought about showing it to them, she felt a tug of resistance. *It's mine.*

She'd take it to the studio with her. Tape it to her storyboard for inspiration.

Popping the lid back on, she shoved the box under the bed. She'd kept him waiting long enough. Only, when she came back into the living room, she found him leaning against the wall, his hands deep in the pockets of his jeans, his biceps round and hard under that dark gray T-shirt.

"Grab your suitcase. You're staying at the ranch."

Chapter Three

BEFORE SHE COULD OBJECT TO STAYING ON THE Bowie's three-hundred-thousand-acre legacy ranch, Gray hoisted the luggage into his arms and headed out the door. "Both Callie and Delilah work full-time—crazy hours—so they can't be driving out here every time they need to try something on. Besides…" He made a sweeping gesture. "You gonna turn this into your studio? When you get more orders, do you want the customers to come here for fittings?"

Obviously, that would be a hard no. Her heels clanked on the metal steps. "I'm not going to live in the main house with your family, Gray."

"Of course not. You can have the bunkhouse. I've checked, and no one's using it."

She locked up the trailer, thinking about all that space. "If you're sure no one's going to mind, I would love that. It'll give me a chance to spread out all my dresses, see what I can salvage."

"It's yours as long as you need it." He waited in a patch of bright yellow desert parsley, until she caught up to him. "There's something else I want to suggest. I've got the space, and I've also got some people who could help you."

"I'm going to have to look at the dresses first, see if they *can* be fixed before I consider hiring anyone." *But* she couldn't expect orders to come in from the custom dresses if she didn't market them. "Let me talk to Callie and her friend first, figure out their budgets, so I can see what I can afford."

"And that's where my proposition comes in."

She could only smile and shake her head. "Okay, give it to me. What else have you got up your sleeve?"

"I'm thinking we could be business partners. Just like you and Luc were."

She headed for the truck. "I'm not taking your money, Gray."

"Good, 'cause I'm not giving you any. I'm offering the bunkhouse and staff to help you out."

"Help me out how?"

"Someone to help on the creative end, someone to handle finances, marketing. Basically, I can provide the team and the infrastructure."

Where on earth would Gray Bowie get a team to help her make wedding gowns? But, okay, if she wanted to turn this into an actual business, she'd need the help, so she'd play along. "And what would you get out of this partnership?"

They reached the truck. "A new business venture and…ten percent of your earnings."

"Ten percent, huh? You're not a very good businessman."

He grinned. "No worse than you. You're supposed to just take the offer and not point it out. But, since you did,

I'll tell you that you get the better end of the bargain, 'cause I'm the one who got you into this mess."

Before getting in, she stopped to take in her mom's flat, sagebrush-covered property. "Twenty-four hours ago, my biggest worry was Luc's reaction to the alteration I'd made on one of my dresses. And now I'm standing here with *you*"—*of all people*—"forming a business partnership."

"But it's pretty cool, right?" He tossed her suitcase into the bed of the trunk.

"It's interesting, that's for sure." She got in and fastened her seatbelt.

The moment he climbed in, he fired up the engine. "So, we're doing this?"

Salvaging her dresses, custom order requests…yeah, she'd need help. "We're doing this." Ooh, there it was. That crazy connection they'd always had. She'd never understood it back then. Frankly, it had frightened her. Maybe, on some level, she'd been attracted to him, but she'd shut down any possibility because a) she'd been with Robert, and b) Gray Bowie would never see her that way. Ever.

She didn't know why she was thinking about it now, except that, sitting so close to him, breathing in his clean, mountain-man scent, was doing a number on her. He looked every bit the bad boy with his unruly hair and scruff, tattoos, and lazy smile, and yet he exuded this powerful energy.

That's it. The juxtaposition of his carefree, yet take-charge attitude, was a total turn-on.

Well, shut it down, because that's a no-fly zone.

Not only wouldn't he be interested in her that way, if

they were going to work together, they had to keep attraction—sex—out of it.

"I know we're not drawing up formal paperwork or anything," he said. "But I have to ask…you're going to stay in town long enough to make these dresses, right? It's okay if you're not sure. I just need to know before I introduce you to Callie and Delilah. They're good people, and they're excited about wearing them. I'm not going to let them down."

"That's fair." Sometimes, he seemed to know her better than she knew herself. On some level, she still clung to the dream that Chanel would call, and she'd be on the next jet. "I'd like to make an addendum to our business deal."

He cracked a smile. "I'm listening."

"If Jack Abrams calls and offers me a contract, I'm out of here. That goes for Chanel or Givenchy, too." She gave him a teasing smile.

"Got it."

"Other than that, I'm in."

He grew serious. "Okay, then we have to plan the next steps carefully. The launch matters in terms of marketing."

She knew her world had turned upside down—and been shaken violently—when Gray Bowie talked about marketing. But, once again, he was spot on. "Once I get settled, I'll map out the whole game plan. I've got it from here."

"I think you missed the part where I'm in business with you."

"Aren't you heading out to Titans? And God knows where you'll go after that."

"I'm coming back right after. Gotta train."

That pinch of disappointment snapped her out of it. As sincere as he sounded, Gray was not *in business* with her. He'd set her up—which was incredibly generous of him—before taking off, back to his life as an extreme athlete and nomad. "Oh, yeah? Which competition's next?" She didn't follow surfing events.

"I'm training for the big one."

"Wait, you're on the championship tour?" For all his medals and trophies, Gray only entered competitions when he felt like it. He'd never wanted to be tied down, so he didn't join teams.

"Hell, no. I'm talking about boarding."

"I don't understand." Until she did. "Wait, you're going for the *Olympics*?"

"That's the idea."

"Hold your horses. You're committing to a sport?" And then it struck her. "Gray, why're you doing Titans if you're training for the Olympics?"

He shrugged. "I got the invitation. About twenty minutes before we crashed into our living room."

"*Gray.*"

"It'll be fine."

"Does your coach know?"

"First of all, there's no team yet. That won't happen until January. Secondly, my coach right now is Fin, and no, I haven't told him."

"Because he'll lose his shit?"

He tapped his fingers on the wheel. "Probably."

"Oh, man. I don't want to be there when he finds out you're riding sixty-foot waves."

"Won't know the size till I get there. Or whether the event's even on."

Weather conditions controlled when Titans Invitational could be held. The participants would all just hang out and wait in tents and RVs. She remembered, because the guys had always dreamed of getting the invitation. For a while there, that was all they'd talked about. It was on the tip of her tongue to say, *Robert would be so jealous.* But she shut that line of thought down cold. The two guys had been crazy competitive with each other, and she didn't need to stir it up again.

Up ahead she spotted the Masterson's house, right near the turn-off for the Bowie ranch. The familiar white fence of their horse training facility stood out against the green sage meadow. "I can't believe I'm back here. I didn't think I'd ever…" She glanced down at the cuticle she'd been smashing with a fingernail. "Well, I wanted to come back as an established fashion designer. Not as a struggling wannabe."

"Pretty sure you've had a career designing wedding gowns for the House of Bellerose."

She smiled.

"What?"

"Hearing Mr. Rough and Tough Athlete say, 'House of Bellerose.'" She made her voice all cowboy-raspy on the last three words.

"That's what Amelia said it's called." He smiled, big and broad. "Did I get it wrong?"

"No, it's just funny to hear you say it, like you've got some Bellerose tuxedoes hanging in your closet."

"Maybe I do."

"Unless your last girlfriend bought you one to wear to her galas, I doubt it."

"You'd be right. Remember Mr. Santorini?"

"Your dad's tailor? Of course."

"He still makes our suits."

A chill swept through her, so real she rubbed her arms. *This is the world I'm returning to.* The one where the wealthy people went to Mr. Santorini for tailoring. Where teachers pitied her, and classmates barked at her.

The town infested with people she swore she'd never see again.

And she'd just committed to a business here. It would take at least six to eight months to make Callie and Delilah's dresses, so that meant she'd be here at least a year.

Okay, but who knew what might happen. If she marketed well, she could attract Jack Abrams's attention sooner than later. Anxiety pinched the back of her neck. And if she didn't, she could become a seamstress. The plan had potential, but without the backing of Luc Bellerose, it was risky.

Gray's hand came down over hers, so big and strong. "I know this is a big swerve. That show meant a lot to you."

"It meant everything."

"I can imagine."

"Can you?" As long as she'd known him, he'd flitted from one activity to another. Just when he'd gotten good at fencing, he'd switched to jazz guitar. Then, after a couple school performances, he'd dropped out of that. No wonder his dad hadn't gotten him that electric guitar he'd wanted for his birthday.

He took his eyes off the road to give her a searching look. "I'm not sure where you're going with that question."

"Have you ever wanted something so much that you'd just die if you didn't get it?"

He went quiet for a moment, attention back on the highway. She thought he wasn't going to respond—which was an answer in itself—until he looked her right in the eye and gave a dead-serious, "Yes."

It had never once occurred to her—she was just so

used to the bachelor Bowies—but with Fin and Will settling down… "Are you and Amelia…"

"What?" He seemed genuinely confused.

"Together?"

"*Amelia*? Hell, no." He shrugged. "We're friends."

He entered surfing and snowboarding competitions on a whim, jumped from one activity to another, and had never had a girlfriend. *That's Gray. Not all that invested in anything.*

Passion. That was the difference between them. Knox's career meant everything to her. She *loved* designing and making gowns, loved the materials, the beads and crystals, the feel of the seed pearls in her fingers, the smell of fabric freshly unrolled off the bolt.

Maybe things had come too easily to him, but Gray didn't have passion for anything. That was sad. He'd never know the extreme ends of the emotional spectrum.

Then again, maybe that's a good thing…he'd never experience the crushing disappointment of failure.

Nah. It was passion that would get her back on the right path. Passion that would make her dreams come true.

Gray Bowie was just a ship carrying her to the next port on this dark stretch of night.

With the windows open and the warm mountain air whipping Knox's hair around her face, it took Gray back —way back—to all the times they'd hung out together.

He'd craved that time alone with her, even when he'd known it was wrong. He'd had no business hanging out with his best friend's girlfriend.

Not when he'd loved her so fucking hard.

It sucked that, after all these years, being with her stirred it all up. Enough time had passed, he should be over it. Maybe it was muscle memory. The habit of wanting her.

"What're all these cars doing here?" She unbuckled before he'd even hit the brakes.

"We're just getting the place cleaned up." He slowed, parking haphazardly at the side of the bunkhouse.

"You move fast."

"Well, I've got a plane to catch." He hauled out her suitcase and caught up with her. "You can use one of our trucks while you're here. Get your own groceries, whatever you need."

She stopped on the patch of grass and turned to him, put a warm hand on his arm. "Thank you."

The thrill of it scuttled down his spine. *What are you, fourteen?* No, he was a grown man, and there wasn't a chance in hell he'd topple back into that hellhole of wanting a woman he couldn't have. He gave a taut nod and continued on.

"It looks exactly the same," she said.

Fifty years ago, back when this had been a working ranch, the cowhands had lived here. But neither his dad nor his uncle had had any interest in ranching, so Gray and his brothers had turned it into a hangout. They'd had the best parties in the large, renovated rectangular building. Over time, they'd covered the entire façade with reflective road and animal crossing signs.

Climbing the porch steps, he breathed in the familiar smell of wood and the musty cushions from the hand-hewn rockers his uncle had made. "Come on in." He held the door open, following behind with her suitcase.

Zach, his most recent hire, had rounded up some dress forms and sewing machines. In the kitchen, a crew unpacked overfilled grocery sacks. Music came from somewhere down the long hallway that led to what were once dormitory-style bedrooms. Several years ago, they'd knocked down walls to create master bedroom suites.

She swept a hand down the back of a dress form. "How could you possibly get supplies like this so quickly?"

"We have connections."

"Okay, hang on. A team, connections, *marketing*?" She fingered some bright blue nylon. "You have fabric swatches in the bunkhouse. Gray, what's going on here?"

"I dabble in some clothing lines."

"You *dabble*?"

"Long story. Let me introduce you to everyone." He started off towards the long dining room table.

"Gray."

Her serious tone stopped him.

"Is there a business already going on in here?"

"No. We run ours remotely or out of our homes. I'm sure Zach just brought some stuff with him. We're in the middle of launching a new line."

"A new *line*?" Her expression said, *What in the world are you talking about?*

He didn't like to talk about it. It was just something he and his friends did together, but he supposed he should fill her in. "Okay, well, a couple years ago, we had an idea for a better snowboard, so we designed it and sold it. Thought we were pretty badass, until we saw the sales report. It was pretty dismal. So, one day, we were sitting around the fire, shooting the shit, talking about marketing and how we could boost sales, and it struck me that what really sells are the things people need to buy new every season. Like socks and gloves and board shorts. Shit like that."

"You and your friends sat around a campfire talking about marketing?"

"You givin' me shade?" He smiled, when what he really felt was frustration. *This is why I don't talk about it.* People didn't take him seriously. They had one idea about him and didn't want to see him any other way. "Let me introduce you to my Creative Director."

Following, she muttered, "He has a Creative Director."

"Zach," he called.

The hipster dude looked up from the screen of his laptop, where he'd been clicking away like a maniac.

"This is Knox Holliday. Knox, this Zach, he's the Creative Director for Duck Dive Haberdashery."

"Duck Dive? That's the name of your business?"

He couldn't tell if she liked it or not. She sounded more surprised than anything. "Yeah. Like I said, we didn't take it too seriously at the start."

"Don't believe a word he says." Zach set the laptop on the coffee table and got up off the couch. "He's a magnate."

"Nah." He shook his head. "Not even close."

"Zach Martin." He reached out a hand. "It's great to meet you, Knox. Wish it were under better circumstances."

"It's nice to meet you." She shook his hand but turned to Gray with a confused expression. "Can I talk to you for a sec?"

"Yeah, sure." He clapped Zach on the shoulder. "Listen, I hate to leave you guys like this, but I have to head to the airport. I'm hoping you'll have a chance to get to know each other, see if you'd like to work together."

"Are you kidding?" Zach smiled as he shook Knox's hand. "Working on something other than board shorts? Hell, yeah."

His creative director must've caught the crease between Knox's eyes, because he continued. "Before I came here, I worked at Hugo Rossi."

"Really?" Knox sounded impressed.

"Yeah, so getting back to higher end products is cool."

"All right. I'm out of here." Gray hoped like hell she'd like his staff. He wanted this partnership to work. It was more than wanting to make things right for her. The challenge of helping build her platform excited him. "Walk me out?"

"Yeah, sure." She blinked away the tears glistening in her eyes.

When he hit the porch, he turned back to her. "Amelia's got a professional preservationist coming in to pack up your dresses. We'll expedite shipping so you don't lose any more time." But that only made her sadder. "You okay?" What else could he do to make it right for her?

She turned glassy eyes toward him. "You're the kindest man I've ever known. I don't even know what to say." She looked lost. "Thank you just seems so hollow."

"I think you forget that I'm the one who caused all your problems."

"No, I'm not forgetting anything."

He wanted to hug her, press a kiss in her palm, and tell her everything would be all right. But he knew where that would lead, because his tongue would wander toward her delicate wrist and then trace the ink on the inside of her forearm.

Starting just below the elbow, black thread unraveled from a spool and turned into a fanciful dress on a hanger.

It continued its merry path to a stitched heart and ended through the eye of a needle. It was awesome.

But there would be no arm licking. "I've got to head to the airport. It'd be great if you could get to know Zach and Amelia. If they're not a good fit, we can hire other people. It's all up to you."

She gestured to the bunkhouse. "This is better than anything I could've imagined. Gray, you've…set me up nicely."

In that moment, he knew he'd give up Titans Invitational just to stay with her and get more of that softness, to be part of this journey she'd just started. He wanted…*fuck. Look at me, going right back there*. "Okay. I'm out." He trampled down the steps. "You need anything at all, text me."

The early September air swept over his heated skin. Even from this distance, he could see the kaleidoscope of emotions moving across her beautiful features. She was completely overwhelmed, and yet, in spite of her panic and confusion, she was rallying, moving forward.

It drove him crazy, what they'd done to her. How they'd ruined things. And he just had to help her. Had to.

Nobody felt things deeper than Knox. When she laughed, it was with her whole body, doubling over and clutching her stomach. When she was angry, hellfire flashed in her eyes. When she was hurt, she'd pull into herself like a turtle.

He'd loved all those moods, and no sixty-foot wave or twenty-two-foot halfpipe wall came close to the thrill he got from simply being with her.

His phone vibrated, and he pulled it out of his pocket to see a text from Sarah, his pilot.

Fueled up and ready to go.

Before hopping into the truck, he glanced back at the bunkhouse and caught a glimpse of Knox through the open door. Her long, surfer-girl hair gleamed as she headed toward the kitchen. The boy in him who'd never gotten to hold her hand wanted to stay, revel in her smiles and laughter and fierce attitude. But the man knew there was nothing between them. Not like that anyway.

He typed his response. *On my way.*

Chapter Four

"I can't believe how fast Gray got these here." Knox gently pulled the pale pink tulle over the dress form and smoothed it. He'd expedited the shipping, getting them preserved and delivered to the bunkhouse in one week. She was just so happy to see them outside the wreckage of that house. This one, the *Pirouette,* didn't have much damage at all.

Zach used his cutter to open one of the other boxes. "He's a great guy." He pulled out a lavender organza so pale it looked like stardust and handed it over to her.

Moving to the next form, she eased the skirt over the top. "Yeah, but he's got so much going on." The strong scent of coffee permeated the huge space, and she worried about the dresses. "Maybe we shouldn't cook here."

Zach looked up, obviously trying to make sense of her comment.

"The fabrics will absorb the smells."

"Ah. Gotcha. I'm used to polyester and nylon. I can hit up Calamity Joe's, though, right? Bring in my own cup?"

"Definitely. It's just better not to brew any here."

Slicing open another box, he pulled out a glittery white fairy gown. "I don't know squat about wedding dresses, but these are pretty damn amazing. I don't even want to touch them."

Normally, she wouldn't let him. An uneven fingernail or a callous could ruin a dress. But these were already destroyed.

Her loss hit her. Full-on body blow. Sacked, she lowered her arms, stopped breathing for the count of one…two…three. *God.* Yes, she was glad to have her dresses back, but seeing what she'd spent a year sewing with her own hands ruined…*hurt.*

She just had to focus on moving forward. She had a plan, a business partner, and a team. *It's going to work out.* And Zach was awesome. "If you don't mind my asking, why'd you leave Hugo Rossi?"

"I'm actually from a small mountain town in Colorado, so when Gray first approached me, I was kind of into the idea of leaving the city and coming back to my roots. But what sealed it was that, at my old job, it was the same button downs, khakis, V-necks…over and over."

"And Duck Dive?"

"Gray's got a really creative business mind. His brain's always working, always thinking of the next idea, and he likes what I bring to the table. As soon as I convinced him to expand into women's swimwear, it opened the door to cover-ups and tunics. He lets me run with it, and I love that."

"And here I've been worried about trusting a surfer with my career."

"Gray's not a surfer. He's an elite athlete, who runs a

successful business. And he's focused on getting your career back."

"I hope I can."

"You don't sound convinced."

"It's an extremely competitive world. The best path was through my old boss." Who had yet to return her calls. She needed to talk to him, tell him her new path. "He had access to the kinds of unique fabrics and material I can't get on my own. I'll get there…it's just going to be harder, that's all."

"Don't sell Gray short." Zach's smile was filled with awe for his boss.

"I know his intentions are good, and I've already benefitted from his good ideas, but he does have a short attention span." She said it with a laugh.

But he didn't smile. "Why do you say that?"

"He's training for the Olympics, but he gets the call for Titans, and off he goes? There isn't much he takes seriously."

"You sure about that? Not sure you can surf sixty-foot waves and heli ski if you don't take it seriously. I know he comes off all easy-going, but I've seen him in action." He tipped his head with a thoughtful expression. "Actually, I don't know why he downplays his achievements."

Had he always been like that? Knox stopped for a moment, considering. For years, both Gray and Robert had been rabidly competitive with each other. Literally, everything was a challenge. They'd hike up to Dead Man's summit and, about a mile before the top, they'd both take off, race-walking. A drive to Bozeman would turn into a drag race, with Knox bracing against the dashboard and shouting at Robert to cut it out.

It only struck her now that Gray's competitiveness had

ended with Robert's addiction. Except...now that she thought about it, maybe he hadn't lost it at all. Maybe he'd only acted like he didn't care. *Isn't that what they'd had to do for Robert?* They'd been so careful not to set him off.

Had Gray started downplaying his wins? Had he stopped acting like he cared because he didn't want Robert to feel bad? It certainly made sense.

Of course, it hadn't worked. Gray figured out long before she had that you couldn't control someone else's behavior. She'd spent half her life fighting that losing battle. But had it become a habit for Gray, downplaying his achievements? Because Zach was right. Gray wouldn't be a champion if he didn't take his training seriously. "You know what? You're absolutely—"

Before she finished her sentence, the door opened, and cool, fresh air swept in. Two gorgeous women—one, Callie Bell, a tall, elegant brunette, the other a sexy, gorgeous blonde who must be Delilah—sashayed into the bunkhouse. Callie put a hand over her heart and said, "Oh, my God. Look at those dresses." Her gaze skimmed along the line of frothy gowns. "Is this for real?" She glanced up with a grin. "Can I have all of them?"

"You bet." Knox knew she sounded a little stiff, but her heart was racing. She'd gone to school with Callie, which meant the woman knew everything about her past. The other one, Delilah, was she local, too? Knox hadn't thought to ask Gray about her, so she tried to process her features, her attributes, anything that might trigger a recollection. The bullies had made a permanent imprint, so she'd recognize them a hundred years from now. She'd rather sell cars for a living than design dresses for anyone who'd ever barked at her. But, no, nothing about Delilah rang any bells. "You can have anything you want."

"Careful what you offer me. I can't even set a date for my wedding, let alone choose a dress."

"Zach," Knox said. "Do you know Callie and Delilah?"

"No, we haven't met." He shook both their hands. "It's nice to meet you both. How about I let you ladies alone to talk gowns, while I finish unpacking them?"

"Thanks, Zach," Knox said.

Turning back to the forms, Callie moaned. "How am I supposed to choose? These are the most gorgeous wedding dresses I've ever seen."

"And trust me when I say she's been looking," Delilah said. "She's got wedding magazines all over her house, her car, the museum." With a bright smile, she reached a hand out. "I'm Delilah Lua, and you must be the magic maker."

Knox clasped her hand. "That's the title on my business card."

"We are *so* excited that you'll be making our dresses," Delilah said. "Just to be clear, I've recently opened a restaurant here, and I'm in way over my head, so I'm in no rush to get this done. Also, I'm not going to be that crazy bride who takes up every second of your time making changes every time she sees something she likes better." She gave an exaggerated tip of her head toward her friend.

Callie's eyes went wide. "Are you seriously making fun of me right now? Look at these."

Delilah burst out laughing.

My God, she's dazzling. Knox was positive she'd remember her. "You're not from here, are you?"

"Oh, no," Delilah said. "I just moved here this summer. I'm from New York."

Thank God. "That's where I went to college."

"FIT?" Delilah asked.

"Yep."

"How many pounds did you gain eating Mort's French fries?"

Knox found herself relaxing. "Ten in my freshman year. And I don't regret a single one."

"I went to school there, too." Callie shook her head. "I'm sorry. I got carried away. I'm Callie Bell, Fin's fiancée. Do you remember me?"

"Of course. It's good to see you again." *Please don't bring up the past.*

"Delilah's marrying Will."

"What voodoo did you practice on him?" From the look on the chef's face, Knox instantly regretted making the joke.

"Why does everybody say that?" Delilah looked genuinely confused. "Will's got the biggest heart of anyone I know."

"That's because you cracked it open." Callie came closer to Knox. "I remember you, you know."

Her smile faltered. *Don't let her go there.* "Well, who wouldn't? I had quite the reputation." Dread got a good, solid grip on her as she waited to hear Callie explain about Knox Holliday, the junk yard dog. *Awesome.*

Callie nudged her friend with an elbow. "She was a year ahead of me, and she had more style in her pinky than everyone in the whole town combined—and that includes the rich people. I swear, everyone in our school wore Uggs, jeans, and hoodies. But Knox?" Callie took in Knox's slim-cut black velvet pants, the leather, studded ankle boots, and the boat-neck blouse she'd made herself. "She rocked scarves and leather jackets, ripped tights and baby doll dresses."

"My mom was a child of the eighties," Knox said. "I borrowed a lot of her stuff."

"I remember making this list," Callie said. "Pretty much writing down everything I saw you wear that I thought was cool. And I spent the entire winter break trying things on and playing with different looks. And then, the morning before we went back to school, my room was this explosion of clothing and accessories, and I wound up going to school in Uggs, jeans, and a hoodie, because I just couldn't make anything work."

"You have gorgeous style now." Knox thought Callie looked as sleek and elegant as Audrey Hepburn.

"Yeah, well, I didn't have the confidence back then," Callie said. "You had it in spades."

"Thank you. That's nice to hear." Though it wasn't confidence so much as defiance. She wouldn't let the assholes win.

"I can't believe Gray destroyed your dresses." Callie cringed, as though witnessing the accident right then.

"It wasn't Gray behind the wheel, but he's the one going above and beyond to make it right."

"So, what's the plan?" Delilah asked. "Are you fixing them for a show?"

"We're…assessing." She didn't have the money to fix them, but she wouldn't bring that up.

"We are definitely doing something with them," Zach called from the long kitchen table, where he was laying out dresses since they'd run out of dress forms. "They're amazing."

"We're hopeful." *Change the subject so you don't break down in front of them.* "But I'm excited to make your wedding gowns. Since neither of you has a date set, we can take our time. I'll go over styles and fabrics with you, make some sketches, and we'll start from there. Sound good?"

"Sounds fantastic," Callie said. "I have to say, now that you're here and this is happening, I'm really excited."

"I'm glad. This'll be fun." She gave them a smile, but inside she was a little panicky. She had no idea where she'd buy the material for two dresses. The high-end vendors she worked with had a minimum amount of fabric they'd sell. Maybe since they knew her, they'd give her a break. *Hopefully*. She had good relationships with everyone.

Her phone vibrated on the table. "Excuse me." Reaching for it, she turned away from them to face the French doors. *Luc*. Finally. Last time they'd talked, he'd completely freaked out before abruptly hanging up on her, and she hadn't heard from him since. "Hey." A million thoughts ran through her head.

Are you still mad at me?

I hope you know it wasn't my fault.

I'm freaking out, and I just want you to fix everything and get my life back on track.

"It has taken me several days." He spoke in a measured tone. "But I am finally coming to terms with the loss of our collection."

Her heart squeezed painfully. Gray had mobilized so quickly to get her back in action, and she truly appreciated his help, but he didn't get it. Only Luc would. It was such a relief to confide in him. "I know." She stepped away from the others. "I'm devastated but trying to hold it together. I was so close, you know? So close to starting the career I've always dreamed of. And to have it ripped from me…God. I just…" Tears spilled down her cheeks, and she swiped them away. "I just can't stand it. I lie awake at night, and it's like I'm plugged in. Like there's an electrical current running through me. I just can't believe it. I want to wake up from this nightmare."

"Mon petit chou, it is a nightmare. I had the Lincoln Center. I had Marie-Thérèse, who wears your gowns like she was born in them. But I have salvaged everything by giving your show to Antonia. She is as close to your talent as I've got. Close, but simply not the same."

Antonia? A sting of jealousy shot through her. That woman was so full of herself. A true mean girl. "Well, good for her."

"Yes, she is floating on air. Now, for you, ma chère, my favorite designer, all is not lost. I have a plan."

"A plan?" Would he back her for April's Bridal Fashion Week? She didn't know if she could have twenty-five dresses in that time—some had to be redone completely.

"You will come back to Paris and work for me again. While you're designing fabulous collections for me, you can create your own line." He paused. "Which we will debut at *next* October's show."

Going back with Luc meant couture, for sure. Her pulse pounded, she wanted it so badly. So what if he stole her designs again? *No, you know what? You go in there knowing he'll steal something. Keep a notebook just for him and leave it out as bait.* And then she could just keep her own private sketchbook hidden somewhere.

Oh, my God. What are you even talking about?
Do you hear yourself? Planting a sketchbook?

If she took his deal, even if she designed the most gorgeous dresses in the world for him, nothing would stop him from claiming her private sketches as his own. *You know he'd do it.* And then another year would go by, and she still might not have her own line.

She wanted her own haute couture atelier with all her

heart…but at what cost? Her pride, her sense of self, they were worth more to her than that. *Oh, dammit, dammit, dammit.* She could not *believe* she was going to do this. "Thank you, Luc. You've believed in me since my senior project fashion show. You've given me a wonderful opportunity in this business, and I will always be grateful for your support." *There's never just one path.* And she liked the one she and Gray were building together.

"But?"

"But I'm going to stay here."

"In the States? Surely, you don't mean that cowboy town you're from?"

"I'm going to—" She closed her eyes, envisioning his expression as she told him. "I'm going to make luxury knock-offs of the dresses and sell them in a pop-up bridal boutique." *What?* She almost laughed out loud. That idea was either genius or utter stupidity.

Actually, though, it was pretty brilliant. That, plus the custom gowns could very well get Jack Abrams's attention. She just needed the right marketing approach.

He wasn't responding. Each moment of silence yanked the strings of tension in her body. "Luc?"

"Why limit yourself to a boutique? Why not sell them on eBay, too?" The venom in his voice was reserved for people who'd crossed him, people he hated.

"It's not like that." She'd find a high-end boutique in New York or Los Angeles. Chicago.

"No. You don't have my permission to sell my dresses."

"They're not your dresses, Luc." She said it softly but firmly. "You don't own this collection."

"We are partners."

No, they weren't. "Luc, you supported me in fashion

week in exchange for my designs. That's the extent of our agreement."

"I put up the money for the material. Textiles that came from my looms."

"And I designed collections for you. I met the terms of our contract."

"Money is not the point. I only backed you because we are building your reputation. It must be done the right way."

"It will be done the right way." She glanced over at Callie and Delilah and found them listening avidly. Zach, too. "I'm also creating couture gowns for high profile brides."

"From Calamity?" he asked.

"Yes, from Calamity." *For now, anyhow.*

"Wonderful. So will you incorporate lassos in the design? Instead of Swarovski crystals, you will have turquoise? Will the brides wear cowboy boots?"

"Thirty percent of the homeowners here are millionaires, and if they choose to wear cowboy boots under their gowns that's their prerogative. All I know is I'll be designing luxury wedding gowns." *Think marketing.* She needed to exploit the meme. "And I'll be recording the entire process on social media." *What's this now?* Oh, she'd hit on her plan. "Last summer a text message someone sent went viral, turning this man I know into a meme. Well, that guy happens to live here, and he's getting married. So, I'll be making the wedding dress for The World's Worst Boyfriend's bride." She thought of all those pages she followed with stylized images. "I'll be setting up a page called *The Making of a Couture Wedding Gown* and filling it with photographs of every step of the process."

Now, this would work. She'd get tons of custom orders from it.

"What is the matter with you?" Luc sounded horrified. "Stop this. Stop it right now. You are destroying your career."

"Christian Navarre built his whole business from an online presence."

"You are not Christian Navarre. You are Knox Holliday, and you are the most talented, gifted designer I know. Your gowns are 'extravagantly feminine, wildly unique, and lushly romantic.'"

Bridal Salon magazine had attended her senior year fashion show and given her that astonishing review. Knox had framed it and hung it on her wall to see every time she felt down or frustrated. Luc hired her not only because she'd won first place but because of that review. "I can't wait another year to start my career." *And I'm not going to work for you.*

"So that's what this is. You're trying to blackmail me into giving you your show?"

"What? Blackmail how? I don't have a collection to show." Why was he attacking her instead of trying to help her? God, he was making this all about him. "You know me better than that."

"I know that I am very upset right now. Listen to me, Knox, along with being creatively brilliant, you are headstrong, impatient, and stubborn. You want everything right now, but in our business it doesn't work like that. You must carefully construct your career. If you want to be a fashion house that endures, if you want to be Balenciaga, McQueen, or Bellerose, then you need to stay the course. Trust me on this. Come back to me, create another collection, and we'll show it next October. You will take the bridal world by storm, I guarantee it."

"You know I want that, but I'm going to get there another way." She took a deep breath to calm her nerves. "I think this is a good plan, Luc." It was scary, risky, but she really did believe in it.

"Don't do this, Knox. This is a mistake. You are capable of Dior, and you're settling for Walmart."

She sucked in a sharp breath. He didn't know much about her past. He certainly didn't know that people had called her the junkyard dog and barked at her, so he didn't know the direct hit to her deepest wound. She loved Walmart—that was where she bought her food and soap and cleaning supplies—but she didn't want to launch her career at the lowest price point. She wanted couture.

"Come back to me," he said. "I will get you where you need to be."

"I'm sorry, Luc. I'm going to swerve, because it's the only way I know to get what I want and keep you in my life." God, she hoped she was making the right choice. Because she *was* headstrong, impatient, and stubborn.

"All right. Your dreams were crushed just two days ago. You think about this, and when you change your mind, come back to me."

She knew he'd come around. "Thank—"

"And if you don't, things will not go well for you."

Chapter Five

Breathing in the ocean air, woodsmoke, and weed, Gray let the heat from the bonfire warm his face.

Ingrid, one of the Central Coast locals who'd come to hang out with the surfers, passed him a joint, eyes squinting, as she held the smoke in her lungs.

He waved a hand. *No thanks.* Most of his life was spent riding monster waves and uncharted mountains. He didn't do drugs or booze. Never had.

She nudged him, breathing the smoke out the side of her mouth. "One toke?"

"I've got a date with a barrel in the morning. No, thanks."

She leaned across him, her breasts grazing his arm, and passed it to the woman sitting on his other side. Instead of leaning back, Ingrid stayed where she was, watching him with invitation in her eyes. "You were amazing out there today." Her long blonde hair spilled over his bare skin, her gaze fixed on his mouth.

With her skimpy bikini and toned body, Ingrid offered him a few hours of pleasure. But…he just wasn't feeling it.

"Thanks. We got some good sets." Over the crackling fire and murmur of conversation, the ocean pounded against the shore. He could feel each thunderous crash under his ass. Tomorrow, he'd be out there. *Fuck, yeah.* Couldn't wait.

Ingrid sat back, slipping an arm under his, like they knew each other. With two fingers, she traced figure eights on his inner thigh, slowly inching closer to his dick. It was a good move; he'd give her that. But he wasn't attracted to her.

Because she's not Knox. A roiling frustration had him pulling out of her hold.

Her eyes went wide, and she looked mortified, which sucked, but come on. He wasn't some playground she could crawl all over. He hadn't given her a single indication of interest since he'd met her a couple hours ago. "Excuse me." He got up and headed toward the surf, feeling the spray from this distance. Pulling out his phone, he was disappointed to see no signal. He'd have to climb to the top of the cliff to download messages.

He had to get in the zone, stop thinking about Knox. Zach had texted to let him know how things were going, and he'd told him about Knox's marketing plan. It was genius. She'd also formally agreed to work with his team, including Wyatt, who'd handle her finances, so she was all set to kick some ass.

But that's the issue right there. He wanted to work with her. By the time he finished competition season five months from now, she might be gone.

Some big designer will scoop her up, and she'll be out of my life again.

Which was her goal, so that would be for the best. She

couldn't have the career she wanted in Calamity, anyway. *Let her go.*

The ocean called the tide back, way back, and a massive swell rose. *That'd be sweet to ride.* It hung suspended for a long, threatening beat, before curling over and…*boom.* It exploded. Cold water barreled onto the shore, knocking him back a step.

"Bowie," someone called from behind.

He looked back to see a fellow competitor.

The guy tipped his head toward the white press tent perched on top of the cliff. "You're up."

"Pass." He wasn't interested in interviews.

"Sorry, man, not only do you have the highest score." The guy gave a teasing smile. "But you're the 'sexiest.' They're waiting for you." He laughed, jogging off to the bonfire.

If he went up there, he'd get a signal. That got his ass moving. Skirting around the gathering of surfers, he hit the narrow dirt path that climbed the nearly vertical face of the cliff.

Once on solid ground, he pulled out his phone. Two bars. *Score.*

"There you are." The reporter held open the flap of a roomy, white tent propped with aluminum bars. "Come on in."

Gray stepped inside to find tables crammed with monitors that tracked currents and weather conditions, cameras, and all kinds of equipment. The bright lights and bodies drove the temperature up, and his skin pebbled from the contrast of the cool night air.

"Gray Bowie." She shook his hand. "Marnee Fletcher. Great to meet you, and thanks for taking a moment to talk to us." She led him to a corner.

"Marnee?" someone called.

With a touch to his arm, she said, "Give me one second."

As he waited for them to set up, he checked his phone again. Messages rolled in, his phone vibrating like crazy. Nothing from Knox, though. *Because she doesn't need you.* Yeah, well, they were business partners. He could fucking check in with her. But, right before he started tapping out a message, the reporter cupped his elbow.

"Ready?" She got him situated, and then stood on the taped X on the floor facing him.

The cameraman held his fingers up over the camera. *Three, two, one.* And then he sliced a finger through the air. *Go.*

"We've got Gray Bowie with us, pretty much an enigma in the world of extreme athletes. He seems to ride the waves as effortlessly as he performs technically perfect tricks on the halfpipe. As the surfer with the highest score today…" She turned to face Gray. "Where's your heart?"

He froze, as a toxic mix of shame, embarrassment, and sharp, painful awareness erupted in his core. *In Calamity.*

The reporter continued, as though his features hadn't flamed. "Do you have a preference for either sport?"

Obviously, she wasn't talking about Knox. And, just like that, he dropped back into the moment. "Nah. It's all good." His phone buzzed against his thigh. More messages coming in.

"Just a basic adrenaline junky, huh?" She gave him an encouraging smile.

"There's probably some truth in that."

The reporter covered her frustration with his brief responses by brightening her smile. "You're leading the pack today. And, if you win tomorrow, you'll be ranked the number one surfer in the world. How is it so effortless for you?"

"It's not effortless." *What a ridiculous thing to say.* "Not for anyone. Look, twenty-four surfers got the invitation for Titans. That means we're all at the same level. It's Mother Nature who decides who wins. I just happened to get a tight barrel today."

"Let's talk about the Olympics. I know it's on everyone's mind, now that your brother, Will Bowie, announced his retirement. First Brodie, then Will...the whole world's wondering, are you going to step up and take that medal home for your family?"

"A lot of things have to line up just right to even get to the Games. We'll have to see how it all plays out." Who knew if he'd even make the team?

"It's the one award none of your brothers has managed to bring home, so it would make you stand apart in a family with some of the greatest extreme athletes in the world."

He looked at her, feeling more exposed than he ever had in his life. She was saying all the things that pinged him hard—but it wasn't like she knew him. She didn't know anything about Knox or his complicated feelings for his family.

He supposed it was obvious—his dad had died, and none of his brothers had managed to fill the one empty trophy case built for an Olympic medal. And, yeah, he did want to be the one to put it there.

Hey, look at me, Dad. For once in my life, look the fuck at me.

But he forced a casual smile and just said, "No lie, it'd be cool. But the coaches make those decisions."

"But you want it, right? You wouldn't win competitions if you didn't have the drive. People like to think of you as easy-going, not driven like Will, but I can't imagine you outscoring the world's top surfers like you did today if you didn't take your training as seriously as they do."

Of course he did. He trained as hard anybody. He just didn't want to commit to a team, a coach...one sport. His phone chimed with a call, and he checked out the screen. *Callie*. "Hey, man, sorry to cut this short, but I've got to take this."

Clearly disappointed, she waved a hand at the cameraman. "Sure. Thanks for your time."

He headed away from the tent, hoping he didn't lose the signal. His brother's fiancée never reached out to him. "Hey, Callie. Everything okay?"

"No. Listen, Knox had a tough call from her boss yesterday. He made it clear if she didn't come back to work for him, things 'wouldn't go well for her.'"

"What the hell does that mean?"

"Hang on. I'm about to tell you. While she was talking to him, she came up with an idea to do something with her twenty-five dresses. She wants to make knock-offs to sell in a pop-up boutique."

Brilliant. "Great idea."

"It is, and she got really excited. Soon as she got off that call, she was pumped. Ready to go."

"Sounds good. What's the problem?" But he could think of a hundred problems. She had no start-up capital, for one.

"Well, she can't do anything without fabric, right? So, the first thing she did was get on the phone with a vendor she's worked with in the past, but guess what?"

"Just tell me."

"He won't sell to her."

"Why not?"

"She tried a bunch more, until she figured out that her asshole boss must've told all his vendors not to sell to her. Gray, he blacklisted her. She can't even get the fabric to make our dresses, let alone recreate the ones from her show."

Tucking a hand under his arm, he stared out at the churning ocean. The clouds had parted, and a single shard of moonlight beamed down, like a spotlight on the thrashing surface.

"Are you there?" Callie sounded pissed. "Did you hear me?"

"Yeah, I heard you. Not sure what I can do about it. I don't have any connections to luxury fabric vendors." *Fucking hell.* What had they done to her?

"We have to do something."

"Yeah, I know, but there's not a damn thing I can do from here."

"Well, what do I tell her?"

"I don't have any answers for you right now. Depending on the weather, I've got my last heat tomorrow. I'll think about it then."

Last night, Knox had barely slept. She'd paced the length of the room, moonlight casting long, eerie shadows. She'd trusted her whole career to Luc, and he'd turned on her.

What had she done, though? *She* hadn't wrecked her gowns, but it had happened, and now she needed to find a new path. Why would he cut her off from the suppliers, ensuring her failure?

The startling crack from the air hockey table made her flinch.

"He said he'd only be gone a few days." Fin, the youngest Bowie brother and Callie's fiancé, watched the puck intently, the thick muscles in his arm bunching and flexing as he drew back the paddle and whacked it. "It's been nearly a week. Where the hell is he?"

Weird that Gray hadn't told his brother—his *trainer*—where he'd gone. It wasn't like he was afraid to tell him. Gray was too confident for that.

Sitting on a bar stool at the kitchen island, Callie twisted around to see him. "He's got other things going on."

Fin shot an apologetic look at Knox. "Sorry. I know he's working with you."

The sound effects went off, giving a tinny shout, "Score!" Fin tossed the paddle onto the table. "But he's not here, so he's not doing that, either." Stepping back, he shoved his hands through his unruly hair.

Knox hadn't heard a word from Gray, but she couldn't be angry. He'd done everything he could to get her set up. *There's nothing more he can do.*

"What is that?" With both arms wrapped around his fiancée, Fin nuzzled her neck and eyed her laptop.

"Gray's friend Amelia is setting up a social media account for us. We're going to make really pretty photographs documenting the making of our wedding gowns."

"Will there be pictures of you on it?" Fin asked.

"Of course." Callie leaned back into him.

"I don't want the whole world knowing about our wedding."

"I told you we were taking advantage of the meme."

She gripped his forearms. "It's going to be great for Knox's business."

"You realize that's basically an invitation to get the paparazzi here, crawling all over town?"

"It's going to happen anyway," Callie said. "The meme might've died down, but we're still feeling the effect of it. Look at my museum. Last weekend, that soccer team from Germany came, remember? They came out here specifically to see The Museum of Broken Hearts. And I'm still getting more donations than I can handle. The attention's unavoidable, so why not throw some of it Knox's way?"

The French doors opened, and Delilah and Will came in, their cheeks rosy, their hair windswept. The little girl in Will's arms—the half-sister he was raising—wriggled to get down. Once her feet hit the floor, she took off for Brodie, who quit resetting the hockey table to greet her.

"Hey, how's it going?" Delilah came right over to them, bringing in the cool mountain air. The scents of pine forest and sage swirled around her.

Callie turned the laptop toward her. "This is what Amelia's done so far. What do you think?"

"Oh, that's a pretty banner." Delilah smiled at Knox. "I hope you're ready for this, because once we go live, the orders are going to start rolling in."

"Not without fabric." Knox said it quietly, but she felt the tension squeeze hold of the room. All eyes were on her, so she pasted on a smile.

She'd find a vendor. Luc didn't have a lock on the entire market. She just couldn't understand *why* he'd do this to her. Well, intellectually she knew. If she went off on her own, he wouldn't benefit from her talent. Emotionally, though, she'd thought—well, not that he was like a father to her. That would be stupid. But that he cared about her.

As a person. That, sure, he'd be disappointed to lose her, but he'd still be rooting for her.

She didn't want to worry them—her customers—though. "I've reached out to some people." She'd emailed her college advisor and some friends she'd made over the years. *Friends?* Well, acquaintances. "They'll hook me up. No worries." People made custom gowns all the time—and they certainly didn't have access to couture's unique textiles.

"In this section here." Delilah tapped the screen. "It'd be fun to put in photographs of some of your gowns." Her gaze flicked up to Knox. "Would you want to do that?"

"That's a great idea," Callie said. "One look at them, and they'll be hooked."

She had dozens of dresses she'd love to post, but they all belonged to Luc. He'd never given her credit for anything. "I'd rather not show the ones in the pop-up, but I'll dig some up from my senior year project." She thought of the sketch she'd taken from the trailer—the gown she'd designed for herself. "I've got some sketches, if you want." Maybe not that one, though.

"Oh, I like that idea," Delilah said.

Just thinking about what Luc had done to her got her all worked up. "I'm going to check my email. See if anyone's gotten back to me." And then she'd start sourcing her own suppliers. "He couldn't have blacklisted me from the entire market." Just his personal connections.

Luc could throw up roadblocks all day long, but he couldn't keep her from succeeding.

Knox didn't have a lot of confidence—*you don't grow up being barked at and ostracized for living in a trailer and come out feeling like a champ.* But she did believe in her talent as a designer.

The moment she sat down beside Callie on a barstool at the kitchen counter and opened up her laptop, Delilah handed her a glass of wine. "Yassss. Thank you." As her email loaded, she skimmed the subject lines.

In the background, she heard the clacking from the air hockey game, two of the brothers shouting and laughing. On the couch, Will read a picture book to Ruby, snuggled up on his lap, her stuffed chicken wrapped tightly in her arms. Beside her, Callie and Delilah talked quietly about the profile picture they wanted for the social media pages.

And then the door flung open.

Chapter Six

GRAY BOWIE STRODE IN LIKE AN FBI AGENT ON A bust. In his black Henley, faded blue jeans, and black boots, his body vibrated with purpose.

Mother of God, that man is so freaking hot. Their gazes locked, and a thrill sizzled through her.

"Hey, man." Will set the book on the table and rose off the couch, effortlessly lifting his sidekick. "Where've you been?"

The brothers were tight, loyal, honest, so it made her sad that Gray hadn't told them about Titans. They'd love that one of them had gotten such an elite invitation.

With a subtle shift of his shoulders, as though girding himself, Gray said, "Half Moon Bay."

The game table rattled, as if Fin had shoved it. "You did not do Titans." The youngest brother stormed over.

"I did. Had some trouble with the weather, but we managed to finish it off." Gray grinned. "Good times."

"You're training for the *Olympics*. What the he—"— Fin shot a look to little Ruby—"heck are you doing surfing *Titans*?"

"I got the invitation." He gave a careless shrug. "Not gonna turn it down. I came out alive."

"You win?" Brodie asked.

"Heck, yeah."

Brodie and Will burst out laughing, surrounding him with back slaps and hugs. Ruby pumped her little arm, the chicken's bright yellow legs flopping around.

"You're an ass—" Fin cut another look to the little girl. "Idiot. Your first competition's in five weeks. Are you going to commit to this or not?"

"Starting tomorrow, I'm yours." But Gray only had eyes for her. Pushing through his brothers, he came right over. "Can we talk?" He directed all that power and urgency on her, and it made her heart pound. "Got something to run by you."

He still cared about her business. Deep down, she'd known it. No matter how nonchalant he acted, he'd always been there for her. Her heart beat furiously, because it *mattered*. "Yeah, of course."

He side-eyed his brothers. "Outside?"

"What?" Callie said. "No. Is this about the dresses? Tell us. We're invested in this, too."

Gray turned to Knox. "I heard we can't get fabric."

She loved when he said *we* when she kept thinking *I*. Made her feel ten thousand times lighter. "I'll find a vendor. Luc's just making it harder for me."

"He can bite me." Happiness glittered in his bright blue eyes. "After Cali, I flew to New York."

"Are you serious?" When Fin's arms lifted, he knocked a spool of thread onto the floor. It clattered and rolled under the table.

Ruby wriggled for Will to set her down. "I get it."

"Maui, Cali, New York." Fin's eyes went wide. "What're you *doing*?"

"She can't get her business started without material, and there's only one connection I know that could hook us up." Gray shot her a look. "Mrs. Granger."

Worry pulsed in her body. *Robert's mom?*

He watched her carefully. "She was the only person I could think of who'd have the kind of fabric producers you need."

"Did he just say fabric producers?" Brodie asked.

"He sure did." Will reached for Ruby, lifting her up and securing her against his hip.

"And she does. She's got someone." Gray's expression said, *That okay?*

No matter her concerns about working with her ex's mother, shock turned into a buzz of excitement. The Granger Collection was like Ralph Lauren. It had a range of collections at a variety of price points, including couture. If anyone had the connections she needed, it was Mrs. Granger.

"But it gets better. I told her you needed the fabric because you wanted to do a pop-up bridal gown event in some fancy boutique." He paused, and trumpets blared in her veins. "She wants to host you next spring."

"Holy moly," Callie said. "This is incredible."

"She wants four of each dress, and she'll pay you twenty-five hundred each up front so you can buy the fabric, machines, and supplies, and hire the help."

"I don't even know what to say," Knox said. "I can't believe it."

"She said she'll price them at her discretion on her end and, after she gets her money back, you'll get ten percent of the profits."

"Ten percent?" Callie said. "That doesn't seem fair. They're Knox's dresses."

"It's a boutique on Fifth Avenue across the street from Central Park," Gray said. "The least expensive thing in the place is a tie that costs a grand. Besides, Mrs. Granger's taking all the risk." He turned back to Knox. "It's a take-it-or-leave-it deal."

"I'll take it. No questions." She'd have to hire several sewers in order to make a hundred dresses in time for a spring show. Still, it was Mrs. Granger. "She knows it's me, right? You said, Knox Holliday?"

"Of course. Right while I was in her office, I showed her the pictures Zach sent me. She loves them."

She still couldn't believe Gray had flown across the country to talk to Mrs. Granger about a fabric vendor. *For me.* She couldn't help worrying, though. "I'm a little surprised she'd work with me, given our history." Just days after her son had gone into rehab, Knox had bailed on him. Mrs. Granger couldn't have understood it was the only way to leave him.

If she'd told Robert to his face that she was breaking up with him, he would've charmed and manipulated her into staying.

With a wave of his hand, Gray erased the guilt that had plagued her for seven years. "She knows you did the right thing." Reaching into his back pocket, he pulled out a folded sheet of paper. "Wrote all the details down right here. You want the gig, it's yours."

"I want it." She turned to Callie and Delilah. "I'm still making your dresses."

"Oh, thank God," Callie said. "I'm happy for you, but I really want my gown."

"I want this, but…" It was exciting…but also overwhelming. "A hundred dresses in time for next spring… we're going to need sewers, pattern makers, materials."

"The up-front money will cover all that." Gray always sounded so confident. "It's all good. We've got this."

"Is Mrs. Granger going to work on it with her?" Callie asked.

"No," Gray said. "She's writing the check and hosting the pop-up show. The rest is up to us."

"And when you say *us*, I know you're not talking about you, right?" Fin said. "Because the first qualifier's in October in *New Zealand*."

"Dude, I'm here, and I'm ready to train, but I've got a business to run. It's what I've been doing all along, so nothing's changed."

"Hang on there," Brodie sad. "You've been doing what all along?"

It broke her heart that Gray kept so much of his life from his brothers. She'd seen it growing up, how much he'd wanted them to be involved in his life. How many times had she watched him scan the spectators at one of his events, only to be crestfallen to find no one in his family had shown up?

She guessed he'd eventually wound up shutting them out.

"My friends and I have a company," Gray said. "And, while I'm training, *they'll* be doing most of the work. I just oversee things. Now, let's stay on point." Gray reached for her hand, nabbing her attention. "So, what do you think?"

"What kind of company?" Fin stood with his hands on his hips, his tone sharp.

"I make socks, scarves, gloves, stuff like that." He said it with his usual casual stance, but there was no hiding the alertness in his eyes.

His brothers looked like he'd just pulled off his mask to reveal his true identity as an alien.

"Okay, that came out of nowhere," Brodie said.

"It's called Duck Dive Haberdashery," Gray said. "You can look it up."

"It's got a *name*?" Fin said. "I don't know whether to be impressed or pissed. You run a company, and you've never told us about it?"

All the slacker went right out of his posture. "Never came up."

Oh, Gray. The brothers had always been this tight, impenetrable unit, communicating with a simple look. Since they were always training or competing, they hung out with each other almost exclusively, so she knew how much he'd want them to be included in something so important.

But they'd never been before. "Did you ever ask?" Knox said.

All the attention in the room snapped over to her.

"Ask what?" Brodie said. "If he's made any socks lately?"

Gray's shoulders tightened. "It's no big deal. Just something me and my friends have been doing."

"When? On the flights to Portugal?" Fin said. "At a bonfire on Bondi Beach?"

Anger sparked in Gray's eyes, but he didn't say anything.

"We're talking about your posse, right? Amelia and Wyatt and those guys?" Will, the unofficial leader of the pack, cocked his head, as if trying to make sense of the information. "You guys are in business together?"

"Amelia's the head of marketing, and she's damn good. Wyatt's our accountant."

73

"Wyatt?" Brodie threw his head back and laughed. "I wouldn't hire that guy to walk my dog."

"He's a whiz with numbers," Gray said. "Look, we can talk about it later."

"No, hang on," Fin said. "I want to know why you didn't tell us."

"Well, I have a pretty good idea." Yeah, she might be overstepping here, but she wasn't going to let them attack Gray. "I can think of a dozen times in high school when he asked you guys to come to his fencing tournaments or his jazz ensemble shows…and none of you showed up. I mean, maybe I've got it all wrong, but at some point, he probably just stopped bothering to let you know what he was doing." *Because it hurt.*

"That right?" Will asked.

"Why would I tell you guys about anything that isn't directly related to training and snowboarding competitions?" Gray's tone bared teeth.

"What the fu—" Fin clamped his jaw shut and turned away, as he worked to get his temper under control. "What the heck does that mean? We're your brothers. Of course, you should tell us."

"You say that like it's obvious," Knox said. "But let me ask you this. If you kept inviting someone to your competitions and they never bothered to come, would you keep trying? If you kept talking to someone about freeriding, but they never asked a single question or expressed any interest, would you keep talking about it? Or would you eventually just stop?"

"I don't remember you asking," Brodie said.

"Well, I did." Gray pointed a finger at his older brothers, Will and Brodie. "How many times did I ask you guys for a ride, but you couldn't be bothered?"

Callie shifted uncomfortably, and Delilah reached for Will's arm, giving it a gentle caress.

"Are you talking about that fencing tournament?" Will asked.

Fin looked between his brothers. "He never fenced."

Gray gave a bitter laugh and shook his head.

With the chicken tucked tightly under one arm, Ruby slowly unwound the thread from the spool in her chubby little hands. She gazed up at Will and said, "Okay, Wheel?"

"Yeah, sweetheart. I'm okay." He looked at his half-sister with pure adoration.

Will had always been this uber cool, aloof guy. Seeing him all soft and affectionate with a two-year-old melted Knox's heart.

He kissed her forehead and turned back to his brother. "I'm not going to apologize again for blowing off your tournament. If I'm remembering correctly, I had a big competition coming up, but it sounds like we're talking about more than that one event." He looked to Knox in acknowledgment.

"I don't recall a single time seeing any of you guys in the audience," she said.

"And she knows because she was the only one there." Gray's voice was filled with warmth. "Look, no harm no foul. You guys weren't into the things I was into, but you wanted to know why I didn't mention it. That's why. Now, I'm trying to talk to Knox." He gave her a look that said, *See why I wanted to go outside?*

Will looked lost in thought. "That jazz group you were in. You got pretty good on the guitar."

"How would you know?" Gray's tone sharpened. "You never came to any of our shows."

"I guess I thought—" Will began.

"You thought what?" Gray drew in a breath. "Look, I could've gotten a ride to that tournament with anyone on the fencing team, but you promised you'd take me. The only reason I didn't go with someone else—after being burned by you ten times before that—was because I really wanted my older brother to come and watch me."

Will looked hit with remorse.

"But you said you had to work on your trick before the next competition." He waved to his brothers. "None of you gave a damn about anything I did if it didn't have to do with snowboarding."

"You were always switching from one thing to another," Brodie said, a little confused. "I thought it was because you didn't care enough about anything in particular."

"Yeah, whatever. Like I said, no harm no foul."

"Look, we've got Mrs. Granger's attention right now, so..." Gray caught her fingers. "Are we doing this?"

A bottle rocket of joy shot straight up her spine, lighting her up inside. "We're doing this." And it was only a small surprise that a good amount of her happiness came from the idea of working with him.

He lunged for her, lifting her off the ground and hugging her to him. For one heavenly moment, she gave him her weight, turned her head so she brushed her cheek against his scruff. But when his grip tightened, the energy between them changed. Turned sharp, electric, and hot. It scared her, so she pulled back.

He set her down, looking like he hadn't noticed a thing. "Awesome. Because once I confirm, it's on like Donkey Kong."

Wind rushed over Gray's face, stinging his eyes, as he slid down the slope at his brother's training facility. As his speed picked up, he just knew. He didn't think, didn't plan. His body just went to work. Bending his knees, he sailed up the ramp and exploded off the lip.

Fuck, yeah. The boost gave him massive air. He pulled his board up, grabbed it, and held. Keeping his eyes on the airbag, he spun once...twice...*spot it, spot it*...and landed backwards, toe edge.

Stomped it.

"Holy shit," someone shouted.

Breathing hard, Gray pumped his fist. Damn, that felt good.

As he flicked off the bindings and bounced his way to the edge of the bag, he tuned into the chatter from the onlookers gathered on the grass.

"Did he just do a double cork twelve-sixty?" someone said.

"Sure as hell did."

"I thought he was just supposed to do a rodeo five-forty?"

"Fuckin' Gray," someone else said.

Fin rushed him. "Holy shit, man, that was perfect."

"Thanks." He needed to talk to his brother, and Fin wasn't going to like what he had to say. "Got a second?"

"Yeah, sure. What's up?"

"I'm taking a couple days off."

"Like hell you are. You just got back to town."

"Yeah, I know. And I wouldn't leave again if it weren't important."

"Dammit, Gray."

"I need to fly out to LA with Knox and meet with the new supplier. She's hired some sewers, bought some machines, and now we've got to get moving on the project. It'll just be a few days."

"It's not like I can stop you."

No, you can't. "Two days max, okay?"

Fin nodded.

"Cool. I'm going to head back now." He'd been at it three hours, done ten runs. *Enough.* Now, he just wanted to tell Knox the good news.

"Yeah, sure," Fin sad. "You had a great day. See in the morning."

Arms behind him, hugging his board to his lower back, he started off. Footsteps crunching on dry grass had him turning around to see Brodie catching up to him. "Hey."

"That was some serious amplitude for an airbag," his brother said.

"Yeah, I could feel it. That's why I took my shot." They walked in companionable silence. "You heading back to the ranch?"

"Mmhm." His brother seemed distracted.

Of all the brothers, Brodie was by far the most intelligent. His brain was like an incubator for ideas, and when he latched onto one, he was off to the races. Which explained how he'd turned an old ghost town into a high-end resort in one year. Their dad had liked to call Brodie the visionary.

Will had been the captain, and Fin, the wild child.

Had his dad been aware he'd never given Gray a nickname? In his heart, Gray didn't believe it had been intentional. It wasn't like he'd ever questioned his dad's love. He just didn't think his dad *saw* him.

"How did Duck Dive start?" Brodie asked.

Ah. So that's what's on his mind. "So, you know how the more sidewall on your board, the deeper you carve?"

Brodie nodded.

"But the heavier the board, the worse it'll perform aerodynamically, so we kept talking about it, trying to come up with ideas. What kind of material would enable us to get a thicker edge but not increase the weight? And then we talked to an engineer, who came up with something. Built it. Sold it. And that's it. That's how it started."

Brodie had his head tucked down, watching his boots eat up the trail. "Would've liked to have been in on those conversations."

"Would've liked to have you."

Brodie's gaze swung up, and in that moment something broke inside Gray.

He hadn't paid attention to how much he'd wanted to include his brothers in the other aspects of his life in a very long time.

And it felt damn good that Brodie was in it now.

Chapter Seven

JUST BECAUSE THEY HADN'T BEEN ABLE TO SECURE AN appointment with the vendor yet didn't mean Knox wouldn't get the dresses done in time. As soon as she got the green light, she'd fly to Los Angeles, take a look at the fabric and embellishments and—fingers crossed—place her order. Everything would be fine.

It'll be fine.

In the meantime, she'd get started on the custom gowns. While she brewed tea, Callie sat at the island, clicking through Knox's inspiration file, a portfolio of every wedding gown that had caught Knox's fancy over the years.

On the couch, Delilah had her feet up on the coffee table, bridal magazines scattered on the table and cushions around her. In her lap sat a local chef's cookbook; her eyebrows were pulled tight in concentration as she read.

"What do you think of this one?" Callie leaned back.

Twisting around to see the computer screen, Delilah said, "That's really pretty."

"You don't think that poofy skirt's too much?"

Delilah set the book down and nearly tripped over the magazines that had toppled onto the floor. "It's stunning, if you're into the whole Cinderella ball gown thing."

Callie laughed. "Okay, so maybe all those Disney movies did a subliminal number on me, because my heart does backflips when I see the princessy ones." She cocked her head. "I just…I don't think I like that neckline."

Setting her elbows on the counter, Knox leaned in. "You realize you can have anything you want, right? You can pick and choose tops and bottoms, colors, design elements…the whole shebang is your invention."

"I'm not sure I have that kind of vision," Callie said.

Delilah nudged her. "You're an artist. Of course you do."

"Not when it comes to wedding dresses. I have no clue what would look good on me."

Knox reached for her sketchbook and a pencil. "Let's start with a ball gown." She made broad, sweeping strokes. "How sexy do you want the bodice?" She reached for the laptop, opened a folder and clicked on a revealing top with sheer panels of lace covered in hand-embroidered petals. "Like this. Or…" She scrolled down the page to another style of top. "A sweetheart neckline." She scrolled some more. "Or we can do an off-the-shoulder cap sleeve. This one's more fairy princess."

"Oh, wait, let me get my phone." Delilah dashed to the couch and dug it out of her bag. "Amelia wants me to get some pictures. Can you lean in a little? Knox, point like you were doing before. Perfect." She took a couple shots. "I'll send these to her right now."

Callie took over the mouse and contemplated the bodices. "I think I like the simpler, more elegant ones."

Knox figured that. She sketched out a top she thought

Callie would like, then turned the book toward her. "Something like this?"

"That's really pretty."

Knox found a similar style in her portfolio and then turned the screen back to Callie. "The dress will look something like this."

Callie gasped. "Yes. Oh…" She blew out a breath. "Yes. Just like that."

"As for bling," Knox said. "We can embed tiny Swarovski crystals in the bodice to make it sparkle."

"How lame am I to want the crystals?" Callie asked.

"All I can say is, if you're drawn to ball gowns, then for one day out of your life, go all-out Cinderella. If that's not your thing, you can wear a pantsuit. Delilah, you could rock the hell out of one. That's the fun in what we're doing. You can create anything you want. Whatever feels right for you."

"I want Cinderella." Callie said it quietly, almost shyly.

"Then, that's what you'll be," Knox said.

"I just feel like…Fin makes me feel like a princess every day. I know that sounds sappy, but it's true. And I guess I want to look like one when I walk down the aisle to meet him."

"Why am I tearing up?" Delilah said. "Are there onions in here? Because I know I'm not crying over the idea of you marrying the love of your life."

"Gray says you've been sketching fancy wedding gowns since you were a kid," Callie said. "How did you even know about couture back then? Not to make fun of Calamity or anything, but it's not exactly on the cutting edge of fashion."

"Oh, I didn't. Not when I first started." Was she really going to open the vault for these women, when she'd only known them a few days? *Looks like I am.* "When I was a kid, I'd tell these stories in my head. I called them dream sets." She watched to see if they'd think she was a freak but, really, they just seemed interested. "Each one would play out over a couple of weeks, before some character from a movie or a book or a TV show would trigger a new one."

"Oh, my God, I had dream sets, too," Callie said. "I didn't call them that, but that's a great name for them. Sadly, mine were about Fin. I'm not kidding. I'm that much of a cliché. I actually couldn't wait to go to bed at night, because it meant I could slip back into my"—she cut a mischievous look to Knox—"dream set and continue the movie playing in my head about our love story."

"I want to fit in here so bad," Delilah said. "But I daydreamed about recipes. Not the same?" She looked between them. "No, I didn't think so."

All three laughed, until Callie nudged Knox. "Go on. I want to hear about your dream sets."

"Well, not to sound too pathetic, but mine were about imaginary friends. It would be a group of us doing totally normal things—hanging out, sleepovers, getting ready for prom together—but it always led to one of the girls getting married. I kept a notebook with me everywhere—on my nightstand, in my backpack—so I could sketch the wedding gowns."

"I love that," Delilah said. "I'm not that excited about going into a store and buying a wedding gown, but the idea of my friend, who knows me, making one just for me —that fits not just my body but my personality…I like that."

"I never got to do that, though," Knox said. "As soon as I got to college, I got on the couture track. Which really just means I made sure all my internships were with the houses I wanted to work in. And that world…it's not about an individual. A woman with a personality and a backstory. It's about drama, flair. How different I can make each dress while staying within my brand."

"You have a brand?" Callie asked. "But they all look so different."

"My brand is…" She made air quotes. "'Extravagantly feminine, wildly unique, and lushly romantic.'"

"Oh, I see. Yes, that's exactly it." Callie patted Delilah's shoulder. "Well, she's certainly got the market on lushness. I don't know why she won't share some of it with the rest of us."

Delilah rolled her eyes. "I wouldn't mind losing a *few* pounds of lushness, because it's harder than you think to find clothes that fit right. And, to be honest, that's partly why I don't get excited about wedding dresses. Buying clothes has always been such a chore. I can't tell you how many times I've fallen in love with something and then tried it on, only to find out I look horrible in it."

"That's the beauty of custom," Knox said. "I'll make one that fits you just right. It'll feel like you're wearing yoga pants and your favorite T-shirt. Okay, maybe not *exactly* like that."

Delilah's expression brightened. "Oh, I wish."

"Besides, don't you want something amazing when you walk down the aisle?" Callie asked. "Will's going to be standing there in a tux, looking fine as wine, and he's only going to have eyes for you. Imagine what you'll be wearing."

Delilah answered right away. "I want to look like me. I don't want a ton of make-up or my hair done in some strange style and lacquered like a helmet." She turned to

Knox with her hands on her breasts. "I need something that won't make me look like an exotic dancer."

"Trust me, you've got a lot of options," Knox said. "For the bodice, you'll want to avoid high necklines and probably halters, but you could go with a sweetheart neckline, a V or scoop neck. For the skirt, A-lines are flattering on almost any figure. No empire. That'll just make you look pregnant."

"I guess I imagined something really structured, you know? To hold the girls in. I didn't think I could have anything as wispy and feminine as those." She gestured to the dress forms.

Now, Knox totally got Delilah's reluctance. "You can have anything you want. Literally anything. We can work with a strapless bra or put in boning. You don't worry about that. Just show me what you love, and I'll make it fit, so you don't worry for a single moment the entire time you're wearing it." She reached for the laptop and found the dress she thought might work for the hour glass-shaped blonde. "Does it matter to you if it's white?"

"Not at all."

"Then look at this one."

It looked deceptively like a plunging V-neck, but covering the cleavage was a transparent silk tulle in the palest pink. Hand-embroidered flower petals in white adorned the organza bodice. The back, though, that was one of her favorites of all time. It had four pink organza flowers surrounding the keyhole cut-out.

"That is stunning," Callie said.

"It is." Delilah didn't sound as effusive.

And Knox thought she knew why. She suspected Delilah didn't trust that she'd come out looking like anything other than a Vegas showgirl. "Only, we'd do this." She turned to a fresh page in the sketchbook and started drawing. "To keep from popping out." When she finished, she turned the book to Delilah.

"You think I could really look good in that?"

"I know you can. But you don't have to worry, because I'm going to make a mock-up, which is made from muslin and lets me fit you in the dress before I cut the actual fabric." She looked from one to the other. "Sound good?"

"Oh, yes," Callie said. "I completely love mine. Make my muslin."

Delilah seemed more hesitant.

"Even after I cut the material," Knox said. "We can keep playing with ideas."

"I want to play with mine a little," Delilah said. "But that's really close." She gestured to the dress on the screen.

"No problem at all."

Callie closed the laptop. "Let's get some lunch. I'm starving."

Dread smacked her right in the gut. Knox didn't want to run into anyone who'd once barked at her—not in front of these beautiful, confident women.

But then anger rolled in, knocking her fear right on its ass. If they barked at her today, as twenty-five-year-old *adults*, then they were immature idiots who hadn't moved on from high school.

Besides, if she planned on staying in town a while, she couldn't hide out in the bunkhouse. She walked with them to the door, each step bringing the image of downtown Calamity into sharper focus, as if seeing it from the perspective of a drone. An aerial view of the town green, narrowing down to the antler arches at each gateway, the crowds of people roaming, listening to live music in the gazebo…until it zeroed in on individual faces.

Cady Toller. Melissa Singer. Danny Mortimer. Her heart pounded and her palms grew damp.

After the women walked out the door, she said, "You know what? I've got so much work to do. You guys go on."

Chicken.

Relieved not to find any trucks parked in front of the bunkhouse, Gray knocked on the door. Except...he didn't have to sneak around, did he? They worked together. *And she's single.*

All those years of wanting his best friend's girlfriend, he'd hated himself. Worked hard to conceal it. It was only after he'd gotten suspended for shutting down some of her bullies, that his dad had gotten involved. They'd taken a long hike—one of the rare occasions they'd spent time alone together—and, over the course of the day, his dad had coaxed the confession out of him: he kept getting into fights over Knox Holliday because he loved her. And he couldn't stand to see her hurt.

He'd never forget the relief he'd felt at finally saying it out loud, in confiding his deepest, darkest secret. Only, his dad had been *pissed.* Delivering a blistering lecture on loyalty—as if Gray hadn't been struggling with that issue all along—his dad had insisted he stay away from Robert and Knox, since any time spent alone with her was a betrayal to his oldest friend.

Gray had tried—of course he had—but he could no sooner breathe without lungs than live in a world without Knox. He'd never talked about her again, though, and his dad had never asked.

He knocked again and, when he still got no answer, he

opened the door and peered in. "Knox?" A cool breeze rushed in from the open French doors that led to the patio. It lifted the skirts of the frilly gowns and riffled the pages of a notebook laid out on the kitchen counter.

Less than two weeks ago, this place had smelled like gym shoes and roasted meat, but now, with Knox living here, it smelled like the pine and sage of the outdoors mingling with the warm bread and fresh flowers inside.

The work stations they'd set up sat abandoned, and Gray knew she had to be freaking out. But he'd fixed the problem and couldn't wait to tell her. "Anybody here?" He raised his voice in case she was coming out of the shower or something. "Knox? It's Gray. I'm coming in."

As he neared the French doors, he heard huffs of breath and a shushing, tapping sound. "Knox?" He nearly shouted this time, not wanting to startle her. Was she exercising?

Like front row seating to the spectacle of the Grand Teton mountain range, the cushioned chairs formed a half-circle around the fire pit. On the brick lip, he saw a lit candle, a plate of food, a wine bottle, and one wine glass. *One.*

Why did the idea of Knox being alone make his stomach hurt?

Stepping onto the patio, he stopped when he saw her dancing like a wild woman. Her wavy, dark hair shimmied and gleamed in the early twilight. In her fist, she held her phone with white wires branching out and leading to her ears. She whispered the lyrics, the soles of her slippered feet scraping on the stone patio.

He'd washed his hands of her seven years ago, the moment he'd understood she was to him what drugs were to Robert. It had been the harshest reality he'd ever faced, knowing he was as messed up as his friend, caught in the unrelenting, sucking pull of unrequited love.

But watching her dance like this—just as she'd done every time a good song had come on the radio—in the bunkhouse, on the trail, in his Jeep—it all came flooding back.

Not good, man. Not good at all.

Fact: she's only here because you screwed up her career. Stick to business.

He glanced at the plate of food she'd set on the edge of the fire pit—thick slabs of sausage, wedges of cheese, and neatly cut slices of baguette. He'd followed Fin's training program for months, and his mouth watered for some real food. Without even thinking, he headed toward it, hungry for a taste of that cheese and bread—

"Jesus!" Knox yanked out her earbuds and slapped a palm over her heart. "What're you doing here?"

He stood there, frozen, like he'd landed on his back on hard ice and gotten the wind knocked out of him. Everything about her—her hair, wild and loose, her toned, feminine legs in black leggings, even the slouchy sweater covering the parts he most wanted to see—was stunning.

And she was pissed that he'd intruded on her privacy. *Right.* His default lazy smile slid into place. "Got some good news."

"You scared the crap out of me."

"I texted you I was on my way over."

"I haven't looked at my messages since everyone left for the day."

"Sorry 'bout that." He shrugged. "I knocked and shouted. Did everything but burn the place down." He stacked cheese and sausage on a slice of fresh baguette and shoved it in his mouth.

Setting the phone down next to the plate, she flopped into a chair. She raised one eyebrow and said, "Help yourself."

"Thanks. I'm starved." He reached for her glass and drank some of the wine. "Nice."

"It's yours. Not many people have a wine cellar in a bunkhouse."

"Callie's brother got married here in June. We classed the place up."

She took in the slate patio, the barbecue station, and fire pit. "You sure did."

"So. You took on my brothers this morning." Not many people had the confidence to stand up to them like that. "Impressive."

"Well, I didn't like the way they made *you* out to be the bad guy. I mean, I was there. I saw—"

"I know you were." One thing he could count on back then: Knox Holliday cheering him on in the audience. "You remember that electric guitar you got me?"

"Of course." Her features turned pink.

"I'd asked my dad for one for my birthday."

Her lips pressed together in disapproval. "I couldn't believe he didn't get it for you."

All through his birthday dinner, he'd had his eyes on the big, long box waiting for him. His spirits had soared, certain his dad had gotten him what he'd wanted. Damn, it had sucked when he'd opened it to find a new snowboard. "So, for Christmas, you got me one."

"It was just a cheap thing from a thrift store in Jackson."

She could make light of it all she wanted. It had meant the world to him. "Still have it."

"You do?"

"Hell, yeah."

"I'm glad." That soft smile hit him as viscerally as if she'd reached out and touched him.

"Okay, I came bearing news about the fabric situation."

"Yeah?" She tried so hard not to expose her fears and anxieties. A survival technique, for sure. *Can't let the bullies see you vulnerable.* He just wished she knew she didn't have to be anything other than herself around him.

Because there'd never been a single thing about her he hadn't liked and respected. "We got the appointment."

"You did? How?"

"Conference call with the owner and Mrs. Granger."

"That was pretty ballsy for a guy who makes socks."

He burst out laughing. "That's going on my headstone. Here lies Gray Bowie. Ballsy…for a guy who makes socks." He sandwiched sausage and cheese between baguette slices and shoved the whole thing in his mouth.

With her legs curled under her on the big chair, she watched while he chewed and swallowed. "Are you a snake?"

"I'm hungry." He grabbed a napkin and swiped his mouth. "So. We leave tomorrow, and meet him on Wednesday at noon. Mrs. Granger will meet us there."

Her hand spasmed—just the tiniest bit—but enough for the wine to slosh over the rim of her glass and spill on her leg. *Damn, well, guess that answers that question.* Her reaction meant she was still tied up emotionally in Robert.

She reached for a napkin. "That was stupid." She patted the damp spots on her leggings.

"Why're you so worried about seeing her?"

"No matter what you say, she can't think well of me

for taking off the way I did. Not when her son was finally getting the help he needed. It was a shitty thing to do."

"All I can tell you is she smiled when I mentioned your name." If he was this disappointed, it meant that somewhere, deep down, he still held out hope for them.

Why couldn't he get over this woman?

"Have you stayed in touch with Robert?" She tried to sound casual.

"I've seen him, but, no. We haven't stayed in touch. What about you?" He held his breath, and he wanted to punch his own face for even caring about this shit.

"My mom said he came straight to our house after getting out of rehab." She shook her head as if to say it hadn't gone well. "In her usual in-your-face style, she told him to let me go. To 'give Knox a chance in life.'" She tried for a smile. "As you can expect, he didn't like hearing that. He lit into her about the way she'd raised me, said that I wouldn't have had to rely on him if I'd had a mother who'd looked out for me. It was ugly. I'm glad I wasn't there." She went quiet, and he knew what came next. He knew his role well.

Man, he did not want to be the window into her fucking ex-boyfriend. *Why is he acting like this? Did you see him with Shauna at the party? Where is he? He's not answering his phone.*

Kill me now. But, of course, he was the asshole who was going to feed the beast. He didn't think he'd ever denied Knox anything she'd ever wanted.

But, surprisingly, in the shrug of her shoulders, he didn't read any interest. Or even guilt. "Took me a while, but I got it." She looked right at him. "You were right. I wasn't doing him any favors by cleaning up his messes." Then, fiddling with the hem of her slouchy sweater, she said, "Where did you go? Did you even graduate?"

"Of course." In the dwindling twilight, a purple haze had settled over the towering spires of the mountain range. "They were used to us taking off for competitions. That part was easy."

"Oh, I'm sure it was." She said it under her breath, but he heard her.

"What was that?"

"I said, I'm sure it was easy for you."

She was pissed at *him*? "I just accepted things before you did."

"Well, you had other people. Your dad, your uncle, your brothers. You had a huge support network. I had my mom and Robert."

It was like taking a trowel and scooping out whole pieces of his heart. He hated that she'd had no one but an unreliable drug addict.

"When my mom told me about Robert's visit, I couldn't even live with myself. It was like I could feel him, you know? His shock, his hurt. The betrayal. Who did he have other than me? How could I have just abandoned him?"

Incredibly, she wasn't looking at him like she used to —like she wanted answers. A way to resolve complicated feelings. It was more recounting an old story. Dispassionate.

"Especially since he'd finally gotten clean," Gray said. "That was all you'd ever wanted from him. A chance to have a real relationship."

"Actually, what I figured out...finally, was that I wasn't *in love* with Robert. I loved him, I certainly needed him. I thought..." Her finger circled the edge of her wine glass. "Well, I was afraid if I didn't reward him for rehab, he'd go right back to using. But, not for a second did I think, Oh, thank God, we can finally be together."

That was interesting. *Not in love?* And she hadn't wanted to get back with him?

Leaning forward, she set her glass down and clasped her hands in her lap. "I was as messed up as he was."

Whoa—that right there—he'd waited a long damn time to hear that.

"And the reason I didn't talk to him after he got out is because I wanted to be free. I don't regret it, not contacting him. It took a while to make peace with it, but I never missed him. As you once said, it wasn't like he'd been a true friend in a very long time. I hope he's clean and sober and living a good life, but that's it."

Seven years ago, that comment would have been a prompt to get information out of him. Was it still? "You want to know if he's clean, but I can't answer that."

"You talked to Mrs. Granger. How could Robert not come up?"

"Because I was there to talk about you."

"I know, but, come on. It'd be like the elephant in the room. You both had to be thinking about him." She must've picked up his mounting frustration, because she broke into an embarrassed smile. "I guess I must feel a *little* guilty if I'm this worried about seeing his mom."

He snatched another slice of bread and popped it in his mouth. After he swallowed, he said, "Or maybe you're worried it'll lead to seeing him." And how would that feel? He looked down at the slate patio, his gaze landing on a scattering of bread crumbs. "He came to my dad's funeral."

Sitting up straighter, she reached for his arm. "I'm so sorry, Gray."

When it came to his dad, it was like a big tangled ball of emotion. But one thing he knew, for sure. He missed him every single day.

Her fingers curled around his wrist. "That must've been the hardest thing for you."

It took a lot of will power not to slide his arm back just enough to align their fingers. He'd always wanted to hold her hand. Maybe it was the symbolism of it—the gesture of easy intimacy. *I'm yours. You're mine.*

But she wasn't touching him because she couldn't keep her hands off him. She was touching him because she felt bad about his loss. "It was." The thing about losing his dad so unexpectedly was that he'd never had the chance to talk about the issues that bothered him. To ask the questions.

To tell his dad he loved him.

But he did have a fresh start with Knox, and that meant forging a new connection, one without the Robert Granger link. "Anyhow, we got the appointment, and we leave tomorrow."

"We? You can't go with me. Fin will lose his mind."

"Yeah, well, in my world, they send us a few swatches, and then we put in an order. But Mrs. Granger said you'd want to see the fabric in person. So, it looks like I'll be skipping a few days of training so you can touch it, roll around in it, and rub it all over your body. Wouldn't miss that for the world."

She lunged for the plate, snatched a piece of bread, and lobbed it at him. "Freak. I'm not rolling around in three-thousand-dollar-a-yard Chantilly lace. Though, she's right. I do need to touch it, but I can go by myself."

"You want to see Mrs. Granger on your own?"

"I'm a big girl. I can handle it."

"Awesome. Then, I guess you're on your own." With a mischievous grin, he started to get up.

"It's not like I have a choice. Fin's obviously worried about how much training you need to put in to catch up with the other competitors."

He broke into a full grin. "I think I can miss a few days and still hold my own."

"You sure about that? You're looking a little slouchy. Might need to stay behind and work on your core." She pinched the skin above her hip. "You don't usually see muffin tops on Olympic athletes."

He threw his head back and laughed, and damn it felt good. "Look, as the CEO of your company—"

Her eyebrows shot up. "Did you just give yourself a promotion?"

"It's in my best interest to accompany you and check out this vendor, make sure he doesn't take advantage of the pretty little fashion designer."

"If you'd like to watch a professional in action, so you can learn a thing or two for your sock business, you're welcome to tag along." She lobbed a piece of sausage at him, and he nabbed it out of the air. "Because everyone needs a ninja travel companion."

Chapter Eight

A BRISK WIND PLASTERED KNOX'S ARMY JACKET TO her back. Maui—an ocean away from the harsh mountain winds of Wyoming—had spoiled her. *And it's only the middle of September.*

Crossing the tarmac, she shot a glance behind her to the Jetway. Still no Gray.

That's okay. She didn't need him on this trip. Besides, he'd gone above and beyond to right Amelia's wrongs and, most importantly, he needed to stay here and train.

She could recite all the reasons he shouldn't come, but none of them wiped away the disappointment of not getting to spend the next few days with him.

At the bottom of the stairs, she retracted the handle and then lifted her carry-on. The cold from the metal steps shot right through the soles of her black leather boots.

Didn't take you long to fall right back into old patterns with him, though, did it? Gray, stepping in to fix her problems, making her feel like nothing mattered more than helping her out. Her, lapping it up like a rescued kitty, greedy for the attention.

And completely forgetting how easily he'd walked away from her and never looked back.

Stepping onto the plane, she set the suitcase down and pulled out the handle, waiting for the line of passengers to move forward. At least this time she understood him better. Hearing his conversation with his brothers had been eye-opening. Their lack of support for anything outside snow sports had given him an attitude of, why bother?

Which meant, any day now, he could flip the switch and go chasing after the next shiny new thing.

I mean, come on. He's training for the Olympics, gets the call to go ride death-defying waves, and off he goes. If he doesn't take his own career seriously—why would he stick around for mine?

It wasn't like she needed him. She handled fabric vendors all the time. She'd done her research. Knew exactly how much material she'd need to buy for all her projects. *Everything's fine.* Between the pop-up and the custom gowns, things were looking good.

"Good morning." The flight attendant reached for her boarding pass and scanned it.

"Morning." Knox rolled her suitcase down the narrow aisle. She didn't have to go far. *2A.* Gray had put her in first class. She'd have to talk to him about that. Then again, he'd figure it out on his own when he saw the price of lace and crystals. *We're not buying nylon.*

Shoving her carry-on into the overhead compartment, she slid into her seat, too aware of the empty one beside her. Well, if he wasn't coming, she might as well take the window view. She shifted over and watched the baggage handlers toss suitcases into the belly of the plane. Setting her phone on her jeans-clad thigh, she checked the time.

The flight left in twenty minutes. It was cutting it close, but he could still make it.

Oh, stop it. He *shouldn't* come. She swiped the screen, itching to tap out a message, but she wouldn't do it. It would only make him feel guilty. Training had to be his priority.

Then stop looking at the door. She closed her eyes, making a promise to herself to disengage. No good could come out of relying on Gray Bowie. Think about Delilah, instead, who thought her sensational figure wouldn't work in a sexy gown. *Show her how awesome she'll look.*

Yes. She'd sketch, let the ideas flow until inspiration hit.

Delilah seemed to be drawn to the ultra-romantic, almost ethereal look of sheer tulle overlaid with floral lace. A bodice like that didn't have support, but Knox could fix that by making it a V-neck, adding some boning—

"Hey." Gray dropped a backpack and kicked it under the seat in front of him.

God, that voice. It traveled through her, all growly and deep, like dirty talk whispered in her ear. "You made it." She didn't know why that had popped out when she'd been thinking, *Thank God.*

He glanced behind him, stepping forward to allow a passenger by, and then reached for the bottom of his sweatshirt.

Knox's blood started to drag in anticipation of what was to come. Not even bothering to anchor his T-shirt, Gray yanked the hemline up and over his head. The shirt flew up with it, exposing the flattest stomach and most obscenely ripped abs of anyone she'd ever seen.

He'd always had a good physique, but his high school body didn't even compare with this powerhouse of a man.

Flopping into his seat, he clipped his seatbelt. "You stole my window view."

"I wasn't sure you'd make it." She gestured to the flight attendant. "Look, they're closing the doors."

"Had a late night."

The Gray she'd known hadn't partied. Which, of course, had enabled her to feel safe with him. Her mom was no addict, but she definitely liked her weed. She and her friends had a lot of "bake sales," as her mom liked to call them. No one got out of hand, but the smell of pot, the look in the eyes of someone stoned, just…squicked her out.

It was something she and Gray had had in common back then. Had he changed? He certainly wouldn't party before a competition, but maybe he'd lightened up and indulged afterwards?

Are you kidding me right now? He'd just won *Titans*, and instead of celebrating he'd gone right back to training with his brother. Of course he'd take the night to hang out with his friends.

You're doing it again. Getting all wrapped up in him. Cut it out. Reaching into her tote to pull out her sketchbook, she pretty much planted her face in his knee, which gave her a nice view of his muscular thigh.

What would it be like to touch him? Run her hands over all that warm skin? An image flashed, her hands full of the hard globes of his ass, squeezing, as she drew him up against her.

Desire burst, flooding her body and making her hot and achy. She'd never been with a guy that fit, and she hadn't known just how attracted she'd be to all that masculine strength. She could picture him naked, hovering over her body. Sliding inside her, the forceful snap of his hips. Deep inside, she pulsed for that kind of hot, wet friction.

Oh, please don't do this. Not with Gray. *He's going out of his way for you.*

Don't fall for him.

She yanked the notebook out so quickly, other crap fell out, and she had to pat around on the carpeted floor to find her make-up bag, pens, and hair elastic. When she sank back in her seat, she forced herself to focus on the dress. It helped that she knew Delilah better now. She couldn't wait to design something she would love.

Her pencil started moving, creating a deep décolleté corset—the cups generous enough to actually cover and support her breasts—and a fairy skirt with three-D lace flowers and petals. Okay, not what she'd meant to draw, but boy, would that be stunning on her.

Oh. Oh, wait. Wait. She turned the page, as an image formed in her mind. Princess cut, natural waist. Massive skirt with overlapping organza ruffles, tulle at the bottom. The whole thing overlaid in cascading flowers. *Yes. Oh, my God.* The neckline could echo those flowers—aligning with the off-the-shoulder sleeves.

"Can I get you something to drink?" The flight attendant leaned across Gray to hand her a cocktail napkin.

They'd already taken off? She glanced out the window. Wow, she'd gotten totally swept away. "Just water, please."

The flight attendant passed the water to her and then waited for Gray. But he seemed lost in thought. Knox elbowed him.

He glanced up. "Oh, sorry. I'll take a water, too."

"Not afraid of flying, are you?" the flight attendant asked with a grin.

"Nah, just thinking big thoughts."

"Big thoughts, huh?" The flight attendant poured his water. "Well, our country sure could use them right now."

"Oh, I'm saving all of them for my friend here. She's got a new business venture."

"Is that right? What kind of business?"

"Fashion."

"Really?" The woman gave Knox an appraising glance. "I can tell. Nice shirt."

"Oh." Self-consciously, she tugged on the material. "Thank you."

"She probably made it herself." The pride in Gray's voice made her feel warm and soft inside.

"Really?" The flight attendant's eyebrows shot up.

Knox nodded.

"Well, good luck." She flashed them a big grin and moved on.

"Do I get to hear all those big thoughts? I want to make sure I write them down before you move onto something else." *Oh, no.* That hadn't come out of her mouth, had it?

Could you be more pathetic?

She reached for his arm. "I'm sorry. That was meant to be a joke, and it came out completely passive-aggressive. I didn't mean it like that." Except she had, and that made her a selfish jerk.

His phone vibrated, and he pulled it out of his pocket. Smirking at the screen, he tapped out a response.

It struck her how little she knew about his life. She'd only seen one tiny little patch of it. She waited until he shut down his phone and shoved it back into his pocket before saying, "Girlfriend?"

"What?" His tone made it sound like she'd asked if he'd eat a beetle. "I don't have a girlfriend."

She laughed because he sounded so affronted. "You were smiling like you two were playing footsy."

"I was smiling because Mrs. Granger told me to behave myself with her vendor. She said I'm exactly his son's type and not to flirt too much because it'll break his heart, and then she'll have a hard time ordering from him again."

"You guys text each other?"

He leaned in close, like she was slow-witted and needed him to articulate. "Well, we're *working* together."

His scent washed over her, surrounding her in crisp, mountain air, newly laundered cotton, and that distinctly but undefinable essence of Gray Bowie.

"She says she's not coming after all. Something came up."

She'd heard him, of course, and what should have registered was that she didn't have to confront her ex's mom. Instead, she lingered, making it look like she was processing the information—*hm, will it matter if she doesn't come?*—when in fact she was gulping in a whole lungful of his scent and trapping it inside her so her body could revel in it tonight, when she was alone in her room.

"That's fine." She sat back. "I'm actually relieved."

He pulled up the sleeve of her blouse, gently rubbing the tip of his finger on the ink on her wrist. "Is this your reminder to reach for the stars?"

Her skin pebbled. "What?" She glanced down at the perfectly aligned and evenly spaced band of tiny stars wrapped around her wrist. "Not exactly. It's a reminder to keep my focus on the future when I get discouraged that I'm not where I want to be." Sitting so close, skin touching, it almost hurt to look into his bright blue eyes. "You did that for me. Something you said once." He'd probably forgotten all about the Etch-a-Sketch notes he'd left her.

He nodded. "I like it." Obviously, because he kept caressing that one star right in the center of her inner wrist.

"Thanks." It stoked an unbearable sexual tension in her. "I love your ink. That one on your shoulder blade? That's incredible." A vivid image of a snowboarder, arms out for balance, stood out against a backdrop of sharp angles and straight lines that fanned out like a protractor.

"I got it because people are always asking why it's so easy for me, but it's not. We didn't just hit the slopes, you know? Coach used physics to teach us how to carve. If I'm good, it's because of all the hours I've put in on the mountain, along with everything I've studied."

"I know how hard you worked." *I was there.* But she hadn't really seen him, had she? She'd been too obsessed with keeping Robert alive.

Gray finished his water and swiped his mouth the cocktail napkin. "So, what about you?"

That low voice, like they were in bed, the caress of his finger like he was fascinated by the single star, made her insides go all soft and gooey. Desire streamed, hot and thick through her.

What the hell's the matter with you? Why was she suddenly seeing Gray this way? "My ink?"

"No. Do you have a boyfriend?"

"I think you'd have heard about him by now if I did."

"I don't know. Maybe he's in Paris or New York."

"No, definitely no boyfriend. After all those years with the same ridiculously difficult man I'm on hiatus and loving my freedom, and I can't honestly see that changing any time soon."

"Boy."

"Sorry?"

"Robert was a boy. Totally different experience."

"Well, this conversation just got a whole lot more interesting. Please tell me *all* about your experience dating men."

That crinkle around his eyes, the dimples that popped on either side of his lazy smile? Lethal. "I'm saying you probably shouldn't compare what you had as a teenager with what you could have today…with a real man."

She pushed back in her seat, cocking her head. "Oh, this is good. Priceless information from a man who's had so many mature, romantic relationships."

"Just saying. You could be missing out on something good just because you're stuck in the past."

"Well, I don't know about the past, but in the present, I work a *lot*."

"Okay, but in your business, you must hang out with impressive people all the time. Actors, rock stars, international businessmen."

"You think I could pull a rock star?" she asked.

He gave her a long look, from her black knee-high boots, to the navy and white silk charmeuse blouse, to her mouth, where he lingered just a little too long. "I think you could get any man you wanted."

Heat roared through her, and she was quite sure her cheeks had turned bright red. What the hell was going on between them? *Nothing good. Change the conversation.* "Speaking of romance, what's in the water on the Bowie ranch? I can't believe two of your brothers finally succumbed to the goddess force."

"Goddess force?" He chuckled. "Well, obviously, Fin got sucked in years ago. There was no pulling him out of

Calliope Bell's clutches. Will, though?" He blew out a breath. "Never saw that coming."

"He's totally changed. Like, he's still a big badass, but the way he looks at Delilah? The fact that he's a *stay-at-home dad*? I mean that's a total one-eighty." When she shifted, her hand slid lower, fitting perfectly under his. The warmth and strength in it, the *comfort*, gave her a rush of energy, and she immediately withdrew it.

"Delilah works long hours at the restaurant, and Ruby's had her whole world turned upside down. She needs someone to be there for her, and she chose Will. I mean, she *chose* him. That little girl lost her mom, never knew her dad, got dumped in a new house with a bunch of strangers, and she just pointed at Will and said, *You*. Made a whole new family for herself."

"Must be strange. Finding out you have a half-sister."

"Psh. You have no idea. At first, she was just this kid. Didn't really associate her with my dad at all. Basically, I was gone most of the summer, so it was on Will to get her set up. But, once I got home and spent time with her, she just became...."

"Yours."

His genuine, warm smile sent a rush of pleasure through her. "She's ours, and she's awesome."

Wow. To be claimed by Gray. That would be...her heart clutched so hard it hurt. As a teenager he'd been so out of her league, she hadn't even had a single thought about him *that* way. She supposed, on some level, she still felt the same way.

"She's a good kid." He picked up the cup and tipped it, watching the bead of water roll from one side to the other. "She's got a voice, you know?"

"She does sound awfully cute."

"No, I mean she asks for what she wants. She doesn't take shit. She's not waiting around, hoping things go her way. That girl's going to get whatever she wants in life." He gave her a tender and really sweet smile, and she assumed he was thinking about his sister. "She's a lot like you. Whatever shit comes her way, she takes it like a champ and gets right back on her feet."

"She feels it, though." She didn't want the brothers to make assumptions about the little girl based on how she handled crises. "Be sure you guys take the time to talk to her. Listen."

"I will."

The way he was looking at her, with admiration, made her purr deep down. "She's lucky she has you guys in your corner."

He held her gaze, a thousand messages in his eyes she couldn't read. "Are you lucky to have me in your corner?"

"If I can hold your attention, I sure am."

Whatever positive energy rolled between them shut down. She felt stupid for ruining the moment, so she went for levity. "It's not going to be easy holding it when I'm talking about lace and organza and hemstitch needles. You're going to run off screaming to the nearest beach."

"I don't know about the screaming part, but the beach sounds nice." He tugged the hoodie over his forehead, folded his arms, and closed his eyes.

What's the matter with you?

Why did she keep pushing him away?

Gray patted his pockets. Phone, room key, wallet. *Good to go.* Just as he reached the door, he caught a glimpse of himself in the mirror. He looked pretty stupid in a suit with his hair curling up around the collar of his white dress shirt. In his business, appearance didn't matter.

But for Knox and her luxury world? He didn't want to embarrass her. While he couldn't get a haircut now, he could at least shave. *Yeah. At least do that.*

Shrugging off the jacket, he unbuttoned the cuffs and rolled up his sleeves as he headed into the bathroom. With the water warming up, he dug around in his toiletry bag for a razor. Did he even have one?

Yep. Got one. Good news. He needed to get a move on, or he'd be late. Squirting shaving cream into the palm of his hand, he smoothed it along his jaw. *Shit.* He should've trimmed it first. *Too late. Hurry up.*

The blade scraped over his skin, and the water trickled in the basin. Damn, he really should have trimmed his beard first. He had to rinse off the blade with every stroke. *I'm late, and she's going to be pissed.*

Snatching a clean towel off the rack, he patted his face dry. He couldn't help smiling as he hurried to get out the door. Because he knew her. She would absolutely call for a ride and go. Leave his late ass behind.

Knox. No other woman set off fireworks in his heart the way she did. No other scent on this earth stirred his possessive instincts.

Home.

Mine.

Rolling his sleeves down and buttoning the cuffs, he grabbed his jacket and hurried out of the room.

The minute the elevator doors opened, he spotted her. In a lobby crowded with guests, valets, and concierges, one woman drew him like iron to a lodestone. Tall and lean, she stood out with all that luxurious, dark hair tumbling down her back.

She wore white pants—tight around the waist and ass but widening as they got to her ankles—some kind of satiny top with puffy short sleeves and red dots on it, and high-heeled sandals that glittered in the morning light. Her bright red toenails matched the red dots of her shirt, as well as the lipstick on her wide, sexy mouth.

Knox Holliday was fuck-hot.

With a large, tan tote bag slung over her shoulder, her fingers tapped the screen of her phone. A businessman bumped her with his rolling suitcase, and she looked up with a smile and a shake of her head in response to his apology and then, right before returning her attention to her phone, her gaze snapped over to Gray.

Her lips parted, as she took a slow scan of him. From his chest to his pants to his dress shoes, and then back up again, quicker that time. At first, she looked confused but, then, a wash of color tinged her cheeks.

When he reached her, she said, "I was just leaving."

"Glad I made it in time."

"We can't be late." She reached up and swiped a spot under his ear, then pulled a tissue out of her tote and rolled her finger in it, removing the dot of shaving cream. "First, it's a crappy thing to do to Mrs. Granger. But, also, I'm dead in the water if this man doesn't sell to me." She glanced at her phone. "The driver's right around the corner. Let's go." She strode to the revolving door and—*swear to God*—three people, all dressed in suits, stepped aside to make way for her.

"Right behind you." He spent his time with pretty chill women. Adventurous—or he wouldn't be hanging out with them on summits or beaches with gargantuan waves—but easy-going. Knox was nothing like them. She was efficient, organized, determined, ambitious…and he loved it. Not many people could make him fall in line, but there was something about Knox…

She was heading somewhere, and he was going along for the ride.

Wouldn't miss it for the world.

Outside, in the early morning L.A. sunshine, she said, "He's a small supplier whose been around forever and doesn't really take on new clients. Mrs. Granger only uses him when she needs specialty items, so she's not one of his regulars." She glanced up at him. "I can't mess this up."

"Ran a little late because…" He rubbed his jaw, finding a tiny patch under his chin he'd missed. "I forgot to shave."

And just like that the storm clouds parted and a ray of sunshine in the form of a dazzling smile hit him right in the eyes, nearly blinding him. "For a second there, I didn't even recognize you." She ran a hand down his lapel, and it took every ounce of his restraint not to grab it and press it to his chest. "My eyes bugged out of my head when I saw the hottest businessman in the world get off the elevator."

"You got a thing for men in suits?" The car pulled into the portico, and she headed for it, cutting off the valets who started jogging over to open her door.

"I guess so." Her tone said, *Who knew?*

He slid onto the seat after her and reached for the strap to buckle in. The moment the driver took off, he said, "Let's grab some breakfast on the way."

"There's not enough time."

"We're good."

She shot him an impatient look. "Not with L.A. traffic."

They'd chosen the beachfront hotel because the supplier was right off the Ten freeway. "It's a twenty-minute drive. We'll be fine."

"Gray." She let out a huff of exasperation. "I don't want to risk it."

"Did you eat anything this morning?" He already knew the answer, though, since she tended not to eat when she was anxious.

"No. But we can grab something after."

"So, you don't get lightheaded anymore when you don't eat?"

With her chin tipped down, she smiled. "No, I do."

Affection bubbled over and, before he could check himself, he reached for her hand. "Right, so you want to make a quick stop for a breakfast sandwich, or you just want to grab a bag of nuts and an orange juice?"

The way she stared at his hand, like it was a dirty napkin he'd tossed at her, had him pulling it back. "Breakfast sandwich sounds good."

Stung by her response to his touch, he sat back in his seat.

He needed to check this growing attraction, because it fucking hurt to be rejected by her.

Chapter Nine

GRAY LOVED DROPPING IN. THE MOMENT HE TOOK off, his board gliding on crunchy snow. The cone of concentration he fell into, the adrenaline punching through him as hard as the icy air...nothing like it. He loved racing up the wall, gaining speed, throwing his shoulder into the first spin and soaring off the lip. Nailing a trick was fucking exhilarating.

But nothing he'd felt about snowboarding compared to the way Knox felt about textiles. As they walked across the mile-long showroom of AG Fine Fabrics, she scoured the bolts of material, ribbons, and lacy shit like she'd been told a winning lottery ticket was embedded somewhere in those piles.

Her comments about him lacking commitment suddenly made sense. Because, truthfully, medals didn't matter to him. Finally confronting his brothers the other day had cleared the way for him to see that, in choosing snowboarding competitions, he'd gone along with the pack. Not because, like Will, he had the drive to win, but because it hadn't felt good to get a ride to a fencing competition, knowing all his brothers were in Utah at an event. Or to sit at the table with them when they got back as they went over every single thing they'd done...without him.

Gray liked the rush of surfing and boarding, but he always plateaued, needing to tackle more complicated tricks and bigger waves.

But the only thing he'd ever loved as passionately as Knox loved textiles was...Knox.

He caught up with her, dared to brush a lock of silky hair off her shoulder so he could see her pretty profile. "I should probably clear out the store, put up a Closed sign, and give you some alone-time."

Fingering something satiny, she snickered. "Would you? Please?" And then she sighed. "I wish we had more time. I'd love to look around after our meeting."

"You could always stay longer." He was the one who had to get back to train. "Fly out tomorrow."

"No, I can't afford another night in the hotel, but thanks."

He wanted to say he'd happily pay for it, but he respected her for not assuming he would.

They climbed a dimly lit stairwell to the second floor, the clap of their shoes echoing off the close walls, and entered into an open space filled with cubicles. Rows of offices lined the perimeter of the quiet room.

Behind the utilitarian metal desk stationed at the top of the stairs sat a young, well-dressed woman. Knox beamed a radiant smile. "Good morning. I'm Knox Holliday, and this is Gray Bowie. We're here to see Mr. Goldschmidt."

The woman peered at her screen, looking confused. "Uh...I don't think you have an appointment?"

Everything happy and hopeful in Knox's features flattened. "We do. Mrs. Granger arranged the meeting."

"Right." She looked uneasy. "But she called first thing this morning to say she couldn't come."

Gray stepped forward. "*She* can't come, but she's not the one ordering fabric today. Knox and I are."

"I don't know what to tell you. When she said she wasn't coming, we cancelled the meeting."

"Well, obviously, there's been a misunderstanding," Knox said. "But we're here, right on time, and we have a plane to catch this afternoon, so we'd like to meet with Mr. Goldschmidt as planned."

"Unfortunately, he's not here," the receptionist said.

"How long will it take him to get here?" Knox sounded firm but still friendly.

Fierce. Damn, he liked her.

"In traffic?" The receptionist shrugged. "At least an hour."

Knox indicated a couple of hard chairs set against the wall. "We're happy to wait."

"I'm afraid that's not possible." The young woman lifted out of her seat to glance into one of the glass-walled offices across the way.

"Get him on the phone." Gray's tone wasn't nearly as amiable as Knox's, but he didn't give two shits. "Or I can call Mrs. Granger, and you can explain why she won't be getting the dresses Knox is making for her spring show."

"I'm so sorry." The receptionist looked uncomfortable. "I'm sure he'd be happy to reschedule, but—"

"That won't work," Knox said. "I've got a plane to catch and a business to run. I'd like to speak with Ethan."

Who the hell was Ethan?

The woman's concern vanished. "Sure. Let me go talk

to him." She got up, her ballet flats shushing on the carpet as she walked to the office she'd been watching.

He gave Knox a questioning look. "Ethan?"

"The man who's heart you've been instructed not to break. I read that his dad's been pulling back on his hours, gradually giving his son more responsibilities. He can take care of my order just as well."

He wanted to kiss her. Haul that sexy body up against his and feel her curves and heat. He was pretty sure his eyes said what he couldn't, because awareness bloomed in a pretty pink splash across her cheeks.

He'd loved the girl who'd fought so hard to survive in a hostile town. But this woman?

Put it this way: I'm in serious trouble.

Gray needed to get out of the hotel room. *Now.* He tossed the room service menu onto the table and got up. "Let's grab something to eat." Fingers tapping on the doorframe, he peered into her bedroom.

Thanks to the love fest between Ethan and Knox, they'd missed their flight. So, while the two of them had walked through the warehouse, touching, fondling, and petting fabric, gawking over pearls and examining crystals through a magnifying glass, he'd called the hotel.

And stupidly, impulsively, moved them into the two-bedroom suite.

Digging through her suitcase, she barely spared him a glance. "Where are my pajama bottoms? Don't tell me I didn't bring them. No, I'm sure I did."

Even though he could've caught a flight out and left Knox on her own—because, let's face it, he didn't care about the various kinds of lace—he could have happily watched Knox in her element all day long.

And, if he had to be really honest, it had to do with the secret smiles she'd thrown his way, as if he was her very first thought. Countless moments where her eyes widened in a look that said, *Isn't this amazing?* Where she'd reach for him, her fingers tapping the back of his hand to get his attention.

"Here they are. I knew I'd packed them." She yanked them out from the bottom and did a victory pump with them. "What did you say? Oh, right. Dinner. Would you mind ordering me the Caesar with grilled chicken, dressing on the side? I'm just going to change."

"You've just spent hours swooning over miles of fabric and scored the deal of a lifetime, and you want a salad?"

"Swooning is exhausting." Her sexy lips curved into a teasing smile, and he nearly lost his shit.

What would she do if he caught her up in his arms, dropped his face into the curve of her neck, and just breathed in the scent of her sweet and feminine skin? Well, he already knew the answer to that, didn't he? She'd pull away.

Enough. He was not sitting in this hotel room all night with Knox in her jammies. "Let's get out of here."

"We've been going all day. I thought we could order in and talk about all the money I just spent." She clutched the pajama bottoms to her chest. "I might be freaking out just a little."

"Well, while you were swooning, I was going back and forth with Wyatt, discussing the spreadsheet he sent us. I can tell you with confidence that we're good on finances. Didn't hurt that you charmed the pants off Ethan, since his dad's going to beat his ass when he finds out the prices he gave you."

"I just slipped right into saleswoman mode." Her brow creased. "I might've oversold the scope of my operation."

"I didn't hear you misleading him about anything."

"Uh, I'm making *two* dresses right now. I might have some requests, but I don't have any actual orders."

"As of twenty minutes ago, thirteen requests have come in from the social media pages. Now, I know it's not a done deal. You have to talk with them, figure out pricing, but you *are* going to make more than two dresses this year, and you're definitely making a hundred gowns for the pop-up."

She backed away from the suitcase, pressing her hands to her stomach. "Oh, man."

"Hey." He cut around the bed to get to her.

"I think I'm in over my head."

When he reached her, he wanted nothing more than to enfold her in his arms. "No, you're not. We've got this."

"I've never had employees and payroll and budgets. I'm good at designing, and I felt in control last year making twenty-five gowns. But right now...I don't feel like I have a handle on this *business*."

"You're not running it by yourself. Wyatt has payroll and taxes and all the financial stuff. Amelia's got PR and marketing. Zach's got the creative end. And, as the business grows, we can hire as many people as we need to fulfill orders." He tipped her chin. "We got this."

She gazed up at him, so many questions in her eyes. "And you?"

"I'm the CEO. I'm going to oversee the whole thing. You got a problem with anyone, you come to me, and I'll handle it. You're running the show, which means you delegate the work that interferes with what you do best—designing and making the product. If you don't like how things are going, you tell me, and together we figure it out. This is your company, we're just the team backing you up, and damn happy for it."

"You really want to be here?"

"Swear to God, Knox, nowhere else I'd rather be. And I know the others feel the same way. We make fuckin' board shorts. We've never done anything as fun as this. We're into it. Promise."

She nodded, inhaling a sharp breath. "Okay. And it's not like I'm making dresses in a bunkhouse in Calamity forever. It's just for now. Until I get the attention of someone like Jack Abrams...until I have my first show."

All that exhilaration—like soaring off the lip of the pipe—crashed and burned.

For a second there, he'd thought his world was big enough for her. "Now, you want a Caesar salad, or you want to get some tacos and funnel cake at the pier?"

He had two seconds to enjoy the view from fifty-feet above the Pacific Ocean before the roller coaster plummeted, slinging his funnel cake from the pit of his stomach into his throat. *Shouldn't have eaten right before the ride.*

Clutching the bar, hair whipped back off his face, Gray laughed so hard tears spilled down his cheeks. Damn, it felt good, spending time with Knox, guilt-free.

But, no matter how badly he wanted to trail his fingertips along the smooth skin of her inner thigh in those shorts she was wearing, he knew he couldn't. She didn't see him like that. Sure, they got along. The intense connection they'd always had wasn't one-sided. He didn't doubt she felt affection for him, but when she closed her eyes, it wasn't him imprinted on her lids. When she turned out the light and drew the blanket up to her ear, so spiders didn't crawl in—like she used to do in the trailer—she didn't get a shudder through her body as she imagined him sinking into her hot, wet heat.

Hey, now. No wood on a roller coaster. The ride jerked to a stop, the safety device pulled back, and they climbed out onto the platform.

"That was insane." Her eyes went wide from the thrill.

The thing he liked about Knox was that she might be into fashion, but she wasn't obsessed with how she looked. Right then, just off a roller coaster ride, she didn't think to smooth down her hair, which was all over the place. Hadn't thought to refresh her lipstick after downing a corndog. He loved how in-the-moment she was, how thoroughly she let herself go around him.

And how she looked like she'd just rolled onto her back after a wild go of hot sex.

"I did *not* expect that drop." When she glanced back at the ride, the bright lights of the pier made her skin glow and her eyes glitter. She was the most beautiful woman he'd ever seen. "It looks so harmless."

I want her.

And I don't think I can stand wanting this woman all over again. It would kill him, all that yearning and longing, the relentless ache.

He had until October eleventh with her—four weeks —before he flew to New Zealand for his first competition. For a while after that, their only interaction would be via text and email.

So, he'd do like he did seven years ago—take whatever she was willing to give right now.

"I had so much fun tonight."

Gray nodded, setting his keycard on the suite's kitchen counter.

Stretching, she reached her arms over head, twisting at the waist, her hands lowering behind her neck. The move exposed a tiny patch of creamy skin right above the waist-line of her shorts. "I'm beat. I'm going to bed." Instead, though, she lingered.

Was she expecting him to say something? Offer up a game of Battleship? She didn't know the only game he wanted to play with her involved naked bodies. And, oh, fuck, did he want to get his hands on her.

"Goodnight." She wore a simple T-shirt and white shorts, but he wanted her with a fierceness that made his skin feel tight, ready to burst.

Stay. Even if they just watched a movie on the couch, he wanted more time with her. The moment they landed in Wyoming tomorrow, he'd lose her. She'd dive into dress-making, and he'd be training. They wouldn't have another chance to be alone like this.

"'Night." He dropped onto the couch, reaching for the remote.

"You're not going to sleep?"

"I'm pretty wired. I'll just watch some mindless TV."

"Your body's not used to sugar, and you did eat a whole three bites of that funnel cake."

His tongue flicked out, like a cat with a hair stuck on it. "It was disgusting."

"Fried food? Your body's in shock. It might never

recover." She lingered at the door. "Okay, well, goodnight."

"You said that."

She laughed. "I feel bad leaving you here when you're wide awake."

"Go. I know all you want to do is get in bed and start sketching."

"Oh, you know that, do you?"

"I'm wrong?"

She smiled.

"I'll also bet you're itching to draw a whole collection based on amusement park rides. Or 'food you'd find on a pier.'"

"I would never do something like that." Her grin grew wider. "It's not couture."

"So, you'd start with The Funnel Cake, realize it was too tacky, and change it to The Crème Brûlée."

"Oh, good one. I better write it down, so I don't forget."

"The Parfait." He leaned back, stretching an arm along the back of the couch.

She gasped, placing a hand over her heart. "Gorgeous."

"The Ambrosia."

"You're brilliant." She tapped her chin, pretending to think. "The Praline?"

"And my personal favorite, The Pots de Crème."

"How do you even know that name?"

"My future sister-in-law."

"Ah." She made an exaggerated show of melancholy. "That's the saddest thing I've ever heard."

"What is?"

"A world class chef marrying into a family that lives off sweet potatoes and meat."

"This is true," he said. "Although, I've got to say, Will's a changed man. He's actually eating real food now."

"That explains the beer belly."

He tipped his head back and laughed. His brother worked out religiously and still had zero percent body fat.

"Yeah, so…"

Was she lingering just to torment him? "I know. Goodnight." He clicked the power button on the remote.

"And I'm not getting into bed to sketch."

Muting the TV, he said, "No?"

"No, I'm going to take a bath. I smell like fried cheese sticks."

"No, you don't. You smell sweet and soft. Feminine." *Shit.* He'd freaked her out. The more he hung around her, the more he liked her, and it was hard to hide that kind of attraction. But he would absolutely not make her uncomfortable with his unwanted interest. "You don't like baths. Don't like to 'wallow in your own filth.'"

"Oh, my God, Gray. That was when I lived in a *trailer.*"

"You want some time alone. That's okay. I'm good."

"I don't want time *alone.* I just…"

"Want to take a 'bath,' which I think we both know means get into bed, find a good movie on TV, and wind up sketching until you fall asleep."

She rolled her eyes. "That's so last decade."

That mischievous smile squeezed his heart so hard all these warm, sticky feelings poured out. Nostalgia, longing. *This is how it used to be, this connection.* He thought he'd lost it forever, and he was so damn glad to have it back. "Hey, if I'm wrong, I'm wrong. People change." But she still saw him as just a pal, so he motioned for her to close the door. "'Night."

When she hesitated, it struck him that something was on her mind. He got up and came over to her. "What's up?"

She didn't answer, just gave him a searching look.

"If you're worried about anything, lay it on me. Let's talk it out."

"No, I'm not worried. I mean, I *am* worried. Everything's happening so fast. It's been two weeks since I was getting my dresses ready to be shipped to New York for Bridal Fashion Week."

Gutted. She'd gutted him. He'd only ever wanted to lift her up—and instead, she'd had her foot on the last step of the ladder, and he'd jerked her right back down.

"And before I could even process what happened, I'm heading back to Calamity, of all places, setting up shop in the bunkhouse. I mean…it's crazy, right? And I know you and Amelia are doing everything in your power to rebuild what I've lost, but…come on, Gray. Ultimately, this is my problem."

"Actually, it's our problem. We're all in this together."

"I don't know how to say this the right way except to say thank you, but now you're off the hook. And I know you well enough to know that you won't walk away until you think you've restored my life to the way it was before you guys crashed into it. So, I guess what I'm trying to say is, it won't ever look that way again. I'm on a whole new course, one without Luc, and I've made peace with it. I mean, it's a swerve, but one that'll still lead me back to the road I'd mapped out."

He came up close—close enough that he could smell the hint of Funnel cake in her hair. "I hear you, and thank you for letting me off the hook. So, now that we've gotten that out of the way, everything I do from this moment on will be of my own volition, right?"

She gave him a disbelieving look.

"The first suggestion I made—making wedding dresses for my sisters-in-law? That came from them. They saw your dresses and begged me for an introduction. Mrs. Granger? She jumped at the idea of selling your gowns in her store. I hired Zach away from Hugo Rossi, so you can probably guess he's fuckin' thrilled to be working on something more than board shorts for a change. I've known Amelia a long time, and I've never seen her so excited about anything as this project, so stop feeling like we're doing you a favor. We're not. We're all goddamn lucky to be part of this business with you."

He reached for her—because he couldn't ever be near her and not need to be close—but her eyes rounded in alarm and her body stiffened. *Well, shit.* She should know he'd never take anything from her she didn't want to give —including a touch.

She looked like she wanted to scrape him off. "Oh, Gray."

Which pissed him off almost as much as her patronizing tone. "Oh, Gray what? Come on, Knox. I'm not a mind reader. You've got something to say, just spit it out. Say what's on your mind."

"Nothing. Just…this is what you do best." She gave him a wry smile. "Make me feel like you're not giving me charity."

"Charity?" What the hell?

"Yes, Gray. You just told me what Mrs. Granger and Zach and Amelia are getting out of this…arrangement, but you failed to mention yourself. So, tell me. Other than you—once again—riding in on your white horse to save me, what do *you* get out of it?"

Was she really this clueless? *White horse?* "Let's rewind all the way back to middle school. I would've shut down any asshole who was barking at someone. Did it make it worse that you were my friend? You bet. But you reamed me out every time I did it, so I *quit* doing it. The point is that I never *needed* to do it, because you always took care of the situation in your own way. As for now, today? You want to know what I get out of working with you? Another income stream and the chance to hang out with you again. Both of those are pretty fuckin' sweet."

"There's only ever been one context for us being together, and that's you saving my ass. You fought my bullies so many times you got suspended. The whole time we hung out I was tormented over Robert. Look, we're adults now, we can be honest about the past. You're a nice guy. You looked out for me, and I'll always be grateful, but let's not pretend it's ever been anything other than what it is."

Nice? He was a *nice* guy? *Awesome.* Well, at least that explained it. *You're not attracted to nice guys. You don't want nice guys to tear off your panties and pound you into next week.* "Okay."

"What? I'm saying that I appreciate all you've done for me. I don't have a lot of people in my corner, and it's nice that you've always been there for me. But we're adults now, and you're going after something really important that requires all your focus." She looked frustrated. "I can see by your expression that I'm saying it all wrong." She lifted her arms and then dropped them so hard they clapped against her thighs. "You've done more than enough this time. I'm ridiculously grateful, but now you're free."

"I don't want to be in your corner, Knox." *I want to be in your heart.*

Whoa. Calm down.

But he couldn't. An avalanche of words he'd never said rumbled and groaned under the pressure. "And I already told you not to be grateful, because I'm right where I want to be."

She clasped her hands together. "You're mad, and I don't know why. I have very few good memories of my childhood. The best ones are with you. But…at the same time…those are the ones that keep me up at night."

His body went on alert. What was she saying? What had he done wrong?

"I try not to think of them, but when I do, when a memory pops up, my first reaction is just…happiness. You brought me that…" She let out a slow, shaky breath through pursed lips. "But, about a second later, I feel sick to my stomach."

"Because of *me*?" *Oh, Jesus.* He thought he'd done such a bang-up job of keeping his feelings from her, but she'd known. And it had made her sick. He'd made her sick. She'd been in love with his best friend, and there he was stealing private moments with her, letting his completely inappropriate feelings bleed all over her.

He wanted to run. Turn and walk out of this room. Head straight to the airport and not look back. But he couldn't do that. Not when he'd made her sick to her stomach. He needed to stand here and take it. He'd earned it.

"Gray, don't feel bad about it. It's not your fault. It's just how you're wired."

Mortification ripped through him like a flash fire. His palms went clammy.

"But we're adults now, and I'm done being your pity project. You weren't driving that car, Amelia was. The only reason you're here right now is because poor Knox is in trouble yet again. It just…makes me sick. Now, just let me take a bath and go to sleep."

Whoa—his head was spinning. *She's not pissed because I lusted after my best friend's girlfriend. She's upset because…* "Nuh uh. No fuckin' way. You don't drop shit like that on me and then walk away. You give me a chance." How the hell did he clear this one up? "Jesus, Knox. all this time, you thought you were my pity project? That is just…" He shook his head. "Fucked up. Did it ever occur to you that I stopped being friends with Robert but stayed friends with you?"

"Yes, to protect me from him and his druggie friends."

"What? No. I stayed friends with Robert long past when I should have because *I felt sorry* for him. Because I thought I could *help* him—not because I liked him anymore. When I figured out I couldn't, I walked away. It was either that or get sucked into his messed up world. Besides, it's disrespectful to pretend to be friends with someone when you're left with nothing but pity."

Her eyebrows hitched up, as if he'd just proven her point, but he wasn't done yet. "I hung out with you, because I liked you. I *admired* you. Do you remember that fire drill when the entire school had to file outside onto the football field? I was one of the last people out of the building, but I watched you climb the bleachers, watched someone shove you so hard you fell on the stairs. Everyone around you stepped aside, and no one did shit to help you. And then I saw Cady Toller laughing her ass off."

She winced, and he knew she didn't want him to continue, but it was a story that needed to be told.

"Everyone just went on like nothing happened, finding their friends, sitting down, but you just sat there, like you were in so much pain you couldn't even function."

"True story. I landed on my tailbone."

"I hauled ass to get to you, but before I could, I saw you get back up. You kept your eyes on Cady. When you hit her row, you made your way down it until you got to her. You stuck your ass out, forcing your way in between Cady and Melissa. You remember what you did?"

"Of course." She said it nonchalantly, like it was no big deal.

But it was. "I was racing up the stairs when I saw your expression, watched you lean right into her ear. What'd you say, Knox? Say it to me right now, what you said to the most popular girl in our class who'd just hurt you in front of the whole school."

"What's your point? You think I want to remember my past in that town?"

"The point is that you're a badass. You said, 'You know the interesting thing about people who have no fucks to give?"

Knox arched a brow and gave him just a hint of a smile. "'We're dangerous. Like, really, scary dangerous. Watch your back.'"

That's right. "And then you sat with them until the drill ended, and we were allowed back into the building." The best part came afterwards, though. "The entire school talked about what you did for weeks."

"Yeah, well, the Bible calls for an eye for an eye."

A smile cut through the tension. After school that day, Cady had been getting into her boyfriend's truck, when Knox came up from behind and yanked on the waistband of her jeans. Cady had fallen onto the asphalt hard—into a dirty puddle—but Knox had just sashayed away. "I hung out with you because you were fierce. I liked you. I liked hanging out with you, more than with anyone else. I—"

"Bullshit. Don't feed me—or yourself—some stupid lines. I wasn't your friend. I was nothing to you."

"Are you out of your mind? Is this what you've been thinking all these years? What the fuck did I ever do to give you that impression?"

"You left me." It was the flatness in her tone, dead as roadkill, that impacted him way worse than if she'd screeched. "You walked out of that hotel room, and you never looked back. Friends don't do that. I get it. I'm not angry. You were pissed at me for hanging onto Robert long past the end-date, I got that. But if you cared about me at all, you would've contacted me at some point. There are plenty of ways to keep in touch with someone, and you didn't find one of them." She reached for the door, like she might close it. "How's that for the truth?"

Five pellets fired with pure menace. Each one hit the target. His body shook with fear, hurt, and wild frustration. "I did what I had to do." He spoke through gritted teeth.

"No, you did what you wanted to do. Just like you always do. That's your MO. You washed your hands of your pity project. And, believe me, I don't blame you, but we should at least be honest about it." She took a step back and slammed the door in his face.

His body was on fire. His pulse thundered. "You want honesty?" It was like fighting against the undertow, reaching the surface, and filling his lungs. "I'll give it to you. I was in love with my best friend's girlfriend. *That's* why I left and never looked back."

Chapter Ten

LOST IN THE WORLD OF HER DESIGNS, KNOX contemplated the idea of a detachable skirt, so the bride could take it off and wear white satin shorts to the reception. *Oh, I like that.* Her pencil flew across the page as images came to mind. Yards and yards of organza, cut to look like feathers, big—bigger—*ach, so feminine*—and then the shock of hot pants underneath. *Edgy.*

Excitement flooded her, making her fingers shake. This was when she knew she'd come upon a great idea. Her body's visceral reaction. Wait, what if the shorts weren't white? What if they were pink? She reached for a different pencil. No, stronger contrast. Purple. And, to give a little hint of what lay beneath the lavish skirt, she'd tie a purple sash around the waist. No, purple petals—two satin flowers at the back. *Wait. No.* She flipped the page to draw the back of the dress. A bustle, with a row of three purple organza flowers along the seam.

Yes. Love it.

Until fear crept in and clamped its jaws into her heart. *What're you doing?* Random sketching wasted precious time, because she wasn't designing collections anymore. She was making two custom dresses. And, while she might have all these requests, until she spoke with the brides and discussed pricing and specific details, she didn't have any actual orders.

I'm giving up my dream.

No. You're not. The pop-up show is at Granger's. The social media campaign could very well get her the kind of attention she needed. She knew it, because the dress page already had several thousand followers. People seemed to love watching the process, and the camaraderie between the women, too.

Amelia had done an amazing job with it. Each post was clever, the photographs stylish and fun. She'd get that call from Jack Abrams, and this would all lead to a couture show on a Paris runway.

Canned laughter caught her attention, yanking her out of her reverie. She looked up to see that the movie had ended, and the TV was on, which meant she must've switched over at some point. She patted the sheets, looking for the remote, and thumbed the power button. The room went dark. Setting the sketchbook on the night-stand, she shoved a pillow between her legs, rolled onto her side and closed her eyes.

You're going to get in bed, find a good movie, and wind up sketching until you fall asleep.

Gray knew her. He just did. And that made it easier to believe the bomb he'd detonated at her feet. Finally, after losing herself in her sketches—blocking out his confession —she let it come flooding in.

I was in love with my best friend's girlfriend.

Shock waves rolled through her, slamming into every cell in her body. *In love with me?* Her brain sorted through snapshots from their childhood, trying to catch a glimpse of his expressions. But what could she make of them? She could mold a memory into anything she wanted.

Gray didn't lie. He didn't have to—he had enough confidence and self-possession to own everything he said and did. Which meant…he'd loved her. *That's why he hung around me.*

All her life she'd felt less than Gray Bowie. He was handsome and powerful, confident and competent. In high school, he'd walk down the hallway, and people would look up from their conversations, pause while reaching into their lockers, just to watch his easy gait, his infectious smile. He radiated authority. He was that unicorn who seemed to fit perfectly in his own skin, while the rest of them were gangly and awkward and unsure.

Gray's bombshell opened up a whole new perspective. It made her see just how deeply she'd let the bullies shape her perceptions about herself. Tonight, Gray had removed that lens.

Not that anything could've happened between them. Robert would never have let go of her. She'd had to move to New York with no forwarding address in order to free herself.

She kept skimming the edge of the bomb site. It was too bright, too scary to look in. He'd loved her? He'd *loved* her.

Gray Bowie had loved her.

Now, it almost seemed ridiculous to think of all that time he'd spent with her as anything else. No one spent that much time with a pity project. *You invited her to party here and there, you heard of an opportunity and tossed it her way. But you didn't spend every free moment with your project.*

He'd dropped the bomb, and she'd slammed the door in his face. She'd let him tell her a truth so big and horrible—he'd been in love with his best friend's girlfriend—and then walked away.

Was he still on the couch, watching mindless TV?

She needed to find the guts to go out there and respond. Because what kind of person just closed her eyes and went to sleep with a confession like that hanging in the air?

More, she missed him. She never should have locked him out. He was right—she'd never planned to take a bath in a hotel tub. *Ew*. Not unless she had an arsenal of cleaning supplies.

Not having a clue what to say to him, she threw back the covers. She hadn't been in love with him. That had been so far out of the realm of possibility, she hadn't even contemplated it. But she'd liked him better than anybody. *Tell him that.*

She flung open the door, ready to talk...only to find the suite dark, the couch empty.

Why did she feel like she'd missed an opportunity? Should she knock on his door? Wake him up?

Yes. Do it. He deserved a response, even if it had taken her an hour to find her lady balls. She pressed her ear to his bedroom door but didn't hear a sound. Lightly, she knocked. "Gray? You up?"

"Yeah. Yep." His voice sounded gravelly.

When she opened the door, she saw a flash of white, as he flipped the covers back and swung his legs off the bed. He snatched his boxers off the floor, jamming his legs into them and yanking them up. Scrubbing his face, he stalked towards her. "You all right? What's going on?"

"I believe you."

"Sorry?" He looked so adorable, this big mountain of a man, wearing nothing but bright red boxers with a green Grinch printed all over them. His broad, hairy chest, so toned, so fit, those bulging biceps, and rock-hard thighs —*my God*.

This man had loved her.

"I believe you." This time she smiled because those were the three most powerful words she'd ever said.

"Still not getting it."

"I've been working through what you said. I started with total dismissal. No way did Gray Bowie have feelings for me. Then I moved on to, okay, yeah, you don't spend all that time with a pity project. You put on latex gloves and feed her Thanksgiving dinner once a year. You don't lie on her bed, feet against the wall, and talk about her dreams of being a fashion designer."

He watched her, like the glitter was settling and the image inside the snow globe was becoming delightfully clear.

"But then, the truth started to sink in. You had a busy life. Not just your competitions, but your brothers, your dad, and uncle. And then—bam—it rose right up out of my subconscious and smacked me in the face." She came closer to him. "Gray, you chose *me* over time with your brothers. Well, over a lot of things. And I didn't see it because of *them*. Of what assholes like Cady and Melissa trained me to believe. That I was trash. I thought flipping them the bird made me rise above it. I thought my little revenge plots made me invincible. But I didn't see how my impressions about myself and the world came from them. Gray, the idea that you loved me? It just didn't compute. A guy like you?"

His eyes softened, and he cracked a shy grin. Oh, Gray

Bowie all vulnerable like that? That was hotter than his abs, his medals, and his lazy smile combined.

"I don't know how it would've changed my life if I'd seen the truth," she said. "But I can tell you it changes me now."

He didn't say anything, and awareness broke over her like a cracked egg. *Don't forget that he walked away, stayed away for seven years. He'd had no intention of ever seeing you again.*

Oh, God. He was talking about a childhood crush, and she was standing here gushing at him. "I mean, I know you don't love me anymore. Of course. Obviously. I'm just saying that you've given me a whole new perspective on my childhood, and it's pretty damn amazing. We're good, though. We can work together without you thinking that I'm, like…that I expect…you know, that I think you're still in love with me." She laughed, but it sounded as phony as it felt. "Anyhow. I just wanted to say I believe you. That's a big moment for *me*, not you, so I obviously shouldn't have woken you up to tell you. I could've kept that one to myself. So, anyhow. I'm a weirdo. Goodnight." She gave him a smile she was pretty sure could only be found in a Fun House hall of mirrors and started to go.

But his years of training served him well, because his arm shot out, wrapped around her waist, and jerked her against his hot, hard chest. "Never keep anything to yourself." He leaned in until she could smell the toothpaste on his breath and the clean-linen scent on his skin. "I love every fucking thing that comes out of your mouth."

And then he pressed those beautiful lips to hers, and her heart exploded. Desire, sharp and fierce, burst in her core, the current so strong it flooded every fiber and tissue in her body. Immediately, she lost herself in the feel of his smooth, warm skin and the command of his tongue as it took possession of hers.

Gray's kiss started with supreme confidence, making it feel like he was in charge, that she was along for the ride— a thrilling but controlled ride. One you knew couldn't go off the rails.

And then it faltered. He let out a sigh that sounded desperate. The power of his touch gave way to a tremble in his arms, and his body heated up to blistering.

His control turned reckless, wild. She'd never been kissed like this—like he needed to gobble her up but couldn't get all of her in at once. Like he needed to consume her, get his fill before she was snatched away. Everything about Gray—his scent, the way his strong hands roamed her back as though he couldn't believe he got to touch her—the passion in his embrace—lit her up, flipped on all the lights—and she wanted it. She wanted this torrent of yearning and desire and need.

Until those strong hands slid down and cupped her ass and gave her a lusty squeeze. The press of his rock-hard erection against her stomach sent up warning flares—*sex*— and, God, sex with Gray Bowie?

Panic had her pushing him away. "I…" Her fingertips brushed across her sensitive lips.

Those blue eyes worked hard to read her, his chest pumping, arms still curved around her, so that if she took one step forward her bottom would fit snugly back in his hands.

And it struck her—like really hit her hard—how much she wanted that.

"I'm sorry." What was she *doing?* "I…goodnight."

Wind—too cold for mid-September—cut through Gray's sweatshirt. People gathered at the bottom of the ramp, his brothers and a bunch of guys who'd come out of the training facility to catch his final run of the day.

He sucked in what was meant to be a calming breath, but it hurt, like there was a vise around his lungs. That damn kiss. It kept popping up like a game of Whac-A-Mole. He'd stomp it out, and then, out of nowhere, it'd pop back up, taunting him. Landing like a punch to his solar plexus.

Breathe. He took in the dark gray mountain range, the bright snow draped across the summits like a sparkling, white blanket, and the brilliant blue sky. Hurt like fuck to fully accept it, but…

His heart didn't want him.

She'd responded to his kiss—her body had gone hot, her hands clutched at him, no question about that—but when she'd pushed him away, he'd understood it was different for her. She'd never seen him as anything other than a friend, and then out of nowhere he'd declared his love for her and…it had been a shock. So, yeah, she'd responded.

But he'd seen her expression afterwards. She didn't want him like that.

"Dude," Brodie called from down below. "Time for your afternoon snack? Need a juice box?"

He let his middle finger answer for him. *Focus.* Bending his knees, he took off, gaining speed down the inflatable ramp. Anger and frustration propelled him until he launched like a rocket. A wild sense of recklessness took hold and, during that first rotation, he knew he had the speed and amplitude to pull off a triple. He shouldn't do it —not here, not now—but, dammit, she didn't want him.

Gripping his board, he threw himself into a third rotation, the world a blur of green, brown, and blue. As he spun, a tumult of emotion roiled like carbonation in a soda can. He spotted the airbag and...stomped his fucking landing. *Hell, yeah.*

His brothers went nuts, shouting and clapping.

Except Fin. "Jesus Christ, Gray." His hands clutched the side of his head. "Are you out of your mind? You don't pull a triple twelve-sixty on a *training* ramp."

"I know, right?" Electrified, Gray made his way to the edge of the bag and jumped off, where Brodie met him with a fist bump.

"Solid," his brother said.

Still vibrating with the rush of his trick, Gray sat on a bench and unclipped his boots. The chatter around him—the guys excitedly going over his run—tamped down the volume of his thoughts.

Until Brodie broke away and dropped onto the bench beside him. Arms folded across his chest, he watched the group talking and laughing. "He's pissed because you took off for a few days. Not because you pulled off that trick."

"Yeah, well, I've got a business to run."

His brother tipped his head back, closing his eyes against the bright sun. "I never realized how alike we are, you and me."

"How's that?"

"We're businessmen, like Dad." Brodie pushed back, stretching his legs out in front of him. "That's not a bad thing."

"I'm not apologizing."

"No, but our family's all about sports, you know? Mom made out like Dad's business was evil because he wasn't around much. And then, when she took off, he quit, so…nobody said anything, but it was like being a businessman was bad. Being an athlete was good."

He could see that. Still, that hadn't been his issue.

"I'm just saying, I get it. You need more than this."

That's true. "Yep."

"I just wonder if your heart's in it."

His back straightened. "What's that supposed to mean? I just pulled off a—"

"I know. I saw. I just think Dad created this… mentality when he made that damn trophy case for my Olympic medal."

Brodie had been eighteen years old and weeks away from the Games when a childhood injury had reared up and forced his retirement.

"That was some kind of pressure to put on a kid, you know?" Brodie said. "Like I had any control over whether I'd get on that podium. And if I didn't…I'd have to look at the empty case the rest of my life."

"Yeah, but that came from Coach. He drilled it into us, about visualization. I think Dad just wanted you to have absolute confidence, like that medal was yours."

"True, true." Brodie still looked troubled. "But it wasn't, and now it sits empty, and…I guess I want to know why you're going for it."

"Who else is going to?" He side-eyed his brother with a mischievous grin.

"I'm serious, man. You don't give two shits about it."

"You think I don't want an Olympic medal?" He sure as hell did.

"I don't know. I'm asking."

"Don't strain your brain. It's not that complicated. I'm going for it."

"Yeah, okay."

He couldn't be pissed at his brothers for not being interested in his life and then shut them out when they asked. "On some level, I want the medal to honor Dad and everything he did for us. It'll close out an era, and we can all move on." *And figure out who we are outside of snow sports.* "But, also? I'm going to win it because I'm sick of you guys thinking I'm a fuckin' slacker."

Brodie cut him a hard look. "We only know what we see."

Well, he'd taken care of that, hadn't he? *Cat's out of the bag.*

"And if you're going to win it," Brodie said. "Then you'd better get your head in it."

He started to argue, but his brother was right. He dropped his head into his hands. "Got a lot on my mind."

"Work stuff?"

Last time he'd opened up about Knox, he'd gotten shut down. His dad's words still reverberated in his head.

Every minute you spend alone with that girl is a betrayal to your friend.

Walk away, son. No good can come out of this.

What if she falls for you? What happens then? You going to be boyfriend and girlfriend right in front of Robert?

And the worst one of all, *A man makes choices, not all of them easy. Listen to your gut. And if your gut's not telling you to keep away from that girl, then you're not the man I raised.*

Because his gut hadn't told him to walk away. And that meant he wasn't the man his dad thought he knew.

It meant his dad hadn't known him at all.

And now here he was, seven years later, right back in the mess of wanting a woman he couldn't have. Only this time, he'd gotten the taste of her. He'd mapped the flare of her hips and curve of her ass with his hands.

Sensation shot through him, practically lifting him off the bench.

Worse, he'd felt her surrender—if only momentarily. *There's no going back from that.* It might've been a mistake for her, but for him? It had been a game-changer.

He looked down at his boots, kicked a tuft of crab grass. "I've got a thing for Knox."

Brodie stiffened.

It shouldn't have felt this good to get it off his chest. "Always have."

"Back when she was with Robert?" his brother asked.

"Yeah." He let out a harsh exhalation.

"And now?"

"She doesn't see me like that."

Brodie looked at the inflatable ramp, watching some guys do flips. "Shit timing."

"Timing doesn't matter. She's just not into me."

"No, I mean running into her now. The next five months, you need your focus."

"I know."

"And you're not going to be around much."

"Yeah, I know that." He must've been a slow learner. Why the hell did he think it was a good idea to open up about this shit again?

Brodie shifted his ass back on the bench. "You're a winner. And not because you're lucky or a Bowie." Brodie turned and looked him right in the eye. "You're a winner because you're smart and you work your ass off. So, come back in five months and win the girl."

Knox felt the eyes in the restaurant on her like a thousand red ants swarming on her back. She wrapped her hand around the glass of ice water, wishing she could bring it to her temple to cool herself down.

The only thing keeping her from bolting was logic. Since she'd chosen the seat facing the wall, she couldn't see the patrons, but in all honesty, how many of them were her bullies from high school? How many recognized the back of her head and were ready to chuck their dirty napkins at her?

Besides, it was her first Ladies Night Out…ever. And the company was awesome.

"I gave it up at sixteen. To Fin." In her slim-fitting black leather pants, suede ankle boots, and magenta-colored blouse, Callie looked like a New Yorker through and through. Chic, gorgeous, and totally sophisticated. "It hurt. It was messy. And it was over so fast I didn't ever want to do it again."

"Truth." Delilah reached for her cocktail. "To the first time sucking."

They all raised their glasses. Knox tried really hard to play along, but she couldn't keep the creepy-crawly feeling at bay. Did anyone recognize her? Were they talking about her?

She needed to shut it down and pay attention to the conversation. The problem wasn't that someone would recognize her—she was honestly so over the immature idiots. It was that they'd embarrass her in front of her friends.

"I lost it to Saxton Montgomery, the third." Delilah made a comical expression. *Yup, I did that.* "This famous chef did a culinary program on Cape Cod the summer between junior and senior year. Sexy Saxy 'summered' on the Cape, and we met on the beach. He was tan and fit with floppy hair and—looking back—unnaturally white teeth."

Knox hadn't known Delilah long, but it was becoming clear the woman had no particular style. One day she wore kitchen clogs with leggings and a rock band T-shirt, another day she had on baggy boyfriend jeans and a slouchy cotton sweater, and tonight…tonight she rocked a dark red sweater dress that accentuated every curve on her voluptuous figure. She was a knockout.

"Sounds like boy-band hot," Calle said.

"Totally," Delilah said. "Anyhow, I crushed hard on him, showed up at all the places I thought he might be. Finally, he asked me out. Just the two of us for a fancy dinner. I thought it was weird, you know? Like, we're seventeen but going out to an old school fancy restaurant. But my sister goes, 'Well, he knows you're there for culinary school and wants to take you somewhere nice.'" She shrugged. "I bought it."

"Turns out he just wanted to get in your pants?" Knox said.

"Exactly. But it didn't work. That date was so boring, I immediately lost interest in him. God, he was obnoxious, talking about his dad's yacht and their second and third and fifteenth houses around the world." She faked a yawn, patting her mouth. "But I guess that got his attention, because the rest of the summer he worked hard to get me."

"He stopped being obnoxious?" Callie asked.

"He did. He dropped the act. We had some good moments. Until we finally did the deed." She lifted her eyebrows in a look that said, *Can you guess what happened next?*

"Don't tell me he ghosted you?" Callie said.

"Yep. Right after I slept with him. Never heard from him again."

"Oh, ouch. What a dick." Callie lifted her wine glass. "To good men who don't objectify women."

"To good men." All three clinked glasses

Callie tipped her chin to Knox. "I'm guessing you gave it up to Robert."

Knox hesitated. At the end of sixth grade, her class had taken a field trip to the community garden. She'd worked alongside Lisa Bettner. For the first half hour, Lisa had chattered nonstop, while Knox remained quiet.

Eventually, though, she'd found herself relaxing, and at one point, when Lisa had asked what her mom did for a living, Knox had said she was an artist. That she used scraps of metal she found in junkyards to make sculptures. It had all seemed innocent enough, until she'd gone back to school the next day and found herself tagged the junkyard dog, a title that had stayed with her until she'd left town at the end of senior year.

So, Knox didn't trust easily. But there came a point when a woman couldn't use her past as an excuse anymore. And that point was now. "I did."

Callie started to raise her glass and, while Knox was curious to hear what the toast might be, she cut it off when she blurted, "But I was too young."

The smiles abruptly died, and both women waited for more. Not in a salacious way but with interest and concern. "Robert and I were inseparable. His mom spent more time in Manhattan than Calamity, and his dad was always in Los Angeles, hanging out with starlets and getting high."

"What about your parents?" Delilah asked.

Oh, yuck, yuck, yuck. This is why I don't make friends

easily. Because I hate talking about my life. There was no fun way to spin her childhood. "My mom's got what her friends like to call a *joie de vivre.* Which means she lives for adventure. She hates to be tied down, so she's a seasonal worker and an artist. As far as my father...well, like I said, she's a seasonal worker, so, he was gone by the time she found out she was pregnant."

"So, you were alone a lot," Delilah said.

"I had Robert. We did everything together." She had great memories of those early years. Hanging out by his pool all summer, doing stupid diving contests and trying peanut butter on everything they could find in the pantry and refrigerator. They'd wander the hills and trails, free to say whatever was on their minds. "But then we reached an age where..."

"Hormones hit," Callie said.

She loved that they understood so readily and without judgement. "Exactly."

"Can I ask a weird question?" Delilah said.

Knox tried to nod, but it felt like her neck had been bolted on too tightly. She might be sharing but that didn't mean it felt good.

"Did you love him? Like, the way Callie and Fin were in love?"

Knox closed her fingers around the glass salt shaker in the middle of the table and tapped it against the pepper. "No." The word came out a whisper wrenched from a dank, secret place inside her. "I needed him. We were inseparable. But it was only after I left—and I mean a long time after—that I realized it had never been romantic love. I think we went from kids who hung out to me trying to keep him clean all the time. There wasn't a time where we could have been *in* love. Does that make sense?"

"Totally," Delilah said.

Callie nodded. "I get that."

"And the same went for sex. We had urges, and so we experimented with each other. It felt safe and totally comfortable. Like, we laughed through every awkward moment. I could tell him what he was doing that wasn't working, and it was like building a car engine together. Here, you do this, and I'll do that. Put this over here and that over there."

"…junkyard dog?"

Two words rose above the chatter in the bar. She could've misheard out of her own insecurities, but it sent a chill down Knox's spine. She forced herself to roll right through, barely missing a beat. "I know it sounds sad, but there was no better person to have all my firsts with." Because the addiction didn't kick into high gear until sophomore year.

"It is," a woman said. "I'm sure of it."

Was it just that her antennae were out and scanning for trigger words? Had to be. *No one's sitting in this fancy restaurant talking about you. Get over yourself.*

"Holy shit, you're right. It *is* the junkyard dog." The voice was loud enough to get Callie swinging around to see who was talking, so, unfortunately, no, she wasn't over-reacting.

In an uncharacteristically loud voice, Callie said. "Ignore them. People are assholes."

"What's going on?" Delilah leaned in, clearly aware of the tension.

The old Knox would've looked them right in the eye, flipped them the bird, and then come up with a plan for swift retribution. But, not only didn't she have the energy for that kind of crap anymore, she wouldn't embarrass Delilah in her elegant restaurant.

She would, though, prepare her in case things got ugly. Focused on twisting the ring on her finger, she said, "In school, they used to call me the junkyard dog." *Brace.* "And just to be sure I fully got the reference, they'd bark at me. My mom wasn't home a lot, so I got to hear it all by myself in the trailer as they'd drive by."

For a long, tense moment, neither of the women said anything. *So help me…*if she saw even a hint of pity in their eyes, she was out of there. Instead, Delilah grabbed both her hands, and said, "No wonder you haven't wanted to go out with us. I wouldn't want anything to do with these jerks, either." She gave them a firm squeeze. "I'm sorry. That's a terrible way to grow up."

"Want to get out of here?" Callie said.

"Nope." Now that the truth was out, the bullies couldn't hurt her anymore. "I'm good. Let's finish our drinks.

"Okay, so, back to losing it too young." Callie lifted her wine glass. "Here's to finding the right man to have mind-blowing sex with."

"Oh, here, here." Delilah squirmed. "Nothing so good as when it's the right guy."

"What about in Paris?" Callie asked Knox. "Did you have a hot Parisian boyfriend?"

Finally, something fun to say. "I did. It was never serious —believe me, I was working all the time—but he definitely wined and dined me. His family had a chateau in the Loire Valley, and we basically traveled all over Europe together."

"Arf arf arf."

A burst of laughter followed the yipping, and it rattled

her bones. Knox was stunned. Stunned that, at twenty-five, they hadn't outgrown their evil ways.

And then, a deeper, more booming voice, barked. Before Knox could even devise her eye-for-an-eye plan, Delilah shot up so quickly her chair actually toppled over. She strode the few feet over to the cluster of idiots laughing at the bar. In a quiet, but hard, voice she gestured for the bartender and said, "Settle up their tab right now, Clarence."

"Oh, we're not done," a man said.

"We just got here." *Cady*.

Knox would recognize the whine in that voice anywhere.

"And now you're leaving."

Wait, what? Knox had to turn around to witness Delilah taking up for her.

The man scoffed. "You can't tell us what to do."

"Sure, I can," Delilah said. "I'm the owner, and we don't serve juveniles here."

"You think I'm underage?" The man laughed. "You want my ID?"

"I want you out of my restaurant. Only a soulless person could bark at another human being, and we don't serve the undead. You're banned. For life."

Cady hitched her Louis Vuitton bag up her shoulder, the get-out-of trouble card played by so many daughters of rich parents. "Do you know who I am?"

"I know that you're a heartless bitch. Now, get out of my restaurant or I will not hesitate to make a scene and embarrass the hell out of you."

Chapter Eleven

The minute Knox walked in the door that evening, she tossed her tote onto the couch—the only surface in the entire room not loaded with sewing materials—and hit the kitchen. She needed tea. Warm, soothing tea.

Holding the kettle under the tap, it made her sick to see her hands shaking. She couldn't believe Callie and Delilah had witnessed the barking. Did Cady Toller have no life? Hadn't she had a single life experience that would've taught her some compassion?

God, she hated Calamity. Hated it. The kettle landed on the stove with a clatter, and she flipped the dial to high. Pulling down a mug from the cabinet, she dropped a tea bag into it.

To bark at her in a fancy restaurant…in front of Knox's new friends.

Horrifying.

Opening the bottom drawer, she snapped a square of chocolate off the bar she kept hidden in a piece of aluminum foil. When that first bite of dark, creamy goodness hit her taste buds, she pulled in a deep breath and took in the bunkhouse, crammed now with work stations.

Some of her employees left theirs a mess of fabric, scissors, and measuring tape. Others left not a single item out of place.

This is who Callie and Delilah know. Not the girl in the trailer.

I'm a fashion designer, and I'm kicking ass.

Well, in the bunkhouse on the Bowe ranch, but still. She wouldn't be here long.

The knock—no, pounding—on the door startled her. "Knox? It's Gray."

She hadn't seen him since they'd returned from LA. The morning after the kiss.

Her fingers brushed over her lips. *That kiss.*

"Knox?"

She quickly wrapped the chocolate bar back up and stowed it in the drawer, before hurrying to the door. All these hours later, and she could still feel the hot imprint of his hungry mouth.

"I'm coming." She sounded irritated when, really, she was thrilled.

She'd lain awake that night for hours, her body electrified, stunned that Gray Bowie wanted her with that kind of passion. But, also, scared witless, because nothing could happen between them. She would never compromise their friendship or their working relationship for a hookup—no matter how spectacular. And that's all Gray had to offer.

A scorching, unforgettable round of sex.

He just wasn't a relationship kind of guy.

Well, maybe he could make it work with someone in his posse, someone who shared his nomadic lifestyle. But she needed to be in one place, working.

She threw open the door. "What's the matter?"

He looked her up and down, chest rising and falling, like he'd heard she'd been attacked by a mountain lion. But he didn't say anything.

"What?" she asked.

"Nothing."

He'd heard. *Just awesome.* "Okay, well." She turned and walked away from him. Word had obviously gotten around about the barking, and the very last thing she needed was anyone's pity. "Come in. I'm just making some tea. Want some?"

"No."

Even before the kettle boiled, she poured the water.

He stood at the counter, watching her. "How's it going?"

"Good." She held the tea bag up by the string and dunked it just to have something to do. "Just...busy."

"Anything I can do to help?"

"No, I've got plenty of help. Everyone's doing an amazing job. I've just never run a whole operation. I design, you know? Luc was kind enough to let me see the whole process, so I learned a lot, but my focus has always been on designing."

He watched her carefully, like he was looking for scars. He wouldn't find them. They'd embarrassed her, nothing more.

"Amelia says requests are rolling in," he said.

"I'm going to have to start making some calls, but I've just been so busy." What Ethan had overnighted was enough to get them started, but the rest of the fabric would come in different shipments. "At some point, I should probably take down the request for information link."

"Why would you do that?"

"I've decided to follow Luc's lead. He makes eight couture dresses a year. That's what he's learned he can manage and still maintain his level of quality. I've already got three times that many requests, so it doesn't make sense to keep the door open when I won't be taking on any more projects."

"Sounds reasonable." He leaned forward, those inked forearms and strong wrists standing out against the black granite counter.

She wanted to trace the massive black wave rising out of a churning ocean. It was so vivid her fingertips itched to brush away the spray. "You know what your dad said to me once? He said, start out at the top. From there, the world's your oyster. But, if you settle for less, it's going to be a fight to get to the top."

One half of his mouth curled up into the cutest grin. "That sounds like him."

"So, what's up? What brings you by?"

"I haven't checked in for a while."

"You check in with Amelia and Zach all the time."

"I want to check in with you."

I miss you. We shouldn't let that kiss keep us from each other. She should just put it on the table, whisk away the weirdness. "It was a good kiss."

Color spilled into his cheeks, spreading like a sunburn to his earlobes. There was something incredibly sexy about a boyish vulnerability in an extremely masculine, powerful man.

It gave her the courage to go on. "It might've been the best kiss I've ever had."

He swallowed hard, making his Adam's apple jump. "But…?"

"But we can't cross that line."

"Right. Because…?"

"Because I like you. I like you better than anybody I've ever known." Although Delilah had leapt to the top of her list tonight. "And we work together."

Need crackled in his eyes. He wanted her.

Would she ever get used to the idea?

His fingertips tapped on the granite. "And I'm leaving soon." The four simple words sounded like he'd pried them out of his throat with a tire iron. And, yet, he kept that nonchalant stance of his, like nothing mattered.

But *she* mattered to him. She knew it not just because of what he'd told her that night in the hotel room, but because for the very first time she could read the truth in his eyes and the tension in his body. And it was just so profound that she could see the world through something other than the bully lens. That she could see desire in his eyes and not aggravation or pity or whatever she might have interpreted in the past.

"Gray." She didn't even know how to deal with such a volatile cocktail of emotion. Affection for him, because it sank deep that she wasn't—had never been—a pity project. Attraction, brand new, but potent and alive, like magnetic waves of energy flowing, colliding, *sparking* between them.

And fear. God, it scared her to death to have romantic feelings for a man like Gray.

She could fall so hard for him.

"We're on totally different paths," he said.

Love was complicated for her. Her mom hadn't been reliable. She was the type of person who checked in with her daughter—*You good?* Texted pictures of her adventures, woke her up in the middle of the night to watch a meteor shower, and routinely stood at the sink to shovel dinner into her mouth before "heading out." She sought her own pleasures in life, and while she cared about Knox, it was in a detached way.

Other than Robert—and that hadn't been healthy— Knox hadn't really loved anyone else.

What she felt for Gray was so much richer, deeper, more profound, because it involved her head and her heart, her body and her soul. It had the power to consume her.

"Right." He tapped his knuckles on the counter. "So, that's it. Glad everything's going well." He turned abruptly and headed for the door.

Panic fluttered in her chest. She set her mug down. Logically, she was making the right choice. But in her heart, she was freaking out. She didn't want him to go, didn't want this distance. She'd meant to bring up the kiss to dispel the weirdness between them but managed to drive him away with a conversation about the impossibility of a relationship.

You're expert level at driving this man away.

Right when his hand closed around the door knob, she gave him what he'd come for. "It was awful. Tonight. Like tumbling back through time and being that girl again." She came around the counter but didn't move any closer to him.

He tensed, his whole body hard and alert. He tipped his forehead to the door. "I fucking hate that they did that to you."

She shrugged. "They made fools of themselves." And then she smiled. "But you should've seen Delilah. She was fierce."

"Yeah?" Slowly, he turned toward her. "That's what I

heard. Good thing she was there. Otherwise I'd be in jail right now." He opened the door and strode out onto the porch.

Don't leave me. Stay, and we can lay in my bed on our backs, our feet against the wall, sharing a pack of cherry Twizzlers.

He sailed off the steps, landed on the grass, and turned to her, walking backwards. "Can you get away tomorrow morning?"

Happiness danced all over her skin. "Of course. What for?"

"A little field trip. Be ready at eight."

"Shouldn't you be training?" In the old days, Knox would be in nothing but a T-shirt and jeans. Today, the sharp chill in the air had her wearing a down jacket. She hadn't lived in the mountains in a long time.

"Got in a few hours this morning. I'll be back at it this afternoon."

At a bend in the trail, she let him stride ahead of her. Mostly, because she wanted to take in all his rugged badassery. She'd always noticed his arms—who wouldn't? Bulging biceps and hard forearms inked with unique and sexy art—but she'd never imagined them lifting her against the nearest tree. His hands on her body, skimming down her bare back and gripping her bottom.

The sizzle ripped through her, making her hairs stand on end.

No, she'd never imagined him doing *that*.

Since that kiss, though, it was all she could think about. "Where're you taking me?"

"To my house." He glanced at her over his shoulder. "Is that okay?"

"You don't live in the main house?"

The canopy of pine trees cast a dark, cool shadow over the trail, and a gentle breeze made the branches shush overhead.

"Nah. That's for Will and his family. Ruby doesn't need a pile of us living there. She needs stability."

The trail widened, and she caught up with him. "So, you...bought a place?"

"Built it."

"You built a house?" Was there anything this man couldn't do?

"Over time. It was just a little project."

"I'm going to guess your brothers don't know about it." He opened his mouth to answer, but she cut him off. "And don't say they never asked."

His deep rumble of a laugh kicked her pulse up a few notches. "They know. They helped build it."

Their shoes crunched over pine needles, and the air smelled like rich soil and damp forest. He went quiet for a minute, and she could tell he had something on his mind.

When they emerged into bright sunlight, he said, "Been thinking about your business. You ever consider building a digital platform?"

"Oh, my God, Gray. If I left it to you, you'd build me an empire." She smiled. "You know you're pretty amazing, right? You don't have a girlfriend, and I doubt your brothers tell you, so I just want to make sure you know."

His fingers flexed, and for just one second hers automatically reacted, reached, as if he'd meant to grasp her hand. But, just as quickly, he balled them into a fist. "Just thinking about financial independence."

Well, that rang like a bell inside her. "I think you know how much that would mean to me." She'd never dreamed of being rich. Didn't really need much to be happy. But she did want *enough*. Enough to pay her bills and not have to struggle. "What're you thinking, exactly?"

"Every year two and a half million people get married. That's seventy-five-billion bucks of revenue in the US and three-hundred billion globally."

"You've done your research."

He snapped a bright yellow flower off a shrub, gave it a brief sniff, before handing it to her. "But bridal's the slowest growing arm of the fashion industry, because it's just not adapting to digital trends. And this generation seems less interested in marriage—specifically, in spending money on a ceremony. They'd rather spend their money on adventures." He cut her a look. "Did you know sixty-four percent of brides use Pinterest? There are thirty-eight million boards about weddings created by brides."

Tucking the flower behind her ear, she said, "I didn't know the exact number, but I'm on there a lot. I like to see what brides love."

"Yeah, so, while the rest of the fashion world's adapted, the bridal sector's dragging its heels." He shrugged. "Which is dumb, because the vast majority of your buyers are technological natives, so you're missing out on a huge sector."

"That's because there's a different level of craftmanship to a wedding dress. It's a different animal."

"Okay, still. Wedding gowns are a two-point-five-billion-dollar industry, and you could tap into that by going digital."

"It's a good idea. Maybe one day I will."

"I just worry that, in making this 'couture' designation your goal, you're not seeing the broader picture."

"You want an Olympic medal. How is that different from me wanting to hit the highest level in my business?"

"Is it the highest level, though? I guess I'm thinking the highest level is having your brand the most sought-after in the marketplace. In any event, I'm not steering you away from your dream. All the big names have multiple lines. I'm suggesting you have something going at every level. I'm talking about creating a digital atelier."

Oh. That was interesting.

"Nothing really changes. You'd still do the pop-up show and the custom orders, which leads to your eventual runway show. But the money maker, the business we'd build behind the scenes, that's the digital shop."

"It's interesting, but I'm not looking for an empire just yet." She had her eye on the prize. *Jack Abrams, come at me.*

"I get that. But it's a way to make sure you never have to work for assholes like Luc again."

"He's not an asshole." He could be petulant and immature, but Gray didn't understand him the way she did.

"Yeah? You hear from him since he blacklisted you from the suppliers?"

"No." That sharp look he'd just given her meant she'd had more hurt in her voice than she'd intended. "You have to understand. He plucked me out of the mass of students graduating fashion schools all over the world, and then he took me in and mentored me—in a way he's never done with anybody else. That's so incredibly rare and special."

"That's because *you're* incredibly rare and special." The

158

trail intersected with a gravel driveway, and he turned onto it. "Your talent is."

"Gray, I quit my job. I left that amazing, once-in-a-lifetime opportunity he'd given me, and he still supported me. He gave me my dream." The reminder that Bridal Fashion Week was three weeks away, and she wouldn't be there, still stung.

"He did it to get more designs from you. No matter how you spin it, he's an asshole."

"No, he's a businessman."

His eyebrows hitched up. "You're saying your relationship was strictly business?"

"Of course." The lie pinched her heart. "What else could it have been?"

"When you first moved to Paris, did he have you over for dinner?"

Oh, dammit. Don't do this. "Yes, but I'd never been overseas before, never been away from home." But, of course, she'd been away at college for four years, so that wasn't exactly true.

"He get you presents on your birthday?"

She nodded.

"Did he get them for his other employees?"

No. "I don't know what he did in private. Everyone got a fabulous gift basket for Christmas with soaps and candles and macarons."

"But he gave *you* something special on your birthday?"

Again, she nodded. What could she say? Luc had made her feel—

"So, he pretty much positioned himself as family."

Hearing the truth out loud was like taking a sip of too-hot coffee. It scalded. "I don't know about *family*. But he looked out for me."

"And, again, I'm going to ask, did he do that with other employees?"

"Maybe he did." Why was she even arguing? Was she really going to hold onto some sense of loyalty when she knew without a doubt Luc had behaved differently with her than he had with anyone else? "No, he didn't." There's no way he'd dropped by anyone else's apartment with chicken noodle soup and a baguette, a brand new Kindle, and a bouquet of flowers when they'd been down with the flu.

Which is how he'd had access to your sketchbook.

That galvanized her. "He did try and make me feel special. Everyone else had to come into work every day, but he understood my creative process and gave me the freedom to run with it." She glanced at him. "I can't work in a cubicle with all that noise and activity around me."

"You get distracted."

"Exactly. So, he let me work at home a lot. Well, not literally at home. I walked for hours, watching people, looking at buildings, touring museums. He saw the results, so he gave me the space to create, the exposure to all the things that sparked my imagination." She looked at his handsome profile. "I thought he was encouraging me by bringing me presents or food or whatever. At the time, I didn't think he was manipulating me."

"When did you realize he was?"

"After he stole my private sketchbook. From my apartment."

"Fucker. He wanted your talent, so he groomed you to be loyal to him."

"No, I mean, he was always perfectly clear. When he gave me a gift, he'd always say he was offering sacrifices to the Gods so that I'd create a dream collection for him. He was honest about it."

"Except when he stole your designs?"

"Yeah, that…that was awful. But my point is that he was very upfront about what I was to him. He'd flat-out say, *This line's going to make me a superstar*. He never pretended to be doing me any favors."

Thick foliage, heavy with white and yellow flowers, bracketed the driveway, and the forest grew denser.

"But the fact that he'd blacklist you means he thinks you owe him something," he said. "And I'd bet my future gold medal that he thinks you do *not* because he was generous enough to back you in fashion week, but because he worked so damn hard to make you feel like family. I bet that doesn't come naturally to him."

"Considering how little that medal means to you, you make it too easy to take that bet."

"Why do you say that?"

"Because you're twenty-five years old, Gray. You could've been in two Olympics by now. Not to mention you're taking me on a field trip when you should be at the gym." No matter what he said about getting a work-out in…it was still eight in the morning.

He chuckled.

"No one else on the Olympic team would take a day off for anything other than an emergency."

"I'm running a business. Besides, it's just a few hours."

"Pretty sure your work ethic is going to give your coach an aneurism."

"Fin's not fond of my work ethic, but he respects my results." Right where the driveway curved, blocking the view of what lay ahead, Gray stopped and looked at her.

"But that's the point, isn't it? You keep pushing me away to see if I'm going to bail on you, too."

Yes. It was like biting into a fiery pepper, the heat burning a path all the way down to her stomach. *He's right. That's exactly why I keep pushing him away.*

They continued on, and the road gently crested, revealing a fairytale pine forest. Nestled in the center sat a charming log cabin. Bright purple and red flowers danced in a breeze in the window planters, and a stone walkway led to a wide, wraparound porch.

"Gray." She took in a sharp breath. "It's gorgeous." Leaves fluttered overhead, and she felt totally encased in the cool shadow of the pine trees. "I can't believe you live here."

"I like it." He held her gaze, like he wanted to say something. Instead, he pressed his lips together, the muscle in his jaw working. There was some kind of powerful meaning in his eyes that she couldn't read. It was a little tortured, a little pleading, and painfully vulnerable. "Now, come inside and let me make you breakfast." His voice sounded rough, gravelly.

She glanced at his home, aware that somewhere deep down, she thought maybe she did understand.

She was just having a hard time believing it.

Chapter Twelve

Knox soared, her hair flying around her face.

"Flip," Gray called.

But she hadn't gotten enough air, so she dropped back down and, this time, sprang off the trampoline even harder. Arms pumping, she urged her body higher.

"Come on, Knox. Do it."

Coming back down, she punched the surface with both feet and took off. *There you go.* Hurling herself forward, she performed the most awkward flip of all time. She landed on her back, bounced, and started cracking up.

"You have the grace of a puppy running on ice." Gray bounced onto her trampoline from an adjoining one, making her flop around. He kept jumping, his torso straight as an arrow before twisting in ways no human body should go—more proof of his insane core strength and stamina.

"Stop." Unable to take being tossed around, she crawled to the edge, turning just in time to watch him execute some quick, twisty maneuvers.

He kept going, jumping ridiculously high, bending his

legs and turning sideways, then rotating once, twice—*oh, my God, a third one?*—before landing and doing it all over again. Watching him, her chest got tight, and her pulse flickered in her neck.

He was…everything. Powerful, confident, kind, thoughtful, protective…and she wanted him. So fiercely, her whole body seized with it.

Tonight, he'd found her alone in the bunkhouse. He'd brought her burgers and fries from Skeeter's, and they'd eaten them outside in the purple twilight. When she'd mentioned she hadn't exercised since the day she'd left Maui, her routine of surfing and yoga destroyed along with her dresses, he'd brought her to the training facility.

Bounding onto the trampoline nearest her, he curled up tightly and did three fast flips in a row before landing on his back. He held out a hand. "Come here. Let's look at the stars."

"We're indoors, genius." But she lay down beside him anyway.

"For a creative sort, you're not all that imaginative."

"I think it has something to do with the fact that you filled my belly with greasy fries and burgers and then made me shake it all up on the trampoline."

"I haven't seen you laugh since I crashed into your living room. I call it a win."

"You, Gray Bowie, are pure win."

He rolled onto his side, hiking up on an elbow. "Tell me more about my awesomeness."

She loved being with him like this, when it was just the two of them alone, no cares, no worries. "I think you're my most favorite face in the world."

"I know you're mine. Always have been."

Oh, Gray.

"What's that look for? Do I make you uncomfortable when I say things like that? Because I spent a lot of years shutting it down, and I don't want to do that anymore. But I know you don't feel the same way, so if it makes you uncomfortable, I'll stop."

She rolled to her side and faced him. "What do you mean, 'you know I don't feel the same way?' Are you sick in the head? Gray, you are seriously the hottest, smartest, kindest, most handsome man on the freaking planet."

"Well, yeah." He gave her a smug smile, and she poked his ribs. "But that doesn't mean you're attracted to me. Attraction isn't intellectual. It's visceral. It lives in the body, not the mind."

Underneath that lazy smile and sleepy eyes lay an alertness that phrased an unspoken question. And the idea that Gray Bowie lived with that kind of doubt hurt her. "You're not giving the mind enough credit. How we see the world comes from our experiences."

"What does that have to do with chemistry? You're either attracted to someone or not."

"What if your mind shuts down even the possibility of that attraction?"

"Why would it do that?"

"A bunch of reasons."

"Like?"

"Like…maybe you couldn't imagine that the guy would ever be interested in you, and so your mind doesn't list it as an option. Life does a number on us, Gray, and it twists our perceptions."

"What're you saying?"

He wanted her to say it out loud. He deserved that. "I'm saying that I never imagined in a million years you'd see me as anything other than a hot mess."

"But you weren't a hot mess. Knox, I don't know where you got that idea. Cady and her friends envied your sense of style. It killed her that you owned Robert so completely that she could strip naked and still not get his attention."

"What now? Who stripped naked?"

"Remember that night you told me to go find Robert?"

"I remember a hundred of those nights. Which one?"

"You might've asked me a hundred times, but I only went once. I found him at Kevin Bowman's house. He was having one of his usual parties, the whole place jammed with people, everyone wasted. Robert was there. Of course, he was the life of the party. And Cady was grinding on him."

"And he let her?" A prickly heat spread through her. She'd always believed Robert had been true to her. "When was this?"

"Beginning of senior year. She had her hands all over him, whispering in his ear."

"And you just stood there and watched him cheat on me?"

"How many times did you ask me if he was fucking around on you? You had no idea what he did when he was wasted, and I was sick of hearing about it, so I let it play out. To see what he did. Anyway, something she said got his interest, so he followed her into the room off the kitchen. I saw her dig around in her purse and hand him something."

"What a bitch. She gave him drugs just so she could be with him?"

"Yep, and he didn't even look at it, just popped it in

166

his mouth. Then, she pushed him back onto the couch and straddled him. Pulled off her top and bra."

"You never told me this. I can't believe it. Why would you not tell me?"

He held up a finger. *Hang on.* "I got my answer, and I knew if I didn't leave right then I'd smash my fist in his face, so I turned to go. But then I heard him say, 'Ya done yet?' And she goes, 'Oh, honey, I'm just getting started.'" Gray raised his voice to sound like a lusty woman.

"Cheesy."

"And Robert said, 'Good, now finish by yourself.' He got up and knocked her on her ass and said, 'You think I'd touch you when I have Knox? You're out of your fucking mind.'"

"He said that?"

His smile faltered, and he seemed to search for something in her eyes. "I never went looking for him again. He never cheated on you."

Knox closed her eyes, doing a full body scan for any residual emotion where Robert was concerned. Nothing. "I was so messed up. My obsession with him…God. I wanted so desperately for him to be normal. I wanted him…"

"To be there for you, like he used to be."

"I thought I could save him, and it made me a hot mess. It's just…my circumstances were so different from yours, you know? In my mind, it wasn't even a possibility that you could be attracted to someone like me."

"Well, hopefully that kiss cleared it up for you, because I'm still attracted to you, Knox, and I'm not going to bullshit you about it. The question is…" He trailed his fingertips along the inside of her forearm. "Are you attracted to me?"

Goosebumps exploded along her arm, racing up to her neck, and cascading down her body, but she wouldn't let Mr. Smugness see. "Please. We're pals, nothing more." But he wasn't stupid. He had to hear the tremor in her voice.

"Hm. Interesting." He leaned over, looking into her eyes. "I had no idea your eyes were black. Oh, wait. They're dilated." He gently brushed his fingers over her collarbone, his thumb teasing her pebbled skin. "Are you…attracted to me?"

She squeezed her thighs together. "I mean, you're okay and everything, but…" Her expression said, *Meh*.

"That right?" He shifted closer—but not quite touching.

His body heat, his scent, that intense look in his eyes…*God*. She tried to act nonplussed, but it didn't work. Heat rushed up her neck, and desire pulsed between her legs.

"Let's test it. If you're not attracted to me, this won't take but a minute." He lowered his face into the crook of her neck. "Do me a quick favor? Inhale. Real deep. Get a lungful of my pheromones."

"Shut up." She tried to push him, but he was solid as granite.

"I just want to see if my scent works for you. Go on, breathe me in."

"You're such an idiot. Get off me."

He lifted his head, bringing his mouth right to her cheek. "I'm conducting an experiment, and I'm going to need you to stay very still. Quit squirming." His lips brushed across her cheek—barely touching—until he reached her jaw line. Then, he glanced up at her. "Okay, that's fascinating. I'd hoped for some pink, but you're beet red. That's way beyond blushing, sugar buns."

"Okay, we're done here."

"Not yet." He gently cupped her jaw. "There's one last study." The moment their gazes met, the mischief turned into pure, unadulterated lust. "This is the one that counts." He brought his mouth over hers and kissed her.

Everything inside her turned creamy and hot. She wanted to slide her hands through all that thick, unruly hair, wanted to feel his hard, muscled body on top of hers.

But fear had a grip on her. *It's Gray.* She didn't want to know such extreme pleasure, get attached to a man who thrilled her, comforted her, wanted her, and then watch him walk away.

They didn't have a future. Anyone could see that. What would happen after he left for his first competition? Got back into his familiar world of traveling from one country to another, one event to another?

She could have one night with him, maybe two. Three, four, what did it matter? Her heart and soul would get engaged, and then he'd be gone.

Gray pulled away, the pad of his thumb on her mouth, looking utterly crestfallen. "It's okay."

What's okay?

"I was just messing with you." He started to roll away from her, and she realized she'd zoned out, let her fears stand on the mountain of her insecurities and plant a victory flag.

She grabbed his shoulder and yanked him back. His big, hard body fell half on top of her. God, did it feel good. *More.* Her hands threaded through his hair. "*Gray.*"

That was all it took to unleash him, just the sound of his name drenched in urgency and need. His mouth opened over hers, and he licked inside, his big hand clamping down on her hip and drawing her closer. He kissed with such fervor, she got swept away, the undertow so powerful it drowned her insecurities. She clutched his broad, powerful back. *He feels so good.*

His hand slid underneath her, caressing down to her bottom and then squeezing with such lust she literally writhed against him.

How had she ever thought he lacked passion? Holy smokes did he have it—and what a heady feeling knowing he had it for *her*.

When he cupped her breast, sensation burst so high and bright it actually hurt. She needed him, needed more. And he gave it to her. His hand slipped under her blouse, his palm splayed flat on her belly, and he caressed up her ribcage, mindless of the buttons that ripped free of their bindings and flew off.

Shifting her onto her back, his big body loomed over her. He lowered the edge of her lacy bra and closed his mouth over her nipple. Electricity ripped through her, making her arch off the trampoline. He sucked hard, tongue lashing. When she crashed back down, she hitched her leg over his hips, drawing him down to connect the parts of their bodies that were made to join. His tongue pulled, flicked, and she grabbed fistfuls of his hair, holding him to her.

Cupping her breasts, he drew them together, thumbs flicking her nipples, all while his erection rocked against her belly. He watched her, his expression heavy with need and a desperate question. *You want me?*

"Yes." The single syllable came out a breathy whisper.

His hand coasted down, pushed beneath the elastic waistband of her leggings, and curved between her legs. Her hips pumped, need climbing into desperation.

A finger grazed her clit, and she tipped her head back

on a cry. He ran gentle circles over her hard bud. "Oh, my God, Gray."

His hand pulled out, and he grabbed the waistband of her leggings, yanking them down, taking her panties with them. Jacking up her knees, he spread her thighs, and the next thing she knew, his hot, wet mouth covered her, his tongue licking her into a pulsing, burning frenzy.

Clutching fistfuls of his silky hair, she made sounds she'd never made in her life, but she didn't care. Lost in sensation, she slammed her hips against his mouth.

The climb toward ecstasy had her hips twisting, her toes curling. Electric heat drenched her body, pleasure reaching such an unbearable height she had to close her eyes to witness the explosion of a star, its fiery particles soaring through her. He stayed with her until she collapsed on the trampoline and let out a long, satisfied breath.

When all her pieces gathered back together, making her whole again, she opened her eyes to see Gray's smug expression. "What?"

"Nothing. Just pleased with the results of my study."

"You ass." Laughing, she shoved him off, but her heart was pounding, and her chest got tight.

Everything's fine. Chill out.

She couldn't calm down, though, as unnamed fears churned, gaining momentum, building into a full-blown panic attack.

What's the matter with you? Get a hold of yourself. You're fine.

But she wasn't fine at all. It had taken years to build a good, sturdy wall to keep her heart safe, and Gray—this generous, sexy warrior—was crashing through it.

She had no protection from him.

And when it went sideways…

God, she didn't even want to think how devasted she'd be.

———

The moment Gray stabbed the sweet potato, steam wafted out. He dragged the tines of his fork across it to let it cool down.

Knox. Every time he thought of her, it tripped his nerve center, sending a rush of sensation through him. He could still feel her soft skin under his fingertips, smell the floral scent in her hair.

He'd captured the sounds she'd made, trapped them in a little corner of his mind, just so he could replay them whenever he wanted. He'd seen Knox happy, sad, angry, frustrated, embarrassed…he thought he'd seen her every expression.

But he'd never seen her come. Never seen her eyes roll back in her head, jaw slack with pleasure, lust making her cry out in sheer ecstasy.

It had been awesome—all the way up until she'd come down from her high, and she'd shut down on him. And he wanted to know why.

Maybe she thought she didn't deserve him or some shit like that. She seemed fixated on the idea that, because he lived in a big house, and she'd grown up in a trailer, somehow they weren't suited. Like he gave two fucks about where she lived or how much she had in her bank account?

He was crazy about Knox Holliday. Now, more than ever.

"What's that stupid expression for?" Brodie came into

the kitchen and went straight for the refrigerator, jerking it open. Jars rattled, as he pulled out a bottled water and twisted the cap.

"I was just imagining your face when the dude puts the gold medal around my neck." Gray scrunched his features like he was bawling.

"That was cold." He tipped the bottle toward his brother. "And beneath you." He wandered over to the island. "What's that?"

"What's it look like?" Like they didn't eat sweet potato on a daily basis in this house.

"Why're you eating it at…" He shot a look at the rooster clock over the stove. "One in the morning?"

"Because I'm hungry?"

Brodie stretched his arms out on the counter. "Know where I've seen that expression before?"

"In the mirror every morning when you think about me getting the job done for you?" He could only joke because Brodie had stopped caring about the Olympics a long time ago.

"That would be incorrect. And petty. I see it on Fin and, now, on Will. Little red cartoon hearts popping out of their chests every time they think of their women." Brodie's lips twisted in disgust. "I don't get it. Fuckin' Fin's been with one woman his whole life. One." He shuddered like he'd just been offered the brains of a dead antelope. "And *Will*. What happened to him?"

"Delilah's cool."

"Yeah, but you don't have to get all domesticated over her. Keep her in the friends-with-benefits zone. She lives here, runs the restaurant. He can see her whenever he wants. Why lock her down? For *life*?"

"Because he doesn't want anyone else."

His gaze snapped over to Gray. "You say that like you understand."

Gray gave a one-shouldered shrug.

"What…" His brother straightened, tapped his water bottle on the offending shoulder. "What was that?"

"Nothing. People fall in love. That's the way of things."

"No, that's the direction society herds us in. That's what movies and books and conservative politicians *tell* us is the way of things. The truth—the real truth? Is that we're programmed to fuck. Which results in procreating. Then, we've gotta hang around till the kid's three, maybe four, before we can move on again, spread our seed far and wide. It's evolution. Look it up."

Thankfully, the curl of Brodie's lip let Gray know he was just messing with him. "Why do you like to grind my gears?"

His brother tipped the bottle to his mouth. "Because your ears get all red." He drained half of it, then dragged the back of his hand across his lips. "And it's cute as fuck."

"So, where does love fit in this brilliant evolutionary theory?"

"Love's transitory."

"Is that right?"

"Of course. By nature, feelings don't last. You get pissed at someone…it fades. You win an event, you're elated…gone a few hours later. Same with love."

"You ever stop loving Dad?"

Brodie's eyebrows slammed together in a scowl. "We're not talking about familial love. We're talking about romance. And, I can tell you from experience, romantic feelings don't last."

"How the hell would you know?"

"I've had feelings."

Gray cracked a smile. "That right?"

"Sure."

"But other than the feeling in your dick…?"

"I've dated." He lifted both arms in a gesture that said, *Obviously.* "And I happen to know a lot more about it than you. You've never dated anyone."

"You might want to pull out a dictionary, because I'm positive none of the women who've gone out with you would define 'one-and-done' as dating."

"Hey, man, a date's a date. Doesn't matter if it means grabbing a coffee, going to dinner, or spending the weekend together."

"Have you ever even asked a woman out?"

"I've *gone* out."

Gray laughed. "Let's face it, brother, most of the time you don't even know you're 'dating' someone until she tightens the noose. The only thing that gets your attention is when she tries to lock you down. Introduce you to her parents or make you go to a dinner party with her friends. Two seconds after she pulls that trick, the woman you're 'dating' finds herself out on her ass."

"You're talking about Dana. Come on. I was focused on getting Owl Hoot up and running. We'd gone out twice and suddenly she's making me come to her sister's rehearsal dinner? What was that?"

"You'd gone out with her for six weeks. You just weren't paying attention."

"I was busy."

"Fine. But, trust me when I tell you, when you meet the right woman, you'll notice. You'll notice every damn thing about her."

"And now we get to the goofy expression. Does Knox know she's the star of your fantasies?"

"The goofy expression was hunger." He stabbed his fork into his cooling potato. "I'm eating."

"Clearly, you didn't take my advice. You do realize you're leaving in three weeks."

"Got it on my calendar."

"So, you just want to get her out of your system…?"

When the back of his neck tightened and burned, Gray knew he didn't have to bother responding. His expression said it all.

"Hey, just asking. Sometimes, once you hit it, you figure out it isn't all that."

"It isn't like that with her."

"She's talented." He said it like he was making a concession. "Sharp, too."

The burden lifted. "Right? And I like hanging out with her."

"And she's hot."

Gray shot him a look.

"But she's not the girl for you."

He wanted to say, *You don't know shit*. But he couldn't, because it rang true. And he needed his brother to say it out loud for him. "Why do you say that?"

"She's got one foot out the door."

She does. "She's basing her business here."

"For now. Until she gets back on her feet." Brodie's expression turned serious. "You know it as well as I do, man. This town's too small for her."

Chapter Thirteen

It struck Knox, as she pinned another layer of muslin on Callie's dress, that something sleeker, more sophisticated might work better for the elegant woman. She wouldn't say anything, of course. Callie knew her own mind, but Knox couldn't stop imagining a different, more refined style.

Someone laughed, and Knox looked up to find Zach and Amelia talking together. A couple of sewers clustered in the kitchen, picking at a pan of brownies someone had brought in, while the others worked hard at their stations.

Most everyone knew each other. They were either Cooters, the retired men and women who gathered every morning at the local diner in town to catch up with each other and hang out, or somehow related to them.

They always brought in leftovers and cookies and cases of soda. Everyone worked hard, but when they took breaks, it was filled with laughter and food and lively conversation.

She liked it a lot, and it gave her a whole new impression of Calamity. One that included awesome people like Callie and Delilah.

And Gray. The memory of last night kept replaying in her mind, and every time she'd get a shock to her system. Gray had been ravenous for her. His hands gripping, caressing, his tongue so greedy.

Who knew she and Gray would be so good together? So…combustible?

Over the hum of the machines and chatter, someone called her name. She glanced up to find Zach waving her over. She set the pins down and headed over to the long dining table. To accommodate the work stations, they'd had to remove the game tables and couches, and, basically, turn the place into a warehouse. "What's up?"

Zach had a glint in his eyes. "A new order just came in."

Nothing unusual there. "Cool. As soon as I finish the muslins for Callie and Delilah, I'll start calling the brides."

"We might want to call this one sooner." He paused. "Have you heard of the MacAllister twins?"

"Of course." They'd been at Columbia University at the same time Knox had been at FIT. The daughters of a Wall Street titan, they'd somehow managed to graduate with honors, while spending their every waking moment shopping and partying.

"They want you to design their wedding gowns."

What? "Me? Are you serious?"

"That page you created was a stroke of genius. We've almost hit a hundred thousand followers."

"And it brought us the MacAllister sisters?" She could hardly believe it.

"This would obviously be extremely high profile. I don't think we should pass on it."

"No, definitely not." Making dresses for them would absolutely get Jack Abrams's attention. "I'll call them right now."

"Good idea."

"I can't believe this. They could get a gown from Hayley or Bellerose or Vera. Why me?" As soon as the words left her mouth, she knew what she'd done. So, she answered before giving Zach a chance. "Because my gowns are amazing."

He smiled and shook his head, like he couldn't believe she didn't get it.

But she was starting to understand that, for all her confidence in her talent, on the deepest level, she didn't feel worthy of the MacAllisters.

Or of Gray. She didn't believe herself worthy of his love. But who should he want? Someone prettier, more successful, athletic, rich? *Because if you boil it down, the only thing I don't have is family and money. Who cares about those things when you're talking about love?* Lord knows he had enough of both--he sure as hell didn't need them from her.

And whose gowns should the MacAllisters choose over hers? *Mine are special.*

They're sensational.

"Brace yourself," Zach said. "If you score this job, you're going to become the "It" girl in the bridal world."

"I have to finish Callie and Delilah's dresses first."

"Oh, trust me, it'll take the sisters a while to settle on a design."

"You're right about that." She knew from Luc's atelier that anyone spending that kind of money took her time and got involved with every step of the design process.

"Could take months."

"I can't believe the response we're getting to this social media campaign." She glanced up at him. "Boy, am I glad I haven't followed up with the requests that've already come in."

"Looks like you'll need to be selective." He smiled. "All right, let me get you that number."

She was heading back to her station, when the door swung open, bringing in a gust of autumn-scented wind, all dry leaves and crisp air. In strode a man she didn't recognize, holding a tablet and wearing khakis and a flannel vest.

More people spilled in after him. An efficient-looking woman in black slacks and a tan sweater and a man in a short-sleeved white shirt with shiny gold badges and patches on it. *Fire chief.* Warning flares shot off in her brain.

Hurrying over to find out what was going on, she approached the group with a smile and her hand extended in greeting. "Hello, I'm Knox Holliday. How can I help you?"

The man in khakis looked around the room, up at the ceiling, and down the hallway. "Mike Fairchild, Town Inspector." He nodded to the woman beside him. "Elaine Tailor, Fire Inspector." And then gestured to the man on her other side. "And Chuck Bailey, Fire Chief."

Oh, shit. "What can I do for you?"

"Do you have a permit to run a business out of this building?"

An awkward laugh tripped out of her throat. "Uh, no. This...this is all new." The three of them just stared at her with impassive expressions. "Sorry, I'm a fashion designer, and I was getting ready for my first show when a car crashed through the window of my house and mowed down my dresses. So, I came out here—I'm from here, actually; I grew up in Calamity—to fix them. That's what we're doing." *You're babbling. Stop talking.*

"You've got employees." The woman scanned the work stations, before looking up at the ceiling. "Do you have sprinklers? Exits?"

"I don't...know. Like I said, I pretty much just got here. It's temporary."

Footfalls pounded on the porch steps, and a massive ball of energy stormed into the room, causing her guests to whip around. In running shorts, sweaty T-shirt, and hair tousled from the wind, Gray reached out his hand. "Mike. Elaine." He gave them a lazy smile. "Chuck, good to see you. What's up?"

Stern faces softened. They all shook hands and chattered for a moment. Knox cut a look to Zach. *Are we up shit's creek?*

"Gray," Mike said. "You know you can't run a business out of this place, right?"

"We're going to take a look around," Elaine said.

With his back to her, Gray reached behind and found Knox's hand, giving it a squeeze. "Sure thing. Let me take you on a tour."

Zach mouthed, *Without a paddle.*

Thunder boomed in the distance, and Gray looked up to the darkening sky. They'd known the storm was rolling in, so they'd tried to visit as many properties as they could before it hit. *Good thing this is the last one.*

The real estate agent slid a key into the lockbox. "I've

been trying to rent this space for a year, and I've had no takers."

What the listing called an industrial park was really a series of five connected buildings located halfway between Calamity and Jackson. Personally, Gray liked the remote area. Just across the highway was the Bison Sanctuary, a flat stretch of grassland that ended at the dramatic upthrust of the Teton Mountain range.

Right as a raindrop hit his cheek, he followed the women into the building and stood inside the empty, cavernous room. The wide-open space would be perfect for their operation. He listened as the agent answered questions and talked up the space, but mostly he watched Knox.

She'd been knocked sideways when the inspectors had shut her down.

It had sucked, but at the same time, he'd gotten a fierce hit of respect for the way she'd handled it. She'd shifted straight into fix-it mode. Without a word, she'd gone to her laptop to look up real estate agents.

"Why can't they rent the space?" Knox asked. "Is it the location? I mean, it is in the middle of nowhere."

"That's exactly why," the agent said. "The moment anything in town goes on the market, it's snatched up by a business that appeals to tourists, skiers, hikers, hunters… that kind of thing. Thanks to Owl Hoot, we've got new breweries opening up, restaurants, outfitters, you name it, but this location's no use to them. It's too far out. The good news is that you can get a great price and a flexible lease. In fact, the owner will love you because you've got so much growth potential. These walls are removable, so when you're ready, you can expand into the next space."

"It's so pretty from the outside," Knox said. "It doesn't

look like an industrial park."

"Oh, it did. Three years ago, when it opened, it had a karate studio and a shared office set-up. Neither business cared about the façade. But, after they left, a big furniture store expressed interest. They needed a huge showroom, and there's nothing in town with that kind of space. Of course, they didn't think their high-end customers would give them a chance when it looked so bleak, so the owner tarted it up. Put up all that dark wood and fancy fittings. Unfortunately, the furniture store decided to open in Idaho Falls, and that was that."

Knox nodded, her gaze seeking his. He gave her a firm nod. He liked it a lot.

The agent caught the exchange and said, "Okay, I'm heading back to town. As soon as this storm passes over, I'm showing the Hellerman Ranch." She slapped the key in Gray's hand. "I've known you since you were in diapers, so I trust you'll lock up. You know how to put it back in the box?"

Gray pocketed the key. "Sure do."

"Great." She headed for the door. Before, she left, though, she turned back to them. "Knox, honey, I made this our last stop today for a reason. I wanted you to have other spaces to compare this one to, so you'd see what a great deal it is. If you want to hold off, wait for something new to come on the market, that's fine, but I guarantee you won't find a better space for the price."

Knox made an effort to smile, but anyone could see she was having a hard time. "Thank you so much. I'll be in touch soon."

"You got it." The moment the agent opened the door, thunder exploded, and rain pummeled the metal roof. "Oh, goodness," she shouted, before dashing out.

He reached for Knox, clasping her delicate wrist. "What do you think?"

"This is definitely the best place."

Not: this is the one I'm going to lease. She was hedging. "Do you want to keep looking?"

"No, I don't have time to wait for another property to hit the market."

"Then what's the problem?" He wanted to press a kiss to her pulse point, but he checked the impulse. After she'd shut down on him last time, he didn't know where they stood. "Talk to me."

"I guess I just need some time to think. Leasing a building is a huge expense, and one I hadn't considered."

He understood that. "Would it help if we called a meeting and went over finances?"

A clap of thunder startled her. It sounded like the skies unloaded a dump truck full of gravel on the roof. "I don't think that's necessary. I have to relocate, and I'm not going to find a better price. It's just… Remember at the trailer, you asked if I'd want to do fittings there? Well, the same question applies here. Can I imagine my customers coming here? It's not exactly—"

"An atelier."

"No." She tipped her head back and blew out a breath. "But, also, it just sort of drives home that I'm committing to living in Calamity. God."

Brodie's words slammed into him. *You know it as well as I do, man. This town's too small for her.* He couldn't force her to stay—he wouldn't even encourage her. It had to be her choice. He let go of her wrist and took a step back. "I heard about the MacAllisters. I knew big things were coming for you, I just didn't know they'd come this quickly. But here we are. And now you've got to make a choice."

The next boom rattled her so badly, she let out a shout of frustration. "No, I know this is the right choice. It's just a little scary. Leasing a *building*? Hiring all these people? Salaries, benefits, maternity leave…it's a big deal."

"It is. I can't do anything about the location, but one thing we might consider is taking on equity investors."

With two fingers, she rubbed her temple. "Yeah, maybe. I have a lot to think about."

It struck him, what was troubling her. "If you sign a lease, you lose the option to take off when Chanel calls."

She gave him a weak smile. "I think you know that was more a fantasy than a real possibility. No, I'm staying here for at least a year. Signing a lease, though…it's just throwing me off a little."

"Let's call a meeting, so we can talk about it as a team. That's where the great ideas come from, when we're all together in a room, bouncing ideas off each other."

She nodded vaguely, like she was humoring him. "I need a little time alone to wrap my head around all this. It's just how I work."

But she wasn't humoring him, he realized. How had he not seen this from the start? He could change pronouns all he wanted, but she could only think in terms of the personal, because it was all she'd ever known.

Maybe it wasn't about Calamity or couture. Maybe it was just the overwhelming responsibility of being the top of the pyramid in her life. No parents or siblings…no one to catch her if she failed.

It was so far out of his realm of experience, that the idea was deeply unsettling. He knew, no matter what, he had his brothers, his uncle, the ranch. Friends. His inheritance. For one stark moment, he swiped them from his world, imagined himself like Knox, completely and totally alone.

It was…devastating. Just as she turned from him, he caught her arm. "You're not alone. We're all in this with you."

"I know." But she sounded about as firm as dandelion fuzz.

"No, I don't think you do. Knox, look at me. We're in this with you."

"Look, I'm going to sign a lease. I just…I need to look at my finances and think about the location. I need some time to work through it all."

Yeah, he was pretty sure he'd gotten it right. It was the vast well of loneliness she lived in, with only her voice and thoughts echoing against the walls. He cupped her beautiful face in his hands. "You're not alone. You've got us." *Me. If you'll have me.*

She didn't look at him.

He lowered his hand right over her heart, the heel of it pressing down on the plumpness of her breast. "I need you to hear me, Knox. Not just in your head, but in your heart. You're not alone. We're in this together. You and me. All of us. We're with you."

She knocked his hand away, the fire back in her eyes. "That's so easy for you to say. But I saw Amelia's bag. She might look like some free-spirited surfer girl, but she comes from money. This is fun for her right now, because it's new, and it's got so much potential, but it's not her career. It's not her life. You don't understand, because you're in the same situation. There is no rock bottom for either of you. If this fails, it's no big deal. You can move on or *dabble* in something new."

He opened his mouth to challenge her, but her fierce expression shut him up.

"Zach left Hugo Rossi to work with you. He could get a call from Ralph Lauren and take off..." She snapped her fingers. "Like that. You're leaving for New Zealand in a few weeks, and your posse might just decide to go with you. And they can. They can, because there's nothing at stake for them. They can walk away from my business and not lose a single night's sleep over it. So, no matter what you say, the bottom line is I'm very much alone. And that's not a complaint. I'm just saying that I'm the only one completely invested here, because it's my career, my *paycheck*. Without it, I have nothing."

"I don't know what bag you're talking about, but Amelia's parents run a bait and tackle shop in Key West. If she owns an expensive purse, it's because she makes enough money at Duck Dive to afford it. We work hard, and we play hard. As for me..." He went into freefall, like flying off the edge of a cliff and hoping like hell he landed on a patch of snow and not rock, but he forged ahead. He'd hidden the truth long enough. "I have loved you since I was six years old. Every second you spent holding Robert's undeserving hand, every time you got into his truck and drove off with him, it felt like ripping my heart right out of my chest."

"*Gray.*" It was the most vulnerable he'd ever seen her, and it touched him.

"But now that I've had you to myself, I can promise you, whatever I felt back then doesn't come close to how I feel today. Do you understand what I'm telling you?"

"I think so." Her voice came out soft, almost incredulous.

But she didn't trust it. "Then let me make it clearer. It's

more than liking you, which I do. I like your passion for your work, your drive and ambition. I like the way you are with Zach, Amelia, Callie and Delilah, the way you really listen to them. It's also more than being attracted to you, which I am." Anxiety covered him like a fog. Exposing himself to a woman who didn't feel the same way…it could not turn out well. But like hell if he wouldn't take his shot. "It's that my cells are formatted for you. My heart…" How did he explain it? "My heart beats in rhythm with yours. I loved you as a boy, but as a man who's spent time with you, kissed you…this is a whole other level. You might've imprinted on me as a kid, but you're in my blood now. Whether you want me as a man or a business partner or as nothing more than a friend, I'm committed to you. To us."

Beneath the wariness, the thrill of his message shimmered in her eyes. "I don't know what to say."

Then he'd show her. Tipping her chin, he lowered his mouth to hers. He kissed gently, wanting her to feel how much he cared. But the minute her lips softened, parted, and he got a hint of wet heat, he licked inside, and that damn pounding in his blood to own this woman, body and soul, overtook him.

Her scent filled his senses, hurling him back in time to dry summer days when they'd hiked the Bowie Pass, after school in her trailer, laying side-by-side on her bed, feet braced against the wall, as they'd held stupid and hilarious conversations through her Etch-a-Sketch.

To the kiss in the hotel room, when she'd lost control and clung to him with desperation.

To the other night on the trampoline, her hips twisting, fingers pulling his hair. The sounds she'd made from his touch.

With the clatter of rain on the roof, he lost himself in the intimacy of the moment, the privacy…the seclusion. He deepened the kiss, his tongue searching for acquiescence…surrender.

Want me, Knox. Want me as much as I want you.

Jesus, fuck. He'd said it out loud, his voice, deep, growly, like a command.

Everything changed in that moment. She got up on her toes and threw her arms around his neck. "I do." She pressed closer to him, her plump breasts on his chest, her hips shifting restlessly over his painfully hard erection. "God, Gray, of course I do."

His body rejoiced in the invitation. He kissed her, his hands caressing down her slender back and over the rising slope of her ass. When she gave a desperate moan, he lost it. Clutching those firm, round cheeks, he held her tightly to him, bending his knees slightly, and rocking up into the space between her legs.

With a wild look in her eyes, she wrenched her mouth away and said his name on a sigh. "I've never felt anything like this. It scares me, Gray. It scares me so much."

"I got you. I swear…I got you." *Trust me.*

She went wild, hands gripping his hair, kissing him with a fervor that made his composure slip, then fade away. He needed more.

Right the fuck now.

He carried her to the wall and pressed her hard against it. One part of his brain still probed, flashed, waiting for a signal that she didn't want this—because he'd lived with the belief that she didn't return his feelings for so damn long—but her urgency, the desperate sounds she made told him she wanted him every bit as much. He'd never felt so plugged in, so alive.

Hitching her up so he could balance her with one hand, he cupped her jaw and deepened the kiss. She fisted the hair at the back of his neck so tightly it hurt, but knowing she was that turned on? It was fucking everything.

His hand shifted lower, until it closed over her breast, cupping and caressing. She arched her back, pressing her core against him and grinding. He had to have her, had to. His hand shoved under her sweater but got tangled up in all that material.

"Wait." Crossing her arms over her chest, she lifted it up and over her head and sent it sailing. Pressing her shoulder blades against the wall, she arched her breasts to him in invitation.

"Fuck, Knox. Gotta have you." He peeled back the cup of her bra, and all that peachy flesh spilled out, the nipple puckered and hard. He covered it with his palm and rubbed his thumb over it, so fucking turned on by her response.

"Gray. God." Her legs banded around his waist in a possessive hold.

He dove in to kiss it, licking and sucking, as she gasped.

"I've never…I can't…" And then she cried out in frustration.

It sent a spasm of need through him, and he set her down. He ripped open the buttons on his jeans, tipping a chin to her leggings. "Off."

She stripped out of them and kicked them away, her pink panties tangled in the black. Grabbing his shoulders, she pulled him back and kissed him with a hunger that only fueled the ageless, burning desire he had for her. Thunder rumbled, lightning flashed, and electricity tore down his spine, lifting the fine hairs at the back of his neck.

He grabbed her ass cheeks, hauling her tightly against him. "I want you like I've never wanted anything in my life, but I don't have a condom."

With her gaze on his chest and her hands roaming greedily, he thought for a moment she hadn't heard him. But, slowly, she reached for the back of his neck, sifted her fingers through his hair, and whispered, "When was the last time you were with someone?"

Oh, fuck. He reached between them, squeezing his dick to relieve some of the pressure. But nothing helped. He was desperate for her. "Not since spring, when I was tested at the training facility."

She batted his hand away, rubbing his erection with the heel of her hand. "You didn't hook up with anybody during Titans?"

Sensation exploded in him, and he wrapped his hand around hers. *Harder.* "No."

With a half-lidded gaze, she circled the head of his dick with her thumb. "You feel so good."

He needed to come so badly, but even more, he wanted her hands on him. "You'd just come back into my life. You think I wanted some random piece of ass?"

Her complexion, clear and smooth, turned pink, and everything in her softened. But it was that little sigh of pleasure that did him in. He needed her now. With bent knees, he lifted her off the ground and pressed her against the wall. "We doing this?"

Her hands clasped behind his neck, her body trembled as she licked her lips. "Yes, God, now."

Gently, he lowered her onto his cock. He slid in, nice and slow, because he'd waited a lifetime to see the look in her eyes when he filled her. And it was worth all the agony to watch her eyes go lazy, to hear her sensual, erotic moan.

He took his time, so he could feel every nerve-ending in his cock light up as it passed through her slick, hot channel. *Holy fuck.* She felt so good, smelled so good, everything about her just made his heart sing.

"Move, Gray." She pumped her hips.

It might be his only time, so he needed to savor every moment of pleasure. He sank in all the way and then eased back out. *Yes. Jesus, yes.*

"More…need you…" Her voice had gone wispier, her ass wriggling.

Then, with a snap of his hips, it was on. He couldn't hold back anymore. She felt too good, too right. This woman…everything about her called to him, drove him wild.

"Yes. Oh, yes." She moved in rhythm with him, skin slapping, urgency rising.

The heat their bodies generated had their scents mingling, combining in a potent perfume of lust. And he knew—he just fucking knew—this was it. It would never get better than this.

Her legs tightened around him, her hips tilting, swiveling. "Gray." Her voice came out breathy.

Oh, fuck, yes. So hot. She felt so good. So fucking good. Every thrust drove him closer to the edge. The slap of skin against skin, the hot surge of her desire coating him, drove him closer to ecstasy.

Her hands clutched his back, while her hips slammed against him, meeting the fervency of his thrusts. "Oh, my God. Oh, *God.*"

He was so close, on the edge, but he needed to bring her there with him. Needed her to *crash* with him.

"Knox." The sound came out a whisper, a plea. Her chin jerked up, and the moment she caught his gaze, a sting of awareness burst in his chest.

She looked so sexy, so soft and sweet, and catching her in this unguarded moment made him feel so fucking tender toward her. The intimacy was almost too much, too intense. And he knew she felt it, too, because she closed her eyes, fingers digging into his back.

Look at me. He thrust hard, and her eyelids flew open. While he had her right there with him, he reached between their bodies and found her sensitive nub.

Still watching him, she spasmed. "*Gray.*"

Flames singed his scalp, his balls drew in tight, and the base of his spine tingled. The roar of his orgasm powered through him, transporting out of his body, and he let out a shout so loud it echoed in the room.

She grew more frantic, her hips twisting, until her head fell back on a cry with her release. He slowed his pumps, desperate to stay inside her, to stay connected, but he pulled out and lowered his head, trying to get control of his heart rate.

Limbs still trembling, he sucked in a breath. He couldn't believe it. Couldn't believe he'd finally been with Knox…*Jesus.* It had been better than any fantasy he'd ever had of them.

But, while he was riding his high, she was gathering her clothes. "We should probably go."

All the liquid heat in his veins froze at her tone. He reached for her arm. "Knox?"

She shook her head with a fragile smile. "I'm sorry. I'm just…confused and a little lost and…I don't know. Let's just go to the real estate office right now."

Chapter Fourteen

THE STORM HAD PASSED, LEAVING PUDDLES AND dripping leaves. Of course, in a mountain town like Calamity, a little thing like weather didn't deter tourists and locals from coming out and enjoying the town. Bazoo's Mercantile, with its regional gifts and souvenirs, always did a lively business, and the diner was packed with families seeking an early dinner.

As they stepped outside the real estate agency that faced the town green, Gray wanted to pump a fist in victory—Knox had just signed a lease. One glance at her dazed expression, though, dampened his mood.

He didn't know what he could say to make this commitment easier for her. "That was brilliant. I can't believe you got them to go month-to-month."

"Well, we did christen the place. It wasn't like they could lease it to anyone else." Her smile sparked, then died.

"You want to grab some dinner before we go home?"

"I should probably get back to work. I can't afford to

fall behind, and I won't have any help until I can move into the new space."

"What if each sewer takes a machine home and continues working? We could move some of them into the main house. There's plenty of room there. Keep a couple in the bunkhouse, another at Fin's. We could…"

He stopped when he caught her expression. Fond? Actually…a little adoring. "What?"

Grabbing a fistful of his shirt, she tugged him toward her. "You're amazing, that's what." She planted a kiss on his mouth, then wiped the lipstick off with her fingertips. Hope rushed him hard. Until she said, "Thank you."

He didn't want her fucking gratitude. He wanted her to be in this with him—for it to become natural for them to stand by each other, help each other, love each other.

But that kind of closeness took time. Time he wouldn't have, once competition season started. Snugging an arm around her waist, he lowered his mouth to her ear. "There's no obstacle anyone can put in front of us that we can't tackle together."

She gazed up at him, reading into the depths of his eyes. "I'm starting to believe you."

That's all I can ask for. "Come on." He headed in the direction of his truck. "Let's get you back."

They stepped off the sidewalk and crossed the street to the town green. In the summer, there'd be live music; in the winter, sleigh rides. Now, a couple huddled in the gazebo, hands wrapped around Calamity Joe coffee cups, while their two little kids in bright yellow rainboots stomped in puddles. Two teens held hands, as they strode purposefully across the wet grass.

"I still can't believe he did this to me. You know?" She

gazed up at him. "Like, he had to come up with this plan, do an internet search for Calamity, find our town hall...he put such an effort into ratting me out. It's just so...extreme."

Luc. Knox had jokingly asked the town inspector if someone with a French accent had tipped them off. The way his expression froze gave them their answer. Gray doubted they got a lot of calls from Parisians reporting a nefarious business operating out of the Bowie ranch. "He sounds like a punk."

"He's trying to close all my doors, so I have no choice but to go back to him. That's never going to happen. He can go fuck himself." She stopped right there on the sidewalk. "You know what? I don't want to go back to the bunkhouse and eat some cheese and bread. I want chicken enchiladas at the Tavern. You in?"

He loved the gleam in her eyes. "You going to spring for guacamole and nachos?"

"Might even toss in a margarita." She turned back and headed toward Sweet Baby Jane's.

But the moment they hit the sidewalk, she towed him into an alcove and pushed him against the wall. She threw her arms around his neck. "You are..." She drew in a breath and held it for a moment. "Gorgeous. And amazing. And I..."

Is this a brush-off? It sounds like one. Gorgeous, amazing...those are empty words. She could use them on any number of people. "Yeah, I know. You're not looking for a relationship. It's fine. We're cool." He glanced away. "Let's grab some dinner."

"Wait. I want to say something."

Please don't.

"I'm scared. I'm leasing a building in the town I swore

I'd never come back to. My dream's still in reach, but the path has changed completely, and I'm just…"

Yep. Not looking for anything serious.

"I'm falling for you, Gray. In a big way. And that scares me more than anything." She placed both palms on his chest.

Oh, fuck, yes. He wanted to tell her she didn't need to be scared. That they'd figure out everything together. But she needed to get there on her own. "I'm in this, Knox. You have to know that."

"It's just…it feels so dangerous. More dangerous than anything else I'm doing." Worry hardened into determination. "But I want us. And maybe that's what's so terrifying. How very *much* I want us to work out."

"I do, too." *You have no idea.* "This is good, Knox. We're good."

"We are. It's never been like this with anyone before."

For one ugly moment, Robert reared like an apparition between them. And it was time to address it. "That's not exactly true. You and Robert had more good years than bad."

"As kids, we were each other's secret treehouse, but as teenagers…I didn't *like* him."

Anxiety churned its way through his guts. "What're you saying?"

"I'm saying this…us…. This is magic. I've never felt anything like it before."

Relief breezed through him, clearing out the unease and tension.

"I just want you to know that…I never thought in a million years I could have you like this."

When she gestured to his half-hard cock, he burst out laughing.

Her features colored. "I don't know why I pointed there. I'm saying—"

"I get it, and I'm glad you laid it out there." His mouth sealed over hers, and he kissed her.

It wasn't sweet, it wasn't a public display of affection. It was a deep-in-the-night, two-bodies-under-the-covers, take-what-you-need burning, wild passion. And it made his scalp tingle, and his dick go hard.

"You make me crazy." He pulled away before he lost himself completely. "Let's get some dinner." He headed out of the alcove.

He almost couldn't believe this was real. He had his heart.

His whole heart.

Sweet Baby Jane's Tavern was rockin'. Live music by the stone hearth mixed with the loud conversation at the town's busiest bar.

The moment they walked in, the hostess came around the podium to greet him. She gave him a hug. "How's it going?" When she pulled back, her gaze shifted to Knox.

"Great." He watched carefully for a reaction. Tara hadn't grown up in Calamity, so he doubted she knew about Knox's childhood reputation. "Your mom feeling better?"

Whatever she'd been thinking about Knox, her attention snapped back to him with gratitude. "She's out of the hospital, but I think she finally learned her lesson."

Gray gestured toward Knox. "Knox, this is Tara. Her mom broke her hip."

"We keep telling her to slow down. She's eighty years

old and still rappelling." She rolled her eyes. "So damn stubborn."

"I'm sorry she got hurt," Knox said. "But she sounds pretty cool."

"Gray," someone called.

Turning, he found a group of old friends from high school gathered at the bar and waved.

"Let's get you to a table before you're swarmed." Tara pulled two menus out of the pocket on the podium and lead them through the restaurant.

A warm, delicate hand brushed his, and he startled. Looking down, he watched as Knox twined her fingers with his. She held his hand like it was the most natural thing in the world, like they were an old couple, and it sent his blood racing, his heart pounding. She didn't know what the simple gesture meant to him.

He'd waited a lifetime to have her like this, so if he gripped her a little too tightly, he couldn't have stopped himself.

In a rush of emotion, he brought their joined hands to his mouth and kissed the back of hers. He didn't delude himself for a second that she'd stay here. He knew she was bound for better things. She'd become a star, like Luc, and base her business in New York, Milan, Paris. *It's what she's always wanted and what she deserves.* He'd never hold her back.

But, maybe, by then, he'd go with her.

As they wove their way across the crowded, noisy restaurant, people giving him chin nods and waves, he imagined a life with her. He could see waking up with her every morning and talking about their day over dinner at night. But the in-between times—that's what he couldn't see. Because she'd be working nonstop. And, if he left

Calamity, what would he do? He loved his mountains, his family, his lifestyle. He'd always figured he'd run his business from the ranch and help Fin out at the training facility. He supposed he could run his business anywhere.

He swiped it from his mind. He'd figure it out when the time came. Now that he had her, he would do whatever it took to steer them toward a forever.

Tara led them to a small table in the corner and set the menus down. "Enjoy your meal."

"Thanks." He started to pull out a chair, when Knox reached for it. It took a moment for him to understand why she'd want to face the wall, but when he did, his anger spiked. Cady should be glad he hadn't been in the restaurant the other night. Delilah had handled it a whole lot better than he would have.

One day she'll be celebrated in this town for the beautiful, talented, woman she is.

Once seated, she pulled her napkin out from under the silverware. "How does all this attention not go to your head? You're like a movie star."

"Hardly."

"Please. You're gorgeous and charismatic. Not to mention you're the hometown hero, bringing home the gold."

"That won't get much traction until I'm actually on the team. Then, it'll be a big deal. It's really more about the meme. It brought a lot of attention on all of us." His phone vibrated. *Fin. Shit.* He pulled it out of his pocket to read his brother's text.

Where the hell are you?

He'd blown off afternoon training. He wrote him back. *Dinner.* He'd only meant to spend a couple hours looking at spaces, but then…things had taken a turn, and he'd lost track of time.

I'm sorry. I blew it.

You better have a good reason.

He did, but he wasn't telling his brother about it. *Town Inspector shut Knox down yesterday. Had to find a new space for her biz.*

Did you?

Yeah. Signed a lease.

Good reason. Should have told me. Been waiting around with my thumb up my ass.

Sounds uncomfortable. Unless…you're into that kind of thing?

Fuck off.

But bailing on his brother wasn't cool. *I should have called you. I'm sorry.*

OK. See you in the morning.

He pocketed his phone.

"Everything okay?" Knox asked.

"Forgot to tell Fin I wasn't training this afternoon."

She immediately looked guilty. "He must be so frustrated. Well, now that I'm settled, I won't be taking up so much of your time."

"I'm good."

"You're driving Fin crazy."

"I know." And it wasn't right. Gray needed to make a decision. He either gave Fin a full commitment, or he freed his brother up to work with other athletes. "I'll fix it." Candlelight flickered on her lovely features, and he knew right then he'd already made his choice.

He wouldn't give up his time with Knox, not for anything.

"I wish your dad could be there to see you on the podium."

"Me, too." He'd dreamed about it as a kid, seeing his dad's face in the crowd at a fencing competition, beaming with pride. Or in the audience at one of his jazz concerts. He'd get that medal, and it would be great—but it would never be the same as having his dad there.

She caressed the back of his hand. "Where did you just go?"

"What do you mean?"

"Everything in you just softened like butter in a microwave." She smiled. "Tell me."

"Nah. Just…I can see it, you know. My dad's expression when the scores come up on the board. When I step off the podium and make my way right to him."

"He'd be thrilled."

"Hey, Gray." The waiter appeared with a water pitcher. "What can I get you guys to drink? And when I say you guys, I really mean your friend." The guy gave Knox a long-suffering look. "And please tell me you're more fun than the Bowies, who only ever want water."

She took a quick scan of the drinks menu. "How about a blackberry mojito?"

"Now, that's what I'm talking about. I'll be right back with your cocktail and to take your order."

They both picked up their menus, and Gray said, "What looks good?"

"You do." She reached for his knee under the table. "I hope it's not stupid to say it. But I can't remember when I've ever felt this happy."

He lunged across the table, cupped the back of her head, and kissed her. Against her mouth, he said, "Say more of that. Every single time shit like that comes into your head, say it out loud."

"I won't get much work done," she murmured, before resuming their kiss.

Jesus, she got him so worked up. The gentle caress of her fingers on his jaw, the lick of her tongue on his lower lip.

"Well, look at this," a way-too familiar voice said. "If it isn't my two favorite people in the world."

Shock blasted through him, the report so powerful Gray jerked back in his seat.

"*Robert?*" Knox's voice was filled with confusion, surprise, and a hint of fear.

Gray forced himself to stand, though his limbs felt like sandbags. He reached a hand out. "Hey, man."

Robert Granger, Junior, looking healthy and fit, smirked at the hand, grabbed it, and yanked Gray in for a bear hug. He squeezed just a little too tightly. *A message?*

"Great to see you, man." Robert released him and turned his attention to Knox.

Between the rainstorm, Gray's hands in her hair, and all the drama of the past couple of hours, she hadn't had time to shower or change her clothes, but her tousled hair and creamy complexion made her the most beautiful woman Gray had ever seen. Her loose sweater had slipped, revealing a bare, slender shoulder.

Watching the couple reunite…it pierced his heart with a razor-sharp knife of fear. But her mouth was still wet from his kiss, and a surge of want crashed over him. He wanted this woman, wanted her more than anything, and he could not believe Robert had come back into their lives right when he'd finally gotten the chance to be with her.

"Jesus, Knox." The smile left Robert's face. "Look at you." He reached for her.

Jammed between the table and the wall, she stood awkwardly and leaned into his embrace for an upper body hug, but Robert bestowed a brilliant smile to the couple at the table next to them. "Excuse me, I haven't seen this woman in seven years, and an air kiss is just not going to cut it."

His usual charm worked its magic, and the elderly couple smiled. "You lay one on her," the man said.

Robert tugged Knox into his arms, closing his eyes and hugging her with the relief of a man who'd just been reunited with his long-lost love.

Knox's body remained stiff, and when she started to pull away, Robert tightened his hold and murmured in her ear.

She broke out in a smile. *You could always count on him for that.* No matter how fucked up a situation got, Robert could always make people laugh. And Gray saw the moment his heart relaxed in her ex's arms, the moment she leaned into him.

"It's so damn good to see you," Robert said.

All Knox had ever wanted was a sober Robert.

Gray felt sucker-punched. He wanted to flip the table over. Was this reunion going to turn into a reenactment of their childhood, with Gray the third wheel, wanting her from afar again?

No. No. And hell no. He wasn't going back to that, not for anything.

He'd learned his lesson. *You can't make someone love you.* She either wanted him or she didn't.

Slow your roll, man. Seven years was a long damn time. Besides, hadn't she said she'd never loved Robert romantically? That she'd been tied to him because of their past?

Yeah, she had.

Gray was done watching them murmur and giggle with each other. He clapped Robert on the shoulder. "Hey, man, how long you in town?"

Knox pulled away, her features flushed.

With a sly smile at her, Robert said, "Depends on how things go."

And there it was, that rumble of energy between the two men. *Competition.*

"Hey." Robert cupped her cheek. "You all right?"

"Yeah, of course." Looking annoyed, she pulled back. "I'm just glad to see you looking so healthy and strong. It's nice."

"What'd you think?" Robert straightened, jammed his hands into his pockets. "I was living in the underground tunnels of the subway system? Passed out with a needle hanging out of my arm?"

She gave him a hardened look. *Yes, actually, I did. Why wouldn't I?*

Robert turned to the couple behind him. "Sorry. Let me grab a chair real quick, get out of your way."

Gray motioned for a passing waiter. A moment later, the man dropped a chair into the tight space, and all three sat down.

"So, what brings you back to town?" The last time Gray had seen Robert was at his dad's funeral three years ago.

"Are you making movies with your dad?" Knox asked.

"Guess you don't read the rags." Robert pointed to Gray's water glass, *You mind?* When Gray nodded, Robert nearly drained the glass. "My folks divorced a couple years ago. Big scandal—I'll fill you in about it later, but yeah, his funding dried up." He gave a self-deprecating laugh. "Hollywood didn't work out."

"I'm sorry to hear that," she said. "I know how much it meant to you."

"It's for the best." The way he leaned in, turning his shoulder just slightly, blocked Gray from the conversation. "I'm clean. Sober for seven years, so being around my dad…not a good idea."

Gray inserted himself into their warm and fuzzy reunion. "What're you doing now?"

Robert sat back in his chair, legs splayed out, one arm resting on the table. "I'm in fashion."

"You work for your mom?" Knox sounded surprised.

Robert nodded. "Should have done it from the start, right? It's hard enough to make it in Hollywood, but with a pothead dad? Who's burned through every connection he's ever made?" Knee jackhammering, he grabbed a fork, turned it over and tapped the tines on the table. "Shows you how messed up I was that I chose him over The Granger Collection."

Seemed strange that Mrs. Granger wouldn't mention her son in their conversation. Considering the relationship, it seemed an obvious thing to bring up.

"What do you do for them?" Knox asked.

Easy to check. He'd look up the corporate website when he got home. Any hint of guilt he might've felt about not believing his old friend, who appeared alert and clean, didn't stick. He'd learned long ago addicts couldn't be trusted.

With his attention on tapping the fork, Robert said, "I'm not full-time yet. I've got to prove myself to my mom. In the meantime, I do contract work for them.

I'm hoping to be Creative Director for one of their lines."

"I had no idea you were interested in fashion." Knox tugged on the cuff of his dress shirt. "Look at you, Mr. Burberry."

"Man's gotta look the part in this business." He flashed a charming grin. "But, no, I can't say I've ever been interested in fashion. I'm *very* interested in a career, though. I've wasted enough time, and I want to get some traction. The family company's my best path."

"Have you looked into the different jobs, though? Creative Director will be tough to land at Granger's without a degree in fashion or experience in the field." Knox shook her head. "Listen to me, giving you advice five minutes after seeing you again."

"No, it's cool. Tell me."

"It's just that the Creative Director's the one who comes up with the overall vision for the house's lines. And that takes into account the marketing and advertising strategies and retail environments. You'd need those skills. I used to work for a fashion house, and I can tell you they'd never hire someone who didn't have deep experience and a history of success."

"Luc Bellerose?" He said it with a sly grin.

She nodded. "I don't want to discourage you. Just the opposite. I want to see you succeed and, without the right background and experience, Creative Director might not get you on the track you want quickly enough."

Setting the fork down, Robert drummed the edge of the table with two fingers. "What job would?"

"Honestly?" Knox said. "I'd start as an intern. Learn every aspect of the business and figure out where you want to work. You've already got the advantage of being a

Granger, so it wouldn't take as long for you as an outsider. But I honestly don't believe any successful person would just hand over a prime job to someone—even her son. I think you could prove your sincerity by learning her business from the bottom up."

"I can't say I want to start as an intern, but I hear you. I'll think about it."

"It's good to see you so motivated. It's nice."

"Back when you knew me, I was only interested in my next score." He paused. "And you."

She lost her smile. "In that order."

Robert dropped his hands into his lap, and his shoulders slumped. All his shine dimmed. "I know what I did to you guys." He cut a look to Gray. "And I don't blame either of you for bailing on me. I put you both through hell, and you sticking with me as long as you did? That says a lot more about you than me. But I'm going to make it up to you."

"You don't have to make anything up." Though Gray was pretty sure the comment was meant for Knox.

"I'd just like to see you happy and healthy." Knox patted his arm.

Robert nodded deeply. "I can do that. There's also one more thing I can do for you." A smile burst his features wide open. "I can get you into Bridal Fashion Week."

Chapter Fifteen

Knox felt like she'd stepped right off a curb into oncoming traffic. "What did you say?"

Robert sat so close their knees bumped under the table. "Got the run-down from my mom." He tipped his chin toward Gray. "That's what brought me out here. Heard my two best buds were working on a project together."

The temperature in the restaurant soared to tropical. She wanted to fan herself with the napkin. "Robert, it's three weeks away. There's not a chance in hell we can get a show together by then." *Is there?* Whatever words came out of her mouth, he'd already tossed propane on the fire in her belly. *Could* he pull this off?

"Why not?"

Of course, he couldn't. *How?* He knew nothing about the fashion industry. "Because it's a huge production. It took a year to put together the show I lost." She cast a look to Gray, not wanting him to feel bad about it.

But she didn't see guilt. The man was stricken. *Oh, Gray.* She needed to make sure he understood this reunion didn't impact *their* relationship. And, though she was sure the kiss had gotten the message across, she needed to show Robert, too.

She gave Gray a warm smile and held her hand out to him. He grasped it.

"I think we can do this." A light shone in Robert's eyes. "I've run it by some people. Look, it's New York City. For the right amount of money, finding a venue's a no-brainer. Hiring models? With all the agencies out there, no issue at all. Everything else, with Granger's connections… we've got this. Piece of cake."

"More like a whole ten-tier wedding cake," she said. "It's a production and, even for a smaller show, it takes six months to build a set."

"Does it have to be that elaborate, though?" Robert asked. "As long as you have the dresses, you can leave the rest to me."

Excitement buzzed, and she wanted to stomp it out. It was cruel of him to make it sound so do-able. She should shut down the conversation, but she couldn't help herself. "I don't think it's a problem to have one of each dress ready. We'd make it a priority." She gave Gray a squeeze. She loved the feel of his big, warm hand. "What do you think?"

"Your call." His smile didn't reach his eyes.

"If you've got the dresses," Robert said. "Then we've got everything else."

"When you say *we*, you mean The Granger Collection?" Gray asked.

"Yep," Robert said. "We have all the connections, all the vendors and modeling agencies." He set his arms on the table. "Knox, I think we can do this."

She was starting to believe him, and it made her

queasy. Getting her hopes up again felt…dangerous. "Even if you could pull it all together—the venue, models, hair stylists, all of that—we'd still need people to show up. There's no point in showing my gowns to an empty room. And they need to be the right people."

"The buzz is already there," Robert said. "Luc created it for you."

"Once she cancelled, though," Gray said. "All those bloggers and editors and buyers booked other shows. Their schedules are full."

As the two men talked about her show, she pulled into herself, needing a moment to take it all in. It felt surreal, the three of them reunited, talking as if no time had passed. Though it clearly had. The men were bigger, harder. The tension between them thicker.

And Robert was *sober.* Which was…phenomenal. At first, when he'd tried to hug her, she'd resisted. Residual anger? Probably. It had taken a long time to free herself from the bonds they'd forged over so many years.

The memories, though, had formed a hard knot in her gut, and they'd stayed there. Until tonight, when he'd whispered in her ear, "Been waiting for this moment, when I could be the man you always wanted me to be." Those simple words had dissolved the knot. Relief had crashed over her. Seeing him healed was a gift.

He'd joked about her thinking of him as a homeless junkie, but it wasn't funny. Over all these years, when she'd allowed herself to think about him, she'd imagined him holed up in some seedy apartment, doing tricks to score meth.

And now here he was, whole, healthy…and dangling her dream right in front of her.

"You hear me, babe?" Robert snagged her attention.

"I'd bet my trust fund, once they hear you're back, they'll rearrange their schedules to come see what you've got."

Gray rubbed the back of her hand with his thumb. "I think he's right about that."

Robert smiled at him—and just that moment of connection between old friends gave her the peace of mind that they could work together, the three of them.

"Well, before you get all excited," she said. "You should probably see the collection. If you don't love it, you won't be able to sell it."

"I got into town yesterday. Went to the bunkhouse to see you. Saw all those dresses..." Robert let out a slow breath through pursed lips. "Damn. They're dynamite. That's when I got the idea, because, babe, those dresses deserve more than a pop-up boutique. I looked you up online and, I'm telling you, I lost count of how many articles and blogs are out there, talking about Knox Holliday, the White-Hot Wedding Gown Designer." He got a gleam in his eyes. "You're the talk of the town. We can do this. *I* can make it happen."

"You don't know how much I want to, but with just three weeks to pull it off, I can't risk it. When I debut at fashion week, it has to be big. I can't afford anything less."

"The Granger Collection's got a whole department for fashion shows. I've got enough people to guide me that I know I can pull this off."

"It's expensive, Robert. You hire the models for the whole week, because it's not just the show itself they have to dress for. They have to be in the room for presentations and appointments." She'd just made peace with this new path, and now Robert—of all people—was giving the original one back to her.

And the worst thing of all? He was right. She might

not get everyone who'd responded to her original invitation, but she knew without a doubt that plenty of the editors and buyers would come see her collection.

Robert leaned in, giving off a powerful forcefield of energy. "Give me a chance, Knox, to not let you down. I don't know what it costs, I don't know if I can get the editors and buyers to come, I can't guarantee a damn thing, but I want to try. Before you outright reject me, can you give me a couple of days to try and pull this together?"

"I want Bridal Fashion Week more than anything, but I only get one shot out of the starting gate. If I fail, if the models don't know what they're doing, or the right people don't come to the show, then it's ten times worse for me than not showing at all. So, if you want to see what you can do—quietly and behind the scenes—then, okay, let's give it a shot."

"Yeah?" Robert gave her a look that said, *We're doing this. You and me.*

"Yeah."

"I won't let you down."

Knox flicked on the lights, tossed her tote on the table, and headed into the kitchen. "I'm making tea. You want some?" Her brain was spinning so fast, she couldn't make it stop. Bridal Fashion Week was three weeks away. Even with The Granger Collection's connections, they still needed a venue, wedding gown models. The dresses needed to *fit* the models. Stylists, PR.

There was so much to think about. She'd totally relied on Luc last time.

She set the kettle under the faucet and looked up at Gray. "Do you have Robert's number?"

"Yeah, why?"

"I might be changing my mind. It's too risky." She shut off the water and placed the kettle on the stove.

"You want to sleep on it?" Gray pulled down two mugs, the answer to her question.

"You're having tea?"

"I'm having tea with you."

Oh, God. This man. He had a way of saying things that sliced through all the wires she got herself tangled up in. She slid her arms through his.

Pressure bore down on her, though, and her head ached. She pulled away from him and poured honey into her mug. She offered the bear-shaped container to him, but he shook his head. "I just don't know if I can trust him," she said. "He sounded good, but…I don't know. Maybe I'm not being fair, judging him by his past behavior."

"I don't see how we could trust him—especially with something as important as this. But we don't have to take his word on anything. He'll come to us with what he's got, and we'll follow up. Verify that it's all above-board and exactly what you want. You did make it clear you wanted him to do it behind the scenes."

"I'm smarter than I realized."

"You are."

"And his mom *is* doing the pop-up for me, so she would want the show to go well. It'll drive business to her store."

"She's not doing it for you." His tone said, *Can you get that through your thick head?* "It's not a favor. She's a businesswoman. She's not giving you two hundred and fifty grand and space in her Fifth Avenue boutique because you used to date her son. She's doing it because she wants a piece of your very hot action."

She shook her ass. "Pretty sure everyone wants a piece of my action."

He came up behind her and enfolded her in his arms. "Can you blame them? Everyone wants to be associated with a superstar." Kissing her cheek, he rocked her in his arms.

She tipped her head back against his chest. "He seemed sober, right?"

"He did, but he's always hid it well." He looked uncomfortable, and she knew he had more to say about it.

She pulled out of his embrace to face him. "That's the point. He hides it well, and I guess I don't want to go back there, where I'm sniffing his breath and sneaking looks at his phone and wondering where he is every second. It's different now. This is my career."

"You're right. So, if you don't trust him, then we stick to the plan. You *will* get your show. It just has to be when it's right for you."

If it were anyone but her ex, would it seem like such an enormous decision? Like, was it the timing—three weeks to pull it off? No, that wasn't it. She would definitely look into it.

It was Robert.

She pulled two teabags out of the chamomile box, staring at the silver kettle but seeing her ex's hands beating out a tune on the table. It didn't mean he was high. Could've been nervous. *I mean, talk about a surprise reunion…* and at the exact moment she and Gray were *kissing*?

They'd all been nervous. There was so much going on beneath the surface.

"Strange seeing him after all these years." His big palm covered her cheek.

"I always thought, if I ever saw him again, he'd hate me. I didn't see hate." As the kettle started to whistle, she poured the water into the mugs. "And no one's got better skills at reading him than I do. All I ever did was check for signs that he was high or lying or cheating or stealing. So, yeah, my Spidey senses are well-honed."

"And what did you see?"

"He kept moving. His hands, fingers, a leg shaking under the table."

Gray nodded. "I noticed."

"But my senses aren't reliable, because I was so nervous about seeing him. And then he dropped the fashion week bomb. I don't know. I just don't know."

"You don't need to know anything right now."

"You're right. I don't." She brought the mug to her mouth, letting the steam warm her, the scent relax her. Only, it wasn't working. The pressure kept bearing down on her, making it hard to take a full breath.

She looked around the room, the empty work stations. Tomorrow, the sewers would return to pack up their stations, marking each box so it could be taken to the new space.

Committing her to living in Calamity.

Breathe.

And now Robert was back in town.

And she and Gray were together. The world titled, and she reached for the counter.

Leaving his mug on the counter, Gray headed out of the kitchen.

"Where are you going?"

"Gonna grab some blankets. Let's take our tea and sit outside."

"That's a good idea." Except that nothing seemed like a good idea. Everything seemed scary and overwhelming. Images rushed her—the trailer, her comforter, in particular —the tear from Robert's belt buckle. *He ruined everything.*

He did. He always had. There wasn't a single good memory from their last couple of years together. So, why would she trust him with her show?

You want it so much you're willing to take a chance on the least trustworthy person you know?

Gray strode out of the hallway with a big, down comforter in his arms. Something about seeing this man— this big, powerful man—coming toward her with a blanket made her feel scared. And she didn't know why.

Well, she did know. She was afraid of getting too close to him, of relying on him, only to have him take off and leave her alone again. She blinked back the sting of tears and busied herself with stirring her tea. If she looked at him, he'd see it. And she needed to be strong.

He opened the French doors. "Can you grab my mug?"

"Of course. I'll be right there."

He nodded but didn't go out the door. "You coming?"

"In a minute. I want to make a list. For Robert. If we're going to do this, then I need to know he won't mention my name. I also need to make sure he understands about the production. This is a big event. You can't show dresses like these in an ordinary setting. And I need him to know I can't pay for anything. I just took on the lease of a building I don't even know if I can afford. I mean, I haven't even talked to the MacAllister sisters. They might not choose me. I might not get another order at all. And then where will I be?"

Gray dropped the blanket and was at her side in three long strides. "Hey."

She waved a hand. "I'm good. I didn't mean to go off on you like that. It'll work out." Lifting both mugs, she started out of the kitchen. "Let's go."

But he blocked her. "You're not alone."

"I know." She tried to push past him.

He tipped her chin. "Sweetheart, look at me."

Sweetheart? No one in her entire life had called her that term of endearment.

"You're not alone."

"I know that. Come on. Let's go outside. It's a nice night." Actually, it was freezing.

Still, he didn't budge. "We're in this together."

The knot in her throat tightened, cutting off her ability to speak, so she just nodded.

His cupped the back of her head. "I'm going to wrap us up in that blanket, and we're going to look at the moonlight on the mountain, and we're going to talk about every little thing that's on your mind."

Hot tea splashed over the rim, and Gray pried the mugs out of her hands, setting them on the counter, all while talking in his low, growly voice. "Every worry and doubt and concern, and when we're done, if you don't have the peace you're looking for, we'll go to bed, I'll love every inch of your beautiful body, and we'll wake up and talk it through some more."

Tears spilled down her cheeks, the tension banding so tightly around her head, she thought it would pop like a boiled cranberry.

"We won't stop until we've worked it all out." Gently,

he ran his fingers through her hair. "And when the next obstacle comes, we'll work it out together. I'm here, and I'm not going anywhere. Even when I'm in New Zealand, I'm still going to be here with you."

She couldn't see him through the sheen of tears.

"Want to know why?"

Somehow the answer to that question meant everything to her.

"Because I've waited a long damn time to be with you, and there's not a chance in hell I'm going to lose you. I'm going to do everything I can to earn your respect and love. So, if there's nothing else you can be sure of right now, there's this. I'm here. I'm not going anywhere, and that means you're never going to be alone again."

Her knees buckled, and she let out a strangled cry. Hot tears flooded her cheeks, and her body crumpled. Thanks to Gray and his reflexes, he caught her elbows, keeping her from hitting the floor. Lowering them both, he wrapped an arm around her. She drew up her knees and hid her face between them. She couldn't stop the tears or the choking sounds.

Gray hauled her onto his lap, arranging her limp and useless limbs so that she straddled him. She tucked her face into his neck and just wailed.

He didn't shush her, didn't beg her to stop crying, didn't even ask what he could do to help. He just held her while she sobbed. Her brain was nothing but white noise, her emotions at such an extreme pitch she couldn't make sense of them.

Her stomach muscles ached, her skull weighed two tons, and yet every tear that flooded out of her seemed to carry the weight of one worry, one fear, one ounce of anxiety, until…she'd emptied her body of all of it. It was like she'd spent all the pain and loss built up over a lifetime, leaving her deflated as an old balloon. She drew in a shuddering breath and dragged the back of her hand across her leaking nose.

"Sexy." Cupping her bottom, he effortlessly lifted them both. "Here." He snatched a couple of paper towels off the dispenser and handed them to her, lowering them back to the floor.

Blowing her nose, she patted the dampness off her face. Her body felt bruised and battered, as if she'd been jumped in an alley, but her mind felt a thousand times lighter. "So, that happened."

"You do everything next level, including breaking down."

"Thank you?" She let out a long, slow breath. "When I was a little girl, I used to jump out of bed, get dressed, and get ready for whatever my mom said we were going to do that day. But, most of the time, she didn't wake up until it was too late to go. She worked late, she was tired, she'd had friends over. Whatever. And there just came a day when I didn't believe her anymore."

"You haven't had many people you could rely on."

"But I can rely on you. And I think…all that…" She motioned to her face. "Was because I trust you. I trust you enough to fall to pieces in front of you."

"I like that, sweetheart. I like it very fucking much."

Leaving their tea behind, they headed outside. Gray wrapped the comforter around himself and sat down first, then drew her down onto his lap.

She snuggled in, before taking in the wide Wyoming sky, ablaze with glittering stars. "Do you remember that

Etch-a-Sketch I had? You used to write me secret messages on it?"

"Of course."

She caressed his bottom lip. He was such a handsome man. "You made me shake it immediately after reading, so no one would see it."

"So *Robert* wouldn't see it." He grabbed her wrist and pressed a kiss to the tip of her finger.

"You guys were so freaking competitive."

"I wasn't competitive with him." He stroked the hair away from her temples. "I just wanted what he had. There's a difference."

She glanced up at him and saw the worry tightening his handsome features. If she'd known he felt this way back then, would she have broken up with Robert earlier? Not a chance. Not only would she never have believed it, they couldn't have betrayed Robert's trust like that.

He gave her a gentle nudge. "The Etch-a-Sketch."

"Right. Well, I took pictures of every message you ever made me."

He shot her a look.

"I did. And I printed them at CVS and saved them. Every single one. They're in a box under the bed. You had a way of saying just the right thing. Like, I don't know if you remember—"

"I remember everything."

Drinking in the sincerity in his eyes, she ran her fingers through his scruff. "This one day I was walking to my locker between fourth and fifth periods, and I could see it'd been pried open. I wasn't going to be that stupid girl who opened it only to find a dead rat or whatever. So, I went to the office and told them about it, told them I wanted someone to come with me and to bring the janitor. The saddest thing was that they didn't even hesitate. It wasn't like, *Oh, come on drama queen.* No, Mrs. Andretti got her SWAT team together, and we marched over to my locker, all of us totally geared up for something terrible. And, lo and behold, those assholes had filled it with garbage from the cafeteria. And I mean, fresh bits of hamburger and pudding, fish sticks. It was disgusting."

He lowered his head and let out a harsh breath.

"You drove me home that day. We had hot chocolate and hung out and, after you left, I went back to my bedroom and found your note. And, the thing is, you never said stuff like, *Keep your chin up* or...*don't listen to those idiots.* You never addressed the bullies at all." She reached for his hand, threading their fingers together. "You never gave them power."

"What'd I write?"

"You drew a picture of a dress—a pretty lame one, if you ask me." She gave him a teasing smile.

"It was the medium."

"Ah, so if it had been paper, you'd have sketched a masterpiece?"

"Well, yeah."

"You probably would have, Mr. Good-at-Literally-Everything. Anyhow, beneath the dress, you wrote my name. But you didn't spell it out. K-N-O-X. You made it like my signature. And underneath you wrote in parentheses, This is going to be worth a fortune one day."

He grinned. "I meant your autograph, not my sketch."

"Yeah, I know. I'm a lot quicker than I look. The point is that, on a truly shitty day, you made me smile because I knew you meant I'd be a famous designer one day." She shifted so she could face him. "You didn't tell me not to worry about those idiots. You made me focus on the future. On the talent I could rely on to get me out of here. You always made me feel like I had value." She showed him her inked bracelet of tiny stars. "That's where this came from."

He brought her wrist to his mouth and kissed it. "You mean I *reminded* you of your value."

"Yes. Exactly." She clasped his hand tightly. "I never dreamed I could be with a guy like you."

"Knox." He let out an exasperated breath. "I don't want to be some ideal."

"No, I know. I don't mean it like that. Well, I kind of do. Because, back then, you were an ideal. Every time I went to your house, I felt like I didn't belong. Like your dad would pull you aside and go, *What's she doing here?* You're the best man I've ever known, and I didn't think I could have the best guy. I thought—I guess subconsciously—that I could only have someone more like me."

"Do you mean a guy who doesn't let life knock him down? Who doesn't let other people define him? A talented guy who makes shit happen? Because that's what my dad saw—that's what anyone who knows you sees."

"It's funny how different people show you different facets of yourself. I never saw myself the way you see me."

"I will gladly hold your mirror."

"Ugh, not after tonight's ugly cry. God, I can't even remember the last time I lost it like that."

"Pretty sure you've been in crisis mode your whole life."

"What does that mean?"

"You spent a lot of your childhood alone in that trailer, and I've been in there. Those sounds are creepy. Trucks roaring past, wind making it creak. Remember that night you called me because a pack of wolves was howling?"

She did. That had been terrifying.

"You never knew when the bullies would strike or whether your boyfriend was sober. There wasn't much about your life you could control. You moved to New York City and Paris by yourself, spent a year making dresses alone in a house on Maui, knowing that your ability to support yourself rested on your shoulders. I'm going to guess you spent every day worried about whether you'd finish in time or not have anything good enough to show."

"I did." For a moment the truth shone so brightly it blinded her, so that all she could do was live inside the rightness of it. "My whole life, everything has seemed critical, every problem life or death. You're right. I *have* been in crisis mode."

"And I think—I hope—for the first time tonight, you get that you're not alone anymore." He drew her so tight against him nothing could get between them. "Maybe that allowed you to break down a little."

"I didn't scare you away?"

"I'm thinking you're not grasping the situation. All I've ever wanted was for you to see me for who I am."

"And who's that?"

"The one who carries your heart."

Chapter Sixteen

HEAT, LUST…HIS BODY BURNED, HIS HIPS LIFTED OFF the mattress. *More, deeper.* Jesus Christ, he was so hard, so ready to burst.

Gray awakened to the slide of silky hair across his stomach, the firm caress of soft hands on his bare skin, and the sensation of a hungry mouth sucking his cock.

That scent in the sheets—sweet, lightly floral, all Knox —sent him to a place he'd never been. He reached beneath the sheets, his hands tangling in silky hair, and it hit him.

Knox. He got the girl.

I fucking got the girl.

Her hand squeezed the base of his cock, tugging in tandem with her sucking mouth, her tongue flicking and pulling.

"Fuck." *Too good.* His body tightened, his legs went rigid. He was going to come, and there wasn't a chance he'd do that anywhere else but inside her body.

"Come here." His voice sounded gruff, almost mean, as he jackknifed up, grabbed under her arms, and hauled her up the bed.

She straddled his hips, her hands sweeping up his torso and across his chest. When she leaned over, the tips of her hair brushed over his skin. A soft yellow light flicked on. "I want to see you."

She took him in, his eyes, mouth, shoulders. Setting her palms on his chest, she fanned out her fingers, digging into his skin. "I can't believe I get to touch this body."

"You get all of me, Knox. You understand? All of me."

He didn't like the trepidation in her eyes, but he could deal with it. They'd had a breakthrough last night. She'd let him in. *Time.* He just needed more time with her.

With a hand on her lower back, his hip pitched forward, knocking her over. He was glad she'd turned on the light, because he got to see the thrill in her eyes, the greedy desire that had her hands clutching his ass and jerking him to her.

Reaching between them, he gripped his cock, rubbed the slick length of her with it, and then pushed in. He fucking loved the sultry look in her eyes as he did it, the arch of her neck, the sexy gasp. Loved the way her fingers curled into his flesh.

Yeah, time. That's what he needed.

Time to make her believe in them.

Knox slammed the nightstand drawer closed after checking it a third time. Dropping to her knees, she scanned under the bed. Fear had her heart pounding. *Maybe the patio?* It was the only place she hadn't looked yet.

Please tell me I didn't leave my sketchbook outside overnight.

The bathroom door opened, expelling whorls of steam, and then Gray strode out fully naked. Time screeched to a stop as she took him in. Smooth, tan skin covered the tightly defined muscles on his torso, and the black ink and shoulder-length wet hair made him look deliciously bad. He snatched his running shorts off the floor and stepped into them.

"Maybe you shouldn't spend the night."

His brow furrowed adorably. Like she'd suggested he wear her bra.

She glanced at the clock on her nightstand. "You should be at the training facility by now. Your house is closer to the gym...your clothes are there...I mean, I already take up too much of your time."

"I want to spend the night." He sounded affronted. "So I can give you a good morning kiss."

It still knocked her on her ass, Gray Bowie saying sweet things. "Also, you should go to a doctor, find out who's inhabiting your body."

"What's that supposed to mean?"

"You're this buff, brawny athlete. You talk about barrels and pipe, dropping in and triple rotations. You don't talk about 'good morning kisses.'" Then again... maybe he did. "Unless you're this sweet and romantic with all the women you sleep with."

"You're gonna do that?"

"Do what?"

He grabbed her hips and pulled her toward him. "Reduce us to some casual hookup."

"No, you're right. I'm sorry. I was a mess last night, and this morning I can't find my sketchbook. In other words, I'm feeling insecure." She held out her arms. "Just give me that morning kiss so you can forget all about the dumb things I say."

"Good, because I sacrificed clean underwear for it."

He came at her like a man on a mission, eyes on her mouth, intention clear. Her pulse quickened—anticipation of his touch and...fear.

Fear of all the unknowns in her life right now—her career, the show, and knowing she was falling hard for a man she didn't know how she could possibly keep.

But then he caught her around the waist and hauled her to his hot, damp body. "Gonna kiss all those doubts right out of your head." He claimed her mouth, teased it open with his hungry tongue, and let her know just how much he wanted her.

His body went hot, his cock hard between them. Need sizzled and snapped, making her crazy to get closer, feel him deeper. *Swallow me whole.*

But he had to train, and she couldn't become a problem for him. She gently eased back, giving him a few more soft kisses. "You should go. Fin's waiting for you."

"Yep. I should." He grabbed his crumpled T-shirt off the bedframe. "You said you lost your sketchbook? Which one?"

"Fortunately, not the one with Callie and Delilah's dresses. It's the one for the next collection I'm working on. I hate that it's gone missing. I had some really good ideas in there."

Hands on his hips, he scanned the room. "You remember where you last saw it?"

"I take it with me everywhere, but when I come home, I always put it on the kitchen counter." She saw the way he looked at her nightstand. "Trust me, I've turned this whole place upside down."

"Could've been boxed up already." They'd hired a couple ranch workers to pack up the supplies and machinery. "Want me to get the guys back? We can open them up and look through them."

She smiled. He always made everything better just by caring so much. "I can wait until we move into the new space. I just don't like not knowing where it is. It's got some of my best dresses ever."

"Must be the mountain air. Or, more likely, the spectacular sex."

"There *is* something very inspiring about good sex. It really opens the creative channels."

"*Good* sex?" His head popped out of the T-shirt's neckline.

"Well, of course, it's subjective, right? What's spectacular for one person could just be meh for someone else."

"Meh?"

"Sure. Think of it like a scale." She held up her palm. "You've got one for I Should've Just Pretended to be Asleep." She lifted the other. "All the way to eight for Holy Cow I Think I've Gone Blind."

"Why does the scale stop at eight? That's random."

"Not everyone can hit the higher notes, you know? But I'm very happy at eight. I'm sure we'll get there at some point. I have faith in you."

With a mischievous glint in his eyes, he bent over and rushed her, tackling her onto the mattress. "I don't enter competitions I don't think I can win." Reaching under her blouse, he skimmed his rough, calloused hand up her stomach and then cupped her breast.

He had a way of touching her—filled with reverence, passion—almost a desperation—like he had to make each time count—and it made her heart flutter out of control.

"Need you naked." He lifted the shirt, and she sat up long enough to tear it off. Then, he grabbed the waistband of her leggings and yanked them down her legs. "So I can bring all my skills to bear." He surged against her, his hard cock grazing over her clit as he rocked his hips. Electricity lit her up with each pass. He kissed his way along her jaw to her ear, licking her lobe, all while that big hand cupped and squeezed her breast, the thumb flicking over her nipple.

"Gray." She stirred restlessly beneath him, her hands pulling, wanting more of him. Her legs wrapped around his hips, and she ground her core against his thick erection.

He found his way back to her mouth, kissing and kissing and kissing, hungry, desperate, driving kisses that sought an answer to the one question that would finally give him peace.

She reached between them, rubbing his rock-hard erection under the nylon shorts. She tried to push him off, but he wouldn't budge. "Still kissin' you."

She squeezed his hot, hard length. "Kiss me with another part of you."

"You always have the best ideas."

With her feet, she pushed down his shorts. That had him rolling off her and kicking them aside. Taking advantage of his position, she sat up and got a hold of his cock, taking him into her mouth and swirling her tongue around the head.

"Give you an inch…" He gasped. "And you take my whole cock."

She burst out laughing. She loved the look in his eyes, so…delighted. It empowered her, knowing she did that to him. She wanted to do more. Wanted to see him lose himself inside her. Falling onto her back, she reached for him. "Let's see if we can push that scale up to a nine."

He lunged for her, one hand on her waist, the other on her cheek, angling her for his kiss. She'd barely gotten a taste, when his mouth skimmed down her neck and made a necklace of kisses along her collarbone. He cupped her breast, lowered his mouth to it, and she arched up into him when he sucked on her nipple. Her hands went to the back of his head to hold him *right there.*

Reaching between her legs, he parted her curls and slid a finger along her length. His thumb made slow circles on her clit, while two fingers caressed inside her. Pressing kisses down her stomach, he nudged her thighs apart with his broad shoulders and then licked inside her folds.

Her body jolted with pleasure. Fisting the sheets, her neck arched, and she closed her eyes to seal herself in the bliss of Gray's sensual swirls and licks, the possession of his grip on her thighs, and the sensation of his soft, silky hair on her skin.

Her hips swiveled, thrust, pressed closer to his mouth. "You feel so good, Gray. So good."

His hands slid under her ass, and he lifted her, his tongue finding her clit and flicking it in the relentless pursuit of her pleasure. Fire burned along her limbs, tension twisted and bore down on her, her senses narrowing to the euphoria of the orgasm that crashed over, shattered her, and left her totally, utterly, sated.

The front door slammed closed, and Gray sat up, listening.

"Knox?" *Robert.* "You here?"

Gray's eyes squeezed closed before he shouted, "Give us a second."

"Yeah, sure," Robert called. "I'll just grab some coffee."

Gray started to get off the bed, but she didn't like his expression. Did he think Robert would ruin this thing developing between them? She pulled him back down on top of her. "I don't know where we're going, you and me, but I do know I've never felt so whole, so safe, so…what's the opposite of alone?"

He gripped her shoulder. "Us. *We're* the opposite of alone."

Gray only needed two minutes to wash up and dress, so he went out to greet Robert first, leaving her to pull herself together. Now, as she headed down the hallway, listening to the deep rumble of their voices, she couldn't help wondering if they'd slip back into their old dynamic. Robert's possessiveness, Gray's nonchalance, and her alertness. *Is he high? Does he smell like pot? Where was he last night?*

She stood back, watching them drink coffee in the kitchen. Well, Robert held a mug in his hand. Gray drank water. *Here we are, the three of us back in the place we spent so much time as kids.* But it didn't feel the same. *Thank God.*

"There she is." Robert and all his charm.

She joined them in the kitchen. "Hey. Sorry to keep you waiting."

"No worries." Robert watched her over the mug. "Nothing wrong with sleeping in."

Gray snickered. "Look out."

Yeah, you're right, look out. "I've been up since five, working on the muslin for Callie's dress. I only stopped because I can't find my sketchbook, and it's driving me crazy." *The patio.* "Hang on a sec." She cut around the kitchen counter and headed for the French doors, but she could already see she hadn't left it out there.

"I'm sure one of the guys packed it with the other stuff," Gray said.

"Probably." But she wouldn't be comfortable until she found it. She hated misplacing things. Drove her nuts.

"You want us to search the bunkhouse?" Robert came right up behind her. She knew it was him because of his unusual scent—almost like sweet pipe tobacco. She had no idea why his clothes had always smelled like that. "Three sets of eyes are better than one."

"No, that's okay. I've looked everywhere. It'll turn up."

"Water's boiling."

She smiled appreciatively at Gray for thinking to make her some tea, but his expression got her moving toward the kitchen. He didn't like seeing Robert so close to her, and suddenly it was there, that uncomfortable dynamic. The competition between the men.

If Robert kept this up, she'd have to spell it out for him. Wrapping her arm around Gray's waist, she got up on her toes and kissed his scruffy cheek. "Thank you."

Gray tipped a chin to the long dining room table. "Why's there a third muslin?"

"Oh, that." She poured water into a mug, just as Gray handed her a spoon. "I'm making a second one for Callie." She poured the honey and stirred.

"Something wrong with the first?"

"Not technically, no. I just think…I want to give her an option. The one she chose is beautiful, but…"

"Not her?" Gray asked.

"Maybe? I just think she might like this other one better." Catching the teabag with her spoon, she lifted it out of the mug. Gray took it from her and dropped it into the garbage, setting the spoon in the sink.

A low chuckle reminded her that Robert was in the room. She glanced up to see his amused expression. "So." He wagged a finger between them. "How long has this been going on?"

"It's brand new." She leaned into Gray's arm, but he didn't lift it to hug her to him. Which she thought was the sign of a good man, not rubbing it in Robert's face.

"Really? You look like an old married couple." His gaze narrowed on her. "Kind of like we used to be."

"Well, he's sober, so there's that." The moment the words came out, she clapped a hand over her mouth. "I'm sorry. I don't where that came from. That was stupid and immature."

"No." Robert turned serious. "It came from the fact that I never got to apologize for what I put you through."

"I'm over it, I swear. I'm so over it."

"No, you're not," Robert said. "How could you be? We never talked about it. The last time I saw either of you was the prom. I was in rehab for thirty days. Every second of that time I was thinking about you. I wanted to apologize, let you know I'd never fuck up again, but I didn't hear from you. Not once. And when I got out? You were gone."

Never had Robert exposed himself so baldly. It felt like he'd flung the words, wrenched from his gut, at her feet. Did he want an apology? She couldn't give it to him. He'd made her life a living hell.

"I never got to apologize, but even worse, you never got to ream me out for fucking everything up. But we're here now, face to face. So, let's do this. Let's get it out. All the shit you've carried inside for years, you can give me. I can handle it, anything you want to give me, I can handle."

"I appreciate the offer, and it might have made a difference seven, six, maybe even five years ago. But I honestly don't have anything left in me to rehash."

"Bullshit."

"No, Robert. It's true. The thing is, I don't need an apology from you because you didn't do anything to me that I didn't let you do. We were locked in an unhealthy relationship. It wasn't love. It wasn't even friendship. We are *both* to blame."

"Don't say that." He came around the counter, the two of them so close their breaths mingled. "I can handle anything you want to give me, except hearing you say it wasn't love. I'm a selfish bastard, and I put you through hell, but I l did love you. Never question that. I fucking loved you."

"How would you know? You were numb the whole time. Isn't that the point of being a drug addict?" Saying that out loud felt so much better than she could have imagined.

He stood there fierce, intense, and she thought he might blow up at her, but the muscle in his jaw popped, and he watched her behind shuttered eyes. The tension grew unbearable, and just as Gray moved closer to her, Robert said, "My dad exposed me to shit no kid should ever experience. My mom wasn't around, and when she was, she was on the phone or locked inside her office. If I didn't want to feel anything, it was the bullshit from my family. The only good thing in my life was you." His gaze shifted to Gray—and hardened. "Both of you." But then he reached for her hand and held it so tightly her ring pinched her finger. "I was a shit boyfriend, a shit friend, a shit person, but never doubt how much I loved you." He looked down at his brown leather boots. "I'm sorry. I'm sorry for not being a better man for you."

His sincerity had any residual anger and resentment melting. In place of the charming, charismatic guy who'd manipulated everyone around him, she saw a humbled man who seemed to have found his way. "I forgive you." A sheen of moisture filled his eyes, and so she touched his shoulder. "And I hope you forgive me for not being there when you got out of rehab. I hope you understand that it was the only way I could have left you."

He grabbed her wrist and kissed her palm. "Fuck, Knox. If I could take it back—"

"You can't. It's over, and we're both in good places. Just…stay good, okay?"

Their gazes locked in understanding, he nodded.

"I've got to get going." Gray kissed her cheek. "I'll leave you two to it."

"Well, hang on." She gestured toward Robert. "He came by for a reason."

"I did. Got some good news." Robert went quiet for a moment, like he was pulling himself together. When, he did, he drew in a breath, and his expression cleared. "I've got six models lined up."

"Already?" she asked, at the same time Gray said, "How?"

"Called a few modeling agencies. That's the easy part."

"I don't think you mentioned where the money's coming from," Gray said.

"I did. I told you The Granger Collection has a department for fashion shows."

"Right, but Granger's isn't backing me," Knox said. "They don't have a bridal line, and we haven't talked about me designing one for them. So, is it your mom? I'm not sure why she'd back me in fashion week."

"*She's* not," Robert said. "Granger's is."

"I don't get why they'd back me if I'm not designing a line for them. It doesn't make sense."

Robert remained unfazed, which gave her confidence. If he were lying, she'd think he'd be rattled, not looking her in the eye. "My mom doesn't trust me enough to hire me in a full-time role—for good reason. But I've got a chance to prove myself. I don't have a specific budget, but she wouldn't want me doing something like this half-assed. Truth? If we pull this off, I wouldn't be surprised if The Granger Collection offers you a contract to launch its first bridal collection."

She shot a look to Gray. *Oh, my God.* His smile did what it always did—made her feel like they were in this together. "That would be amazing."

"Okay, so six models," Gray said. "What else?"

She elbowed him. "It's been thirty-six hours."

Robert pulled out that luminous grin, the one that made all the girls' knees weak back in high school. Teachers and guidance counselors, too. He'd avoided a lot of trouble with that smile. "I hired the models in the first hour."

Gray swept past them and grabbed his running shoes. Perched on a bar stool, he shoved a foot into one.

Robert watched him for a moment. "I know you've got to train, so if you can't stick around, it's cool."

"I've got a few more minutes." Gray gave a chin nod. *Go on.*

"Okay, best news of all?" Robert said. "I've got a location, and it's fucking awesome."

"Really?" Knox asked. "You move fast."

"Yeah, my dad's got a connection at a gallery in SoHo."

"Your dad?" She didn't trust her fashion show to Robert, senior.

He held up a hand. "I'm the one talking to the owner. My dad just gave me the suggestion. No worries. And it's a great space, amazing location."

"Can you get us the name?" Finished tying his shoes, Gray stood up. "We'll take a look at it online."

"Sure thing."

But she knew Robert well enough to see he was annoyed. *Pretty sure he doesn't want Gray checking up on him.* Well, nothing she could do about that. Gray was in this with her.

"The big question," Gray said. "Is whether or not we can get the right people to come."

"I'm on it." She heard the bite in his tone.

The two faced off for a moment, but she let them work it out. As much as she didn't want tension at a time like this, they had to accept this shift in their relationship. Knox was with Gray now—in all ways.

Just the thought of his hands…his mouth on her… sent a shiver down her spine.

And then Gray said, "I bring it up because our concern is whether you know the *right* editors and blog-gers and buyers. Grangers doesn't do bridal, so their connections are going to be different."

"I told you the other night, Luc created enough buzz for her show that we're not going to have any problem getting people to come. I've already been in contact with a few of them."

"How do you know Luc's contacts?" Gray folded his arms over his impressive chest.

"You want to know my big sleuthing secrets? How I hacked into the Bellerose database?" Robert whipped out his phone. "Here, let me show how I put in *Who goes to the shows at Bridal Fashion Week.*"

"Okay, you know what?" Knox stepped between them. "Gray asked a totally fair question, but whatever's going on between you two has nothing to do with my business. Work out your issues somewhere else."

Robert shoved his phone back into his pocket. "Look, if this is going to work, you're going to have to give me a clean slate here. I'm not high. You want to drug test me?"

"This isn't about you. It's about Knox. In order for her to decide if she's going to move forward with the show, she has to know the details, which means it isn't enough to say you're inviting people. She needs to know who you're thinking of contacting."

The tension left Robert's shoulders, and the muscle in his jaw relaxed. "Fair enough. I'll get you a list."

"That'd be great," Gray said. "Do you have anything else?"

"Hell, yeah." Robert grinned. "I found a florist in New Jersey far enough away that no one's ever thought to use him for events in the city but close enough that he'll do it for the shot at getting future contracts."

A tingling at the back of her neck set off a shower of energy down her limbs. *This might actually happen.* She might get her show.

"Good thinking," Gray said—a little tightly, but still.

"It was." After a moment, the tension broke and they high-fived each other. "Yeah, so that's it so far. The five models, the venue, the—"

Hang on. "You said six models."

"I've confirmed five of them, but I'm talking to a sixth.

I'm pretty sure she's in. She doesn't work much anymore, but she's sending me a portfolio today. I'll put her in the win category for now."

Knox couldn't help the little bubble of marvel that broke over her. "You're really going to pull this off, aren't you?"

"Or die trying."

"What about the presentation?" She thought of the set at the Lincoln Center that Luc had built for her. The idea that Antonia would get it…it was like a splash of alcohol on a fresh blister. But she couldn't go there, to what she'd lost. She had to stay focused on what she was building.

"I haven't really thought about that yet," Robert said. "But we've got this great gallery space, which, honestly, is a lot hipper than the Lincoln Center. Your dresses are too fresh and contemporary for an old school venue like that anyway. If you're cool with it, we'll just keep it simple." He looked to her for confirmation.

"Simple's fine." Her gowns were the showstopper. "But it has to be the right backdrop for the style of the dresses."

"Good to know." He flashed a mischievous grin. "Because the gallery owner offered some gold cages and polyurethane swings leftover from an opening she had over the summer."

"Uh…" They all looked at each other, and the burst of laughter broke down the barrier between them. Warmth flowed freely, leaving her with affection for her two oldest friends.

"In this space, there won't be a traditional catwalk," Robert said. "But we'll form a path for the models with chairs set up to face each other."

"Like a path through a garden." She could picture her dresses billowing in a breeze.

"Exactly."

Inspiration struck. "Let's do that, then. We need to keep the pathway clear so the models don't trip, and we can't have the fabric catching on anything, but it would be awesome to create an English garden."

"That's a good idea," Gray said. "It'll keep costs down."

"Maybe we can hang some fans," Knox said. "The fabric would look amazing fluttering in a breeze. We could bring in some planters with trees to make it look like a hedge."

"I should write this down," Robert said.

As Gray reached for a pad of paper and pencil, Knox continued. "If there's time, we could cover the walls with *trompe l'oeil* canvases. A manor house in the distance on one, a view of the countryside on another." But they didn't have time—no, wait, it was an art gallery. The owner must know an artist who could put something like this together. "Can you talk to the florist about planters and trees and pink and white roses? We can't have colors that will overshadow the dresses."

While Robert took notes, Knox shared a smile with Gray. *This is going to work, isn't it?*

She loved his answering expression. *Looks like it.*

"The gallery owner's got the champagne covered," Robert said. "She gets a nice discount. So, that leaves stylists and makeup artists. There's no shortage of talent in the Tri-State area, so I'm not worried about any of that." He looked between the two of them. "Sound good?"

Gray nodded, and she said, "It does." She felt like she'd breathed in helium, like she was about to lift off. But it wasn't a done deal, so she needed to stay grounded. "Let's hope we can get the right people to come."

"I'm not worried about that," Robert said. "But I do

think our best bet is to show as early in the week as possible. Once they see your collection, they'll clear some room in their schedules to meet with you. We'll keep the gallery open every day for presentations and hope to hell someone makes an appointment for a private showing."

"The models understand they're booked for the week?" she asked.

"Oh. A *whole* week?" Robert feigned shock. "Is that how it works?"

She whacked his arm with the back of her hand. "Excuse me for being careful, you ass."

And then he let loose his signature cocky smirk, and his charisma and magnetism flowed all over her. "I got this."

She felt almost drunk from the crazy cocktail of emotions sloshing inside her. Hope, fear, relief. It was too good to be true, standing here beside a clean and sober Robert who was competently putting together a fashion show for her. "Thank you."

For being the man I always wanted you to be.

And giving me back my show.

"I'm not going to let you down. I did enough of that in the past. It won't happen again. You're going to get your fashion week. And we're going knock it out of the park."

Chapter Seventeen

GRAY DUMPED HIS BOARD AND BOOTS IN THE BACK OF the truck. They'd had a great day on the mountain, but he needed to get home. Today, Knox had moved into the new space, and he wanted to help her unpack. Hopefully, she'd find that sketchbook.

As he rounded the truck, he pulled out his keys, only to find his brothers heading into the resort. "Where you going?"

"Take a leak," Brodie said.

"It's a thirty-five-minute drive home." *Dammit.* "You can't wait?"

"Nope." Brodie led the way inside the ski lodge.

Pocketing his keys, Gray took in the rustic decor. Pretty busy, considering they hadn't had the first snowfall, when the cross-country skiers would start showing up. His brothers headed across the lobby to the restrooms, but Gray pulled out his phone. He'd just check in with her, see how the move was going.

But before the call could connect, one voice snagged his attention in the noisy bar. It didn't make sense to hear it in this town on the other side of their mountain. He turned to look, sure he'd find some other guy who sounded like his friend.

But, no, there he was. Robert, sitting at a bar in Idaho in the middle of the afternoon, yucking it up with some older men. Anger broke out across his skin like a rash.

Was he playing them? Striding over, he clapped a hand a little too hard on his friend's shoulder. "Hey, man. Small world."

It was just a flash of fear—a flinch around the eyes—replaced by Robert's winning smile. "What the hell are you doing here?"

"Big storm's coming in that'll close the pass for the winter. Thought we'd drop in for one last run."

"Saw the heli. Should've known it was yours." He twisted around. "Knox here?"

"Nope. She's working her ass off to get those dresses done in time." His tone made his point for him.

Robert gave him a shit-eating grin. "Got it all under control."

"Yeah? You line up the rest of the models? Hire some stylists?"

Robert slid off the stool, forcing Gray to take a step back. "You don't trust me, I get that. But you're out of your mind if you think I'm going to mess things up with her."

"What things are we talking about, specifically?" *Because that sure sounded like he meant more than a fashion show.*

"All the things she wanted from me before, but I couldn't give her because I was too much of an asshole."

"Top of that list…" He tipped his head toward the bar. "Sobriety."

"Ah, come on, man. I've been sober seven years. I can handle a beer or two."

"You sure about that?" He was pretty sure an addict shouldn't be in a bar.

"I'm sure about a lot of things."

"Seems like you've got something to say to me," Gray said. "You weren't man enough back in high school, but I'm hoping you are now."

"Yeah, okay. That's fair."

And right when Gray girded himself to hear about Robert's intention of winning Knox back, the man shocked the hell out of him.

"It felt like you used my bad behavior to make yourself look better than me. And, a lot of the time, when I'd take things too far and you had to save the day, I think I just wanted to take you down a notch, to my level." He dug his hands in his pockets and looked down at the floor. "And I'm sorry for that. Been waiting a long time to say that to you." He looked him right in the eye. "I'm sorry for being a dick."

The humility hit him right in the gut, as powerful as a fist. Made him think Robert really had changed. Except... a bar? And not just that, but one in *Idaho*? "Thank you. It's good to hear."

"Truth is, you're the only one who didn't put up with my shit. I wore everyone else out, but you were smart enough to bail on me junior year."

"I didn't bail on you."

"Hey, I'm trying to apologize here." And yet the words sounded pointed. Barbed.

"Apology accepted."

"When your dad shut me out, that was the beginning

of the end for our friendship. I don't blame you. Your dad was a good guy. You wouldn't go against him."

Like hell he'd let that comment stand. "My dad didn't give up on you until you stole his watch and showed up wasted for a competition."

Robert had never admitted to the crime, had been offended at the very idea that he would steal from the man who'd been more of a father to him than his own dad had been. Gray waited, because his response would make all the difference in determining whether Robert was sincere or playing them.

Head lowered, Robert drew in a deep breath. When he looked up, his eyes were filled with a mix of challenge and remorse. "I was an addict." He shrugged. "I stole from everybody. My parents, my friends, even my girlfriend. Who I loved more than anything."

Was that a warning? *Had* he come back for Knox?

It needed to be addressed, here and now. "You want her back? Is that what you're really doing in town, making her dream come true?"

An ugly curl at one side of Robert's mouth sent a shiver down his spine. "You love her?"

He wouldn't stir his friend's competitive instincts. "It's new, what we have. But it's strong." He tried to read Robert's expression but couldn't. "What's your point?"

"Just asking."

"Why? Because if you're going to make a move on her, I want to know. I have a right to know."

"Why is that, now? Because you never made a move on her when I was going out with her? Tit for tat? Is that something like Knox's eye for an eye? Because I don't subscribe to that philosophy myself."

"Yeah? And what, exactly, are you into?"

The tension rose, crackling between them, and Gray's body braced for action.

But then—just like that—it broke. And Robert's features turned slack. "Look, man, I don't want any trouble. I'm twenty-five years old, and I just wasted seven years trying to get things going in LA. I want a damn career. That's it. That's all I want."

The anxiety dropped fast and hard, and he almost felt sympathy for the guy. "Glad to see your mom's giving you a shot. You can't do better than The Granger Collection."

"Don't I know it."

"Your mom staying on top of this?" If she was, Gray would have absolute confidence.

"She's in Milan, but yeah, I'm working with someone." He straightened. "So, you don't have to worry. I'm not gonna fuck this up."

In her new office, Knox zipped up the muslin for her very first actual bride. It was about a thousand times more emotional and rewarding than working with models.

Callie smoothed the fabric around her hips, twisting around to see her reflection from behind in the full-length mirror. "You'd think as an artist I could imagine what the actual dress will look like."

"Well, hopefully the sketch makes it come to life for you," Knox said. "A few layers of drab muslin won't give you the princess effect."

"What if I gain ten pounds? I haven't even set a wedding date yet."

"Do you plan on gaining weight?" Knox hoped her

friend wasn't pregnant. That wouldn't work out very well. "It's easier to take a dress in than let it out."

Callie cut a stern but playful look to Delilah. "Maybe if someone stopped trying out her amazing recipes on us, I might have a hope in hell."

"Sorry-not-sorry for cooking something other than sweet potato," Delilah said.

"Literally never apologize," Callie said. "Whatever you did to that chicken the other night? Pure witchcraft."

"Here." Knox reached for her sketchbook and flipped to Callie's gown. "Hold this up while you're looking in the mirror."

Callie's gaze shifted from the sketch to the mirror.

"Okay, that's not exactly the kind of look we're hoping for when you're imagining your wedding gown," Delilah said.

"It's the prettiest dress I've ever seen." But Callie looked unsure. "I love it."

"Hey, can I show you something?" Knox reached for the sketchbook. *Flip, flip, flip.* "Take a look at this."

Delilah got up on the dais with Callie, and they both looked at the sketch.

Knox saw the moment it happened, awe dawning over Callie's features, and it filled her with more joy, more satisfaction, than seeing any of her dresses on models over the last several years.

Callie looked from the sketch to the mirror and back again.

"Now, that is you," Delilah said.

Callie's gaze found Knox in the mirror, and she looked incredibly conflicted.

"If you want it, you can have it." Knox gave her a reassuring smile. "It's not too late."

"But we ordered the material," Callie said.

"And I'll use it. All of it."

"You're not mad?" Callie asked.

"Hey, I designed it with you in mind. This one…" She gestured to the muslin. "Will be perfect for someone else."

"I guess I just had this idea in my head," Callie said wistfully.

"But *this* is you." Delilah pointed at the sketchbook.

"It really is." Callie turned around, forcing Delilah to step off the dais. "So, you really don't mind if we do this one?"

"You want to see the back first?" Knox motioned for her to turn the page.

"Oh, my God." Callie's eyes bugged out. "That's crazy sexy." She snapped the book shut and held it to her chest. "I'm so in love with this dress."

"Fin's gonna cry like a little bitch when he sees you walking toward him," Delilah said.

"Aw, you're so romantic," Callie said.

"So, that's the one?" Knox asked.

"For sure."

"Speaking of which," Delilah said. "While I'm here, do you think I could look through your sketchbook? The one you said had some ideas I might like?"

"Unfortunately, no. I lost it in the move."

"You what?" Delilah looked horrified.

"Don't worry. Your dress wasn't in that one—"

"You must be devastated," Delilah said.

Oh. The woman had been worried about Knox. Not her own wedding gown. "I am, actually."

"Maybe it's in one of the boxes." Callie stepped off the dais.

"I don't think so. We've opened all of them." Knox

glanced through the office windows overlooking her new space. The sewers were already back at work. Phone cradled on his shoulder, Zach paced, one hand gesticulating. "And I've turned the bunkhouse upside down."

"Gray's truck?" Callie said. "A different purse?"

"I've searched everywhere. It's just gone. Things always get lost in a move, but don't worry about your dress. I always have new ideas."

"I'm not worried at all," Delilah said. "Besides, you have more than enough on your plate. How about you get through fashion week, and then we'll talk about finishing my dress?"

Knox gave her a grateful smile.

"Okay," Callie said. "I have to pick up some Coco's chocolates I ordered for an event at the museum tonight. Want to come into town with me, and we can get a coffee?"

Knox unzipped the muslin. What the new dress lacked in volume, she could make up with some subtle but dynamic bling. Like embedding tiny crystals—

"Knox?" Callie said.

She peered at the future bride. "Yeah?" Had she missed something?

"Coffee?"

She spit the pins out again. "Oh, me? I thought you were talking to Delilah."

"I'm talking to both of you. Coffee at Calamity Joe's?"

She bit down on her go-to response. *I have to get back to work.* Because she'd been working since five in the morning and would continue to work long after the sewers went home, so taking a half hour to hang out with her...friends was absolutely fine. Besides, she'd already been barked at in the fanciest restaurant in town. There was literally nothing those idiots could do to hurt her now. "I'd love it."

"I must be in the wrong studio," a deep voice said from the doorway.

They all turned to see Robert breezing in with a to-go tray of two hot beverages.

"Hey, Robert," Callie said. "Good to see you."

He leaned in and brushed a kiss across her cheek. Then, he gave Delilah the full wattage of his brilliant smile. "Well, hello, there. I'm Robert Granger."

"Delilah Lua. Nice to meet you."

He turned back to the muslin. "So, is this the new Amish line?"

"Ha ha," Knox said. "This is the mock-up. It's how we make sure the dress fits perfectly before we cut expensive and rare fabrics."

"Well, that's a relief." He held the tray out to her. "Got you tea."

"Oh, thank you." She reached for it and cupped it in both hands. "What brings you out here?"

"Bringing you tea isn't reason enough?" Robert said. "No? Okay, fine. I've got news."

"We'll get out of your hair," Callie said.

"Don't leave on my account."

Callie headed for the door. "I have to take this off, and I'm one hundred percent sure I don't want to listen to your news in my underpants. Besides, I left my clothes in the bathroom." She reached for the door, then called back to Knox. "Meet us at Joe's, if you can."

"Will do." Once the women left, she turned to Robert. "So, what's the news?"

He took a leisurely sip of his coffee, obviously toying

with her. "If you only needed one person to show up to make the show worthwhile, who would it be?"

She didn't even have to think. "Alayna Chaumier."

"Now, I'm new at this, but would she happen to be the senior editor at *Bridal Couture* magazine?"

"Oh, my God, don't play around. Is she coming? Did you get her?"

That smile—God, it threw her back to her childhood. Robert had always been ridiculously handsome. He had a sexy mouth and mischievous eyes, thick, dark hair and a trim frame. He dressed well, smelled expensive, and was utterly charming. Her heart swelled to see him so healthy. So vibrant.

This was the man she'd wanted him to be in high school.

This was the man she'd wanted to take her to prom, when she'd worn a sensational dress and wanted to go out on a high note. "How did you get her?"

"Seriously, you completely underestimate yourself. All I had to do was tell her your show's back on. That's it. She wants to come. So much that she's already booked a private appointment with you."

She turned away from him, one hand over her heart to keep it from bursting, and blinked back tears. Her skin felt hot, itchy, and she wanted Gray.

"Hey. You okay? I know I didn't get your approval, but after our conversation the other morning, it seemed like we were all on the same page. You liked everything I'd set up so far. I thought...if I got the right people to come, you'd be happy."

Lost in a cloud of emotion, she couldn't get the words out. She was showing her gowns in Bridal Fashion Week. *It's going to happen.* Alayna Chaumier would see them.

And Knox wasn't scared—not a bit—about what kind of review she'd get. Because she *knew*.

"Babe." His hand landed on her shoulder, and he turned her to face him. "Tell me those are tears of happiness. Tell me that I made you happy."

"So happy." Her voice came out a whisper. "This means everything to me."

"I know."

"Did you get my text?" Knox leaned into the passenger side window.

"Been driving. What's up?" Fact: right after his late afternoon conditioning, Gray had jumped in his truck to go pick her up. Didn't check his phone, grab a water, nothing. Just raced over here to see her.

Highlight of my day.

She opened the door and climbed in. First thing she did was close the window. "It's freezing." She dumped her tote on the floor and lunged for him. With her cold hands on his cheeks, she planted a kiss on his mouth. Nothing sexual, but he didn't care. He just wanted her hands on him.

Holding him close, she said, "Hi," with her dazzling smile.

Fuck, she made him happy. "Hi, beautiful. Good day?"

Before letting him go, she scraped her fingernails through his scruff. When her thumb caressed his lower lip, he about died. And then she sat back in her seat and buckled herself in. "The best. Robert stopped by."

Robert had made her this happy?

"I can't even believe it, but he got the biggest editor and blogger in the bridal business to come to my show. I mean, Luc's PR firm had already booked her for the original one, and she'd made a big deal about it on her page, but the fact that she rearranged her schedule for me is huge."

"That's great." *Dammit.* The pieces just didn't fit. The Robert he found in the bar yesterday didn't align with the Robert who was hitting all his marks for this show.

He sure as hell wished Mrs. Granger would get back to him. He'd sent a text and an email. *No response.*

"I mean, even if no one else comes, I'm still going to have the single biggest influencer there." She tipped her head back. "Oh, my God, Gray, it's going to happen. I'm going to be in Bridal Fashion Week."

He flashed her a grin before turning onto the highway. "I'm happy for you."

"And it's Robert. Of all people. Like, out of the blue he shows up and within a week, I've got my show back."

He sure as hell hoped she did. If Robert was fucking with her…well, they wouldn't let him. They'd stay on top of everything.

"Is everything okay?" She shifted in her seat to face him, hitching up a knee.

Pulled out of his thoughts, he pasted on a smile. "Of course. I'm happy for you."

"Oh, come on. I've known you practically your whole life. I know your smiles."

"My smiles?"

"Yes, and that one says you're withholding information."

"What?"

"You've got the lazy, hey-man-how's-it-going one." She

showed him with half-lidded eyes and a stoner grin. "And the you're-seriously-the-most-delightful-person-I've-ever-met one." She gave him a lovelorn look. "That one's reserved for me."

"I've never smiled like that in my life."

"And you've got the one you just gave me, so what aren't you telling me?"

Bringing up the bar would stir up a hornet's nest of trouble. She'd confront Robert, who'd, in turn, come after Gray, accusing him of throwing shade on him just to look better in Knox's eyes. Stupidly competitive, but that was just the way it had always been between them. With two weeks until the show, she didn't need their drama.

He did, though, need to address his concerns. "So far, Robert's delivered on all of his promises. We've checked into the gallery, the florist...we've seen the agency contracts. Everything's above-board. How can we be sure he's got this blogger?"

She dug into her tote and pulled out her phone. "She'd definitely post it on her blog. Say something about the fact that Knox Holliday's back, that my show's actually going to happen." It only took her a minute to find what she was looking for. "No. Not yet. But that doesn't mean anything."

"He just heard back from her today."

"True. And her last post is from yesterday." She dropped the phone into the tote. "Okay, so I can be happy but not too happy."

"Cautiously optimistic."

"But is that your only hesitation? Like, if we find out the gallery's real and the blogger's actually coming, are you going to bounce around in your seat and pump your fist?"

"You won't see it, but it'll be happening inside." He

reached for her hand and kissed her palm. "He'd have to be a sociopath to lie about things we can easily verify."

"True. Okay, so…I'm going to just sit here and be a little bit excited."

He'd like to not be driving while she did that, so he could watch. "You want to get dinner?"

"I'm too excited to eat." She glanced at his clothing. "Besides, don't you want to shower and change first?"

"Yeah, sure."

"Actually, you know what I want, what I really, really want? I want to drive. No destination. Just…drive. You and me, in the truck."

"Highway or four-wheelin'?"

"You did not just ask me that question." Her smile lit up the cab, and he wanted to bathe in it, read by it, live inside its heat.

Just ahead was a turn-out that headed across the meadow and right to the base of the mountain. He took it. She reached for the radio, flicked it on, and played around until she found a song she liked.

Rolling down her window, she stuck her arm outside and danced along with the country tune. It threw him back to high school, when they'd drive aimlessly, blasting tunes. When he'd loved her, wanted her, but couldn't have her.

Only this time he could have her. And, fuck, if that didn't make his blood hot.

The truck lurched, then bounced along the rutted road. At the base of the mountain, he shot her a questioning look, and she nodded, a gleam in her eyes. So, he floored it, clots of dirt pinging against the truck, the growl of the engine overpowering the radio.

She turned up the volume, singing along with the

country tune. The narrow road didn't afford him a chance to watch her. He wanted to see her skirt ride up, exposing more of her tights-covered thighs, her hair flying in the chilly breeze. Wanted to get his hands and mouth on her.

At the first turn-out, he pulled off, drove right up to the edge and killed the lights. Jackson Hole spread out before them, clusters of light indicating the small towns spread out within the basin.

Just as the song ended, another one came on. "Oh, I love this one. Come on." She threw open the door and started dancing. He cut the engine but kept the radio on and, when she drifted out of sight, he got out of the truck. Knox was rocking out, her hips swaying, arms waving, completely letting loose. Every now and then she'd double over, letting the tips of her hair brush the ground, then fling back up, a cascade of shimmering beauty. Her ass shook, and he wanted to clutch it, but if he did that, she'd stop dancing and singing, and that wouldn't do.

He lowered the back of the truck and leapt onto it, sitting on the edge to watch her dance in the moonlight.

She held her arms out to him. "Dance with me."

Not a chance would he miss the show.

"Come on, sexy pants." With a hand on her stomach, she rocked her hips slowly as she got low to the ground then climbed back up. She cupped her hand, fingers waving him over. "Get over here."

He shook his head, joy filling his body to overflowing. She was the sexiest woman he'd ever seen. *And she's mine.*

The song ended, and the next one was slower. A ballad. She sashayed over to the truck, hitching a foot onto the bed and climbing on. Eyes on him, teeth biting into that plump lower lip, she made her way over to him, crooking a finger. She didn't know what all that untamed hair did to him. Didn't know that her playful smile made his heart pound furiously.

He swiveled around to her, parting his thighs when she got up close.

Hands on his shoulders, her hair brushing across his cheeks, she leaned over. "If you dance with me, I'll make it worth your while."

He got up, but she didn't take a step back, which meant he grazed her, every cell in his body bursting into flames as it came in contact with her lush body. Not a single word in his vocabulary could express how fiercely he wanted her, how her beauty made him wild, and so he showed her with a grip on her ass and a kiss so consuming that need ripped through his body like wind at the summit of a mountain.

Licking into her mouth, he tasted her hunger, reveled in the feel of her hands tangling in his hair. He needed more. More skin, more taste, deeper, harder connection.

Trailing sucking kisses down her neck, he filled his senses with her scent—vanilla, flowery shampoo, and a hint of fresh peaches.

"Gray." She pressed up against him so hard his cock ached.

He slipped a hand between her legs, fingers stroking. Her head tipped back, her eyelids fluttered closed, and she made a soft exhalation, before pushing him off. Lifting her dress, she pulled down her tights and panties and kicked them aside. Then, she turned around. "Unzip me."

His fingers barely managed to latch onto that tiny pull tab, but he got the dress off her shoulders and, before she could turn back around, he reached under the silky fabric to cup her breasts. She moaned, her hair spilling forward, moonlight making the back of her neck glow milky white.

He didn't want a handful of satin, he wanted *her*. One flick of his fingers undid the bra clasp. He nudged the bra straps off and filled his hands with warm, plump flesh, the nipples hard beads against his palms.

She bent over just a little, hands braced on the lip of the truck, and pressed her ass against his cock, swishing it back and forth. *Jesus*. He had to have her. Unbuttoning his jeans with one hand, he grasped his cock and slowly eased inside, the pleasure so intense he had to stop and get a hold of himself. "You feel so fucking good."

Cupping her breasts, she rubbed her nipples roughly. She took what she wanted, and that was hot. Gray pulled out, then slid back in.

"Yes," her voice a breathless hush over the music floating in the air.

Sweat beaded at his hairline, as his hips pumped hard and fast. She arched her back, bringing that spectacular ass higher, slamming it back against him in time with his thrusts.

With the black velvet sky ablaze in glittering stars and the pine-scented air swirling around him, Gray had never felt more connected, more perfectly plugged into his life and the world. This woman, she closed his circle. With her, he was complete.

A deep and profound sense of love swept over him, as he lost himself in her wet heat. Her cries grew more frenzied, her fingers turned white where they clutched the metal. The rush of his climax came in hot and dark, and he didn't know how he could keep it from crashing over him.

He reached around to caress her clit, and the sound ripped from her throat was all it took to push him over. Gripping her hips, he held her in place, as he slammed hard into her and held, his release so intense he about blacked out. But he kept pumping until she threw her head back, cried out, and spasmed in his arms.

This woman was a shooting star.

He just didn't know how to hang onto her.

Chapter Eighteen

IT HAD BEEN BOTHERING HIM ALL NIGHT, SO THE moment she stirred beside him, he said, "I have to tell you something."

"With your hands?" Her arms rose out of the covers, and her body twisted with a crazy stretch. She let out a tortured groan that ended in a shout. "Because I love when you tell me things with your hands."

"No." He hated to douse her playful mood. "It's about Robert."

She stilled. "What about him? Did something happen?"

"Remember I said we dropped in on Gros Ventre to do some backcountry skiing? Well, we parked at the resort in Victor and, before we headed back, we went in to use the bathroom."

"I'm pretty sure peeing in a hotel bathroom isn't the punchline."

"Nope." He scratched the back of his neck. "Robert was there."

"In Idaho? That's weird. What was he doing?"

"He didn't say, but I found him in the bar."

She sat up. "The *bar?* Was he wasted?"

"No. He seemed sober. And that's why I didn't tell you right away. I didn't want it to become—"

"Who was he with?"

"Don't know. Looked like a bunch of older men."

"But you didn't recognize any of them?"

He shook his head, growing uneasy with her line of questioning.

"What was he drinking?"

And here we go again. "I couldn't tell."

"Did he smell like booze? Because you can't hide it. He gets this gluey kind of smell. It's hard to describe."

"If I thought he'd been drinking, I would've told you right away. I didn't smell his breath, but he didn't seem intoxicated."

"So that's why you were subdued last night, when I told you my news."

"That's why."

"I don't understand why he'd be in a bar in the middle of the day in *Idaho*. What's in Victor?"

He didn't bother answering, because it just felt too damn familiar. Knox, drilling him to try and make sense of behaviors that didn't add up. She said she didn't want to go back there, but she was doing it. "I only know what I just told you. Nothing more." *And maybe this is why I didn't tell her right away.* He couldn't stomach this version of her.

"Well, it couldn't be good. First of all, he shouldn't be in a bar."

"I brought that up, and he said he'd been sober for seven years. He could handle a beer or two."

"Which is problematic in itself. Should I talk to him

about it? I mean, I have a right. I can't afford for anything to go wrong, and if he's using—well, I think we all know how spectacularly bad things can go if he's high."

"If you want to talk to him about it, go ahead." He threw back the covers. He needed a shower and a power shake before he hit the gym.

"Are you angry with me?" She got out of bed. "Gray?"

He turned back to her. "I'm not angry. I'm annoyed. I don't want to dissect Robert's behavior." But, no matter how frustrated he was with the situation, he wouldn't leave her to the internal dialogue he knew from past experience she'd be embroiled in for the rest of the day. "I believe two things. One, he needs a career, so I think he's as invested in this working out as we are. If it fails, he looks bad not only in front of his family but in the one industry where he's got a shot of kick-starting things."

"I agree with that. What's the other thing?"

"That he wants to do right by you." He watched her carefully for a reaction, a little disgusted with himself. And when she softened, when she smiled, he felt it like a corkscrew twisting in his heart.

"Yeah. I think so, too."

He wasn't going to do it again, be the third wheel. He wasn't going to watch her reunite with her first love. He went into the bathroom and shut the door. Didn't even wait for the water to get hot, just stepped into the stall and let the cold water crash over him. It startled him, woke him up fully. He needed to hit the trails, run the madness out of his pores. Closing his eyes, he tipped his head back, the warming water saturating his scalp. He poured shampoo into his palms and attacked his hair like it was on fire.

Cold air swirled around his ankles, and he whipped around to find Knox stepping in beside him.

Looking chastised, she stood there in her loose tank top and boxer-style bottoms, water pummeling her, drenching her clothes. "I time-traveled, and I'm sorry. Dialed back the clock a full seven years. I thought…" She shook her head. "Well, I'm aware of it now and I promise to be better about it. But can you do me a favor?"

He reached for her, so damn happy when she stepped into his arms. "I'll do anything for you. You know that." *Except compete with Robert. That…I won't ever do again.*

"I need you to tell me when I'm doing it. Don't shut me out, and don't walk away, okay?"

"Yeah, okay. But Knox?"

She tipped her head up, immediately shutting her eyes against the spray. Shielding her, he walked her back till she hit the wall.

"If you have feelings for Robert, you need to tell me right now. Don't fuck with me about this."

"*Feelings*? Oh, God, no. *Gray.* I just meant I fell back into the old pattern. I don't have any romantic feelings for him." She looked genuinely confused. "I'm with you. How could I possibly want anyone else?"

Relief sideswiped him, knocking him back a step.

She scraped the wet hair out of his eyes. "You okay, there?"

He answered with his hands.

Since she liked the way they talked to her.

"What the hell?" Robert stopped to take in the costumed actors performing a staged shoot-out on the street in front of them.

Owl Hoot, the wild west ghost town Brodie had turned into a living museum, looked right out of an old cowboy movie with its jail, saloon, and general store, but it'd been modernized with working shops, bars, and even an upscale resort.

Strolling on the boardwalk, a group of women in period dresses and parasols nodded to an actor tying his horse's reins to a hitching post.

Robert winked at them. "This place is amazing."

"Yeah, Brodie did a good job." As his friend took it all in, Gray stepped behind Knox, bracing his hands on the wooden bannister, and nuzzled her ear. "Good day?" They hadn't had a chance to catch up yet. He'd prefer to be alone with her, but Robert had wanted to update them on the show.

She touched his hands, leaning back into him. "Really good."

"Tell me after dinner?"

"Is this what it was like for you?" Robert's voice shattered their quiet intimacy. He observed them with a smile, but since Gray knew first-hand what it felt like to be the third wheel, he knew it wasn't sincere.

It sucked not to be the one who got to go home with Knox. "It was a thousand times worse." *Because she's my heart.*

"We going to get some grub?" Robert asked.

"You bet." Gray needed to be more careful. He didn't want to make his friend uncomfortable. "Delilah's expecting us." They continued along the boardwalk, crossed the street, and headed into the resort hotel. Keeping with the wild west theme, the lobby had deep red carpet and shiny brass sconces and chandeliers. The staff dressed in the style of the early nineteen-hundreds, when Calamity was founded.

Reaching for Knox's hand, Gray led the way to Wally's, the elegant restaurant with one-hundred-eighty-degree views of the sage meadows and dark gray Teton range.

"How the hell did Brodie do this?" Robert marveled at the décor, before heading into the restaurant with them. "I thought he designed terrain parks."

"A little over a year ago, his friends were making noise about moving to Seattle or San Diego," Gray said. "They couldn't make a decent living here. My dad always called him a visionary, and I guess he was right, because Brodie came up with this idea and then, a year later, here we are. It's a work in progress, of course, but he's gotten a lot done."

Robert looked to Knox. "See that? Brodie's no architect. He's not an engineer or a contractor. A year from now, I could be Luc Bellerose."

"You absolutely could," Knox said. "Though it might take a teeny bit more than a year."

"Hey, Gray," the hostess said. "Delilah's got a table all set for you guys. She's prepared a tasting menu. Come on."

They wove their way through the light wood tables and pale green booths, greeting familiar faces, until they reached their four-top. Just as Gray moved to slide in next to Knox, Robert did the same, and they collided.

Robert grinned. "Old habit." He took the chair across from them. "Okay, so, the florist's all over your idea. He's working with the gallery owner, who's got concerns about her floor, but they said not to worry, they'll take care of it. I've got three more models, which means we're good to go even if I can't get any more since they can repeat."

"I have to ship the dresses to New York this Friday,"

Knox said. "Are they going to the gallery? Can she store them for me?"

"She can't close down that long," Robert said. "But she does have a storage space we can use."

"Well, they can't just be in a storage space." Knox looked worried. "They're fragile, and the fabric picks up odors."

Robert raised a hand. "It's actually the unoccupied building right next door. We have to pay the landlord the same amount we'd pay for a pop-up store."

"The person you've hired," Gray said. "Does she know how to pack wedding gowns?"

"Of course." Robert sounded offended. "I'm flying someone in from LA."

"Hey, it's a valid question," Gray said.

"At some point you have to trust me. Have I fucked up yet, even once?"

"That's got nothing to do with making sure the person you hired can handle seventy-five-thousand-dollars-worth of couture wedding gowns," Gray said.

"Let's put ego aside," Knox said. "This is my show. I have to be on top of everything. I'd be stupid not to." She pulled her napkin out from under the silverware and spread it across her lap. "Okay, so, we've got nine models."

"Ten." Robert smiled, pleased with himself. "That retired one I mentioned? She's in."

"Can I see them?"

"Yeah, sure." He pulled out his phone, scrolled until he found what he was looking for, and passed it over. "I've got their portfolios in a Dropbox file."

While Gray downed his water, Knox flipped quickly through the file. "I don't recognize any of these women.

Oh. Wait." She looked up at him with a strange expression. "That's Marie-Thérèse."

"Yeah. She retired a couple years ago. After she had a baby."

"I thought she only came out of retirement for Luc."

"Apparently, she'll do it for Grangers, too." Robert took his phone back. "I can be pretty persuasive."

"Oh, I'm well aware."

"I'm sure you are, since you learned on the first day we met." Robert grew animated. "You remember that day? I told you I'd followed a coyote."

"How could I forget? Not many people spend Christmas morning alone in a park. It shocked the hell out of me to see someone else there. Especially a kid from school."

"What were you doing there anyway?" Gray knew the story, of course, but as a kid he hadn't thought to ask. It only struck him now that she'd been *nine* at the time. "You lived pretty far from any parks."

"Christmas Eve, we spent the night at the lodge, where my mom worked," Knox said. "I don't really remember much, just that she wasn't waking up, and I was getting impatient to open my presents."

"I'll tell you why she left the room." Robert only had eyes for Knox, and they glittered with a private joke. "You wanted hot chocolate."

She leaned closer to Gray. "How do you even remember that?"

He lifted his arm and wrapped it around her, ridiculously pleased when she settled in against him.

"The lobby had a coffee and tea station, and you wanted cocoa. But you couldn't reach it. You spilled something, and when people started coming over, you ran out of there like you'd just pulled off a heist."

"That's exactly what it felt like."

"And you ran across the street to the park. As soon as I saw you, I wanted you to stay with me, but I knew you'd want to go back inside when the coast was clear." One side of his mouth curled up. "So I told you I'd seen a coyote in my backyard, and that I'd followed him."

"And there I went, trying to track down an imaginary wild animal. Nice job."

"Well, it started *us*, so…no regrets."

"All I really wanted was to open my presents." She didn't acknowledge his sentimental comment, and Gray appreciated it.

"And the hot chocolate," Robert said.

"And the hot chocolate." Knox turned to Gray. "We wound up spending the whole day together. Forgot all about the stupid coyote. My mom went nuts trying to find me, and I never did get my hot chocolate."

Gray breathed in the scent of her floral shampoo. "Did you get what you wanted that Christmas?"

She rewarded his question with a sweet smile. "I did. My mom came through and got me the Deluxe Magnadoodle."

"Oh, my God." Robert slapped the table. "Do you remember those walkie talkies we had?"

"That was hilarious." She straightened, looking at Gray to explain. "We—"

"—wanted to see how far apart we could get and still hear each other." Robert deliberately cut Gray out of the conversation. "But I took it too far and started climbing down the cliff. Shit, do you still have that scar?"

"Of course."

Robert reached across the table to cradle her hand, turning it over, and running a finger along the fleshy part of her palm. "I told you not to follow me down there."

"Where did you think I should go?" She pulled her hand back. "I was completely alone in the woods, it was getting dark, and there were creepy sounds out there." She pointed a finger at Robert. "And you weren't using the walkie talkie anymore, because you wanted to go home in time for—"

"The Sopranos."

Knox shook her head. "Nope. *The Amazing Race.* You wanted to enter with Gray." She nudged him with an elbow. "Do you remember how obsessed he was? He was so worried they'd end the show before you guys were old enough to be on it."

"You're right," Robert said. "You're totally right. It was *The Amazing Race.* In fact, that's why I tried to climb down that cliff."

"You were in training."

"Exactly. But then you came after me." He squeezed his eyes shut. "Jesus." When he opened them, he clasped his hands behind his head. "I thought my heart was going to beat right out of my chest."

"What happened?" Gray asked.

"You don't know?" Robert asked, at the same time Knox said, "I found him. He was making his way down the side of the mountain...more like skidding down. He kept landing on his butt, and I called out to him to wait for me, but he couldn't—"

"Dude, gravity had me fuckin' careening down that mountain. But I turned around and saw you *jump.* You jumped off the ledge, and I thought you were good, you landed, but then you lost your footing. Slammed onto a boulder and sliced your hand open. Jesus. I felt so bad."

"Yeah, but you took really good care of me," Knox said. "You gave me a piggyback ride to your house. Cleaned my wound. Gave me the last Klondike bar."

A phone chimed. Knox reached into her tote bag and pulled it out, reading the screen. "It's Delilah. She wants me to come to the kitchen and say hi. I'll be right back." She got up and took off, both of them watching until she disappeared behind the double doors.

When she was out of sight, Gray turned to his friend. "Come on, man. Don't do that."

"Do what?" Robert reached for his water and took a long, slow drink. He set the glass down, pulled the napkin out from under the silverware, and dabbed his mouth.

He was *not* going to play games. Not where Knox was concerned. "I thought you were all about your career."

"I am."

"Then, why play games with me?"

"Oh. Is that we're calling it? Because I call it catching up with my ex-girlfriend."

"I get what you lost, and it sucks. But it's been seven years. You made your choices. Don't try to mess up what Knox and I have."

All civility left, as Robert planted his feet on the floor and lunged forward so fast water sloshed out of glasses. "And you don't think it's fucked up to hook up with my ex? What about the bro code? You wouldn't go after one of your brother's exes."

"No, I wouldn't. I wouldn't go after any woman who'd been with any of my friends or brothers." He paused to make his point very, very clear. "Except for Knox. And I think you know that."

"Oh, I knew." Robert's smile turned hard and mean. "Everyone knew. You had it bad for my girl."

A flood of heat washed up his neck, burning the back of his neck, but he kept his mouth shut.

"You had everything a guy could ever want," Robert said. "Brothers, a dad, money…and everything you touched turned to gold. You had everything…except the one thing you wanted most." He leaned in so close, Gray could see the birthmark on the edge of Robert's jaw. "My girlfriend."

And that was it. Gray'd had enough. "My dad treated you like his own. You were part of my family until you stole from him. You had money, *and* you had skills. If you hadn't chosen drugs over boarding, you could've competed with us. You made your choices. And, yes, I wanted her, but I never touched her, never made a move. I respected your relationship even through all the years you treated her like shit."

"Right, Saint Gray. Perfect fucking Gray Bowie. You want to lay it all out on the table, then let's do it." He stabbed a finger at Gray. "You don't bail on friends when they need you most."

So, he'd lied about being cool with everything. *No surprise there.* "I didn't bail on you. I tried everything I could to help you, to get you clean. You didn't want it, and when I finally figured that out, I backed away. I wasn't going down with you."

"You stayed for Knox. You wanted to be her hero…it's the only reason you stuck around as long as you did. Don't pretend it was anything other than that."

"Are you fucking serious? You *know* how hard I tried. You want to blame me, but *you're* the one who ended the friendship. You ended it when you chose drugs over me.

When you chose to get high over hanging out with me. Every time you asked me to bail you out of trouble? That was using me. It sure as hell wasn't friendship. Stealing my dad's watch, showing up wasted to a competition? Friends don't do that. But you're right about one thing. Nothing —*nothing*—made me sicker than watching you hurt her. That was the deal-breaker for me. How many times did you let her down? Break her heart? I couldn't stand it."

"And yet she still chose me. Must've sucked, huh? Mr. Perfect couldn't get the girl."

He'd never seen this side of affable, charming Robert, and suddenly the picture came into focus. "Jesus, did you ever love her? Or has it always been competition with me?"

"Everything okay here?" Knox sat down, looking between them.

"Just clearing the air," Robert said.

She gazed up at Gray with concern. "You okay?" She stroked his thigh.

"Fine."

"You don't look fine." She drew in a breath. "Guys, whatever issues you have to work through, I'm going to ask that we deal with it after fashion week, okay? Please? Can we do that?"

"Of course." But Gray wasn't sure they could.

Because he'd never been less sure of Robert's motives.

Knox patted her face dry, then pulled the elastic out of her hair. "Gray?"

"Yeah?"

Leaning back, she looked through the doorway

into her bedroom and found him facing the window, stark naked, stretching the resistance band. *Holy mother of God.* Feet braced, he stood there with one arm stretched all the way out and the other bent at the elbow and crossing his chest, making his biceps bulge. The muscles of his back flexed, his broad shoulders tapering to a trim waist and rock-hard bubble ass.

That ass started moving, bunching and releasing like some *Magic Mike* dancer. When she glanced up, she caught his big grin in the window's reflection. "Perv."

He glanced over his shoulder. "You're the one thinking sketchy thoughts about my ass."

"It's really nice." She made a circling motion with her finger. "Why don't you face me when we're having a conversation?"

"It's just safer for me this way."

"Safer?"

"Yeah. Once I show you the frontal view, you'll leap across the bed like a mountain lion."

"If you're talking about your wiener...I don't know, Gray. At this point, it's just kind of...same old same old, you know?"

"You sure about that?" He turned around to reveal a hard-on like a steel bar.

"Oh, my God, Gray. Is that from staring at your own reflection?" She balled up her hand towel and tossed it at him. Of course, he snatched it out of the air. "If you're about done with your Mr. Universe poses, do you think we can go to bed now?"

"That depends. You going to keep me up all night with your insatiable needs?"

Pretending to give it some thought, she let her gaze

wander from those strong shoulders to the sculpted pecs, down his ripped torso, to his thick, long erection. "Yes."

He got back to stretching. "Then I've got to stay in shape."

"You're very disciplined." She flicked off the light and sashayed toward him. "I admire that." When she reached him, she set her hands lightly on his chest. He dropped the resistance band and reached for her, but she shook her head. "Don't let me interrupt your routine."

She skimmed those powerful shoulders, the skin smooth and hot, and down his thickly muscled arms, her palms registering every curve and bulge. Up on her toes, she leaned into his neck and breathed him in. "You smell as good as you look." Reaching around, she stroked his back, the muscles flexing under her touch. When she got to his ass, she squeezed hard.

He grunted. "You've got about ten seconds before I toss you on the bed."

"Hold your horses." With her hands full of his ass, she kissed the hollow at the base of his neck, then wandered to one nipple, which she licked and sucked before trailing wet kisses across to the other one.

His hand came to the back of her hand, and she shook him off. "Dammit, Knox."

"It's not every day a woman gets the run of a body like this."

He cupped her cheeks, tilted her face. "I'm not a body. I'm Gray."

Clarity hit her like an alarm jarring her out of a deep sleep. She didn't know why it had taken her so long to get it. He'd grown up feeling invisible in his family, but then she'd gone and done the same thing when all she did was talk about Robert.

She brought her hands around to his chest, sweeping up and around his neck. "You should know that it's not the hard body that turns me on—lots of men are fit. It's not your handsome face, your medals and trophies, and it's certainly not your money. It's the man who takes responsibility for the actions of his friend, when she drives a Jeep through someone's living room."

"It was *your* living room."

"You would've gone above and beyond no matter whose career Amelia had wiped out. I see you, Gray, and I feel so damn lucky to be with you. Every minute of every day, you're on my mind, and you can bet your very hard ass that the immediate thought that follows is how grateful I am that you chose me." She dropped to her knees, and the vulnerability in his eyes only made her want him more.

Grasping his erection with both hands, one on top of the other, she stroked him in twisting pulls. She took pity on his strained expression by licking the head with the flat of her tongue.

His fingers dug into her hair, barely touching her scalp, but poised to grip her if she dared pull off. It made her smile. Until she sucked him deep into her mouth, one hand tugging on him, the other clutching his ass to keep him right where she needed him.

His hips flexed, and he started pumping. She watched his chest rise and fall, his eyelids lower. Loved the way his hands clamped down on the sides of her head, the tremble in his thighs, and the groans deep in his throat.

"Fuck, Knox. Fuck."

He was moving too fast for her to flick her tongue, so she used suction instead. He had that just-showered scent of soap and man, and his fingers digging into her hair, the rough punch of his hips, made her drenched with desire.

"I'm gonna come. I'm gonna come so fucking hard." His fingers shifted to the back of her head, holding her in place, while he released in short, hard thrusts.

She sucked and licked, drawing out his climax, and she was rewarded with animalistic sounds and the twisting of his hips.

He let out a harsh exhalation, before letting her go and sliding out of her mouth. "Jesus. You're going to kill me." He fell back onto the bed.

"It's a good way to go, though, right?" She got in beside him.

"The best."

"Come on. Get under the covers."

"I can't feel my toes."

In the cover of dark, she eased off the bed and lowered to a crouch. His legs hung off the mattress, elevating his feet. She gathered a lock of hair and brushed the strands over his bare soles.

He jerked. "Okay, okay."

"You said you were numb. Just making sure you're all right."

She *loved* the rumble of his sleepy laughter. He reached for her and hauled her onto the bed. They both got under the covers, and his big arm wrapped around her, enfolding her in his heat and strength.

It didn't take long for his breathing to even out, and his muscles to slacken.

But she was wired and knew she wouldn't be sleeping anytime soon. Gently, she lifted his arm from her waist.

"Hey." He sounded adorably sleepy. "Where you going?"

"Go to sleep. I'll be back in a bit."

His head popped off the pillow, and he squinted at her. "What's wrong?"

It would have been so easy to say, *Nothing*, but she didn't want that kind of relationship with him. "I'm scared."

"You think Robert's going to screw us over?"

"You know, you always think it's Robert who's got the power to hurt me the most, but you're wrong."

"Wrong?" He sat up, shoving the hair off his face. His powerful body belied his confused, boyish expression. "What're you talking about?"

As a kid, she'd gotten the concept of love all wrong. What she had with Robert was loyalty, obligation, guilt. Because he was her boyfriend, she'd forced the jumble of powerful emotions to fit in a box labeled love.

But with Gray, she had respect, awe, gratitude, affection…it was love. Pure and simple. How did she know? Because losing Robert had made her feel guilty. Losing Gray had ruined her. "It's you."

"*Me?*"

"You think I left town because prom night was my wake-up call, but it had nothing to do with Robert crashing into a plate glass window. There was absolutely nothing new about that."

"Then what was it?"

"It was you leaving me. You were the one constant in my life. The one person who seemed to like me unconditionally. No matter how hard people tried to humiliate me, no matter how many times I lost my shit over where Robert was or what he was doing, how hard I took it when I got a rejection letter from Parson's, you were always there. You were the only barrier between me and loneliness. Until you weren't. Until I was so twisted that you couldn't stand me one more second."

"That's not why I left."

"Yes, it was, and you don't have to lie about it. You didn't leave because you were in love with your best friend's girlfriend. You'd put up with that for years. You left because I disgusted you. And that was the coldest, harshest wake-up call I could have gotten." She got out of bed, too upset to lay beside him. Because in a week, he'd leave for New Zealand, while she took off for New York.

And she was terrified to lose him all over again.

"It gutted me," she continued. "I didn't think I'd ever recover. I felt shame and…horror. I couldn't even live in my own skin. My mom was working on the ranch, so she wasn't around, Robert was in rehab, and you were gone, so all I had was myself, and I thought if I didn't change my life I would die. So, I left. Packed my suitcase, got on a bus, and moved to New York, where I could grow a new skin."

"You got it wrong." He shifted to the edge of the mattress, elbows on his knees, gazing up at her with an earnest expression. "I was disgusted with *me*. All those years I saw myself as the outsider looking in. But that night, I realized that I was as caught up in my relationship with you as you were with Robert, and I needed to cut myself off. I needed a clean break. When you wouldn't come with me, I got that you'd never be mine, and so I left." He stood up. "I'm sorry I hurt you. I honestly thought you wouldn't even notice, that you'd be so invested in Robert's rehab and in keeping him clean, that you wouldn't even notice I was missing." He stroked the hair off her face.

"Robert was my job," she said. "He was responsibility,

and that was fueled by the terrible guilt that if I took my eyes off him, he might die, and I couldn't live with that. You, you were my happy place. You made me laugh and listened to my dreams and fears. You were everything good. And when you left me, my world went dark. I have never been so scared in my life. Not as a teenager alone in New York City or a young woman in Paris for her first job, not when Luc stole my sketchbook, and not when Amelia drove into my living room. The worst day of my life was when I understood you were gone for good. And I'll be honest with you. Deep down, I'm not sure I believe you're going to stay this time."

Chapter Nineteen

KNOX STOOD IN THE PARKING LOT, LEAVES skittering across the asphalt in a crisp autumn breeze, and watched the truck spew exhaust as it turned onto the highway. Every time she blinked, she saw the profusion of tulle, organza, and lace imprinted on her eyelids.

Her dresses were headed to New York.

I'm doing this.

It's happening.

She was so giddy with excitement she wanted to scream.

The wrong arms came around her from behind and lifted her off the ground. "It's done, baby. We're on our way to Bridal Fashion Week." Robert set her down and opened his arms, but when she didn't step into them, he faltered.

"You have to cut it out. We're not together. I'm with Gray, and you can't call me 'baby' or touch me like that."

"Pretty sure he can handle a hug between old friends, but whatever. You can be excited from over there." He grinned broadly. "And I'll do it right here. Because, honey, it is *on*."

"I can't believe it." She pressed her hands together. "I just can't believe it."

"Believe it. It's real. We did this. We made it happen."

"No, you did. I'd put it in my rearview mirror." He'd gotten fifteen models, really good stylists and make-up artists, and even some of the best influencers. In the space of a few weeks, he'd pulled it all together.

"Hey, good news. I was able to move up our flight."

"What are you talking about?" That dimmed her mood.

"Did some smooth talking with the airline to get us on a flight the day after tomorrow."

That would mean leaving Gray two days earlier. She'd counted on that time. "I don't know that I can leave before Friday. I've got so much to do before then."

Robert bent his knees to look her in the eyes. "Three words. Bridal. Fashion. Week."

"I know, but…"

"We have to fit the dresses to the models. And I know you want to be there while the florist sets up the space."

He's right. "I do." Besides, she and Gray were strong. They'd only be apart ten days. She let out a breath. "No, you're right. This is good." She was about to launch her career, and she was worried about spending two extra days with her boyfriend?

The whole world is waiting to see this collection, Knox.

Word had spread, so Luc would know about her show by now. Would he try to ruin it? *I mean, for goodness' sake, he called Calamity's town hall.*

Okay, but really, what's the worst he can do? She knew that answer. Claim ownership of her collection. Her word wouldn't stand a chance against The House of Bellerose.

"You can trust Amelia and Zach to take care of things here."

"Of course. No, it's all good. Can you send me the booking information? I might try and see if Gray can come."

"What? No. He's got a competition next week. Don't do that to him. You know if you ask him, he'll come. He needs to get in the zone."

"You're right. I'm being selfish."

"These competitions are life-or-death, and you can't perform when you're distracted. It's ten days. You do your thing, he'll do his, and then you'll be back together like I never happened."

The night of her going-away party, Knox sat curled up in a chair, a glass of wine in her hand, as the flames from the fire pit cast an orange glow on the patio.

The Bowie brothers stood talking to each other, Callie nestled in the shelter of Fin's arms, and Delilah sitting on a low wall, one hand in Will's back pocket. The crack of pool balls reminded her that Gray's posse was inside, and that they'd become more than work associates to her.

The fire crackled, wine warmed her blood, and the hum of conversation and laughter made her feel utterly content.

Gray parted from his brothers and dropped into the chair beside her. He patted his lap. "Come here, beautiful."

She curled up on him, resting her head on his shoulder. "I'm going to miss you."

"We'll talk every day."

"It's not the same. Promise me we won't drift apart."

"Are you kidding me?" He tipped her chin. "I first laid eyes on you in Mrs. Flint's kindergarten class. I remember to this day the funny feeling I got just from looking at you. That night at dinner, I told my mom I was worried about my heart because I'd felt it flip over. My asshole brothers teased the shit out of me, so I never brought it up again. But, by the time I was ten, every time I saw you or talked to you or got anywhere near you, my heart got too big for my chest. I didn't know what it meant. It was just a physical reaction to you. And then, when I was thirteen, you got out of the lake in your bikini and my dick went hard."

She grinned at him.

"Yeah, real funny when you're surrounded by little kids and parents and guys from school. But you came right over to me and sat down, blabbing away, and I couldn't hear anything because my heart was thundering, and I thought I was going to die." He shifted, holding her in both his big, powerful arms. "I finally figured it out."

"Figured what out?"

"You're my heart."

Her skin pebbled and went hot at the same time.

"So, ten days or ten years…makes no difference," he continued. "Nothing can ever change my feelings for you." He kissed her, slow, sexy, and achingly sweet. Then, reaching for her hand, he pressed it to his chest. "Because you're right here."

She flung her arms around his neck. "There's nowhere else I want to be." Her mouth turned toward his ear. "Ever."

And she'd do whatever it took to stay there.

. . .

The art gallery two blocks south of Houston Street was the coolest Knox had ever seen. With music blasting and the florist and his team setting up the English garden, she'd never felt closer to her dreams.

Wishing Gray could be here, she pulled her phone out of her tote and shot a quick video of the scene and sent it to him.

"What're you doing?" Robert asked. "We don't want anyone to see our set."

"It's just for Gray."

"Cool. Just make sure he doesn't show it to anybody. Then, again, he doesn't know anyone in our world. You up for some good news?"

"Always."

He showed her the screen of his phone. "Check it out."

It was an email. *Subject: Knox Holliday Show.* She skimmed, trying to get the gist. Someone was coming to her show. *Who?* Robert's finger tapped the From box.

Jack Abrams. Her body exploded with adrenaline. She read the message again. Just four words. *Would like to attend.* She whipped around to him. "You invited Jack Abrams?"

"Babe, I invited everyone I was told mattered. He was top of the list."

"Yeah, but he's not an influencer. How did you know about him?"

"His name kept coming up."

"I can't believe this."

He held her gaze. "This is it, Knox. Your ticket to couture. He's going to see your dresses and lose his shit.

He's going to offer you a contract. You're going to be a designer with Jack Abrams Couture."

"Thank you so much. I'm so happy." Amidst the noise and chaos, the anxiety and nerves, she sank into the arms of the man who'd held such a huge part of her childhood.

And who'd been the one to deliver her dream as an adult. *Full circle.*

"You know I'd do anything to change what I put you through."

She tried to pull away, but he tightened his hold. She saw what he needed, and she gave it to him. "I know. I forgive you." But he didn't look in any way relieved. "You've made up for it, believe me."

"But I haven't. Nothing can erase the hell I put you through. You were the best girlfriend ever. The best *friend*, and I treated you like shit. I just want you to know—not that it helps—but it was the drugs treating you like shit. It wasn't me. If I were in my right mind, I would've listened to you. I would've stopped hanging out with those assholes. I would've stopped filling my body with poison." He let out a huff of breath, color rising in his cheeks. "I would've been a better man for you."

She'd never seen him so overcome with emotion. He'd learned as a kid not to show any—his mom hadn't been around, his dad couldn't handle anything, and his nannies didn't care. So, to see him experiencing real, deep, true remorse...it meant he'd really changed. She rubbed his arm. "We can't change the past. It's over and done. What we have is the present." She pulled away and gestured to the room. "And this is what we've done together."

"We make an awesome team. You know, I'm not looking for us to get back together—I know you're with Gray—but if there's a place for me at Jack Abrams with you, I want it. Swear to God, Knox, I'll bust my ass for you."

"I have a feeling Granger's is going to hire you full-time, and that's your legacy. That's where you belong."

He shrugged. "But if it doesn't work out that way, then think about hiring me, okay?"

That wouldn't happen. For many reasons, but mostly because of Gray. "One step at a time, right? Let's hope they fall in love with my dresses."

"They will. Guarantee it."

Everything was in place.

Now, all she needed was for Luc not to undermine her.

The four brothers stood in the empty expanse of living room, taking in all its…starkness. Gray breathed in the scent of fresh paint in the newly-built house.

"Gotta say, there's a lot of light." Hands planted on his hips, Will glanced at the floor-to-ceiling windows that overlooked the lap pool in the tiny backyard.

The marble floor looked shiny as a frozen lake. What the hell were they doing here? Brodie would never go for a house like this. It did, though, make him wonder if Knox would ever live in the house he'd built. He had no idea what had possessed him to take her there. She had to have seen it in his eyes, what he wanted. He'd jumped the gun on that one.

She'd texted him the good news about Jack Abrams coming to her show. If she got that contract—which she would—where would she set up shop? New York, most likely.

Did he want to live in New York City? Not really, but he'd go. No idea what he'd do there, but it wasn't like he'd break up with her. They could have houses in both places.

"What happens in a hailstorm?" Fin drifted into the kitchen, all white and chalkboard gray. "What is all this?"

Gray followed him in to find a platter of mini quiches, four wine goblets, and two bottles of red wine. "The real estate agent set this up?"

"I guess so." Brodie came in from the terrace.

"Watch out," Will called. "Or she'll wind up as your future wife."

The guys burst out laughing, forcing Brodie to look up from his phone. "Huh?"

"We came here for you," Gray said. "You might want to get your head out of your ass and look around."

"You wanted me to look into three-D modeling."

"Not now," Gray said. "We're looking at houses."

"I thought Knox doesn't want to do the digital platform," Fin said.

"She'll change her mind." Brodie tapped out a text. "I've reached out to some people. Got someone whose work I really like."

"So you're not just a visionary," Gray said. "You're a psychic, too?"

"Writing's right there on the wall for anyone to see," Brodie said. "It's the future of her industry."

Gray knew it made sense, given the digital world they lived in, but Knox had a dream, and she'd stop at nothing to achieve it. He turned to his older brother. "You want to live in town?"

"We're just getting started," Brodie said. "And she's showing me what's on the market in my price range."

Fin stood in front of the sink, looking out the window

to the neighbor's house. "You can't walk around naked." He glanced behind him. "Which eliminates a lot of fun activities."

"Ones that involve countertops," Will said.

"And walls," Gray added.

"And kitchen tables." Will picked up a quiche and sniffed.

"What're you assholes talking about?" Brodie said.

Fin gestured toward the living area. "The agent obviously wants you to buy this house."

"I told you she's showing me lots of places."

"And does she set out quiches and wine in all of them?" Will asked.

Brodie stared at the offending items, almost like he'd just found out a Russian spy had planted them to get intel on him. "No." He slapped the quiche out of Will's hand. "Let's get out of here."

As they headed out, Gray took a picture of the food and the house and sent it to Knox. *Brodie's future home.*

While his brother locked up, the guys headed down the walkway to the sidewalk.

Knox responded. *No way. But those hors d'oeuvres look tasty.*

"Learned something new about you, brother." Will clapped Brodie on the back. "Never knew you were a wine-sniffing—"

"Quiche-eating—" Gray said.

"Glass house dwelling—" Fin said.

"Did you just say 'dwelling'" Will let out a bark of laughter so loud, some tourists up the street turned to look.

"You guys are assholes," Brodie said with a grin. "I'm just looking."

They turned onto Main Street and walked right into Mrs. Granger and a group of her well-heeled friends.

"Oh, hey." Gray touched her shoulder and leaned in for a quick hug, sucking in a cloud of her expensive perfume. "I'm so glad I ran into you." His brothers had continued across the street to the town green.

A warm smile lit her face. "Gray. How nice to see you." She gestured to her companions. "This is my team. We've just returned from Milan and have so much discuss. We hold our annual retreat here in Calamity." She touched his arm. "I know I owe you a call. Can we catch up tomorrow?"

He'd been trying to get confirmation from her about the show, and since he had her right here and now, he'd just go for it. "I just wanted to thank you for all you're doing for Knox."

"I see it quite the other way. She's going to bring customers into my store with her fabulous gowns."

"True, but I actually meant Bridal Fashion Week. She and Robert are there now." The moment he said her son's name her smile faltered. The punch of alarm had him pressing on. "He's done a great job. Surprised us how he put everything together in three weeks. And it wouldn't have happened without your support."

"I thought you said Knox's dresses were ruined? That she'd lost her show? Isn't that why I'm hosting the boutique?"

Christ. If Granger's wasn't funding the week-long event, where was Robert getting the money? Where had he gotten the connections? "We were able to get at least one of each dress made, and Robert took care of everything else. It's an expensive undertaking, and we appreciate that you believed in her enough to back it."

"I'm sorry. I'm confused. I'm not backing anything."

His pulse spiked, but he wouldn't lose it yet. The Granger Collection was a big company. She might not know what the fashion show department—or whatever it was called—did. "No, but Granger's is. The department that handles fashion shows."

"We don't have a 'department' for that." She gave an irritable smile to her team. "Can you excuse us, please? I'll just be a moment." She waited until they were heading into the restaurant. "Gray, dear, Robert doesn't work for me."

"I know. He told us about your arrangement."

Confusion turned into annoyance. "What arrangement?"

"That he's doing contract work for you until he proves himself."

Releasing a weary breath, Mrs. Granger looked unspeakably sad. "I love my son, but he doesn't work for me or my company. Not in any capacity. I don't know what he told you, but I know nothing about fashion week, nor are we in any way supporting him. Not with finances or connections. I'm sorry if he misrepresented the situation to you."

Fucker. "Well, I guess it's good I found out before the actual show. Thank you. Have a great retreat, Mrs. Granger." Hopping off the curb, he had his phone out and the pad of his finger pressing on his pilot's speed dial. Jogging across the street, he caught up with his brothers, who'd gathered around the truck.

"Hello?" his pilot answered. "Gray?"

"Yeah, Sarah, listen, how soon can you get me to New York City?"

"Whenever you want. You buy my fealty," she said. "When would you like to go?"

"It'll take me twenty minutes to get home and pack a bag. Another twenty to get to the airport." Fin could handle getting together what he needed for New Zealand.

"So much for that deep exfoliating mask I just put on. Let me check into it, and I'll get back to you. But it shouldn't be a problem to get out tonight."

"Great, thanks." He swung open the door of his truck.

"What's going on?" Fin climbed into the passenger seat and reached for the seatbelt.

"That fucker lied to us. Again. I knew it. I knew when I found him drinking in a bar in Idaho that something was wrong."

"We talking about Robert?" Brodie asked from the back.

"What'd he do?" Will asked.

"Told us he was a contract worker for his mom's company. That they were backing the show." He grimaced. "His mom said he doesn't work with her in any capacity."

"Okay," Brodie said. "But you and Knox have checked everything out. It's all legit."

True. That brought his temper down a notch. "I have to tell her."

"You want me to drive?" Fin asked. "Pull over. You can call her right now."

"I'll call her from the airport. I have to pack."

"What?" Fin said. "No. Gray, you can't go there. We leave for New Zealand in four days."

He had no idea what Robert was up to, only that he had to find out for himself. "I know that. Soon as I check things out, I'll fly there straight from New York." He turned onto the highway.

"Do you see why getting involved with Knox right now isn't the best timing?" Brodie asked quietly.

"There is no circumstance under which I wouldn't be with her, do you understand? I've wanted Knox Holliday all my life, and there isn't a damn thing—including a fucking medal—that will ever come before her."

The moment the cab turned off Houston onto Broadway, traffic snarled. "This is good right here." Gray fished four twenties out of his wallet and handed them to the driver. Hauling his duffle bag, he got out onto the street, jogged between idling cars, and hustled over to the row of art galleries.

Without checking addresses, he knew which one hosted Knox's show. A string of white lights framed a plate glass window, and passersby peered inside. Well-dressed people gathered outside the door, waiting to get in.

This is everything she's ever wanted.

That fucker better not have screwed anything up.

Avoiding the crowd, he hitched his bag onto his shoulder and headed down a narrow alleyway between two brick buildings. Knox would be in back, anyway, getting her models ready.

He'd hoped to get into town before the show, but mechanical issues had grounded his plane for hours, which meant he hadn't been able to get out of Calamity until morning. While he wouldn't tell her about Robert's deception right now—not in the middle of her show—he wanted to be here in case something went wrong.

Heading for the yellow light at the end of the alley, he heard laughter. *Robert.* He stopped, peering around the building to size up the situation.

Christ, this is too familiar. At twenty-five, he was back to checking up on Robert, protecting Knox from him.

Yep, there he was. With his back to him, Robert talked quietly to some guy with shaggy hair, skinny jeans, and a pork pie hat. Disappointment slammed him—which meant he'd held out some small hope that Robert wasn't out here buying drugs.

"Okay, man, cool. I gotta get back in." Robert pulled his wallet out of his back pocket, fiddled with it a minute. "What the fuck?" He let out an uncomfortable laugh. "Come on."

Gray was close enough to see the tremble in Robert's fingers, his inability to grasp a bill. Anger welled up hard and fast. *Fucker's wasted at Knox's show?* It took every ounce of restraint not to charge out there and confront the asshole. Except he knew from experience not to mess with someone on drugs. He couldn't do anything that might jeopardize the show. So, he waited while they made the exchange. Immediately after the dealer quickly took off, Robert unscrewed the small cap, tapped the container onto his palm, and swallowed some pills.

Jesus Christ. Gray strode right past him and reached for the door handle to get into the building. "Hey, man."

Robert spun around. "What the fuck are *you* doing here?"

Forcing a casual stance, Gray said, "Came to support Knox."

"You just can't stay away, can you?" He stepped closer. "Don't you have a competition to get to?"

"Sure do. I'll head out the day after tomorrow." He gave him a chin nod, biting down on everything he wanted to say. Gray grasped the handle, but the moment he pulled, Robert lunged and yanked on his arm.

"You're not going in there. We're in the middle of a show." His pupils were blown, his body shook with energy.

Gray wanted to say, *Really? Because it looked like you were in the middle of a drug deal.* But it wouldn't help Knox, so he got his temper under control. "Yeah, I know."

"You want to see the show, go around to the front and wait to get in like everyone else."

Holy shit, what he wanted to say to this fucker. But he knew…he *knew* stirring him up when he was already agitated would have disastrous results. So, for Knox, he'd back off. "Sure." It came out tersely, but that was the best he could do. "I'll do that." But, the moment he turned around, Robert shoved him against the brick wall.

"Don't fucking patronize me, you dickhead. I know why you're here. My mom told me." He gripped Gray's shirt in a fist and jerked him forward. "You're not going to tell Knox. She doesn't need to know."

In one swift move, he could have this asshole on his knees, his arm twisted behind his back. *Knox.* Instead, he said, "Not here to tell her anything. Like I said, I just came to support her."

But if you don't let go of me, this won't end well for you.

"I didn't do anything wrong." Robert grew more anxious. "I'm giving her what she's always wanted."

"All she ever wanted from you was sobriety. The career she could handle on her own."

"Ah, did I steal your cape? Sorry, Superman, but you couldn't give her what she really wanted, so I had to step in."

Gray's hands fisted, his chest pumped. But he wouldn't lose it. He'd save all his words for when the show was over.

"We're on the same side, man. We both just want her happy. There's no competition here."

"You sure about that? Because I'm pretty sure you're fucking my girlfriend."

Gray's elbow cocked back automatically, but he caught himself before following through. *Not fighting a drug addict in the alley outside her show.* He sucked in a deep breath and took a step back. "I don't know why you lied about Granger's backing you, but it looks like it's all working out, so we're cool." Oh, fuck, his jaw ached; his joints felt raw and brittle.

Calm down.

"I didn't lie. I told you I don't have a job at Grangers. I *told* you that."

"You said you're a contract worker for them."

"Yeah. And, after I pull off this show, I'll get a job there. I'll prove I'm an asset."

"The only reason you don't have a job there now is because you're not clean. Christ, man, you're smart, you're—"

"Shut the fuck up. You don't know shit. I can take the edge off and not be an addict. There isn't just one way to live. We don't all have to do it the fuckin' Bowie way. Now get the fuck out of here."

The door opened, and a young man peered outside. "Hey, everything okay?"

"Everything's fine." Needing to diffuse the situation, Gray hitched his duffle higher and started to head back down the alley.

But Robert wrenched the strap, knocking Gray off balance. With a feral look in his eyes, he slammed his fist into Gray's cheek. Out of control, he started raining punches and kicks. Gray jumped into action, bending low and ramming into him with his shoulder.

The men crashed through the open door and tumbled inside the building. A tower of boxes toppled over. Gray landed on top of his friend and pinned him.

His features livid, veins protruding from his neck, Robert fought to get free. "Fucker. Get off me."

With a brutal grip on his wrists, Gray got right in his face. "Stop it. This is Knox's show. If you care about her at all, you'll get a hold of yourself."

"What's going on?" someone said. "Is that *Robert*?"

"Call nine-one-one. Someone's assaulting him."

"No." Gray shot them a look. "Don't call nine-one-one. Don't ruin her show. I'm Knox's boyfriend."

Taking advantage of the momentary distraction, Robert wrested an arm free. He tried to stab his fingers into Gray's eyes, but Gray head-butted him.

He gripped Robert's wrists and slammed them onto the floor. "You will not fuck up her show. Do you hear me? I'll put us both in jail before I let you ruin this for her."

Chapter Twenty

WITH EVERYTHING UNDER CONTROL IN THE
dressing area, Knox snuck out to take in her show. The
florist had done an amazing job of turning a modern,
brick-walled space into a verdant, colorful English
garden.

In its elegant simplicity, it had turned out even more
beautiful than what Luc's set designer had created.

The models worked the room perfectly, as they
strutted to Tame Impala's *Elephant*—a perfect juxtaposition to the old world gentility of the setting.

Her dresses…seriously, in this setting, they looked as
'extravagantly feminine and lushly romantic' as the *Bridal
Salon* reviewer had once described.

She thought she heard a shout—but it could've come
from outside. Didn't sound like it, though. She'd better get
back. As she slowly made her way through the standing-
room only crowd, she pulled out her phone and texted
Robert. *Everything okay?*

A scream pierced the room. Quickening her pace, she
made it to the front row of chairs when a man roared—a

sound unlike anything she'd ever heard—pure, unleashed rage.

"Excuse me." Knox pushed through the agitated crowd.

The unmistakable sound of a fist slamming into a gut had chairs scraping back and people getting to their feet.

"Let's get out of here," someone said.

And then a man crashed through the trompe l'oeil canvas, taking a set of track lights down with him. Sparks flew, and the man rolled onto his back moaning. A moment later, another man—*Gray?*—came out and dropped to a crouch to pick up—*oh, my God, Robert?*—as if he were nothing more than a rag doll.

Why was Gray here?

Why were they fighting?

With Robert slung over his shoulder, Gray stood up. He looked horrified, scanning the hundred and fifty faces staring at him. With a look of utter defeat, he swiped the blood trickling at the side of his mouth.

Oh, my God. What has he done? She could not believe she was watching Gray Bowie carry Robert away in a fireman's hold.

"So much for the white-hot wedding dress designer," the woman in front of her said.

"More like white trash."

Knox closed her eyes, the faint sound of barking echoing in her mind. "Excuse me." She made her way through the crowded room to the back, where she found Gray carrying a subdued Robert out the door.

She followed him into the alley. "What have you done?" Crouching, she smoothed the hair out of Robert's eyes. "Are you okay? Are you hurt?" When he groaned, she glanced up at Gray and shook her head in disbelief. She gestured helplessly to the gallery. "How could you do this to me?"

"Me? I didn't…Jesus, Knox, he's high as a kite right now."

"He's not *high*. Are you kidding me? You ruined my show because you think he's on drugs? I've been with him this whole time. He's fine. God, Gray." She covered her eyes with a hand, blinking back scalding tears. "How could you do this to me?"

"Where to, sir?" the driver asked.

"Teterboro airport." Adrenaline rocked his body. Gray held his hand out, watching it shake. *Fuck.* He'd come out here to help her…and he'd screwed everything up.

He felt sick. The look of betrayal in Knox's eyes gutted him. Took a knife to his insides and slashed, slashed, slashed, leaving him a bloody, gory mess.

Only now, in this horrible, sickening moment did he fully get it. What that couture designation meant to her. It obliterated the junkyard dog. It liberated her from her past. Enabled her to fully reinvent herself based on her true self.

Her mom had chosen to work seasonal jobs and live in a trailer and litter the property with chunks of mangled metal. The blowback hit Knox. But, from the time she'd left Calamity until half hour ago, she'd been on a whole new path, one of her own making. She'd been building toward the highest level of art in the fashion world.

And now he'd destroyed her reputation.

White trash wedding designer. He'd heard it. Someone had said those actual words.

Jesus.

He lowered his head, closing his eyes—and there it was again, that scene he'd replay for the rest of his life. Knox rushing over to Robert.

Are you okay? Are you hurt?

And then…shooting Gray that look of utter betrayal.

She hadn't believed him, of course.

What had he expected? Those two had a lifetime of intimacy and secrets, and he would *always* be shut out from it. He'd wanted to save her from Robert's bullshit, and instead he'd ruined her reputation.

He was an asshole to think the dynamics between them would ever change. She owned his heart, but *Robert* owned hers.

The cab jolted to a stop. The driver slammed his steering wheel with the palm of his hand, cursing out the bike messenger who'd veered into his lane.

The jarring motion rattled the broken pieces in Gray's brain into a clear picture.

I'm out. Done.

He was living the definition of insanity, trying to win the heart of a woman who would never get over her first love. And he was done.

He pulled out his phone and dialed his pilot.

"I miss you, too, Gray," Sarah said.

"How soon can we take off?"

"Depends on where we're going." The humor left her voice.

"New Zealand."

"I thought…okay. You got it." But she didn't hang up. "You okay?"

"Let's just say I'm a slow learner. But I think I've figured it out, so yeah, I'm just fine."

He'd walked away seven years ago for this exact reason. Because it would never change. Their little trio was set in stone—Robert in his addiction to drugs, Knox in her addiction to making him well, and Gray in his obsession with winning Knox's whole heart.

It was time. He could hear the snip in his chest, severing the string that kept him tied to her. He was done.

Fin would get exactly what he wanted.

Gray's full and total focus on winning.

At least Knox's childhood had prepared her for this moment, when the bridal world referred to her as the white trash wedding gown designer. It didn't mean she'd built up an immunity to it—of course not—it still hurt in ways that knocked the breath right out of her lungs—but at least it wasn't so unfamiliar that she'd go off running to lick her wounds.

Quite the contrary. It was more her nature to come back swinging. Which was how she felt right then, as Jack Abrams and his people watched her models strut down the same path they'd walked only yesterday, when Robert and Gray had crashed her show.

Because, in the end, she knew what mattered. Her dresses were glorious. They were light and airy rooms with all the windows thrown open and gauze drapes fluttering in a breeze. They were fields of sweetly scented wildflowers and bathtubs billowing with iridescent bubbles. Her gowns were lush and feminine and sensual. They made women feel beautiful, sexy, and powerful.

In other words, the haters could go fuck themselves.

The people who got their power from making others

feel small? She'd stuff them in the box, along with Cady and Melissa and the other idiots from her childhood.

So, yeah, a new, hateful moniker she could handle.

Losing Gray, though? Nothing could have prepared her for this kind of crushing pain.

She hadn't heard from him once since he'd left her standing in the ruins of her show. Robert had gone back to the hotel to clean up, and she and the gallery owner had slapped on smiles and continued with the program. Some of the guests had left, but so what? People in the arts loved drama.

But any joy she should be experiencing had gone flat as the champagne left in uncorked bottles.

Because she'd lost Gray.

"Oh, I like that one." Jack Abrams wore a skinny plaid suit. The lime green set against light brown and dark green actually looked really good. "Magnificent." He pulled the cap off his Montblanc pen and twisted around in his chair to find her. "What do you call that one?"

She moved closer to him. "That's Le Danseur."

He scribbled it down in his notebook. Then, getting up, he walked away from his people and led her to a corner. "I'm going to tell you something. The press did some digging."

"Okay." Her muscles clenched, body going into battle mode.

"They know you grew up in a trailer and what the kids used to call you."

Cady's voice rang through her body. *Junkyard dog.*

"It's given steam to the whole white trash designer thing. God knows why people get off on other people's misfortune." He shook his head dismissively. "It is what it is. But none of that matters because I love your gowns."

303

Oh, my God. Is he going to offer me a contract? *Gray, get back here. You need to hear this.*

"You're the freshest voice I've seen since Hayley Page, and I mean that sincerely." He cupped his hand toward his people and flicked it. *Let's go.* They all got up and headed out the door. Jack reached for her hand and gave it a firm shake. "Stay the course."

"Oh, you can count on it." She walked him to the door. "Thank you so much for coming." But he was already ducking into the town car waiting for him at the curb.

Without offering her a contract. Why would he want to be associated with the white trash wedding gown designer? Who would want to back her now?

Oh, God. She might lose the MacAllister sisters. They wanted gowns from a hot up-and-coming designer. Not one who was ridiculed during fashion week.

Then, so be it. She had no control over the decisions people made.

This will all blow over. She'd get the custom gowns done, do the pop-up. She'd be fine. This moment would pass. She was young, and she'd only get better. One day, she'd get that contract.

This I'll recover from.

But she would never get over losing Gray. Because she finally understood he was more than a great man, a good friend, and the best business partner imaginable. All of those things she could replace. What she couldn't replace was her soulmate. And Gray Bowie…he owned her, heart and soul.

When she turned back around, she found the gallery staff picking up the champagne flutes and little party plates from the hors d'oeuvres they'd served. Her phone vibrated, and she pulled it out.

Callie. She answered right away. "Hey."

"I just heard," Callie said. "I'm so sorry."

Oh. Well, that's mortifying. "What did you hear, exactly?"

"About the show. My idiot future brother-in-law and his idiot friend."

"It's okay. I just had an appointment with Jack Abrams, and he really liked my work—"

"Knox. I'm not talking about your career. I'm talking about Gray and Robert."

She heard a muffled sound, and then Delilah came on the line. "Knox? Robert's an asshole for lying to you like that."

She closed her eyes, as her fatal mistake spread through her like red wine on a white tablecloth.

Gray hadn't randomly attacked Robert. Of course he hadn't.

And yet…she'd jumped to that conclusion.

"What did he lie to me about?" Her voice sounded like it came from inside a tin can.

"You don't know?"

No, because I never asked. I jumped to conclusions. "Please just tell me." The anticipation made it hard to breathe. She was still pissed at Robert for getting into it with Gray, so she'd barely spoken to him since the show, but she hadn't cast him out. No, she'd done that to Gray.

"The whole reason Gray flew to New York was because he ran into Mrs. Granger. Knox, she didn't know anything about Robert putting a show together for you. He doesn't have an arrangement with Granger's."

Once, on a late spring day, they'd hiked to the summit in T-shirts and shorts. It had been twenty degrees up there, and the icy cold on her bare skin had burned. That's what she felt like right then, finding out that Robert had deceived her. That he'd lied about something so critical to her. "I didn't know."

"Didn't Gray tell you?"

She hadn't let him. An image flashed in her mind, of her crouching beside Robert, looking up accusingly at Gray. "What have I done?"

"You didn't do anything. You have no fault in any of this."

Callie came back on the line. "Robert's in all kinds of trouble with his family, though. They don't appreciate him using their company name like that."

"Then who backed him? Where did he get all those connections?" How had he pulled this off?

"No idea. You haven't talked to Gray about it?"

The owner swept into the gallery, her hair tossed about by the autumn breeze. She flashed a grin, immediately glancing up at the monitors placed around the room, where another fashion show livestreamed. "Isn't that your former boss?"

Knox glanced up. A reporter held out a microphone to Luc, and he spoke in his animated way.

God, he must be so happy to be free of her. Being associated with the white trash designer would be the worst thing in the world for him.

"That must be why he's not feeling well," Callie said. "Fin says he's lost his focus."

"He can get hurt if he's not focused." *Oh, my God.* What had she done? "He has to get his head on right."

"Hey, slow down. Fin's got this. You know he wouldn't let anything happen to his brother."

"This is my fault. I blamed him for the fight. I thought he was being competitive with Robert over me."

"Oh, honey, no. Gray caught him in the alley buying drugs from some guy."

Her heart lurched. Her stomach roiled. "I didn't…" She was going to say she hadn't known, but what she really meant was that she hadn't bothered to ask.

On the screen, the camera panned Luc's body, taking in his pink Tattersall dress shirt and silver metallic sateen pants, a black leather messenger bag slung over his shoulder.

"Fin says you guys aren't talking," Callie said. "Look, I've known Gray most of my life, and I've never seen him as happy as he is with you. Just…maybe talk to him. Whatever it was you were building together, it deserves a conversation."

"I will." Peeking out of the messenger bag was a notebook. "Listen, I have to go."

"Sure. But we're here if you need to talk."

"Thanks, Callie." She pocketed the phone and moved closer to the monitor.

"I'm most excited about my next collection," Luc said. "It's some of the best work I've ever done." Absently, he hugged his messenger bag closer to him. "In fact, I've already sold one of the gowns to Princess Rosalina. She happened to be in my studio as we were working on the spring collection and saw it." Gesturing with both hands exposed more of the bag, enabling Knox to catch a clearer look at the notebook. It was the gold trim that confirmed what she already knew. A cold fluid seeped into her bloodstream.

Her missing sketchbook.

How had he gotten it?

"Did you want us to set up for your next appointment?" the gallery owner asked.

"That would be great. Listen, I have a quick meeting uptown. I'll be back in plenty of time to get the models ready." She pushed out the doors into a brisk October afternoon. The rush of traffic, the flow of pedestrians, only compounded her anxiety.

Luc had stolen from her again.

But how?

She hailed a cab, got inside, and said, "Lincoln Center."

By the time the cab pulled up to the curb, Knox had contacted Zach and asked him to speak with Duck Dive's attorney. She'd also explained the situation to Amelia, who'd vowed to do whatever Knox needed to help her nail Luc to the wall.

She had a team. And it felt damn good not to be alone in this.

But it didn't diffuse the anger. Not one little bit. In fact, every step up the Lincoln Center's staircase and across the wide travertine promenade, around the fountain, and through the glass doors, only ramped it up.

When she pulled open the door to the venue, she found it mostly empty.

Seriously, big let-down. She'd been prepared to call him out publicly, had imagined snatching the sketchbook out of the bag and waving it in his face.

Instead, she found a few clusters of people talking and staff cleaning up and folding chairs. She called out to the nearest group, "Excuse me? Do you know where Luc is?"

"Knox?"

She whipped around to find him entering the room with a to-go cup of coffee. It was *on*. She stormed over to him. "How the hell did you get my sketchbook?"

Like the moment before a crack of thunder, the energy in the room crackled. A screech of chair legs lingered in the startling silence.

"What, do you have magic fingers that can steal all the way from Paris? Did you plant spies in the bunkhouse?"

He pulled her sketchbook out of his messenger bag. "You're talking about this?"

His tone, so casual, so open, had a few people sneering at her.

"Come. We'll talk." He led her up the stairs, across the dusty stage, and behind a thick velvet curtain.

"You stole my sketchbook again, and this time you can't claim ownership because I. Do. Not. Work. For. You."

"I didn't steal." He was eerily calm and unaffected. "We made an exchange."

"And when did this exchange happen? While I was sleeping? When your thief crept in and tucked it into his luggage?"

Now, his chin tipped up. "I have never stolen from you. I used the designs you created while under contract with me. It is standard operating procedure for any fashion house to own anything its designers create."

"That sketchbook was my private one. You had no right to it."

"It falls under the category of trade secrets. You would not have designed those dresses had it not been for my tutelage, the exposure to my designs, my fabrics…the environment of my studio."

He would never understand that taking a book off a

coffee table in her apartment did not fall under the category of Intellectual Property. "I don't work for you, Luc. There is no contract." She waved the notebook. "So, what the hell are you doing with this?"

"But we do have a contract. I entered into a verbal one with your business partner."

My partner? He couldn't be talking about Gray. Gray would never…

Robert? It all became clear. He would do anything to start his career—even steal from his ex-girlfriend. And, she'd bet, in Robert's twisted logic, he believed he was doing a great thing for her, delivering her dream on a silver platter. The price? A simple sketchbook.

"He contacted me," Luc said. "Asking how he could get you back into fashion week. We agreed on a trade. In exchange for your show…" He tapped the notebook. "I got this."

"Well, he lied to both of us. He didn't have my permission to take that notebook."

"You really did not know? This is not some game you're playing because your show went so disastrously?"

Briefly, she closed her eyes. *Thanks for the brutal reminder.* "I didn't know." She leveled her gaze at him. "So, you can tell your princess, if she wants one of my dresses, she'll have to contact me. Because these are *my* designs. I had no knowledge of whatever deal Robert brokered with you." She'd had her mic drop moment. *Go.* But a strange resistance kept her rooted.

"This is unfortunate," Luc said. "We have both been deceived."

The anger subsided, the fog cleared, leaving nothing but the truth. "You know, I wasn't that little girl who longed for a daddy. I didn't stand on stage during recitals and look out at all the men in the auditorium wishing one of them was watching me with an adoring smile. I didn't feel anything at all about not having a dad, until you came into my life and acted like one."

His forehead creased in concern.

"Do you remember that day I called you, frantic, because I'd gotten lost on the subway? You'd sent me out on all these errands—buttons from Madame Michelle and crystals from Swarovski's—and I'd missed my stop and wound up in a really dangerous *banlieue*."

"I remember."

"You told me to stay put, your driver would come for me." She gave a bitter laugh. "If you'd just given me the right Metro directions, I'd have been grateful, but sending your driver? That was really sweet. But when I saw you *get out* of the car? Knowing you'd taken time out of your day to pick me up and make sure I was safe? That...it made me feel like I mattered. Not that my *talent* mattered, but that *I* did."

She searched his gaze for something—anything—and found a hint of remorse. But it wasn't enough. "Maybe you didn't mean to, but it felt like something a dad would do. I trusted you, Luc. And all you wanted was my sketchbook. If you've lost your creative fire, then bow out gracefully. Don't become the guy that has to steal someone else's talent to stay relevant." She lifted the notebook again. "Well, I guess it's too late for that."

Chapter Twenty-One

PHONE PRESSED TO HER EAR, KNOX ROLLED ONTO her side, reaching for a tissue to dab her nose.

Finally, he picked up. "Hey." His voice, all deep and rumbly, made her spirits soar.

She was desperate to talk to him. "Gray—"

"It's Gray. Leave a message."

Dammit. She quickly blew her nose and sat up. "Hi. It's me again. I wish you'd talk to me. I'm sorry. I'm sorry for jumping to the wrong conclusion. I'm sorry I didn't ask you what was going on. I'm just so damn *sorry.*"

How did she get through to him? "I know you think it was about believing Robert over you, but the truth is…" Shame, fear, regret swamped her, suffocating her. "The truth is that it was about hearing them call me white trash. It's so stupid." Fresh, hot tears streamed down her face. *Stop with the excuses. Just tell him how you feel.* "You're… you're everything to me, Gray. I miss you. I can't stand it. I just can't…" One beat passed, two, three. *Say something or hang up.* "I don't want us to end." *Oh, come on. That's the best you can do?* "Call me. Please."

How did she make this right?

He'd called her his heart. He couldn't just dump his heart like this, could he?

A knock startled her. *Gray?* She threw off the covers and dashed to the door. That would be just like him to fly out here and talk to her in person. "Just a minute." *Stupid. Of course it's not him. He's in New Zealand.*

Peering through the peep hole, she found the distorted image of a room service waiter. "Oh. Hang on." Releasing the lock, she opened the door and stepped back to let him wheel in the cart. "I don't think you've got the right room. I didn't order anything."

The guy pulled the receipt out from under a plate. "Knox Holliday, room 1262?"

"That's me."

"Enjoy your treat." He started to go.

"Don't I have to sign anything?"

"Nope. It's all been taken care of. Including the tip."

"Oh, well, thank you so much." She caught her image in the mirror behind the coffee station. No wonder he'd raced out of there. Messy hair, streaks of mascara...she looked like a woman on the edge.

On the linen-draped cart, she found a silver tea pot, white porcelain cup and saucer, a folded white napkin with a knife, fork, and spoon tucked inside, a plate, and a three-tiered cake stand. Beautiful pastries filled each level. Flaky puff pastry oozing with whipped cream, custard-filled fruit tarts dotted with glazed strawberries and blueberries, pastel-colored macarons, slim cannolis, and chocolate chip-studded biscotti.

A cream-colored envelope had *Knox Holliday* scrawled on it.

We can't be there in person, but we're there in spirit. Love, Callie and Delilah.

She hurried back to the nightstand to grab her phone. Taking a picture, she sent it to both of them. *You guys are the best. Thank you.* Just as she sat down to pour her tea, the phone chimed. *Bowie.* Her heart jumped into her throat. "Hello?" *Please be let it be Gray's voice. Please.*

"Hey, honey," Delilah said.

"Oh. I…" Working hard not to sink into despair, she turned back to the cart. "I can't believe you guys did this."

"I only wish we could be there to stuff our faces with you," Delilah said. "Because that looks amazing."

"Hey, girl," Callie said. "How are you?"

"I'm good," she said. "But I think I'm going to move my flight up and come home. I have a ton of work, and there's nothing left for me to do here."

"What about the gala?" Callie asked.

"I don't care about that." As if she wanted to see Luc win a lifetime achievement award off the backs of all the young, hopeful designers he'd plucked out of college.

"But isn't it a big deal?" Callie said. "A chance to get in front of everybody and promote your brand?"

"I don't want to promote *this* brand. I'll work on a whole new collection, come back next year, and blow them all away."

"That's great," Callie said. "And you should definitely stick with that plan, but *after* you wow them tomorrow night."

"I'd rather come home."

"Honey," Delilah said. "I don't like the idea of letting the bullies win."

Oh. Was that what she was doing? "If I leave quietly, no one will notice. If I stay, I'll give them more opportunities to post pictures of the White Trash Wedding Gown Designer. It'll only draw attention to me."

"That's offensive and racist," Callie said. "And we're going to ignore it, because we don't give attention to bad people. Your show was a hit."

"When does Alayna's blog come out?" Delilah asked.

"She's been posting randomly throughout the week, but she always does a couple of major posts after she gets home and sorts through all her photos. She does a Hits and Misses column, predicts the up-and-coming designer to look for. Stuff like that."

"How do you feel, honey?" Callie asked. "And I'm not talking about the gala."

It all came rushing back, the horror of her loss. "I ruined everything, and I don't know how to make it better. He won't talk to me."

"The competition's happening right now, sweetie," Delilah said.

"No, I know. That's not the issue. Seven years ago, Robert ruined the prom. Gray told me to leave with him, and I didn't. I chose Robert. And, now, during my show, Robert messed up again, and instead of asking what happened, I immediately blamed Gray."

"You'd been around Robert the whole week," Delilah said. "He'd been sober, he'd done everything he needed to do...why would you think he was high? I don't think you did anything wrong."

"I think," Callie said. "It's more about the past than the present. The three of you have some pretty intense history, and once you talk it out, I'm sure you'll get through it."

"I'm not so sure. I think this time he's done with me for good." The pain engulfed her. Streaming tears had her snatching the napkin off the table, the silverware clattering onto the table. She swiped her cheeks frantically. *Make it stop.* "I never dreamed I could have him like that. He was my best friend. He was…everything. And I didn't think enough of myself to see him as the man of my heart."

"What if he's just upset that he had a hand in ruining your event?" Delilah said. "I mean, they fought on your catwalk."

"No, I know him. He's disgusted with me for jumping to the wrong conclusion. It just never entered my mind that Robert was doing drugs. I thought Gray was being competitive over me."

"I think you're being too hard on yourself, hon," Delilah said.

"I don't," Knox said. "He always felt like he was invisible in his family. And, now, I just showed him he's invisible in his relationship with me and Robert."

"Then I guess you just have to prove that you see him," Callie said.

Go time.

Body tense with electric energy, Gray twisted his board in the fresh, packed snow.

Visualize. But the only thing he could see was Knox's horrified expression, thinking he'd instigated the fight with Robert the night of her fashion show.

I lost her.

For good this time.

Because he couldn't—wouldn't—do it again. Love someone who didn't love him back.

"Hey, man." Fin came up to him, snow crunching under his boots. "You good?"

"What're you doing? Get out of here." The prequalifier got a lot of attention in the freestyle world. It set the tone for the season, introducing the world to the contenders. Gray was already in the lead, going into this final run.

Fin tugged on his scruff, glancing at the halfpipe. "Don't need to tell you how important it is to get your head on right."

"Sure as hell don't. Now back off and let me get in the zone."

"Yeah, that's the thing. Not sure you're anywhere near the zone."

"What's going on?" a staff guy asked. "Is there a problem?"

"Fixing it," Fin said.

The guy gave a curt nod and said something into his headset.

"The thing is." Fin looked anywhere but at Gray. "When Mom left, Dad got a pretty serious wake-up call."

"You're not seriously talking to me about our parents right now?"

But his brother ignored him. "He quit his job and had to raise the four of us wild-ass kids by himself. I think herding us all into snow sports was the only way he could handle it."

By the twist in his heart, he knew his brother was right. "You want me disqualified? Keep talking."

"Dad saw you. I know he did. He just couldn't be in four places at one time. He was in survival mode, and I think he raised us the best way he knew how."

"Okay." *I still would've liked a nickname.* He actually

cracked a smile at how dumb that sounded. But it was true.

"Brodie skied to win a medal, Will did it to prove to Mom that he was a good guy. But you and me? We've always done it because it's fun. Freeriding's our jam. Remember?"

That simple reminder got his energy flowing, kicking up the adrenaline he'd been missing.

"Yeah, so, anyhow," Fin said. "Remember to have fun. That's when you do your best."

He gave his younger brother the side-eye. *Fun? I just had my heart ripped out of my chest, so fuck you.*

"I love you, brother. And when you're done here, you can take your trophy and head out wherever you need to go to fix whatever you broke. But for right now? It's time for you to fuckin' explode. Can you do that?"

He smiled at his brother, coach, and friend. "Yeah. I can do that." He turned to the course, bent his knees, and slid down the slope to the starting point.

Explode. The word did something to him. Visualizing his first trick, Gray took off. Right before hitting the lip, he threw his shoulder, looking over his shoulder—*spot it, spot it—and again—fuck*, he loved the smell of snow, the rush of the wind on his face as he rotated a second time and…stomped his landing. *Fuck, yeah*. He stayed low to gain speed as he raced up the wall.

And then he was in it—completely lost in the muscle memory of his tricks. As soon as he hit the lip, he knew he was going for it. *Switchback twelve*. Didn't think, just threw himself into the flip, kept his focus right between his arm and leg to spot his landing, and grabbed his board.

Landed. *Nice. This is it, man, go for it*. Back-to-back twelve combos. *Do it*.

His back foot hit the lip, every muscle in his body contracted, and Gray just fucking exploded. And when he landed, he knew.

He'd nailed it.

Sliding down, snow spraying off his board, he pumped his arms in the air. The crowd went wild. As soon as he scraped to a stop, he unbuckled his helmet, tore off his gloves, and tipped his head back, letting the sharp sunlight hit his face.

For one moment, he imagined his dad right there in the crowd, fighting to get to Gray, expression bursting with pride. It made his eyes sting, and he glanced up to the sky. "Love you, Dad."

In that tense moment while waiting for his score, his heart pounding, lungs heaving, he felt a peace settle over him and knew Fin was right. His dad had loved him just as much as his brothers. And, when the crowd roared, he knew he'd won.

This one's for you, Dad.

Immediately, he was swarmed. A reporter shoved a microphone in his face. "Congratulations, man, that was outstanding."

"Thanks."

"Gray," another reporter called. "Please don't tell me you're going to pull a Will and retire after a perfect run like this."

"Oh, hell, no. I'm no quitter." He gave a teasing smile. "We're going to the Olympics. One of us has to get the job done."

In a spectacular crystal gown with a deep V neckline and cap sleeves that she'd made in Maui, Knox stood in the New York Public Library's Astor Hall.

Decorated in a *Midsummer Night's Dream* theme, with dramatic lighting and lavish greenery, the event was sponsored by the fashion council, and the coveted invitations were issued only to the who's-who of the bridal fashion world.

She'd wondered how Robert had scored her a ticket, considering she wasn't officially part of the week-long event, but now she knew the truth. *Luc* had gotten it for her.

A fresh wave of anger rolled through her. The only comfort she took from the whole sickening situation was that she'd confronted both men. She'd knocked on Robert's door and reamed him. Hadn't let him get in a single word. She'd left him with the threat that if he tried to make any headway in the fashion industry, she would expose him for the lying bastard he was. She was pretty sure his own mom would back her up on that one.

You've gone to all this trouble to attend the gala…why are you standing here thinking about bad things?

Tonight, you're a talented wedding gown designer.

Leave your baggage at the door.

Her gaze swept the room. Nearly a thousand stunningly-dressed guests chatted in the dramatic space, dimly lit to accentuate the glowing sprites and fairies gracefully chasing each other through the crowd. Copper cocktail glasses and flower pots stuffed with gourmet charcuterie lent a whimsical touch to the décor.

"Ladies and gentlemen, if I may have your attention." On the podium, a tuxedoed woman she recognized as Esther Delgado, the president of the fashion council, leaned against the lectern. "It's time to introduce the recipient of this year's Lifetime Achievement award." She paused while the room quieted down to nothing more than a few clinking glasses and a low murmur of conversation between the wait staff.

"Persistence," Ms. Delgado said. "Is the word I'd use to describe this couturier who grew up in the suburbs of Paris, son of a single father who held three jobs to keep food on the table. Tonight's recipient had no formal design education but, rather, racked up hours of experience while sitting on the stairs of his apartment building and watching the newly wedded couples emerge from the church across the street. Never without a pencil in hand, he would sketch gowns and send them to every designer in Paris. Until, finally, one of them responded. Jacques Tournier hired him to apprentice in his atelier and, from there, he went on to become the most famous bridal gown designer in the world. Ladies and gentlemen, it's my great honor to present this year's Lifetime Achievement award to Mr. Luc Bellerose, couturier of the esteemed House of Bellerose."

The ballroom burst into deafening applause, and Knox watched her former boss disentangle himself from a sea of greedy hands, all wanting a piece of his magic, and climb the steps to the podium. He waved to the crowd, his smile so bright and wide, it stretched his features unnaturally.

What killed her was that Luc had never even bothered to talk to her. To verify that she was actually behind the exchange.

Some guy contacts you out of the blue, and you just go along with it?

That's how desperate he is for inspiration. He's bone dry.

When Luc reached the lectern, the audience quieted

down. Everyone watched him with adoring expressions… except for her. She willed him to find her in the crowd, look into her eyes as he took credit for all the collections of the past several years that he hadn't designed. She wanted him to feel shame, remorse…*something*.

He couldn't hurt her anymore, but maybe she could stop him from preying on some other young designer with stars in her eyes and a hunger in her soul to be something different than the way her childhood had painted her.

"Thank you, thank you, thank you." In his electric blue velvet tuxedo jacket with a thin yellow military stripe on each side, he hoisted the heavy crystal statue in the air before clutching it to his chest.

He looked down, noticeably moved. "This means everything to me. You see, as a little boy, my father did not approve of me drawing dresses. He enrolled me in athletics at the community center, believing I could be cured of my obsession with satin and lace. But, still, as Madame Delgado said, I persisted. I persisted when, instead of going to college, I apprenticed with a designer who saw my sketchbook and said, 'You're a hard worker, Luc, but I'm afraid I don't see any potential here.' I persisted when my very first review in *Bridal Couture* magazine called my designs 'nothing terribly extraordinary.'"

He panned the room, as though taking a moment to work through his emotions. "Each failure, each rejection, each person who told me I wouldn't succeed at the job I wanted more than anything, fueled my ambition. Each one made me work harder. I took classes—all kinds—not just fashion design but figure drawing and watercolors, so I could understand shape, shading, and tone. I visited ateliers and fashion shows. I persisted until the Fédération granted me membership. And I continue to persist to make my way in this field that, to this day, makes my heart and soul rejoice."

He held out the award. "So, to be here tonight holding this in my hands…this is the moment when I can let out a breath and say, I did it. And if *I* can do it, anyone can. As long as you persist."

Amidst the explosion of applause came whistles and shouts of support. A wave of heat barreled across the room, as if he'd sparked a fire in the attendees souls. When Mrs. Delgado approached to lead him off the stage, he held up a finger and leaned into the microphone. "And, unfortunately for you, I'm going to persist with this speech, so bear with me." The humor left his expression. "Following your dreams, never giving up, is good. It's essential. But, as someone recently pointed out to me, it is equally essential to know when it's time to step back. Ladies and gentlemen, friends, colleagues, I have lost my creative fire."

Shock burned hot and cold on Knox's skin.

"Years ago, in fact. And in its place, I've devoted my life to discovering the brightest talent." He seemed to search the crowd. "In the beginning, I believed it would rekindle my spark. But, it has occurred to me this week, perhaps instead of rekindling I should just step aside to make room for the next generation. And, so, I am retiring. I'm going to set this beautiful symbol of all I've accomplished on my bookshelf, where I can look at it every day, while I enjoy, for the first time in my life, some peace. There is so much talent in the world of bridal fashion design." His gaze landed on her, and she felt it like a jolt of electricity. "And the brightest light of all is in this room tonight. Knox Holliday *is* the White-Hot designer. And I want you to remember her name because, mark my words, in twenty years, she's going to be standing on this podium accepting this award." He held it over his head. "From the bottom of my heart, thank you. And goodnight."

All around her, everyone stood in place, mesmerized and shocked by the announcement.

He's retiring?

Still reeling from the speech, that acknowledgment of her as the hottest up-and-coming designer, Knox wandered through the ballroom. But, really, what had hit her the hardest was the comment he'd made about peace. She'd felt that comment viscerally.

She'd been on the run from bullies her whole life. She could admit, finally, that they'd chased her to Paris, to Luc's atelier, to this very moment where she'd forced herself into Bridal Fashion Week on the promises of an ex-boyfriend who had zero experience in her industry. A man who had never told the truth about anything.

There's no peace in that.

That's what Luc meant. He didn't mean the hard work it took to become a well-known designer or to run his business. He meant the constant fight to prove his dad wrong. That was exhausting.

Knox had what it took to succeed. The talent, the work ethic, the ambition—but trying to prove the bullies wrong depleted her.

She didn't need the couture designation to live her dream or accomplish her goals. She just needed to design her beloved wedding gowns.

And she needed Gray. Her feet ached in the rented shoes, and she was tired of sucking in her belly in the form-fitting dress. It was time to go home.

"Excuse me, Miss Holliday?" Jack Abrams stood before her with a warm smile.

"Mr. Abrams. It's so nice to see you again."

"I had to finish out the week, just in case we found an even hotter star in the bridal gown galaxy but, of course, my first instincts were correct, and my board unanimously voted to extend a contract to you."

The moment couldn't have been more surreal if he'd started belting out show tunes.

Here it is, the moment you've dreamed of for years. "I'm so…" *What?* She did a quick check-in with herself. "Pleased." *You're pleased that Jack Abrams just offered you a contract?* "Honored." She gave an awkward laugh. "Shocked, I guess." Shock, frankly, that she didn't feel as elated as she would've expected.

Why on earth wouldn't she want the coveted the contract?

But, then, she knew. Take away the quest to prove the bullies wrong, and she was left with the truth in her own heart. She knew exactly what she wanted.

"I'll cover your expenses," Jack continued. "Sewers, pattern makers, all the start-up capital you need. You'll have access to our textile mills. But the dresses will be *yours.*" He dipped so they were eye-level. "Under your name."

She caught his deeper meaning. "You knew?"

"Everyone knows. It's a small world, this bridal market, and everyone knows what everyone else is doing. With me, you can design your gowns, and I'll take care of the business end. You'll get all the credit."

"I can't tell you how much this means to me. From the moment I learned about your company during my sophomore year at FIT, I've set my sights on working with you." She allowed herself to imagine setting up an atelier in New

York City. Or Paris. Not hard to do, since she'd dreamed it a hundred times over the years.

She pictured a life of designing collections based on what would wow the fashion world. Of living—like Luc had—to outdo the other top designers. Doing whatever it took to stay relevant.

And then she imagined a life of designing gowns for clients. Real women who shared their love stories with her. Of living in Calamity surrounded by friends and a team of people she loved and trusted.

There was no comparison.

"Excellent." Jack gave her a warm grin. "If you have some time tomorrow, come by the office—"

"I'm sorry, as incredible as it sounds, I'm going to pass. Your offer really is a dream come true, but I think…I think my dream has changed."

His features fell in disappointment. "I see. Well, if you change your mind, my offer has no end-date. Best of luck to you."

"Thank you." She watched him disappear into the crowd. And then she kicked off her heels and ran for the exit.

Knox Holliday was going home.

Alone in the gym, Gray bounced and flipped from one trampoline to the next. Throwing his right shoulder down, he twisted his hip into a spin. Once he got some air, he tucked, held, and made a safety grab, spotted his landing and—

What was that? The flash of white in his peripheral

vision jarred him in a gym filled with black trampoline beds and blue throw pads. *Someone's here.*

He landed on his back, then jumped to his feet, making out the form of a woman.

In a gown.

A ball gown.

What the hell? He leaped onto a throw pad and braced to get a stable view of the gorgeous woman with thick, wavy long hair. "Knox?" She looked ethereal, like a fairy princess.

"Hi." She stood on a trampoline in one of her extravagant dresses, all lace and an abundance of feathers and creamy skin.

"You're here." *Thank Christ.*

She started to walk towards him, but between the profusion of feathers and the bouncy launch pad, she wavered.

"Hang on." He leapt from one pad to another, until he reached her. Leaning down, he held out his hand to help her climb out.

Her hands fisted in the skirt, as she lifted it off the ground. "That's better."

"What're you doing here? In a wedding gown?"

She fixed him with the most heartbreakingly earnest expression. "I'm here because I see you. I see how much you love me."

Emotion crashed over him, dragging him below the surface. It took a moment to paddle his way out, because she needed an answer. "I do."

"With all your heart."

Why the hell was he shaking? He squeezed his hands into fists to make it stop. "You *are* my heart."

She broke into a luminous grin. "I'm your heart." And

then she turned serious. "It isn't about competing with Robert. It never was. All you've ever wanted was to be with me."

Something broke inside his chest, spilling out warmth and light, rushing so fast it swept away the ache and crushing disappointment that lived deep inside him. "That's right."

"And I'm here because I want you to look into my eyes and see *me*. See how deeply and completely I love you. How I have never loved anybody the way I love you, and I never will." Lifting the skirt of her gown, she awkwardly got down on one knee. When he reached out to help her, she shook her head. She gazed up at him, her expression so full of love, it knocked him senseless. "Gray Bowie, you're the best man I've ever known. In my whole life, I've never felt so loved, so protected, and so happy. I want you, love you, lust you, crave you, need you, miss you, dream you, ache you, joy you…I *choose* you. I want to spend my life with you, make babies with you, get your good morning kiss every single day for the rest of my life. I want to make you feel as cherished and protected as you make me."

He couldn't take it one more second. Dropping to his knees, he scooped her and her endless yards of feathers into his arms. "*Yes.*"

"I haven't asked you yet."

"You don't have to ask. I love you. With everything in me, I love you."

She leaned back within the shelter of his embrace to give him a confident smile. "I know. And I'm gonna put a ring on it."

Epilogue

THE TRAIN PULLED INTO THE STATION AND DOZENS of tourists climbed off to explore Owl Hoot on this spectacular June day. Knox waited at the crosswalk for them to pass, before turning into a parking spot in front of the resort hotel.

Cutting the ignition, she glanced at the stack of Etch-A-Sketches piled on Callie's lap. "Anyone going to tell me what's going on?" She peered at Delilah in the rear-view mirror.

"She's really not very good with surprises, is she?" Callie asked.

"So impatient," Delilah said, before getting out of the truck.

In her log cabin in the middle of a fairytale forest, Knox had awakened to an empty bed. On Gray's pillow sat an Etch-a-Sketch that said, *Come get your morning kiss.* She'd found the next one on the kitchen counter. It had led her to Callie's house, where she'd had her make-up done. The one after that had led to Delilah, at the main house, which was filled with a stunning array of flowers. The three women had put together gorgeous bouquets.

But no one would tell her what any of this was for.

The fourth Etch-a-Sketch had led to the hotel. "I don't know why I need make-up this early in the morning." But she followed them inside, where the concierge's expression lit up at the sight of her.

"Good morning, Knox." He handed her a *fifth* one.

"You're in on it, too?"

He grinned, eyes sparkling, and returned to his desk.

"Okay, then." On the screen, someone had drawn a crude image of a storefront. Written across the top: Knox Holliday Atelier. "What is this?" She turned to her friends for an explanation, but they were nowhere to be found. "What's going *on*?"

To her right, guests checked into reception. Straight ahead, a grand staircase led to the second floor ballrooms. Shops and restaurants made up the left side of the building.

Butcher paper covered the window of one of the stores. A comfortable wrought iron bench sat nestled between planters filled with brightly colored wild flowers.

And written across the top of the black wood façade, in magenta-colored letters: *Knox Holliday Atelier.*

She nearly dropped the Etch-a-Sketch.

This store is mine? On legs as shaky as a newborn colt's, she headed over and tried the door. It opened to a roomful of familiar—and expectant—faces. The Cooters, Zach, Amelia, Wyatt, the realtor, the hostess from Sweet Baby Jane's…Good Lord, half the town had come to celebrate the opening of her…the breath whooshed out of her lungs.

My atelier.

So many people surrounded her, reaching for her hands, kissing her cheek, congratulating her. "Where's Gray?" she kept asking. But no one gave her anything more than a secretive smile.

Wearing a suit, Zach broke through the crowd. "What do you think?"

"I think I'm having a crazy dream, and someone needs to give me a good hard slap to snap me out of it."

"Not a dream," Zach said. "While you've been working on the custom gowns and launching your digital platform, the Bowie brothers built out this salon for you. Wait'll you see the rest of it."

The guests blocked her view of most of the room. But what she could see—plush magenta couches facing a long glass coffee table, one whole wall of windows bringing in stunning natural light, and crystal chandeliers hanging from the ceiling—was absolutely stunning. The black wainscoting and the pin-striped wallpaper with a pattern of tiny magenta fleur de lis made the space elegant but whimsical. It had personality.

Mine.

"I think it's the nicest thing anyone's ever done for me."

"Just wait."

"There's more?" She searched faces for her fiancé. "Where's Gray?"

"He's waiting for you." With a hand on her elbow, he moved her toward the velvet-draped dressing rooms. "But, first, let's get you dressed."

He brought her to a dress form. It took a moment to make sense of it, but it was the wedding gown she'd designed as a teenager. "Is this my dress?" Tears blurred her vision, until she couldn't see it anymore. "Who made this?" Furiously, she swiped her eyes, desperate to see what was going on.

"We did."

To see the sketch she'd designed as young, hopeful girl come to life…"Wait, why did you make my wedding gown?"

"Come on," Callie said. "How 'bout we make sure it fits?"

"I'm *wearing* it?" *Wait.* "Oh, my God, is that why you used me?" With her as a model, Zach had recorded the exact process of taking measurements and posted it on the website.

He smiled. "I'm so clever, right? You didn't suspect a thing."

"Make-up, bouquet, wedding gown…you guys." She tried with all her might not to bawl like a baby. "Am I getting married?"

"For six months, you've been pushing Gray to either elope or do it at the courthouse," Callie said.

"And he wasn't having it," Zach said. "So…" He gestured to the room. "He planned the wedding for you."

Delilah smoothed a hand on her arm. "Is this okay?"

"It's better than okay. It's the most amazing thing anyone's ever done for me."

"Then, let's get you dressed," Callie said.

Wearing her frothy, extravagant gown and holding her gardenia-scented bouquet, Knox stepped out into the salon.

When the first strains of Tim McGraw's *My Best Friend* started playing, she could no longer hold back the tears. As she moved toward the center of the room, the crowd parted to reveal a row of chairs facing...a white, wooden wedding arbor. Wrapped in lace, it was adorned with white, pink, and magenta zinnias.

And standing there, waiting, was Gray in a sleek black tuxedo.

The tremble began deep inside her. Because she understood all at once that her morning kiss was also her *I do*.

His brothers stood beside him, all three of them dashing and imposing in their tuxes. The guests took their seats, chairs scraping on the wood floor, amidst the low hum of conversation.

But Knox only had eyes for her man. That look of love, like she was his gift, the source of his joy, made her heart flutter out of control.

Because she would be blessed with that expression for the rest of her life.

Little Ruby came crashing from behind, ramming into her. "Sowwy." She peered up at Knox with an earnest expression. "I gots fowers." She held up a basket of magenta rose petals, before breaking away to do her job.

The three year old stomped down the aisle, carefully dropping them one at a time. The guests watched her with gentle smiles, some placing a hand over their hearts at all the cuteness, and some with actual tears.

But the stuffed chicken under her arm made it difficult to toss flower petals, so Ruby wound up tripping. The adults seated closest to her lurched forward, everyone ready to come to her rescue, but everyone froze because Ruby only had eyes for Will. Splayed out on the shiny wood floor, she watched her half-brother with a question in her eyes

Will smiled, but the intensity in his gaze radiated confidence, encouragement. *You can do this, little one.*

Everyone waited to find out whether Ruby would burst into tears. But, no, the little girl got back up. "I okay, Wheel."

A titter of laughter broke out, but Ruby was too busy picking up the spilled petals to notice. Once she finished her task, Will scooped her up and pressed a dozen kisses all over her chubby cheeks, before setting her down. Giggling she ran to Marcella, the Bowie's house manager, who was the ceremony's officiant. The older woman leaned down and pointed to Uncle Lachlan, their dad's tall, lean, and bearded brother. The man got up and in two long strides, whisked the little girl into his arms and plopped her into his lap.

"Okay, here we go." Before heading down the aisle, Callie pressed a kiss to Knox's cheek, leaving her awash in her subtle but elegant fragrance.

"You look gorgeous, and I'm so happy for you." Delilah gave her a big hug before making her way down.

Fin and Will watched their women with pure adoration in their eyes.

And then it was Knox's turn to make the walk down the aisle to her groom.

A breeze ruffled the feathers of her dress, making her turn to find her mom racing in the door, hair windblown, cheeks ruddy. Dressed in holey jeans, black patent leather Dr. Marten's boots, and a peasant blouse, she hustled over to Knox. "Hey, hon."

Tucking an arm under hers, her mom leaned in. "Got the car idling, full tank of gas. Just say the word."

She couldn't help laughing. "Mom, seriously, there's nowhere else I'd rather be." And then, together, they headed down the aisle to her groom.

Knox handed off her bouquet to Callie, her mom took her seat, and Marcella gave her a beaming smile.

And then she was standing beside Gray Bowie, the love of her life. Her heart and soul.

He brushed a kiss across her cheek. "Took you long enough."

"Too long." She placed her palm on his chest. "But my heart's been here the whole time."

"Friends, family," Marcella began. "We are gathered here to witness the commitment shared today between Gray Bowie and Knox Holliday." With glittering eyes, she looked from one to the other. "Today signifies the creation of a new home and a new family for you both. May you be fulfilled by each other's love and friendship. May you be overjoyed by the life you will create together. Remember that in every marriage, there are good times and bad, times of joy and times of sorrow. Marriage is a journey, an adventure filled with excitement enhanced by the love, trust, dedication, and faith you share in one another."

Reaching for her hand, Gray kissed her palm and mouthed, *I love you.*

"Gray and Knox," Marcella said. "Will you promise to care for each other in the joys and sorrows of life, come what may, and to share the responsibility for growth and enrichment of your life together?"

"I will," Gray said.

She couldn't keep her body from trembling, her heart from thundering. "Yes," Knox said. "I will."

"Our groom has a thing or two to say to you," Marcella said. "Gray?"

He turned to face his bride, clasping her hands. "Knox,

people have always liked to joke about my lack of commitment, but that's because they didn't know I was committed to you. It happened the second I first saw you in Mrs. Flint's kindergarten class. My heart recognized you, and I just knew. You used to talk about me finding my passion, but that's because you didn't know that *you* were my passion. Always have been, always will be." He shrugged, as if he'd just accepted the way he was wired long ago. "I love you. I promise that I'll always make your tea, hold your hand, and give you a good morning kiss. There is nothing I wouldn't do for you, so you can skip all the sickness and in health crap, because I'm thoroughly devoted to you, my heart."

"That's my boy." Marcella cupped his cheek. "I'm so proud of you." And then she turned to Knox. "I know we're springing this on you, so I'll just go through the questions. Do you—"

"No, I want to say something." Her heart was so full it hurt. "I love you, Gray. There isn't anything I cherish more than that commitment you've given me throughout my entire life. It's made me strong, confident, and deeply, profoundly, content. I vow to wake up every morning and ask myself what I can do to make your day better, to hold your hand every chance I get, and to sit down with you for dinner every night so I can find out how your day went. I love you with my whole heart, soul, mind, and body."

"Now can I have my good morning kiss?" Gray asked the officiant.

"Hang on," Marcella said on a laugh. "The rings."

Will dug into his suit coat pocket and pulled out a rose gold band. Gray lifted her hand and slid it on her finger. "With this ring, I *finally* get the girl."

Callie handed the simple gold band to Knox. "With this ring, my life is finally complete."

"Ladies and gentlemen," Marcella said. "May I present to you, Gray Bowie and Knox Holliday, husband and wife."

Gray wrapped his arms around her waist and pulled her up against him, not wasting a single second before possessing her mouth with a searing kiss. Her body went hot; her heart jubilant. She flung her arms around his neck, unable to keep from smiling.

While their friends clapped, she tucked her face into his neck. "You're amazing. I can't believe you did all this."

"Better than eloping or the courthouse?"

"A thousand, billion times better."

Delilah tapped her shoulder. "Come on, you two. My pastry chef made you the world's best cake. Let's get slicing."

As they made their way through the crowd, everyone stopping to hug and congratulate them, Knox had never felt so full. Of love and happiness, of the absolute rightness of her life.

Just as they reached the table with a stunning four-tiered white cake with wild flowers cascading down it, the door opened, and the hotel manager poked his head in. "Brodie?"

"Yeah, man, what's up?" Her brother-in-law broke from the crowd.

"The princess of St. Christophe is here."

They all turned to check out the lobby, where black-suited security detail surrounded a blonde-haired bombshell in stilettos and enormous sunglasses.

"And she's demanding to speak with you."

Thank you for reading THE VERY THOUGHT OF YOU! You're going to love the next story in The Calamity Falls series about a princess gone wild! A member of the royal family, Rosalina's always been expected to be refined and dignified in her home country. So, imagine how much fun she has going incognito in this wild west town in America where no one knows anything about her. And who could be a better tour guide of badassery than Brodie, the last single Bowie brother? Check out JUST THE WAY YOU ARE!

Do you subscribe to my newsletter? Get on that right now because I've got an EXCLUSIVE novella for my readers in 2022! You'll get 2 chapters a month of this super sexy, fun romance! #rockstarromance #whenyourcelebritycrushbe-comesyourboyfriend #teenidol

Need more Calamity Falls, where the people are wild at heart?

KEEP ON LOVING YOU
WE BELONG TOGETHER
THE VERY THOUGHT OF YOU
JUST THE WAY YOU ARE
IT WAS ALWAYS YOU
CAN'T HELP FALLING IN LOVE
COME AWAY WITH ME
WHOLE LOTTA LOVE
YOU'RE STILL THE ONE
THE DEEPER I FALL

LOVE ME LIKE YOU DO

Have you read the Rock Star Romance series? Come meet the sexy rockers of Blue Fire:

YOU REALLY GOT ME
I WANT YOU TO WANT ME
TAKE ME HOME TONIGHT
MORE THAN A FEELING

Look for LOVE ME LIKE YOU DO in September 2022! Grab a FREE copy of PLANES, TRAINS, AND HEAD OVER HEELS. And come hang out with me on Facebook, Twitter, Instagram, Goodreads, and Pinterest or in my private reader group.

Excerpt of Just the Way You Are

I DID IT!

With her jar in hand, Princess Rosalina Anais Isabella Villeneuve crossed the lawn, breathing in the scents of freshly mown grass and clean, crisp June air. Sunlight glinted off a sleek blue BMW, and her heart clutched with happiness. *He's here.* She couldn't wait to show her fiancé. *He's going to love it.*

Climbing the stone steps, she opened the back door of the castle to find the staff eating breakfast at the weathered table. "Something smells delicious." On the island, she found a platter of buttery eggs, sliced bread, and strawberry jam.

Everyone looked over at her and smiled. "Morning, Miss."

Chef started to get up, but Rosalina shook her head. *Don't bother.* It was her fault she'd missed breakfast. *Again.* "I'll eat later. I'd like to catch Marcel before he takes off." She grabbed a croissant from the basket and bit into it. "Mm. So good."

"It would've been warm and flaky if you'd had it fresh

from the oven three hours ago." Chef got up anyway and filled herself a mug with coffee from the French press, dropping sugar and cream into it.

"But then I wouldn't have this." She lifted the tiny glass bottle.

"Oh, you've got it, then?" Her father's valet scraped his chair back on the stone floor and came over. Twisting off the cap, he closed his eyes and inhaled. "Ah. It's perfect." He broke out in a big grin. "Spot on."

"Here." Rosalina dipped a finger in and smeared a glob onto the back of his age-spotted hand.

The older man, in a black suit and a full head of salt and pepper hair, rubbed it in. "Rich...creamy." With two fingers, he tipped her chin, and she caught the exotic scent of her family's perfume. "It's lovely. You've got it just right."

"And it only took two and a half *years* to nail it. But, whatever, it's done, and they can't possibly say no this time."

As if jerked by a string, they all looked down at their plates.

Rosalina's stomach pinched with dread. "No, it's different this time. You'll see."

Chef patted her shoulder. "We have all the faith in you, my love. It's the tide of history you're swimming against we're worried about."

She knew the challenge she faced—after ninety years of running a successful business off one product, her family wasn't inclined to shake things up. But this time, she'd come up with an idea that would fit seamlessly.

Chef offered a fork and a bowl of mixed fruit, but Rosalina couldn't eat a thing. "I'll be back for a proper breakfast, but right now I have to catch Marcel before he heads to the airport." At the doorway, she turned to the staff who'd loved and protected her all her life. "And then we'll celebrate the new product line." Taking another bite of the croissant, she waved the jar at them with a mischievous grin.

A few rallied with warm smiles, but the others focused on their breakfast.

Well, obviously, if she went straight to her parents, they'd reject it outright. *That's why I'm going through Marcel first.* Her fiancé's father was the business manager for House of Villeneuve, and he oversaw the family's Nocturne perfume company. Once she convinced Marcel and his father of the value of her idea, she'd let *them* present it to her parents.

They wouldn't ignore advice from the people running their business.

Besides, she had a different angle this time. While at school, she'd created several truly lovely perfumes, and they'd rejected all of them. *They don't fit our brand.*

This time, she'd simply expanded the product line by creating bath and body products based on the same essential oil that had been in the Villeneuve family for centuries. And she'd created proprietary ingredients to make them every bit as luxurious as the perfume itself.

She was *adding* to what they already had. They couldn't say no.

As she headed down the cool hallway, her ballet flats shushed on the hundred-year-old runner. On either side, her ancestors lined up as though forming a gauntlet. *You're wasting your time*, their expressions said, noses in the air.

"You're wrong," she whispered. Anyone who bought the perfume would want the soap and body lotion to reinforce the scent.

The thick stone walls of the castle muffled sound, so she only heard the quiet conversation when she reached the grand parlor. *Shoot.* She didn't want to get pulled into one of her mother's meetings. Hanging back, she peered into the room crammed with antique furniture, the walls covered in *trompe l'oeil* murals.

Sitting demurely on the embroidered sofa, her mother spoke quietly to a woman in a pastel-colored skirt and beige flats. On the glass coffee table, tea service had been set with fine china and silver.

Having only just crested the corner of the parlor, Rosalina figured she could quietly step back before being noticed.

"Oh, darling, there you are." Her mother got up, her hand gliding toward the guest. "I'd like you to meet Marguerite, the wedding planner."

The shock hit her system like a car crash, the jolt reverberating throughout her body. *Wedding planner?* For one unbearably long moment, she heard the ticking grandfather clock as if it were inside her head.

But, of course, she snapped out of it and shifted into full princess mode. Flipping on her royal smile, she gave the woman a nod. "Good morning."

"Good morning, your Highness."

"Come." Her mother strode purposefully out of the room. "She's brought her portfolio and samples."

"Unfortunately, this isn't a good time. I'm already late for my meeting with Marcel." If only she'd brought her phone with her, but she'd left it charging in her bedroom before heading to the lab that morning. *Please don't go until I talk to you.*

"This won't take but a moment." Her mother's low

heels clacked across the marble foyer. "It's just a preliminary meeting."

Rosalina stopped just under the massive crystal chandelier. "Mother."

Her mother slowly turned to her, one brow arched. No one used that tone to speak to Her Serene Highness the Princess of St. Christophe.

But, while her mother's haughty expression made her cringe—she would normally never challenge her mother publicly—she truly couldn't spare a moment. "Marguerite, I'm so sorry I don't have time to discuss my wedding plans right now, but I do look forward to working with you."

"Of course." The woman reached into her tote and pulled out a thin silver case. Plucking a white card out of it, she handed it over. "Please call me at your convenience, and we can get started. I'll leave my portfolio with you."

"Perfect." Rosalina tucked the card into the pocket of her capri pants. "Thank you."

As her mother walked the wedding planner to the door, Rosalina spun back around and headed for the stairs. As excited as she was about her formula, she didn't actually know if Marcel's father would support her idea. He was very much of the same mind as her parents. As her American roommate's father used to say, *If it ain't broke, don't fix it.*

"Rosalina," her mother called.

Crap. Her fingers itched to text Marcel and ask him to wait for her. *Why didn't you bring your phone?* He might've left by now. "Yes?"

"Come with me."

She recognized her mother's tone for what it was, and so she did as she was told. At twenty-five, it was time for the Hereditary Princess of St. Christophe to step into her mother's shoes. Get married, give birth to an heir, and devote her time to a few established charities and one of her own creation.

Yes, she knew the expectations, and she would get there. But right now, she needed to see her project through. She had the rest of her life to be a wife and mother.

Her mother led the way into the oak-paneled library. The scents of old books, lemon furniture polish, and her father's spicy shaving cream filled the large room.

Oh, what about shaving cream for women? She'd use synthetic materials for that, though.

As they entered, her father lowered one side of his paper, a tea cup in one hand. "Oh, dear." He shot a look to the door, as if calculating his getaway.

"Exactly." For a moment there, she considered showing them the lotion, just to get the conversation away from wedding plans. As the hereditary princess, it would fall on her and Marcel to keep the company running. She'd be showing them that the family legacy was in good hands.

Ha. Good one.

Let Marcel lead the charge. Her fiancé had her back.

Her mother stood beside her husband's chair. "I don't appreciate you sending away my guest. I invited her here to launch the wedding plans, and I found it rude and disrespectful that you asked her to leave."

"I'm sorry. It did come across as rude, but I wish you'd have discussed it with me first. I wasn't prepared to meet with anyone this morning. In fact, if I don't go right now, I'll miss Marcel. He's leaving for Zurich in a few minutes."

Her father set down his paper, and his tall, lanky frame

rose out of the chair. Pulling his cell phone from his pocket, he tapped out a text. "There. Marcel will wait."

Uh oh. Her dad had something to *say.* Tension pulled at her skin, and she became aware of the cool breeze sweeping through the room, riffling the pages of magazines.

Pulling an engraved handkerchief out of the pocket of his slacks, he took the croissant out of her hand and wiped the buttery remnants off her fingers. Balling it up, he dropped it on the side table that held his silver teapot. "My sweet Rosalina, I think you can agree we've been more than generous in supporting your choices. We assumed, once you graduated from university, you'd come home and marry Marcel, but you wanted to continue your education, and we love you very much, we want you to be happy, so we supported that decision. But it's time, my love. It's time for you to assume your duties here."

"Of course. I know that, and I'm absolutely going to marry Marcel. In fact, when I go upstairs, I'll talk to Fabiana, and she'll set up a time for me to meet with the wedding planner."

"This is not the first time you've put off this discussion," her mother said. "Darling, this is *your* wedding. You must take it seriously."

Impatience rumbled under her skin. Why would she bother thinking about the details when they were already set in stone? "What's to talk about? We're marrying in the church, and the reception will be held in the grand ballroom." She shrugged. "I'm being fitted for my dress next week." A tiny flicker of interest teased her heart.

The designer lived in the United States. A wild west town, Calamity had cowboys and ranches, saloons and gold mining. It even had a *bison* preserve.

Imagine that—bison!

"There is much to discuss," her mother said. "And the top priority is setting a date so we can send out invitations."

"Honestly, whatever works best for your schedule. It doesn't matter to me." Because it would be a performance in front of the entire country.

"Your enthusiasm for this wedding is underwhelming," her mother said.

"Well, sorry, Mama, but it's not like I have a say in anything." Other than the dress and cake, none of the rest reflected her personality at all.

The newspaper rustled, as her father picked it up and sat back down. "Is there something you'd prefer?"

She scanned his handsome features. *Does it matter?*

He gave her a deep nod.

Well, then. "Actually, I'd love to get married in the meadow." The night-blooming flower used in Nocturne only blossomed for a few weeks in June. "If we could have the service at twilight, then the lyantha would perfume the night air during my reception."

Her mother's features tightened. "That would mean waiting a *year.*"

She watched the silent communication pass between her equally strong and stubborn parents.

"As long as the date is set and invitations go out before the vote," her father said. "We can wait for the actual ceremony."

"Really?" Since when did her family break from tradition? "Then I'd prefer a date in the middle of June, so that if we don't get enough precipitation and the flowers bloom later, I won't miss out."

"Then, that's what you'll have," her father said.

She could hardly believe it. "It doesn't have to be in the church?"

"I would *prefer* the church," her father said. "But I've learned to pick my battles with my oldest daughter."

The comment swiped across her heart like a claw. She knew her father wasn't referring to what happened all those years ago. Intellectually, she knew her single act of rebellion hadn't caused his heart attack, but the two would forever be tied in her mind.

"What if, instead of having the wedding in the meadow, we fill the church with the lyantha?" her mother asked.

Rosalina reared back, as if her mother had suggested burning the castle to the ground. "We're not cutting my flowers."

Her father tried to suppress a grin. "Not to worry. The ceremony itself is far more important than the location. No harm will come to your precious lyantha."

"You'll be the first in six hundred years to marry outside the church." But her mother sounded like she'd accepted Rosalina's decision.

"I know, but it's my one and only wedding, and the meadow just fits me."

Her mother broke into a luminous grin. "Then, the meadow it will be."

"This makes me so happy." Her parents were being awfully accommodating. Maybe... Her fingers curled around the glass jar. But, instead of presenting her idea to them, she found herself blurting, "I think I'll go to the States for my fitting."

They looked at her like she was the fly that had just landed in their soup bowls.

Spin it. "Marcel's in Zurich for the week, and we'll

want to plan the wedding together, so the timing works out well. Besides, asking the designer to fly all the way out here seems ridiculous. I'm not her only client."

Her mother pressed a hand to her shoulder. "That is enough, Rosalina. You take your life and your position in this country for granted." She had a fierce look in her eyes. "But we face a formidable opponent with the People's Party, who are passionate in their plea for an egalitarian society. Every minute you're out of sight, still unmarried, still not pregnant with an heir, you reinforce their position that the monarchy's dying out. When they liken us to 'an ancient tree that no longer bears fruit,' they're not only referring to my inability to produce a male heir but to our oldest daughter, who shows no sign of settling into her role." She glanced at her husband—not with an apologetic look because she'd had to stop bearing children after two girls but with a look that said, *Back me up here.*

"You've traveled the world, had your experiences, and now you must come home and embrace everything that entails," her father said. "You must live here to understand the needs of the people so that you can choose a cause you feel passionate about. You need to stand with us in showing that our family may be small, but we're devoted to our country's well-being."

"I understand." With her sister at university, the eyes of the people were on Rosalina. She needed to be seen with Marcel, moving forward with wedding plans, so when the voters went to the polls, they went knowing the monarchy would continue.

And she was fine with that. She didn't need to go to Calamity right now. She would have plenty of time to travel, once she set up her philanthropy, got married…and had a baby.

Marriage, baby…what was this resistance deep inside of her? Why couldn't she just go along with what was required of her?

It's not like you've ever had any other expectations for your life.

"It's fine. Besides, the designer's scheduled to come out here next week, so she's probably already bought her ticket. Okay, well, now that we've set a date, I really do need to go."

"Won't you at least have a look at the invitations?" her mother asked.

Oh, dear. But she appreciated her mother's efforts, so she stepped closer to the table, skimming the choices. "Any of those are fine." Honestly, they all looked the same.

Her father laughed, before shaking open his newspaper.

"I'm glad my choices please you," her mother said with an unfortunate amount of sarcasm. "But you still need to work out the wording, the font…the color of the envelopes."

"Of course. Let me talk with Fabiana, and we'll set up a time to go over all the details." She kissed her mother's cheek. "Thank you, Mama, for doing this for me."

The moment Rosalina left the library, she opened the jar and let the fragrance fill her senses. She waited just a moment for the two scents to merge—the lotion and her mother's perfume. And…*yes*. Perfect match. Given the complex mix of ingredients—the shea butter and ceramides and acids—recreating the exact scent had been difficult. But she'd gotten it. And, even better, the lotion was sumptuous, so it fit their brand.

She made her way up the stone staircase that led to the

business offices. At the landing, she glanced out the rectangular window and got that familiar rush of joy.

Villeneuve Castle sat atop a ridge overlooking the capital city. Wildflowers carpeted the hills, and the snow-covered Alps created a cozy fortress for her picturesque little town. Below, the two-lane highway snaked through the valley like a black river. Heavy mid-morning traffic meant the businesses were thriving, and it made her proud to think how well her father ran this beautiful, safe country.

Hushed, urgent voices upstairs drew her attention. A woman and a man.

But the urgency wasn't anger or frustration…it was passionate. Yearning.

An office romance? Not many employees worked in the castle—only the finance department—and most of them were married and had held their positions forever. She would be devastated to learn someone was having an affair.

As she climbed the steps, she let the soles of her ballet flats slap on the stone to alert them, but their impassioned conversation didn't stop.

"But you don't love her." The hushed, fervent voice came from behind the closed door of a supply closet.

A spike of recognition hit the base of her spine. *Fabiana.* But her personal assistant and close friend wasn't dating anyone.

"You don't marry someone you don't love." Fabiana sounded overwrought. "It won't work. Not when you're in love with *me.*"

One single second had never held so much tension. *Who's she talking to?*

Who?

A man let out a rough exhalation. "It's a different kind of love, Fabi. It might not be wild and crazy like I feel for you, but I *do* love her. I've known her all my life."

Marcel.

Her fiancé was in love with her best friend?

About the Author

Award-winning author Erika Kelly writes sexy and emotional small town romance. Married to the love of her life and raising four children, she lives in the southwest, drinks a lot of tea, and is always waiting for her cats to get off her keyboard.

https://www.erikakellybooks.com/

facebook.com/erikakellybooks

twitter.com/ErikaKellyBooks

instagram.com/erikakellyauthor

goodreads.com/Erika_Kelly

pinterest.com/erikakellybooks

amazon.com/Erika-Kelly/e/B00L0MLWUY

bookbub.com/authors/erika-kelly

Made in United States
North Haven, CT
25 September 2022

24548404R00221